ALLEN STANFILL

# Killer In The Woods

Éditions
DEDICACES

# Contents

# 1

# A Visit From A Stranger

I t was a very warm evening just like always in the Deep
South. But besides that, there was something different
going on this time around at what seemed to be a normal
hospital at first glance. However that was far from the case, if
you looked closer, you could tell it was an insane asylum, and
that asylum held a very unfortunate patient, Bobby Sikes.

He's been in this place for fifteen years of his young life; he is
now thirty-one years of age. His is a very strange story indeed;
he was arrested at the age of sixteen for supposedly murdering
six adults and over thirty young kids and teens. And no matter
how much he told his side of the story, no one would believe
him, not the cops nor the parents of the kids that died.

What's really sad is the fact that not even his own parents
believed him. What's weird is that a few of his friends that he
had made over the years that he went camping with had survived.
Now why in the world would a teen killer let anyone survive
even if they're friends? It doesn't make any sense whatsoever;
these were some brutal murders or so they say.

And what was even weirder was when his so-called friends
were questioned, they claimed they couldn't remember a damn

thing at all, and that sure didn't make any sense now, does it? But it didn't matter they had found a suspect, and that was all they wanted was for someone to take the fall and who better than a sixteen-year-old kid covered in blood and in shock.

They cleaned him up and kept him in the hospital for a few days before putting him in juvenile hall and then tried him for the murders. However, Bobby was lucky; at his hearing, he was found not guilty by cause of insufficient evidence. Even though they couldn't put him in prison, the judge made a call to have him put in an asylum for the criminally insane until he was deemed fit for society.

So here he'd been since the incident; he'd seen many psychologists, some deem him suitable to go back in society, and some believe he's a danger to himself and others. He'd even talked to people that just wanted to know what exactly happened at the campgrounds, only to leave and never come back to talk to him again. Asked why, they replied, "The details he gives are just too gruesome and unbelievable." Even after all of that, there were a few times that he had been released from the asylum only to do something that would land him back in; it was almost like he didn't want to leave.

What really happened out there in the woods that year? Only Bobby knows the real truth, and nowadays he sits in his padded room and rarely talks to anyone. But what's the point? Nobody ever listened to him or believed him—that is, until now. Things are about to change on this day as a stranger makes his way into the insane asylum, he's there to find Bobby, and he had no intention of explaining himself either. He's just there to find and talk to Bobby, and the staff can't stop him or ask this man any questions; he had all the credentials he needed to talk Bobby and made it confidential. The man made his way up to a nurse.

"Can we help you sir?" one of the nurses asked.

"Of course, you can, ma'am," the man replied.

"Well?" This time the nurse asked with a slight attitude.

"Yes, it is, sir," she replied.

"Why's it on a hall to its self?" he asked.

"You'll have to ask him that, sir, if he will see you, that is," she replied again to him. She turned and knocked on the door then looked back at the man. "Good luck, sir," she said to him before walking off.

He stood there and watched her walk off before he began to focus on the door in front him; it took him some time to think about what his next move would be, but it was clear to him he had only one choice but to knock on his door, and that's exactly what he did. "Bobby Sikes. Are you in there, Bobby?" the man called out as he knocked on the door. He stood there and waited a few minutes before he started to knock again. "Bobby. I'm not going away unless you answer the door," he yelled out as he kept knocking at the door.

Bobby finally had answered the door, seemed like the man had annoyed him enough into doing so. "Who are you?" this person had asked.

"I'm not inclined to tell you my name, and honestly I refuse to do so. All I want to know is, are you Bobby Sikes?" the man had said back.

"Yeah, I'm Bobby. What do you want? Since you're not going to tell me your name."

The man wondered if this was the Bobby Sikes he had been looking for, so instead of answering the question, he decided to ask another. "Are you the same Bobby Sikes that lived through what is now known as the Camp Hell incident? About fifteen years ago?"

Bobby then stared at the man for a bit before responding, "One and the same. What's it to you?" Bobby replied.

The man was amazed that this was the man he was looking for. He was expecting a frail man that was out of his mind; instead, he found a man that was somewhat in complete control at least on the outside. He would hope to get a chance to dig deeper into this man's calm demeanor, but that wasn't up to him; it would be up to Bobby. "Well, Bobby, I'm here to listen to your story and help you out any way that I can. And I won't run away, that's if you still wish for someone to hear you out?"

Bobby turned around and headed back into his padded cell, leaving the door open behind him. "You have three hours today, and I'll think about whether or not I will allow you to come back and talk to me tomorrow." The man walked into the room and pulled up a chair.

"Agreed," the man says as he sits down. "Are you going to take a seat, Bobby?" the man asked.

"No, I think I'll stand this time," Bobby replied back to him.

The man smiled before saying, "Suit yourself, and you can start anytime you're ready, Bobby." Bobby begins to pace back and forth nervously, you could tell he wasn't exactly used to visitors anymore, and he definitely wasn't used to talking about that god-awful event either. "Are you all right, Bobby?" the man asks.

Bobby looks over at him. "I'm fine. I'm just not sure where to start from."

"Start from anywhere you like. It can be at the beginning of that week, or you can start from the first day of camp. It's up to you," the man calmly says back.

Bobby paces for a bit longer not saying another word until he stops and leans back against the wall; with his head down

4

Bobby finally talks again. "I'll start from the beginning of the week. It holds some importance as well that I think you should hear about if that's alright with you?"

The man smiles once again and answers, "That's fine with me. If that's what you want, then please start from there."

Bobby nodded and began to tell his tale. "Well, it started like this," he said as he got further into his story. "I was just your normal teenager who had just turned sixteen at the time, lost in my own little world, or maybe I wasn't normal at all. Teens my age had girlfriends and also had their permit to drive, but that just wasn't me. I didn't have a girlfriend, and I didn't know how to drive either.

I wasn't athletic, and I didn't play sports; however, I did take karate for reasons, and that kept me in decent shape, plus I liked to walk. That week I was on top of the world, school was out for the summer, and that meant no more homework and no more dealing with the rest of the ignorant teens either. I remember how the next day started for me. It wasn't near as good as the last.

It started off normal, I had my breakfast, and I was ready to read my comic book, and that's exactly what I did, and I was lost in my own little world, and that's what I had been waiting for. While sitting on the couch reading my comic book, I could hear my mom and dad talking in the kitchen, but I paid them no mind. Then I heard those two words that I thought I would never hear again: summer camp. And that snapped me out of that world. Shit! I thought to myself. Another year of summer camp. Really. I mean, come on, I was to old for that shit now. I can tell by the look on your face what you're thinking," Bobby said to him. "Summer camp is fun for most kids. Right?"

The man just smirked at Bobby. "Never been, so I wouldn't

know," he said back to Bobby.

"Lucky you," Bobby said to him before rambling on. "Well, summer camp sure as hell has never been fun for me; every year it's always the same. I get picked on and beat up on by the bullies; they're a year older than me and have always been bigger than me. I just downright hate it. And on top of that, there's no TV, and you can't even use your cell phone, and if caught with one, they will take it away from you.

All I usually end up with are my comic books, which is fine with me when I get a chance to read them, and nine times out of ten some asshole steals them from me, and the counselors could care less. They're either to busy having sex or to be busy picking on the nerds, which usually includes me.

I can't help I'm considered a nerd because of my love for comic books. Which in my eyes makes the counselors a complete and utter joke! And believe me, I paid for being who I am, and so did many of the other kids throughout the years. If you were a jock, you were loved by the counselors and could get away with anything. If you were a nerd, you were guaranteed a long and harsh summer. "Honestly, just the thought of going back to that place made me sick to my stomach. So I asked myself, 'Why would my parents do this to me? What have I done wrong?' I couldn't come up with any answers to my questions. I knew if this happened it was going to ruin my summer yet again for another year of my life. But what was I supposed to do in this situation?

I decided to calmly wait and listen in on some more of my parents' conversation before doing anything else, so I just sat on the couch and just listened to them talk about me. I was shocked when I heard everything. My mom thought it would be a good idea for me to go one more time, while my dad made it sound like it would be the last time they could get rid of me for another summer. I know they wanted to be alone and all, but why I do I have to go through hell so they can achieve it?"

"Hold on a second, you knew your parents were going to send you to camp again, and you didn't do anything about it?" the man interrupted Bobby's story to ask him that question out of curiosity.

Bobby just kind of glared at him before he answered the man's question, "I was getting to that; if you would give me a damn chance to finish, you would know." Bobby was a bit snappy with his answer, but who could blame him?

"Sorry, Bobby, please continue," the man apologetically says to him.

"All right, but don't interrupt me again. Or this conversation is over. Are we clear?" Bobby said to him. The man shook his head in agreement but didn't say another word; it was clear he just wanted Bobby to continue on with his story. "As I was saying, I was listening to my parent's talk in the kitchen about sending me back to summer camp one last time. "I started to get upset, so on that day I decided since I was close to being a man, I would tell my parents how I felt."

"Sorry, Bobby, please continue," the man apologetically says to him.

"All right, but don't interrupt me again. Or this conversation is over. Are we clear?" Bobby said to him. The man shook his head in agreement but didn't say another word; it was clear he just wanted Bobby to continue on with his story. "As I was saying, I was listening to my parent's talk in the kitchen about sending me back to summer camp one last time. "I started to get upset, so on that day I decided since I was close to being a man, I would tell my parents how I felt."

"Mom, Dad," I said with a very stern voice, "I don't want to go back to that place," I said to them with a hint of anger in my voice. "It sucks and I refuse to go, and you can't make me." And I just kept on running my mouth without thinking. "I'm a man now. I can do what I want."

If only I had used my head, what came next would have been avoided, if I had done so. Before I knew it, I felt my dad's hand land flush on my cheek as he slapped the taste right out of my mouth. It hurt like hell. It's been a while since the last time my dad hit me. Now I was upset, and my face was hurting like hell, I was still in shock that my dad slapped my face, I was just telling my parents how felt, and I paid for it.

Yes, I could have handled things differently, but I was young and rambunctious. It happens, right? Still, I don't feel like I deserved it, but whatever. And I sure as hell didn't deserve what happened next either, because they both started screaming at me. First, it was my mom.

"What in the hell is your problem?" she asked loudly, and then she continued on screaming at me not giving me a chance to answer. "You know what? After that stunt, you're going whether you like it or not!" I knew not to say another word, I wasn't about to get slapped again, and I could tell by the look on my mom's face that she wasn't done with me yet. "Your father busts his ass to send you to summer camp so you can get out there and have some fun! And on top of that, it's not cheap; these things cost money. And it keeps you out of trouble, young man! And if it wasn't for summer camp, your lazy ass would be at home all day with your nose in those damn comic books, all summer long."

Before my mom could even get another word in, my dad interrupted her, "Son, we just want what's best for you, that's all. And if that means you having to get out of the house and going to summer camp, then so be it." And he was being calm about it at first, I could tell by the look on his face he felt bad about slapping me, but I didn't care. At that moment I was going to win the argument this time around.

"But, dad. I'm an adult now, don't I get a say in this?"

He was still trying his best to be calm with me as he said, "No buts this time, son, it's been decided. And no, you don't have a say in this, you may be a teenager now, but you're still a child, and you will do what you're told. No ifs, or buts about it, young man. Are we clear?"

I just looked at my dad with an angry look on my face. To me, it wasn't fair I deserved a summer to myself, and that's why I kept fighting against them both. "Dad, it's not fair. You know how much I hate that place. And yet you still send me there, and on top of that, you and Mom both find excuses to send me back there every year. Think about how I feel for once." I wasn't backing down, but in the end, it didn't do me a bit of good.

My dad was starting to get upset with me. Man did his face began to get red. That's when I decided it was time to ease up a bit, but I knew I was too late. He turned away from me and did his best to calm himself down.

It wasn't good; I could see his facial expression change. The more that he tried to calm down, the angrier he was getting, and now he was really pissed off, and it didn't take long for him to show it either. "Our word is final, young man," he said angrily to me. But he didn't stop there and believe me, it was far from over. Dad was letting me know he was the boss of this house very quickly. "You're going whether you like it or not, and that is that. And don't say another word, young man, or you'll be in serious trouble."

I looked at my dad and gave him the biggest "go to hell" look that you could give anyone, I was upset, and now I was fighting back my tears because everyone knows men don't cry. Feeling my anger boiling over inside of me, I yelled to the top of my lungs at my dad and mom, "I hate you both!" I tried, and I tried and tried to fight back my tears with all my might, and I finally broke down.

With tears in my eyes, I stormed off to my room not saying a word to my parents as I went that way, and I slammed the door behind me. I didn't say another word to my parents the rest of the night, and my parents never came to my room to apologize or try to console me. I didn't have any brothers or sisters. I was the only child, so I didn't have to worry about anyone else trying to bother me either.

So I pretty much laid in bed staring up at the ceiling thinking about the day after tomorrow; that was really the only thing on my mind. Yeah, I felt bad about the argument I had with my parents that night, but at that moment I didn't care; all I know is that I felt like they had betrayed me again. After a while, I knew it wasn't going to do me any good to be angry or to fight with my parents. I had officially given up and accepted my fate.

I now realized I had to figure out what I was going to do for fun on my last day of freedom before I have to go back to that damn place. That's when it hit me, tomorrow I was going to wake up early, eat some breakfast, grab my favorite comic book that I had been reading, and go to my favorite hiding spot.

Before long my thoughts went from thinking about tomorrow to thinking about summer camp. And the more I thought about it, the more I started to feel uneasy about it all. I just had a very bad feeling about camp this year, it was like a warning coming deep from inside my soul, and it scared me. I had a million things running through my head at the moment; however, my eyes were starting to get heavy, and before I knew it, I had fallen asleep. That night I had one of the most horrible nightmares you could ever imagine, something was chasing me, I couldn't exactly see what it was, but all I knew is that it was after me. It wasn't long before I realized that I was running around in circles, so for a reason, I decided to stop and look around, and there wasn't anything there.

And then there was nothing but silence. I stood there in the darkness all alone and waited for whatever was after me to jump out and show itself. I couldn't take it anymore, so I yelled out into the darkness, "Hello! is anyone out there? If so, please stop. It's not funny anymore." Then it began; screams started coming from all around me. It wasn't just normal screams either, it was some of the most blood-curdling screams you could ever imagine, and I was paralyzed with fear.

I could also see something in the dark; all of a sudden it leaped out at me. At first I couldn't make out what it was; however, I could hear a creepy laughter as whatever this thing was had a hold of me. I screamed out into the darkness fighting against whatever had me; then I heard a faint voice. I really couldn't make out what it was saying, and I was honestly too scared to pay attention anyways, but I do remember the constant laughing before I knew it, I woke up screaming bloody murder.

It was horrible, and I had a cold sweat all over my body. I jumped out of my bed and started looking around my room as if I was looking for what had me in my nightmare. I guess I was making sure that I was really safe in my own room; it didn't take me long to decide that it was time for me to jump back in my bed and hide under my covers. Yeah, it was childish of me; however, at that time I didn't care.

After the nightmare, I had barely gotten any sleep the rest of that night. For me, it was definitely a sign of things to come, and it wasn't long before the sun started coming up and little rays of light shined through my curtains. I lay in bed still partially under my covers, and to be honest I didn't want to get out of my bed because I knew this would be my last day of freedom. But at last, I knew it was time for me to get up and get myself ready because I could hear faint sounds of footsteps and the sound of dishes clanging together, which let me know that my mom was up and more than likely cooking breakfast for my dad before he goes to work and for me also. And I was sure that they were both still mad at me, so yeah, I was somewhat scared to make my way downstairs.

Before long I didn't have a choice as my dad yelled for me, "Bobby! It's time to get out of bed and eat! You have a long day ahead of you!"

Damn, I thought to myself. I really didn't want to get yelled at again, so I did the smart thing. "Okay, Dad!" I answered back nicely. I got out of bed and got myself dressed. "I'm on my way down now, Dad!" And I ran downstairs. But I stopped right at the kitchen entrance as I had an idea. I decided I was going to try and pout my way out of this whole summer camp thing. So I slowly walked into the kitchen with my head held low, with a sad look my on my face. Nobody can resist my sad face.

Or so I had thought anyway, but clearly, it didn't work because my mom and dad completely ignored me. Oh well, I thought to myself. It's not like I could do anything about it, so I took a seat down at the table even after trying to suck up by giving my mom and dad a kiss on the cheek and that too had failed. I decided to just give up and start eating the food that was on the table in front of me, at least the breakfast was good though.

I even tried to talk to my mom and dad, but they kept on

ignoring me and talked among themselves as they ate like I wasn't even there. All I could do was sit there and listen in on what they were talking about. My mom looked over at me, "How do you like your breakfast?" she asked.

I looked up at her not knowing what to say at first; then I gave a faint smile and said, "It's really good, Mom, like always." We pretty much just sat there eating and talking. I still didn't say a whole lot though. I tried to think of things to say, but my mind had gone blank; afterward, I helped clear the table and then started my chores without so much saying a word. It took me longer to finish my chores this day than most, my mind was elsewhere, and I figured, what's the point? Like I said before, it took me a while to finish my chores, and before I knew it, I was finally done. I decided to make my way to the living room and catch up on some reading before my journey into hell tomorrow. Just as I was about to take a seat on the couch, my dad told me to go outside, that my mom and he had some things to do and discuss.

Bullshit, I thought to myself. As I turned around and proceeded to walk out the front door, I knew they just wanted me out of their way. Their excuse was that I needed to be outside more and get used to being more active because I would soon be outside more than usual. I wanted to yell and scream as I walked out on the porch, but all I could muster was a, "Yes, sir." And I quietly closed the door behind me.

The way I looked at things was, why start another argument? I was still angry though. This sucks, I'm sixteen years old, and I'm still being treated like a child. I thought to myself as I stomped down the porch steps and down the sidewalk. But then I remembered I had plans for today, and I already had my comic book in hand, so I was ready to go.

What seemed to start off as another bad day started to look up just a bit, but for some reason, my anger boiled over inside of me, and I couldn't seem to shake the feeling of rage, so I started muttering obscenities to myself at first. Before I knew it, I was yelling at the top of my lungs, "How much longer do I have to take this shit." And I kicked at the sidewalk. I kept on walking with a pissed-off look on my face, hoping that when I got to my favorite spot, I would have calmed down some.

I was still a few blocks away from my destination, and the sun was beating down on me. It was hot as hell that day, and I was sweating bullets, but all I could think about was going to that hellhole tomorrow, and that spurred on my anger. Then out of nowhere I heard a noise, it sounded like someone was following me, so I stopped walking and quickly turned around, but there wasn't a single soul around. So I just chalked it up to my imagination and blamed the heat and my anger as well, and I kept walking on.

My thoughts then turned back on having to go to that wretched place in the morning. I snickered as I thought to myself, Guess I could run away. Then I wouldn't have to go. It wouldn't do me any good at all though because my parents would just call the cops, and I know they would find me, and then my parents would kill me. Or I would just chicken out even if I tried; either way, I'm not sure I'm willing to take the risk and find out. I walked a little farther down the sidewalk and noticed a huge tree in the distance.

I was finally there. I breathed a sigh of relief and made my way toward the tree. Finally, I thought to myself. I needed a break from the sun and the heat; I smiled as I sat under the tree. It was definitely my favorite spot in the world to sit and read my comic books. The tree was an amazing one, it was big and beautiful, the leaves were full and green, and the limbs hung over you as if trying to cradle you from the sun. And the grass was soft to the touch and nice to sit upon; it felt good to sit down and relax and forget about the things to come.

I leaned back against the tree and stretched my legs out to get as comfortable as I possibly could be. I opened my comic book and started to read, but I found myself somewhat distracted by my own thoughts. I couldn't help but think about tomorrow. Believe me when I say that I tried to forget and read, but I couldn't; the only happy thought that came from it was the thought of seeing my friends again. Yes, I missed them, that part I couldn't help.

I just hoped they would be there. I knew I couldn't get through it alone. And another happy thought was the fact that after this year, my parents could no longer force me to go back to that damn place. But still, yet I hated that place and wish I could have come up with a way for me not to go, before I knew it I could feel my eyes start to get heavy. I fought it the best I could, but with the cool breeze and my body being tired from my restless night, my eyes started to close, and before I knew it, had fallen asleep.

That was when I had my second nightmare, my dream started off decent at first, it was my friends and myself at camp actually having a good time. Then that dream turned into a horrible nightmare; one by one my friends started to disappear into a darkness that suddenly surrounded me. It wasn't long that I found myself all alone. I ran around in the darkness frantically searching for my friends or any other sign of human life.

Then I realized that there wasn't another soul around, and the more I searched, the more I found myself engulfed in the darkness. All of a sudden the hairs on my arm stood up straight, and a cold chill slowly ran up my spine. The air around me became thick and ice like, and I found that it had gotten a lot harder to breathe. There was nothing but pure malice and hatred everywhere I turned, and I knew I wasn't alone. Out of the darkness came a creepy and sinister laugh that shook me to my core. I tried to scream out. Hell, I even tried to run, but I was paralyzed with fear and could not find the strength to do either. After a brief few seconds, the laughter ceased, and shadows in the distance could be seen along with sounds of footsteps. It was too dark to see exactly what was going on, or what these shadows were. I myself was still too scared to even think about moving, and then it happened: the laughter was back, but it was different, somehow playful.

I swear it seemed like there were little children playing a game with me, or perhaps even picking on me. I remember feeling absolute terror running through my body as the shadows came closer and closer to me. And the laughter got louder and louder, then all became silent. It was so quiet you could hear a pin drop. That's when I gained the courage to check my surroundings. I turned my head quickly in every direction. I took a sigh of relief thinking that it was finally over.

But I was just kidding myself because at that moment I heard someone or something walking up behind me. I turned around quickly to confront whatever was behind me, but nothing was there! Right then I could feel something breathing on the back of my neck! I tried to turn to see what it was, but again I couldn't move! It wasn't like it was before where I was struck with fear, this time I had no control over my body, and I couldn't move a muscle no matter how hard I tried. The worst part, my nightmare was about to happen. I actually started to see what was in front of me, and I wished I hadn't; there were children in front of me poking their small bony fingers into my skin making me bleed as they did so. That wasn't even the worst part of it all. I think what got me the most was how these kids looked.

Their faces and bodies were burned and mangled, and some were even missing their arms or hands. It was horrible. I couldn't get away. The pain was getting unbearable as they jammed their fingers further and further into my skin. Then out of nowhere, this hideous face rushed at me, laughing that bloodcurdling laugh! And that's when I woke up screaming as loud as I possibly could and sweating like no other. It was just like last night. I wiped the sweat from my brow and calmed myself down. I leaned my head back against the tree and closed my eyes for a brief second; that's when I heard a faint chuckle. I quickly rose up and opened my eyes; there was a boy standing over me.

I couldn't make out what the boy looked like at first, that is until my eyes adjusted. Just looking at him I could tell he was about my age, or maybe even a year younger or so. His face was pale, or I guess you could say he was as white as a ghost, his eyes were black as coal, and they were sunken deep in his sockets. His lips were blood red, which I figured was very odd for his complexion, he had on a dirty and ripped pair of jeans and an old, worn-out and torn shirt. He seemed to be slightly taller than me, and his build was that of someone that was malnourished; his skin was leathery, almost inhuman looking.

His facial expression was very odd to me; it was hard to tell if he was crying or laughing. I jumped up frightened from the sight of the boy; now on my feet with my back to him, I did a quick spin around to meet this stranger face-to-face. However, he was nowhere to be found. After gathering myself, I decided to have one more glance around the place; still, there wasn't a soul around. So I shrugged and chalked it up to nothing more than a bad dream like last night; to my surprise, I happened to notice that I had stayed out too late. Damn. I thought to myself.

I knew that if I didn't get home soon, my ass would be in more trouble than what it already has; without even thinking about anything else, I grabbed my comic book and made a run for it back home. I ran and ran as fast as I could, but let's face it, I knew I was a dead man; there was home right in front of me. I didn't even stop or slow down. I bolted straight on in the front door, apologizing as I ran in the house like a madman expecting to get yelled at for being that late, but there wasn't anyone in the living room. I then heard voices coming from in the kitchen.

That's when I decided I would try and pout my way out of trouble. So I slumped over and slowly walked into the kitchen, but instead of getting yelled at, I was completely ignored. No shouting, no yelling, no nothing. I walked further into the kitchen, and still, they treated me like I wasn't even there. The hell with it, I thought to myself and just walked on to my room. I figured this would be the perfect chance to sneak away and not have to deal with my parents.

But as I made my way upstairs and was just about to shut my bedroom door, a voice called out to me. "Bobby. You're grounded. There won't be any supper for you. So clean up and go to bed!" It was my dad.

"Shit." And here I was thinking my mom and dad had completely ignored me; guess I was wrong. I answered the best way I knew how. "All right, Dad. Sorry about being late."

My dad answered me back calmly, "It's fine. You just need to get your rest. You have a very long day tomorrow, and it starts very early." Well, at least on the bright side, I didn't get yelled at. Don't get me wrong, though, I still wasn't a happy camper, but I also knew not to start a fight with my dad. I didn't answer back. I went to the bathroom and cleaned myself up and got ready for bed.

As I lay in my bed I could hear my parents talking, usually, they're pretty quiet when I'm trying to sleep. However, this time they seemed like they didn't care, and I was the topic of their conversation; they talked about the things they were going to do while I was gone. You could hear the excitement in their voices, and to be honest, that pissed me off badly. I grabbed my covers and pulled them over my head; that way I couldn't hear what they were saying about me anymore.

Then this idea came to my mind. All I had to do was stay up for the rest of the night. It was a stupid idea, I know, but at that time it seemed perfect to me. In my mind, I was going to show them who was the boss, but that plan soon fell to pieces as my eyes began to shut, and sleep took my body over. I swear, though, before I fell asleep, I heard a faint voice that said, "See you soon." It was followed by a chuckle. Then off to sleep I went.

That night I got a good night's sleep, I didn't have not one nightmare, and I can say that I really needed that. Before I knew it, the night was over, and the rays of daylight made way through my curtains, and I could also hear faint sounds of footsteps moving around downstairs, which let me know my parents were also awake. If I had to take a guess, I would say my mom was making breakfast, and my dad was more than likely getting my bag packed up and ready to go. As for myself, I did my best to stay under my covers, and that didn't last either.

It wasn't long before my mom yelled out to me, "Bobby. Wake up. It's time to eat and get ready to go now." And of course, as bad as I hated to, I got myself out of bed, got dressed, and proceeded to make my way downstairs and into the kitchen.

My mom acted like she was in a huge hurry; she had everyone's spot set at the table and hurried me down onto my chair. My dad also rushed into the room and took his place at the table; then my mom took her seat too.

I took one last chance to try and beg them not to make me go. "Mom? Dad?" They stopped eating for a brief second to look up at me and ask, "What?" I knew this wasn't going to end well, but I had to at least try. "Please, don't make me go. I have—"

Before I could say another word, I was cut off by my dad, "You're going. End of. Now eat your food. We have to leave here in a minute or two."

I just lowered my head and started eating, there wasn't a point in saying another word, I didn't want to start another fight, and I would lose the battle anyway. Before I knew it, my mom and dad had finished their food, and I had barely taken a bite. What came next was unexpected. My parents pretty much rushed me out the door—hell, I didn't even get to finish my food. It wasn't like we were late or anything like that, but that didn't stop them from pushing me out the door and into our SUV. "Is his bag in the back?" my mom asked him.

"Yes, dear. He's all ready to go," my dad responded.

"Hey! What about me? Why are we in such a hurry?" And of course it was the same as it was last night: they had ignored me. And again they talked among themselves and left me out of the conversation, and off we went toward the meeting place so my happy ass could be sent off to summer camp, or hell, however, you want to look at it.

As we made our way down the road, I couldn't help but think about the place I was going, I just couldn't shake this bad feeling, and I knew something bad was going to happen. And then my mind shifted, and I started thinking about the nightmares I had been having; they have been intense and scary. And I then I wondered about the boy I had seen standing over me yesterday. Was he real? Or just part of my nightmares? And why me? Why was this happening to me? I have never had nightmares in my life until now. I didn't have a whole lot of time to think about everything as I was already there, and I could see three buses in line waiting to take me to my destination.

The vehicle stopped, and my dad looked at me and said, "We're here, son, grab your bag like a man, and walk over to the buses."

"Yes, sir," I said as I reached over and grabbed my bag. My parents got out of the vehicle to bid me farewell, and I put my arms around my mom and gave her a hug, and then I turned toward my dad and did the same to him. I also told them both that I loved them. You could see the surprised look on their faces. I was even surprised myself. I, for some reason, felt like that would be the last time I would see them again.

"Have fun, and we will see you in a few months, dear," my mom said to me.

I stood there and didn't say a word back. I watched as they both got back in the vehicle and drove off. I so badly wanted to run after them, but I didn't. I did as my dad said, and I turned around and made my way to the buses. I had a lot of bad feelings as I walked closer, but those feelings went away when I heard an all too familiar voice.

"Hey, dumbass!" I turned around to see Tommy walking my way. "Hey, Tommy." I was happy to see at least one of my friends there.

"Glad to see a familiar face," he said.

"Yeah, I know the feeling, Tommy." We both paused for a second and then busted out laughing. We started talking again after we caught our breath. "Hey, Tommy. Have you seen any of the other guys around yet?"

"Nope, just got here myself. You?"

"Same here," I replied. Now let me tell you a little bit about Tommy because I'm sure you're curious. First and foremost, he's a hardass, and what I mean by that is that he's been through a lot of shit, and had to earn his status as a jock. He's athletic and on the smart side and actually the first black friend I've ever had.

We talked for a while before another familiar voice interrupted the conversation. "Hey, look who it is, Bobby and Tommy. What's up, losers?" We couldn't help but to start cracking up, because we knew exactly who it was.

"How's it going, Chubs?" Tommy yelled out first.

"Chubs, my friend. What's happening?" I shouted. We walked up to him and both gave him a high five.

"It's going good, guys." he smiled. "Nice to see you guys here as well. Who knows, maybe this year we can take on the bullies." he laughed. It was nice to have almost the whole gang here, still there was one of us that was missing; But still seeing friendly faces put my mixed emotions at ease, yet curiosity had gained the upper hand in me. I looked around.

"Has anyone seen, John Boy?" I asked. Tommy and Chubs just looked at me and gave a faint smile. "What's wrong, guys?" I could tell something wasn't right.

"Let's talk about it later." Tommy replied.

"Yeah, I agree with Tommy." Chubs then lowered his head and looked down at the ground; he gave a fake laugh before looking back up at me and saying, "Looks like we will be the three amigos this time around." Just like Chubs to make a remark like that, always the jokester.

Ah, Chubs, one friend I will always remember. His real name

is Billy McNown; he was a heavyset young man and always the camp clown. He played more pranks on more people than I could count, trouble always seemed to find that kid. I swear he pissed off the bullies just for the hell of it whenever he needed a good laugh.

That would probably explain why Tommy, John Boy, and myself became really good friends with him; we all had two things that brought us together as friends: our hatred for summer camp and the camp bullies. And "Chubs" just seemed like a good nickname for Billy, and it stuck with him through all the years at camp. As for John Boy, he was my very first friend that I made at camp so many years

ago. He was like me: shy and not very social, and she had a love for comic books like I had. The funny thing is, we started off hating each other at first, but later on we had earned each others respect and trust at the end of our first year of camp.

And Tommy? Well, he became mine and John Boy's good friend the second year of camp, and then Chubs, and so on and so forth. Looks like John Boy won't be around this year though, and I have a feeling either Tommy or Chubs know why, or perhaps they both knew something and didn't want to say. I just had a feeling both of them were hiding something, and I was going to find out, it was just a matter of time.

And me being me, of course, I had to ask, "Hey, guys, do you know something about John Boy that you're not telling me?" Tommy and Chubs both gave me that "shut the hell up" look. Right then and there, I knew I had better not push my luck with them on this subject, so I backed off and started talking about something else. I look back on that now and wished I hadn't backed off at all; things might have ended differently if I had pushed them into telling me everything at the time.

But you can't change the past, can you? Sorry, I keep getting off the subject, I do apologize. Where was I? Oh yes, I remember. We talked for what seemed to be hours about how our winters went and about school and how we were all dreading the bus ride to camp. Hell, we even talked about how hot some of them women counselors were; before we knew it, the parking lot had filled up with all the other teens and kids that were also heading for camp.

And then out of nowhere, "Well, well, well. If it isn't the geek squad." Followed by laughter. Then we heard another voice, "Hey, guys. Looks like we get another year with the crybabies." Then more laughter ensued afterward.

"Who said that?" Tommy yelled out as loud as he could, while Chubs and myself looked around in the crowd of kids to find out who was saying that to us.

"Up here, dweebs." and then we heard banging noises coming from one of the buses, and that got our attention. "Looking for someone, nerds?" And there to our demise, right in front of us, on the bus hanging out the windows was the bullies. To the left was Jimmy—we don't really know his last name, but he prefers to be called Spike because it sounds cool.

To the right was big Tony Parks, and in the center like always was Johnny Goodman, the leader himself of the bullies. All were star football players, and all were big-time assholes, and every teen and kid in camp wanted to hang out with them. Which, in turn, all it did was make all of them Johnny's pawns.

It didn't take much longer for Bobby to decide he was done talking to the stranger for the day. "I think I've said enough, for now, sir. If you don't mind, I'm tired and would like some time alone to rest. Come back tomorrow if you really want to know more."

The stranger stood and reached out to shake Bobby's hand and said, "See you tomorrow then, Bobby." Bobby stepped back and stared at the man's hand; the stranger just smiled at him before lowering his hand back down. He turned his back to Bobby, and without saying another word, he walked out the door.

Bobby laughed and then muttered under his breath, "He won't be coming back. They never do; he will be just like all the others and think I'm crazy too." He looked around his room to make sure there wasn't anyone else around before lying down on his bed and pulling out a notebook from in between his mattress and box spring. He had been writing a few things down in a journal, just in case something bad happens to him; he wants to at least let someone know the truth. A strange man came by to visit with me today.

He wanted to know all about the incident that happened at my camp so many years ago. I'm not sure I can trust that man yet, but I have a feeling I will know soon enough. Never believe in what you hear, and your eyes can always deceive you. Trust no one. Hours later after Bobby had fallen asleep, his door opened; it was the stranger again that was there earlier.

# 2

# Let The Fun Begin

He insisted on hearing more of Bobby's story. "So, are you ready to tell me more? I know it's early, but you're more than likely used to this."

Bobby gave the man a sarcastic smirk before saying, "More than you know. But do you mind giving me a chance to get out of my bed?"

The man had a perplexed look on his face before finally getting the hint; he turned his back to Bobby. "Does this work?"

Bobby just shook his head. "Yes, that works. You know I'm surprised you came back. Most people don't bother with me after the first time they meet me."

The man looked at him with that perplexed look still plastered on his face. "Why wouldn't I come back? I have a job to do, and you're a part of that job. I'm not like the rest—"

Bobby didn't even give him a chance to finish his sentence before cutting him off. "And what makes you or your so-called job any different than all the rest and their jobs?" Then out of nowhere, his anger showed at the man. "Every last one they came and went, And after a few hours of talking to me, they deem me crazy. Then they never come back." After that Bobby gathered himself and calmed his nerve. "Answer my question: what makes you so different? How do I know you won't do the same?"

The stranger looked at him and said, "You're just going to have to trust me."

Bobby looks at the stranger and replies, "Trust you? Why should I trust what you have to say?"

The strange man smiled and said, "That's the best I can do for now. And besides, I came back, didn't I?"

Bobby reluctantly agreed, "I guess I have no choice for now. I shall start from where I left off." The man nodded in agreement. This time they both took a chair, and to Bobby's surprise, the man had opened his black bag and pulled out a folder. Is he been taking notes? Bobby thought to himself, now his curiosity was piqued, and he wanted to know what was in those notes. But Bobby was smarter than he looked, and he decided he would wait for the opportunity to do so. "So." He looked at the man strangely. "Now let the fun begin, shall we?" He continued on with the story he started telling yesterday.

Everyone wanted to be like Johnny, and he loved the attention and having the control over them. Tommy was pissed off, and he shouted, "Why don't the three of you get off that bus and say that to my face." Johnny just started laughing at him. "Something funny?" Tommy asked, with a hint of anger in his voice.

"Yeah, we're looking right at it," Spike yelled out, laughing as he did so.

That's when I opened my mouth. "Like you have room to talk." and Spike came running off the bus with a wild look in his eyes.

Chubs were scared and pulling at Tommy's and also mine. "What in the hell are you guys doing?"

Tommy pulled his arm angrily away from Chubs and said, "I'm

tired of this shit. It's time we do something about it." Tommy looked back at us both. "You guys got my back or what?"

Chubs stood there afraid to even move, and I was ready for a fight. "Hell yeah, Tommy. We have your back." I was tired of camp and the bullies and the nightmares. I was honestly on the edge of madness.

Tommy yelled out to us, "Here they come, guys—be ready." Spike was running right at us. With Tony hot on his heels, Tommy and I stood our ground ready for the fight of our lives. Chubs stood there shaking. I honestly thought he was going to shit himself right at the last second Johnny jumps in front of them.

"Guys, you need to calm down. This isn't the time or the place," Johnny hissed.

"What's wrong, Johnny? Not going to let your boys come over here and get their asses kicked?" said Tommy.

Johnny looked at us and laughed. "You and the nerds versus us? Let me ask you. Who do you think will win? And furthermore, this isn't the time or the place, but I will say this. There will be a time and a place, Tommy, and you damn sure better be ready because we're going to make you and your friends pay." Johnny gave a cocky smile, then added, "However, Tommy. I'm willing to let things slide, for you only." He continued on, "The nerds will still pay, just like they do every year." Johnny reached out his hand. "What do you say, Tommy? Friends?"

I was actually waiting for Tommy to shake his hand. Tommy didn't have to be friends with a bunch of nerds like us. What happened next truly surprised me. He stared down at Johnny's hand and slapped it away. "I have my true friends right here. I'm not going to be one of your followers or pawns, Johnny."

Johnny lowered his hand and shook his head and said, "Tsk,

tsk, tsk. What a waste, you chose nerds over us. You could have rolled with the big dogs, Tommy. Now you're a dead man, just like the rest of these losers." he pointed at each and every one of us as he spoke.

Tommy took a step forward and got right in Johnny's face. "If you even touch my friends, not even your lapdogs will save you from the ass beating that I will give to you, 'friend'"

Johnny lifted up his hands laughing at Tommy's threat as he was stepping back. "Whatever you say, Tommy. Whatever you say." He stares at all of us before winking, then looks over at his friends. "Back on the bus boys. We will settle this later. For now, patience." Johnny turned and made his way back toward the bus.

Spike glared and then pointed at us and pounds his fist into his hand before turning and walking off. Tony had given us a look of complete hatred, you could just see the fire in his eyes. He walked away slowly without saying a word to us. I also noticed he had put something back in his pocket that looked like a knife. I had somewhat of a bad feeling that we would find out later exactly what was in his pocket.

"Well, that almost ended badly," muttered Chubs. Tommy shook his fist in the air and yelled out, "Pricks!"

It took me a while to calm my nerves; all I could think about was picking something up, and it wouldn't have mattered to me at that point what I picked up and walked up behind them and bash their skulls in. But I didn't. I stood there and watched as they walked away like a bunch of cowards. I then turned my attention to the crowd that was behind us; there had to have been at least forty, maybe fifty teens, and young kids in all if I could wager a guess.

"Everyone, please leave your bags on the ground and get on

the buses. We will take care of everything from here. Do not take your bags on the buses with you. There's not enough room!" yells one of the counselors.

I sighed and looked over at Tommy and Chubs. "Looks like it's time to go, guys."

Tommy looked at me and replied, "We better hurry so we can take the good seats this time around." He walked ahead toward one of the buses. I just nodded and followed behind him.

Poor Chubs just stood there like he was unsure of what to do next. I turned to him and said, "Hurry up Chubs! Unless you want to be left behind!" I waved him on and added, "And I don't think you want to be all alone out here in the middle of nowhere." Chubs lowered his head and slowly followed behind us like a lost puppy dog. We ended up getting lucky enough to end up on the opposite bus as the bullies, and we also got lucky enough to finally get seats in the back of the bus as well.

For us, it didn't get any better than that, first time for everything I guess. After we got ourselves seated, we looked around for Johnny and the goon squad, just to be on the safe side. And again, lucky for us, the coast was clear. We all took a big sigh of relief before we started talking and catching up on some things.

I was certain this was my chance to find out what they knew about John Boy; however, before I got a chance, out of nowhere, Chubs blurts out, "What in the hell was that all about, guys?" And that wasn't all he rambled on about either. "You could have gotten us a killed or hurt! What in the hell were you fucking thinking?" Chubs looked like he was about to puke or cry.

"Chill, Chubs, I've got this," Tommy replied with a smirk on his face. "What in the hell does that mean, Tommy?" Chubs yelled.

"It means, I've got everything under control," Tommy replied back, still smirking.

Chubs slammed his hands on the back of the seat. "Dammit!"

I could tell Chubs was really starting to get pissed off, I knew I had to do something before a fight started. "Chill out, Chubs," I said to Chubs before turning to Tommy. "What do you mean by 'I've got this' Tommy? Just tell us, please."

Tommy laughed before saying, "Fine. Fine. Ruin all the fun for me why don't you." Then he laughed again and added, "My older brother, Jerry, is the head counselor this year at camp, so, guys, what I'm trying to say is that we have backup this time." Tommy explained.

Hearing that made Chubs calm down a bit. "Sorry, Tommy. I should have trusted in your word to us; you've got this all under control," said Chubs.

Tommy smiled before he said, "It's all good, Chubs. And besides, wasn't that crazy? I mean who knows what could have happened to the three of us, look at it this way. We actually stood our ground this time. It was one hell of a rush."

Tommy was definitely enjoying himself, maybe just a little too much before Chubs jumped into the conversation. "Yeah, we were about to kick some serious ass. Too bad they ran away like cowards, instead of fighting us like men."

After hearing what Chubs had to say, Tommy bent over and started laughing hysterically at him. It took a few minutes for Tommy to compose himself. I've never seen him laugh so hard. And I could see the anger in Chubs's face starting to boil over; at that moment I felt sorry for him, even though Chubs was coming up with quite the lie.

"Chubs, man, you sure do know how to make me laugh." He then looked Chubs straight in the eyes and said, "We? We!

Chubs, all you did was stand there shaking like you were about to piss yourself, and you looked like a damn ghost you were so pale. For a moment I thought you were going to puke on top of that."

He laughed again and added, "But it's all good, Chubs. At least you didn't run away this time like you did last year, so I'll give you that much. You better have our backs next time though, Chubs. We're counting on you to help us out when the time comes. And we stick together no matter what." Tommy then turned his attention toward me. "But at least I know my man Bobby here has my back against those guys." And then he slapped me on the back and then talked some more. "We all have each other's back, and never leave the other behind. Right, Bobby?"

I could tell by the look on Tommy's face he needed my reassurance, even though he said the things he did. But I knew how to answer his question. "That's right, Tommy, I have your back. Just as long as you have mine. That's the way it works, right?" I waited for the usual smart ass remark from him, but this time what he said was reassuring.

"You're right about that, Bobby." Tommy looked over at Chubs and asked, "You have our back too, Chubs?" He didn't answer, so Tommy asked him again. "Chubs. Are you in?" Chubs still didn't answer; he was off in his own little world muttering to himself.

We looked at each other and laughed. "What's so funny?" Chubs asked. He wasn't too happy with us, and you could tell he was still somewhat scared. Hell, I think deep down we were all scared and just didn't want to show it.

"All right, everyone, can I please have your attention?" And of course, it being one of the hot women counselors that were standing there, everyone paid attention. And believe me when I say, everyone on that bus paid attention to her. Especially since she was wearing a tank top that was damn near see-through and Daisy Duke shorts, which was wow. Just wow! "Please take your seats. We are about to head out and also enjoy the ride. Thank you, and we will be at our destination before we know it!" she happily explained to everyone with a smile on her face.

A few minutes after she sat back down, the bus started to move, and we were all on our way to summer camp. All of the smiles we had on our faces soon faded away, because none of us wanted to go. But at that time, parents would always win against us. This, however, will be a summer that none of us would ever forget. As the bus started down the road, I decided that it was time for Tommy, Chubs, and myself to catch up on a few more things. I was smart about it, however, and would slowly work on the subject that I wanted information about.

We started off talking about how each other's school year had gone. Tommy bragged about his grades and then about how he's finally the starter for the football team and how good he was doing and all that shit, but we knew how much that meant to him. Tommy wasn't shy about bragging either; he loved to talk about himself and would have kept on all the way to camp if I hadn't interrupted him.

"So, Chubs, anything new with you?" I asked. He just sat there staring ahead toward the front of the bus, like he didn't even hear me. "Hey, Chubs? Earth to Chubs." I said, this time poking at his arm with my finger. It took a while, and Chubs finally snapped out of it; he gave me a look like he was lost or had been in a trance.

Even his answer had me confused. "Huh?" He was still giving me a weird look. Tommy even noticed his weird reaction. "Are you alright, Chubs?"

"What?" Chub's muttered.

So I decided to be a smart-ass. "Chubs, stop staring at that cute counselor and answer our questions."

Still, with a blank stare, he answered, "What questions?"

I sighed and told Chubs to just forget about it; it wasn't a big deal. I knew something was up, but I was too damn annoyed to actually give a damn. However, after my comment about the cute counselor, I now found Tommy and Chubs both staring at her and now ignoring me. I just rolled my eyes and lay my head back against the bus seat. Camp was still on my mind, and so was the mystery of my best friend, John Boy. And I was going to work my way up to that conversation; however, now their attention was elsewhere, and right now I didn't have a chance in hell of getting through to them. And also I started to think about my nightmares again, even though my mind was preoccupied with all these things. I felt my eyes getting weary, and my body failing me because sleep was beckoning me. Before I knew it, I found myself in a deep slumber, and then I think the bus must have hit a huge hole in the road because the whole bus shook with a violent force. It was violent enough that it woke me up, or so I thought anyway.

I rubbed my eyes and was yawning in the process; also, I was wondering how long I had been out for as I was gathering my senses. After I was fully awake, I looked over at Tommy and asked, "How long was I out for?" No response at all from him. "Hey, Tommy! How long was I out for!" I asked yet again. Still no response from him. Either Tommy was ignoring me or he was preoccupied with something else, but at second glance he was just staring straight ahead—no talking, no moving, no nothing from him. That pissed me off badly. "Damn you, Tommy!" I yelled out. "I didn't want to talk to your punk ass anyways."

So then I turned to Chubs. "Hey, Chubs. Since Tommy is being a little bitch, maybe you can answer me. How long was I out for?" I then angrily added, "And then maybe you can tell me what's eating at Tommy." I waited for an answer, but oddly I didn't get one from him either. Now I was furious with both of them. "Chubs! Tommy! One of you assholes had better answer me! Hey!" I even stuck my mouth by Tommy's ear and yelled at him as loud as I could, and nothing worked. I turned toward Chubs, who was sitting right beside me, and I shook him as hard as I could instead of yelling at him.

Oddly, not a damn thing I did to get their attention worked. I was getting worried and yet at the same time, I was pissed off at them also. But then something caught my attention out of the corner of my eye; it had looked like we were already at the campgrounds, for the bus was surrounded by trees. However, we kept going down what seemed to be a deserted road, and that wasn't all I had seen while looking out the window.

I noticed how different things seemed to look; it was creepy, all seemed dark, almost evil in a way. I started to feel ill. Was this really the same campgrounds? Or was this a different place altogether? I kept asking myself all of the questions over and over again; then to my anguish, the color of the trees had changed almost instantly. They went from full and green, to dead looking, and all the leaves had fallen off the branches. The green grass on the ground started to ooze crimson red.

I kept on looking back and forth, from out the window and back inside the bus; however, it seemed like I was the only one that noticed the change outside at all. To me, it was like everyone was in a trance except for me, and hell, I even yelled to the top of my lungs, "Hey, guys!" And nothing. "Hello! Is there anyone that can hear or answer me?" That didn't even work. Not a single person on the bus moved an inch; everyone just kept staring straight ahead.

Tommy and Chubs were acting exactly the same way. I was beyond scared at the time, and I didn't know what was going on. Why won't anyone answer me? What's going to happen to us?" The thoughts just shot through my mind. I wanted to shut my eyes and hope that when I opened them, everything would be back to normal. Unfortunately, as I went to do so, something came over me, and it seemed like I didn't have control over my body. It felt like I was being made by some unknown force to look out the bus window again; as I looked out, I saw something that startled me badly. What I saw was that creepy kid again.

He was wearing the same torn-up clothes as before, so I knew it was the same exact kid. And if that wasn't proof enough, seeing his horrible face again was. I tried to look away, but I couldn't; my will was not my own. Since I couldn't look away, I stared at him with wonder in my eyes. "What in the hell was he doing?" I asked myself. To me, it looked like he was pointing at something. It was as if he was trying to show me what he wanted; unfortunately, the bus started picking up speed, and I couldn't exactly see too clearly.

He didn't go away either. At every point the bus went flying by with speed, he was there again and again and again. He was there. It was definitely disturbing, and he never stopped making that expression as if to point at something. What really got me was the fact that every time I had seen, him there was another kid with him, each time until he was surrounded by them. And these were not normal kids; they looked as if they were the undead.

The man interrupted Bobby in mid-sentence, "What do you

mean by 'undead'?"

You could tell by the look on Bobby's face he didn't like being interrupted. "If you would let me finish, you would know." The man nodded as if telling Bobby to continue on The other kids were mangled very badly: some had no arms, and some were missing legs, and others were missing eyes, or bleeding profusely. But finally, I understood what was going on: the boy was doing his best to warn me to go back from where I came from, or death would ensue. Seeing all the other kids, that much was clear. I tried again to turn around and give my friends and the others a warning of what was to happen, but I still couldn't move a muscle.

Out of nowhere a hand came from the shadows from behind the boy and was placed on his shoulder. I couldn't make out anything of what was behind him, except for the hand on his shoulder. The hand was thin and bony like, and the skin looked burned in spots, pale and leathery as well, and the fingernails were black as the darkest night, and oh, so sharp. And then the boy let out the most frightening scream I've ever heard, and yes, the scream was so loud that I think the devil himself could have heard it.

I know I did, and I will never forget it. None of it made a damn bit of sense to me whatsoever; the boy had disappeared along with all the other children that had surrounded him. The only thing I could make out now was the outline of some figure, along with glowing red eyes. I couldn't tell you what it was; it could have been man or demon, I wasn't for sure.

If only I could have gotten a better look at it, maybe I could have been prepared later for what was to as well, and the fingernails were black as the darkest night, and oh, so sharp. And then the boy let out the most frightening scream I've ever heard, and yes, the scream was so loud that I think the devil himself could have heard it. I know I did, and I will never forget it. None of it made a damn bit of sense to me whatsoever; the boy had disappeared along with all the other children that had surrounded him.

The only thing I could make out now was the outline of some figure, along with glowing red eyes. I couldn't tell you what it was; it could have been man or demon, I wasn't for sure. If only I could have gotten a better look at it, maybe I could have been prepared later for what was to come. Bobby had lost track of what he was saying and stared off into the unknown, that is until a voice snapped him out of it.

"Bobby? Hey, Bobby?" the stranger loudly said.

Bobby regained his composure. "Sorry about that, I found myself lost in thought," Bobby explained to him.

"Should I come back another time?" the man asked.

"No, I'm fine," Bobby said to him.

"Are you sure you can go on?" the man come. Bobby had lost track of what he was saying and stared off into the unknown, that is until a voice snapped him out of it.

"Bobby? Hey, Bobby?" the stranger loudly said.

Bobby regained his composure. "Sorry about that, I found myself lost in thought," Bobby explained to him.

"Should I come back another time?" the man asked.

"No, I'm fine," Bobby said to him.

"Are you sure you can go on?" the man asked him, seeming worried at the moment.

"Yes, I'm sorry to have worried you. But I assure that I am just fine," the man nodded hesitantly, saying, "Continue on when ready." And hearing the okay, Bobby continued on from where he left off.

After the red blazing eyes had disappeared, I had control over my body again or so I thought I did, but I was sadly mistaken. All I was able to do was turn away from the window; when I tried to scream, not a sound came from my asked him, seeming worried at the moment.

"Yes, I'm sorry to have worried you. But I assure that I am just fine," the man nodded hesitantly, saying, "Continue on when ready." And hearing the okay, Bobby continued on from where he left off.

After the red blazing eyes had disappeared, I had control over my body again or so I thought I did, but I was sadly mistaken. All I was able to do was turn away from the window; when I tried to scream, not a sound came from my mouth, and when I tried to move, I could not. It was like my whole body was paralyzed. I was scared to my core. I couldn't do a damn thing no matter how hard I tried. Damn it! I have to do something! I thought to myself.

Then all of a sudden one by one, the counselors and all the other teens and kids started to burst into flames. Still, I tried to fight and scream, but my body wouldn't move. It was of no use! I had no choice but to sit there and watch everyone burn, even my friends. As everyone had been on fire I expected screams of agony or at least seeing someone, anyone tries to jump up and save themselves.

However, there were no screams, no movement from a single one of them, my eyes widened. My God! They must be like me and unable to move! I thought to myself. I watched in horror as everyone's flesh melted off their bones from the flames around them. Oh, the agony they must feel must now be far worse than anyone could have ever imagined, seeing how they couldn't move to voice their pain or save themselves, I thought, wishing there was something I could do, but there was none.

I could now start to feel the heat from the flames and smell the horrid smell of burning flesh! I knew now it was about to be me that was going to burn in the flames. Now I could hear However, there were no screams, no movement from a single one of them, my eyes widened. My God! They must be like me and unable to move! I thought to myself. I watched in horror as everyone's flesh melted off their bones from the flames around them.

Oh, the agony they must feel must now be far worse than anyone could have ever imagined, seeing how they couldn't move to voice their pain or save themselves, I thought, wishing there was something I could do, but there was none. I could now start to feel the heat from the flames and smell the horrid smell of burning flesh! I knew now it was about to be me that was going to burn in the flames. Now I could hear the crackle from the flames all around me, and then out from the depths of hell came a dark and sadistic laugh in which for some reason scared me more than the flames itself.

But what I heard and saw next chilled me straight to the bone. A voice called out to me, "I will see you soon." And right in front of me, I had seen those red, evil glowing eyes staring at me with such hate and contempt as if for all human life that was in its wake. After I heard that damn voice, the flames started to consume me. I could feel my flesh start to burn! I tried my best to fight and scream yet again, but finally, I had had enough and gave into the crackle from the flames all around me, and then out from the depths of hell came a dark and sadistic laugh in which for some reason scared me more than the flames itself.

Maybe burning would be better than where I was about to go and what I was going to have to endure, or at least that was what my mind was telling me. But my heart was wanting me to live on, so again I fought against what had me paralyzed, yet I was too late; the flames now had me consumed, and I was burning alive.

"Hey man, you okay?" It was an all too familiar voice that was now calling out to me. "Hey!" The voice called out again. This time I could feel someone grab my shoulder and shake me. It was Tommy, and he was doing the best that he could to wake me up.

To his surprise, I jumped up and without thinking I yelled out, "I can move!" Shortly after I started to pat myself down. "Where are the flames? The bus, is it still on fire?" I asked, with a frantic tone to my voice. I was still looking around frantically as I tried to figure out what was happening.

"Bobby? Are you alright, man?" Tommy asked over and over again.

I completely ignored his question, and then I looked over his face and his arms. "You're not burned."

He pulled his arm away from me, and with a look of wonder in his eyes, he asked me, "What the hell, Bobby? Man, what's going on? You're creeping me out."

That's when Chubs raised up his head and rubbing his eyes as if waking from sleep, he asked, "What in the sam hell is going on!" Joy overcame my body at the sound of Chubs's voice that I literally jumped over the seat and gave him a hug.

"What the— get the hell off me, dude." He pushed me off as quickly as he could. "What's up with you?" he asked.

I found myself ignoring his question as well. "Where're the flames," I asked, confused.

"What are you talking about, Bobby?" Tommy asked. "The bus is on fire, you guys," I said to him.

Chubs looked around confused himself and replied, "Hey, Bobby. Look around. Does it really look like the bus is on fire to you?"

I looked around the bus with an insane look in my eyes. "But everything was up in flames. And everyone in it was being burned alive." I made one last inspection of the bus and calmed my nerves. "Was it a dream?" I asked myself. I leaned my head back on the seat. I was pale, sweating, and breathing heavily. My body felt like it was on fire, and I wanted to puke my guts up.

"Bobby?" Chubs tried to get my attention.

"What, Chubs?" I asked. Tommy I guess decided to interrupt our conversation with his own question for me.

"What was that all about, Bobby?"

I looked at him trying to regain my composure, and I answered. "I was having a nightmare. That's all, Tommy." At least that's what I was trying to convince myself it was.

Tommy nudged me. "It must have been one hell of a nightmare to make you act like that, man." Then he looked at me again and laughed. "But, man, you've scared everyone on the bus. Just look around at all the eyes on you, Bobby." He then pointed around the bus. And sure enough, every single person on the bus was looking back at me.

I could feel my face turning red with embarrassment. I smiled and waved at everyone on the bus and reassured them that everything was all right and that I just had a nightmare. A few of the younger kids looked at me like I was crazy and didn't know what to think; the other teens on the bus busted up laughing at me. Hell, even the counselors gave me weird looks and then came back to check on me, just in case. After the counselors took their seats, the bus was off and running again, "So you had a nightmare, and that's what caused you to go nuts!" Chubs asked. "Yeah, seems that way," I replied.

"Man, that's too funny!" Chubs laughed.

"Back off, Chubs, that shit ain't funny," Tommy told him. "Tell us what happened in your nightmare. Maybe you will feel somewhat better if you do." Tommy explained.

"Yeah, I'm curious about this bad dream too," said Chubs.

"I'm fine now, guys. But that nightmare felt so real," I answered.

"It was really weird. All you did was sit there and stare straight ahead you didn't even move a muscle. We tried to talk to you, but you never responded to us. Then your eyes closed, and I shook you, and next, I know you start freaking out. So just tell us, what exactly happened?" said Tommy.

It all sounded very odd to me; I didn't know what to think, or even what to say at first. How could I have had such a nightmare with my eyes open? I've never slept with my eyes open before, so why now? And why did Tommy and Chubs say I was awake and then suddenly fell asleep all at once? Thinking about it all really scared me, and as bad as I wanted to change the subject and not talk about it anymore, I couldn't, or you could say I wouldn't. I knew that since we were on the subject of dreams, I had to ask, "So, guys. I just have to ask you two about something." They both gave me their full attention. I had a feeling they knew what I was about to ask. "Have either one of you had any bad nightmares?" I just had to ask them.

Chubs turned back around in his seat and said, "Nope, not me." I could tell he didn't want to talk about it anymore.

So I turned my attention toward Tommy. "And you?" I asked.

Tommy being a tough guy just smirked. "I don't have time to worry about silly dreams. And besides, I'm not a child anymore either, so that shit doesn't bother me," he answered me like a wannabe badass.

I just glared at them both and then asked myself, Was it just me having these nightmares? And if so, then why me? Or could it be that both Tommy and Chubs were both lying to me? Or maybe it was the hatred I had for camp causing my dreams to spiral out of control? I had a million thoughts going through my head, and I wasn't sure how to handle it all. I didn't have the answers to any of my questions, and I also knew that Tommy and Chubs weren't going to be of much help either. So I dropped that subject and decided to start another conversation instead.

"Hey, Tommy. So tell me, why John Boy's not around?" I asked. I just thought John Boy's parents didn't make him have to go this time around. But after watching Tommy's and Chubs' facial expressions when I asked about him proved me wrong. So now I wanted to know the truth, and finally, I had found out the chilling news straight from Tommy's mouth.

"Look, Bobby. I don't know how to tell you this, but John Boy ended up getting sick." he paused for a moment.

"Just say it, Tommy." my patience had completely run out.

Tommy glared at me; for a moment I could see the hate in his eyes or maybe it was sadness. "Well—"

That's when Chubs jumped in. "Just give it a rest, Bobby."

For a second I could feel my heart race, and I had gotten mad at Chubs. "I have to know. So stay out of this." I yelled. Then I focused my attention back to Tommy. "Tell me now, damn it!" I demanded.

Tommy nodded in agreement; even though he could barely look at me, he went on with what he was telling me. "As I was saying, he got sick. And in the hospital, he rambled on about nightmares, ghosts, and some kind of demon that was trying to kill him. It was just two days later, the nurses found him dead in his bed. He had died of complete shock. And then I got even more shocking news from Chubs.

Yeah, and I even heard that before he was admitted into the hospital, he went insane. He would refuse to sleep, and sometimes he wouldn't even eat. And on top of that, he started to get really violent. At first, he started to hurt himself, and then others. He even attacked his mom with a knife, and he stabbed his dad as he took the knife away from him. I believe that was his parents' breaking point, scary, huh? Poor son of a bitch."

I was sad over everything that I was hearing, and yet at the same time I was getting really scared. I was having the same dreams, and yes, my fuse was starting to get short, and at times my anger would take control over me. Was I going to go insane and start attacking people like John Boy did? Or was I going to end up dying in my sleep as well? What does all this mean? The wheels were turning in my head wildly that it made this trip to summer camp even more menacing. That's when a voice snapped Bobby back to reality.

# 3

# Detour

Sorry to have to stop you there, but it's getting late. I have things that I need to do, and I'm sure you need some rest," the stranger said.

"That's fine with me, you're right it is getting late, and I would like to get some rest," said Bobby.

The man finished up his notes for the evening and put his folder away in his black bag as usual. "Well," he said as he stood up out of his chair. "Don't worry, I'll be back tomorrow." he gave a faint smile and offered his hand to Bobby yet again. He got the same response as last time from him. Bobby just stared at his hand again and turned his back on him. "Still don't trust me, I see." the man said.

That had gotten Bobby's attention, and he turned back around to confront the man face-to-face. "Can you blame me?" he asked.

"You can trust me, Bobby," the man said back to him.

"Yeah right. Sure I can trust you," Bobby said sarcastically. "I still don't even know your name or why you're so interested in me or what I have to say. And most of all, why do you find what happened so many years ago intriguing?" Bobby had a lot of questions for the stranger.

And the man definitely didn't want to answer Bobby's questions either; all he would say to him is, "Good point, Bobby. You will know everything in due time. I promise you that much." he turned walking towards the door.

"Yeah right," Bobby said. "We will see if you actually come back tomorrow. Just know that I will never trust you until I know what you are really up to."

The man smiled at Bobby and then made his way out the door without saying another word to him. Bobby paced around the room for a while; none of it made sense to him. That was fifteen years ago; why was everything being brought up again? This was a mystery he was intent to find out no matter what it took. So he did what he's always done when he has things on his mind; he went over to his bed and looked under his mattress and grabbed his journal. He walked over to the corner of the room where his desk stood; he took a seat and opened up his journal and began to write.

Another evening of talking to the stranger about my horrid past has come and gone. He seems genuinely interested though, which has been a surprise to me. But I still can't trust the man until I learn more about him; still, yet, I'm curious on why he wants to know about what happened fifteen years ago at that blasted camp. I will find out one way or another, no matter the cost. If I have to relive my nightmares, then that man is going to tell me everything that I want to know. Because all I've ever wanted to do was forget about that place and all the gruesome things that took place there as well. That's why I hide here and never do I want to leave because I know what's waiting for me out in the real world.

And yet every time someone different walks through that door wanting to hear about that incident, I can't help but tell them the truth even if it does sound far-fetched. It's like I'm compelled to tell them, or maybe it's because I'm trying to warn them of ghosts and demons that walk among us, I can't say for sure. However crazy it sounds and even if it sounds like the ramblings of a madman, all I say is the truth. However, on top of that, I prefer the fact that everyone thinks I'm crazy even though I'm not.

I just do my best to make everyone think that I'm a danger to myself and to society; indeed, it sounds crazy, but for me, it's not. I feel safe in this place far more than I would anywhere else. Hell, maybe I am crazy. And still, for some reason I hate it when others call me crazy; also it aggravates me when others come here and bother me about what really happened. Yet when I tell them, they don't believe me, and that pisses me off.

However, this stranger that has been talking to me lately hangs on to every little detail like he has some important task at hand. I still can't trust him, at least not yet. For now, I need sleep. I shall make more entries in this journal as each day passes. He places the journal back under the mattress and prepares himself for another restless night of sleep.

Early that next day, there was a knock at the door. Bobby didn't answer at first; he already knew who was at his door anyway. "Looks like Mr. No Name is back. I'll make him wait a minute or two," He said to himself as he smiled. "Come on in! I know it's you!" He called out.

The stranger walked into the room with a slight smile on his face. "How could you tell?" he asked sarcastically.

And Bobby, deciding to be a smart-ass, answered, "Lucky guess." Then he took his usual seat and waited for the stranger to sit down. "Guess you want to know even more now?" Bobby asked.

"That's right. I am sorry, Bobby, but I need you to continue on from where you left off yesterday," The man answered as he took his seat in his usual spot in front of him. And Bobby didn't have a choice; that much he understood.

"Hmm." It looked like Bobby was deep in thought. "What's wrong?" the man asked. "I'm trying to remember where I left off," Bobby responded.

"I believe it was when you finally found out the truth about one of your friends."

"Oh, that's right."

After hearing the chilling news about John Boy, I sat there in silence looking out the bus window watching the scenery go by. That's when I noticed how different everything was; it wasn't like the nightmare though, which was a good thing. Right before I could say anything to Tommy or Chubs, one of the counselors stood up and informed all of us that we will be taking a detour for special reasons this year.

"About damn time they decided to switch things up a little." I could tell by the look on his face that he was overly excited. Now Chubs, on the other hand, didn't really give a shit; all he wanted to do was get to camp as quickly as possible so he could get it over with.

Too bad that it's never that easy; as for me, I was somewhat uneasy about it all at first. Eventually, I came around to the idea. That, however, ended up biting me right on the ass later on. It wasn't long before the bus came to a complete stop at its destination and shortly after the counselors stood up again and started to lead everyone off the bus, explaining things, as we went on, our way.

Candice, the cute one, was the first of the counselors that talked to everyone, saying, "All right, everyone, listen up." It amazed me how she seemed to control a whole crowd with just a few words. "I bet everyone here is wondering what's going on. Am I right? Well, we've decided to treat all of you to a surprise. We're going to a whole new camp and wait until you see it! So here's how it's going to be: we have a two-day hike, and we have to start now." Before she could get another word out, another bus pulled up behind us full of more campers, and just like us, they too were ushered off.

However, Tommy's excitement for change suddenly took a backseat when we noticed the counselors getting off the bus. It was Mark and Steve. Mark was the biggest asshole you could ever meet, and Steve, well, he was Mark's lackey and would do anything that Mark would ask of him, even if it was right or wrong. Almost always it was wrong, badly wrong. "Everyone gather around!" Mark shouted. "Hey, Candice?" he yelled out to her.

She looked over at him. "What do you want, Mark?" she shouted back at him. "Bring your group over here!" he yelled back at her.

"Sure," she responded with a shout. "Well you heard the man, let's head over to him. Now that he's here, he is now the boss." Unfortunately, none of us had much of a choice in the matter.

So yet again the group was ushered over, and as soon as the group we were in merged with the other, Mark's head grew, and he started his shit quickly. "All right, everyone, listen up! I'm the boss here now. You will do what I say when I say it! This is how it's going to work! We will hand you back your bags, and you will all be given backpacks! At that point, all of you will put all your belongings from your bags into the backpacks. Everyone has exactly ten minutes to get done and be ready to go! Or you will be left behind. Is that clear?"

We all had our backpacks full of our stuff in no time flat and was ready to go. We did that with a purpose in mind; it gave Tommy enough time to look for his brother, and we helped him out. "Hey, Tommy? Why don't you just ask about your brother? We really don't have much time until we have to move out," I said to him.

Tommy knew at that moment I was right; as much as he hated the fact, he would have to talk to that asshole, Mark. "Hey, Mark? Have you seen my brother anywhere?" Tommy asked.

"Your brother took another way, one for the more adventurous type. And I was lucky enough to watch the losers. Now get ready to go," Mark told Tommy. "Okay, everyone, we're moving out!" Mark shouted. He pointed in the direction he wanted the group to go; that's when he noticed that Steve wasn't even paying attention to him. So he walked up behind Steve and slapped him upside his head. "Stop drooling over Candice and move out!" he yelled at him. Candice turned and smiled before walking on ahead. Poor Steve's face turned beet red I swear it looked like he was about to cry as he followed on behind. "What are you guys waiting for?" he asked the other counselors. "Get your asses moving now!"

You had to feel sorry for them, but none of us knew the new counselors that well, so we didn't care. The group and the rest of us walked on into the woods; we knew we were in for a long two days.

"Hey, Tommy. Did you find anything about your brother?" I asked.

"Yeah, he's not here. He ended up going a different way than us. That's all I know," he answered.

"Looks like we lucked out on something though," I said.

He looked at me all confused and asked, "What do you mean

by that?"

I smiled and said, "Johnny and his goons aren't here. That's what I mean; that's a plus, right?" then I laughed about it.

Tommy laughed with me and said, "That's a major plus for us right now."

On the other hand, we both knew that by the time they got to camp, he would have more lackeys on his side, and it wouldn't be fun for us. And on top of that, as we walked on for what seemed to be for hours, Chubs was silent, and for some reason, he refused to talk to either Tommy or me. I tried my best to get him to talk to me. "So what do you think about everything we found out?" he didn't reply to me whatsoever. So I tried again. "Chubs! Hey, Chubs! Are you going to answer me or what?" I asked. He still didn't answer me, and this time around I was starting to get pissed off at him. And just as I was about to rip his ass for being a prick, Mark yelled out for everyone to stop here because it was time for a breather.

That's when Tommy confronted Chubs instead of me, not that I didn't want to, but Tommy just ended up beating me to it. "What's your problem, man?"

"Don't worry about," Chubs responded.

"Hell no! I want to know right now what your deal is." I could see the look on Tommy's face, and it was about to get ugly.

"What's my deal? What's my deal! I will tell you what my deal is: I have a problem with you, Tommy!"

Tommy glared at him then he yelled back, "Then tell me, Chubs. Why do you have a problem with me? What in the hell did I do?"

"You lied, Tommy! You said your brother was going to be here and have our backs! I don't see him anywhere, do you! I think you just wanted to play the part of the big shot!" he erupted.

Tommy then got right up in his face. "Don't you ever call me a liar again, Chubs! Unless you want your ass kicked! You got that?"

"Yeah, yeah. Why don't you bring it, Tommy!" Chubs replied as he got right back in Tommy's face.

At that moment I knew I had to do something before a fight broke out between the two; that's when I jumped right in the middle of them. "Knock it off, guys, we have to stick together, or when the time comes for us to stand together as a strong front, we'll be screwed! And besides, this isn't like you two to fight like this—there, see who's watching? It's Mark, and he's laughing at us. Is that what you guy's want?

If you don't shake hands and end this now, he'll leave us behind." I was angry for sure this time and was barely able to control myself. "What's it going to be?" They both looked at me like I was crazy for yelling at them, but at least they started to laugh even if it was at me. So they both apologized, which was a good thing. "Now can we get over this and stop acting like a bunch of babies?" I asked.

We walked back over to the rest of the group. I was happy to see them both back on the same page again. "Break time is over. It's time to hit the trail again!" Mark shouted. It seemed like Mark didn't have anything better to do than yell; then the unthinkable happened.

"What an asshole," Tommy said out loud. Chubs stopped in his tracks, and so did I. We hoped he didn't hear Tommy's remark, but seeing how Mark stopped and looked back at us, we knew otherwise.

He walked up to us and looked right at Tommy. "So you guys want to run your mouths?" Then he smiled at us and motioned for Steve and Candice to walk over as well. "Since the three of you want to be smart-asses, guess who will be carrying our backpacks too?" he asked.

Since Tommy was already busted, there was no point in him holding back, so he pushed it a little more. "I guess that would be us, right?" he asked.

"That's right smart-ass. You three are my new volunteers, so get used to it," Mark answered back. I could tell that Tommy was fired up and was about to start something with Mark, but before he could, Mark threw the backpacks at us that belonged to Candice, Steve, and himself. Then he laughed as the three of them walked off. "Don't fall behind, ladies," he said, walking away.

"I knew this would happen eventually," said Tommy.

"Tell me about it," Chubs added. This was an ongoing thing for us, for the past three years Mark has done this to us over and over again.

"You see what fighting gets us?" I asked. "Sorry, Bobby," Tommy said. I think he could tell that I wasn't exactly happy with either one of them.

Then I guess Chubs felt like he had to apologize too. "Yeah, Bobby. We're both sorry. It's our fault we have bag-carrying duty again this year." I couldn't stay mad at them; if we stood a chance against the bullies and or the counselors, we would have to stick together more than ever this year.

"It's all good, guys," I replied. "Besides, someday, and I do mean someday, Mark will get what he deserves," I added.

"Hey, ladies!" Mark shouted. "Move out! Or I will leave your asses behind!" he shouted again. As badly as we wanted to mouth off and tell that jerk what we think about him and what he can do with the bags, we didn't; we had to hold it off. Out here in the middle of nowhere, it's best to shut up and take it. Not a single one of us had a choice in the matter; out here the counselors were pretty much gods. So we held on to the extra backpacks that were forced upon us and rejoined the group; it was embarrassing for us.

The other teens were pointing and laughing at us, all while Mark had a big shit eating grin on his face. You could tell by the look on Candice's face that she was none too happy about Mark's attitude toward us; however, she knew that there was nothing she could do about it, so she kept quiet.

Steve, on the other hand, thought the whole thing was funny as hell, but he would do anything to impress Mark. Maybe Tommy's older brother, Jerry, can do something about Mark when the time comes; at least we were hoping that would be the case. Mark then motioned for the group to move out with one big wave of his hand, and we followed him like lapdogs. I had a bad feeling this was going to be one long summer.

Anyways, we walked and walked and walked, while everyone around us was having a good time hiking; we didn't say a word to each other or to anyone else. It seemed like we had walked for hours on end; for once I'm glad my parents had kicked me out of the house as much as they did, for that reason alone I was able to handle the hike without a problem.

Tommy, on the other hand, was showing off his athletic prowess as he was ahead of us all. "Damn showoff," I said to myself as I laughed quietly. Then I happened to glance behind me, and I saw Chubs huffing it at the tail end of the group. I knew then that we had to keep an eye on Chubs the whole time, so I decided to whistle at Tommy to get his attention. He turned to see who had whistled at him, and as soon as he did, I made a motion for him to look back at Chubs. Tommy knew exactly what I meant just by looking at my facial expression, so he nodded his head in agreement with me, and each chance either one of us got, we would turn back and check to make sure Chubs was still with the group.

Tommy and I knew that if he got left behind or fell too far behind us, we would never be able to find him without getting lost ourselves. I felt bad for Chubs, I really did, I mean no matter how many stops we made, or how many breaks we got to take, it just wasn't enough rest for him. Chubs pretty much stayed at the far back of the group, not because he wanted to, but he just couldn't keep up no matter how much he tried. The poor kid was walking as fast as he could, and on top of that, he was drenched in sweat, and he was very pale, and you could hear him wheezing very loudly as he walked.

There were a few times that Tommy or myself had to stop and run to the very back with him to make sure he didn't stop for too long. Hell, there were a few times we both had to go to the back of the group with him because he had fallen to his knees, and neither Tommy or myself could lift him up on our own. And every time we would get him to his feet, it didn't take long before he was sitting down again or down on his knees taking deep breaths.

I know one thing for sure is that the three of us got damn lucky that we didn't get left behind. This may sound stupid, but sometimes I wish we had gotten left behind. I'm not sure if that would have changed anything or not though. I seriously doubt it. Anyways, we hiked for a way farther. And before long the sun had started to set slowly behind the trees. "Hold up here, everyone!" Mark yelled out. "Steve, start checking the area and make sure it's safe to set up camp," he demanded.

Steve searched the area very thoroughly as demanded of him. "This looks like a good place to set up camp, Mark," he answered.

"All right, listen up! We are going to camp here tonight!" shouted Mark.

Tommy, Chubs, and I looked at one another oddly, and we weren't the only ones with the confused looks on our faces either. I believe the whole group was confused; none of us had tents to even set up a campsite. I was about to be an ass and bring that up to him, but I was beaten to the punch by another kid.

"What are you talking about? We don't have any tents, so how on earth are we going to set up anything? Let alone a campsite," the boy said. Eventually, that boy would end up being one of our best friends.

Mark walked up to the boy like a complete asshole and said to him, "We are going to teach you how to make a tent out of the equipment in those bags." he pointed over at the bags we were carrying and then added, "And if you can't be taught, or if you don't want to listen to us, then I guess your happy asses will be sleeping out in the cold tonight."

Then out of the blue, we heard Candice say, "Knock it off, Mark. Stop being an asshole. And leave the kids alone!" It was about time that one of the other counselors finally stood up to Mark; it was a long time coming. I think Candice had finally had enough of Mark's crap. "Don't worry, kiddo," she said to the boy. "I promise that you won't be left out in the cold. We will help you out any way that we can to make sure you have a tent to sleep in." She smiled and placed her hand on his shoulder before looking up at the rest of the group. "And that goes for the rest of you as well! If you need help in any way, just ask Mark, Steve, or myself. We're here to learn something new and have some fun in this process toward the campgrounds. Right, Mark?"

Mark raised his arms up in the air and started to back away.

"Whatever you say, Candice. Whatever you say." He smiled his cocky smile, and then he turned to Steve and said, "Come on, Steve. Let's go and get things set up." Mark walked off, and Steve followed right behind him. I think what Mark really meant was Steve was about to bust his ass getting the campsite set up, while Mark was going to sit back and take all the credit for it like always. You weren't about to hear any of us complaining; if Steve has to set up camp, that means less work for us, and Mark's attention will be on him instead of us for now.

Or so we thought, for as soon as we looked over at them, they were already walking our way. "Hey, ladies!" Mark shouted. "We need those backpacks!" he shouted again as they were even close to us. So the three of us sat the backpacks on the ground in front of us without saying a word. Mark stomped right up to the backpacks; he then leaned and grabbed them and threw them over to Steve.

We played it smart and still didn't say a word to either one of them; we stood there waiting for Mark to make a smart-ass remark to us. Most of the time he would call us lazy asses, or sometimes he would try and make us help Steve do the work. Yet this time he didn't do either, not a single word came out of his mouth, nor did he even look at us. We figured he was probably butthurt at the fact that someone stood up to him, which I'm sure he wasn't used to. Or perhaps he was bored with us and had fresh meat to torture now; honestly, we didn't know what was going on, and we didn't care.

"Well, there's no point in just standing around here, is there?" Tommy looked at us and asked.

"I agree, let's go over and introduce ourselves to everyone else." I said.

He looked at me with surprise and replied back, "I never

thought I would ever hear you say that, Bobby. But yeah, man, that sounds like a good idea to me." Tommy then looked at Chubs. "You up for it, Chubs?" he asked.

Chubs never did answer Tommy's question; he just waved us off. "You guys can find me later; my fat ass isn't going anywhere." he seemed like he was pissed off about something. I felt bad for him, and on top of that, he still didn't look all that great either. However, his color to his face was returning, so that was a plus, but he was still wheezing.

"Go on ahead, Tommy. I'm going to hang here with Chubs for a while longer," I said.

"All right, Bobby. We can all meet up here in a bit and start making our tent," Tommy answered before walking off.

"You didn't have to stay with me, Bobby. And I didn't ask you to either, just saying," said Chubs.

Instead of getting mad, I laughed and sat down with him. "A thank-you would have been nice," I said to him.

He just glared at me before sarcastically saying, "Thanks."

I chuckled a little at him. "Good to see you're in a better mood now.

He glared at me again before quickly saying, "Shut up, Bobby!" He did his very best to look like he was still pissed off at the world, so I made a few funny faces at him, and it wasn't long before we both started to crack up.

"You feel better now?" I asked.

Chubs smiled and replied, "I do feel better now. Thank you, Bobby." I was curious now, and I wanted to know what had him so worked up, besides the hike.

"Tell me something, Chubs," I said.

"Sure, what do you want to know, Bobby?"

"What has you so pissed off? You went off on Tommy earlier.

And then you acted like you didn't want to hang with us. So, what's up?" That's what I said to him, and I wanted an answer.

"Look, I'm sorry about how I've acted lately. It's just I hate summer camp and everything about it. We get bullied every year, and the counselors don't help us. They join in with the damn bullies! I really thought this year might be different when Tommy told us about his brother. And when he wasn't here, I flipped out on Tommy. On top of that, now my fat ass is hiking! You should be pissed off too, Bobby!"

Without thinking, I blurted out, "I'm a little upset, but I have bigger things to worry about."

By the look on his face, I knew I had made a mistake saying that to him. "What do you mean by that, Bobby?"

"Don't worry about it, Chubs." That's when I knew I had no choice but to change the subject quickly; it wasn't time to talk about that yet. "So, Chubs. Which one of us will see Candice naked first?" I said as I laughed.

Man did he glare at me; that must have been a touchy subject for him. "Hey! Don't give me that look! What did you expect me to say?" After that, he shook his head and just laughed at me. "Are you good now?" I asked.

"Good to go here." Chub's then looked around for Tommy. "We better go meet up with Tommy now. It's starting to get late by the looks of things." he stood up and brushed himself off. "What are you waiting for, Bobby? Let's get moving!" he said. I was still struggling with all that was going on, but it did make me feel better knowing Chubs was in a better mood. And it didn't take us long to find, Tommy. He was gathering some of the supplies that we needed for our tent, and he made it clear that he had picked out a spot for us as well.

"Hey, Tommy!" I yelled.

"Well, look who's back," Tommy replied. "About damn time."
Chubs walked up and slapped Tommy on the back. "Looks
like the three amigos are back in action," said Chubs.

"That's good to know, man. I needed some help gathering
supplies for the tent. Now that the two of you are here, we can
get this shit done," Tommy explained.

I knew that making a tent for us out of scratch was going to
be a whole hell of a lot harder than just driving stakes in the
ground. And as quick as the sun was setting, it was clear that
we didn't have any time to waste. Lucky for us that Tommy had
most of the supplies ready and the fact that we had Candice to
help us when needed was also a plus for us. What was funny
was the fact that all of the others took our lead and also teamed
up to build their tents, all except one kid that is. He stood there
watching everyone else.

It wasn't like he wasn't trying to join in; however, it wasn't
going well for him. It seemed like he was being rejected by the
other group of teens for no reason at all. Tommy pointed out to
us that he was the boy that mouthed off at Mark earlier that day.
And knowing Mark the way we do, he probably went around
and told the others not to have anything to do with him, or else.
Believe me, Mark had a way with words, or you could say that
he was good with threats, and he enjoyed it when he got the
chance to do so. Let's just say, Mark could be a scary man at
times when he wanted to be.

"Leave him be, we don't need the extra attention from Mark
right now. We're not anyone's babysitter either," said Chubs.

Tommy didn't wait long to say something to Chubs. "Damn,
Chubs. That's cold, even for you." Then he added, "Since when
have we given a damn about what Mark thinks?"

Chubs were about to say something back to Tommy, but he

didn't have a chance to, though, for I walked over to the boy and asked him if he would like to join our group; that actually stunned Chubs enough he forgot what he was going to say. At least that's what I thought when he kept his words to himself. The hell with Mark. I thought to myself. I figured I didn't need anyone's permission to ask if someone wanted to join us. I was going to do what I wanted. It was no surprise to me when he said that he would join our group, so I offered my hand in friendship to him. "Name's, Bobby. And yours?" I asked.

The boy smiled and quickly shook my hand and answered, "My name's Nick. It's nice to see a friendly face here." I could tell this was his first year ever being at summer camp.

"It's nice to meet you, Nick. Let me introduce you to the rest of the group." I said as I motioned for him to follow me. And I led Nick over to our side of the camp. The look on Mark's face was priceless; he was so pissed off I thought he was going to explode. I'm not sure, but I believe something inside of me changed that year. I honestly didn't give a shit anymore. I was ready to take on the world if I had to. We walked up to Chubs and Tommy, and as promised, I introduced him. "Tommy, Chubs, this is Nick. He's agreed to join our group and help us with the tent."

Tommy was the type to make friends with anyone; maybe he was too trusting. "What's up, Nick? It's nice to meet you." He smiled and shook Nick's hand. Chubs just gave a slight nod and went back to working on the tent without saying a word. "Don't mind him. He's just being a little bitch!" Tommy shouted loudly. Chubs looked back up and gave Tommy a huge "go to hell" look and muttered something under his breath before he looked back down. However, we couldn't understand anything he said.

"It's cool. I'm the new guy. I get it," Nick said.

So I said the only thing that came to mind, "Don't take offense to how he's acting. Chubs is just being Chubs." I was just letting Nick know he didn't mean anything by it.

"Enough talking! Let's get this tent up before nightfall, shall we!" shouted Chubs.

"Shut the hell up, Chubs!" Tommy yelled back at him.

"Welcome to the gang of losers, Nick. Hope you can handle it," I said to him.

I know what I said was mean, but I meant every word of it. Well, we did pride ourselves on being the losers, and we didn't give a damn about what anyone else thought about us either. The rest of that evening we worked on our tent and also got to know more about Nick. It even looked like Chubs was warming up to him just a little. As it got even later into the day, it was getting very hard for me to focus. I tried my best to help them finish the tent, but for some reason, I just couldn't. It wasn't that I didn't want to help finish the tent. I was just daydreaming way too much and was still troubled by what happened to John Boy.

I just couldn't figure out what made him snap like he did, or why he got sick and died in his bed in the hospital. Was it the nightmares? Or maybe he hated summer camp so much that he did whatever it took. Perhaps something scared him so bad that he went completely insane? The more I asked myself those questions, the more confused I had become. What troubled me the most was the fact that I was now going through the same thing, yet I haven't snapped like he did, at least not yet anyway. I was still in complete control over everything that I was feeling; however, there was this rage that was slowly building up inside of me. It took quite a bit of willpower to control the the rage, but I kept it in check.

Honestly, though, I think I enjoyed the power I felt when it started building inside of me; maybe that's why I could control it. "Almost done, guys!" a voice shouted in excitement, which snapped me out of my daydream.

I looked around dazed and confused at first, but it didn't take long for Tommy to notice and smack me on the back of my head. "Snap out of it, Bobby!" he shouted. That's when I noticed that our tent was completely finished. I felt like shit that my friends had to finish without my help. I just hoped they weren't too mad at me; when all else fails, start kissing some major ass, and that's what I did.

"Damn, guys," I said. "The tent looks awesome," I added as I got up and walked around it. Though the bottom of the tent didn't exactly touch the ground, and it was leaning somewhat to the right, I was smart enough to keep my mouth shut, and besides, it wasn't like I was of much help to them there at the end. "You're right, Bobby. We did a great job on this bad boy," Chubs said with a smile on his face as he admired the work they had done.

"This works, right?" Nick asked.

Before Tommy even made a comment, he walked around the tent twice; then he said, "Let's face it, it looks like shit." then he starts to laugh before adding, "Besides, all it has to do is get us through the night. If the tent can do that, then we're golden."

Just looking at that ugly thing gave the four of us a well-deserved laugh; it seemed like that all we needed was to laugh to put us all in a better mood. That's when I got the bright idea to walk around and look at the other tents. "Does anyone want to walk around and take a look at the other tents?" I asked.

"That sounds like a great idea to me. How about you, Chubs? Are you in?" asked Tommy.

"Count me in," Chubs answered.

"Me too," said Nick. And so it was settled; we had decided

in favor of walking around the campsite. It was an interesting walk, to say the least, looking at all the other tents that were put together by the other teens, and kids, proved that ours wasn't the worst one in camp. Now, on the other hand, our tent wasn't even close to being the best either, but then we noticed something a little odd to us, which took our attention away from looking at how the tents were built. We noticed that all the tents had been placed close together except for ours.

Our tent was all the way on the other side of the camp, either Tommy wanted to be that far away from everyone else, or we were viewed as the losers, and no one wanted to be near us. Oh well, losers until the end were our way of thinking, and soon Nick would think the same way. We had decided it was time to head back to our tent; walking around was beginning to bore us. Plus at the same time, it was starting to get late, and we knew what that meant for us if we didn't hurry.

"The sun is setting quickly; we need to hurry our asses back to the tent. And now." I said, quickly turning around to head back. Unfortunately, it was too late. Right before we could all turn around, Mark ran up behind us and put his arms around Tommy and Chubs.

"Where are the four of you heading off to?" he asked. I tried to ignore him, and honestly, I was going to try and make a run for it, and by the look on Nick's face, he was thinking the same thing. I think Mark also knew what we were thinking about doing. "Don't even think about it, you two. I've decided that I need the four of you to go and gather some firewood to get us through the night," he said with a shit-eating grin on his face.

I had a feeling I knew what Mark was waiting for; he's done this to us before. He was standing there actually waiting for one of us to mouth off. That wasn't going to happen this year; we were smarter and wasn't going to fall for that this time. There was no way in hell that we were going to play his stupid mind game; however, we forgot about Nick. He was new to camp and wasn't sure how to handle Mark; we didn't even get a chance to shut him up either.

"You're an asshole, you know that?" said Nick.

Damn it. This isn't going to be good, I thought to myself. The look on Mark's face let me know that we were all in deep shit, not just Nick. "Oh, and not only that. The four of you will also be on watch duty tonight as well, while everyone else sleeps. Do any of the other ladies have a smart-ass remark?" Mark said to us.

We shook our heads no; we knew better than to speak another word. What he did was bullshit treating us the way he did, and here I was actually thinking that Mark was finally done bullying us. The only reason he started again had to have been because we befriended Nick. But hey, it's like I said before. When you're out in the middle of nowhere with dip shits like Mark and Steve, you do what you're told, or you suffer the consequences. And we were about to suffer, big time. Mark was walking away with that same shit-eating grin; however, we must not have moved fast enough for him, for he turned around and started yelling at us.

"Hey! Get to it, ladies! We need that firewood, and it's not going to collect itself." He pointed out into the woods as he yelled. We stood there looking at each other, then ahead into the woods in front of us, it was like staring into the unknown. And then all of a sudden it was back, that uneasy feeling that something bad was about to happen, and this time it was stronger than ever. Damn them and their detour.

# 4

# Into the Unknown

"All right, Bobby. I think that's enough for today," the stranger interrupted as he began to stand up out of his chair. "I would offer you my hand in friendship, but we both know you won't accept it." the man said to him before making his way toward the door. Before leaving, the man turned and looked back at, Bobby. "I know that you don't trust me. In time, though, you will, Bobby. You will." then he turned back around and had the nurse open the door yet again for him as he walked away. Hearing those words made Bobby cringe, as that all too familiar feeling of uneasiness came flooding back to him.

As the night slowly crept upon him, the uneasy feeling was getting stronger, and it was growing harder for him to sleep. So he reached under his mattress and grabbed his journal. Well, if I can't sleep. I might as well write, he thought to himself. He then made his way over to the desk in the corner of his room for another night of writing. He reached over and turned on his desk lamp, and with pen in hand, he opened up his journal and began jotting down his thoughts.

July 1, 1999, I'm writing in my journal yet again. Ever since this stranger has shown up, it has been one sleepless night after another. All I can do now is think about what happened all those years ago. I wanted to forget about the past and hide here and never have to relive that past ever again.

I was foolish enough to believe that I could make that reality happen; like I said, I was a fool. And now I'm forced into talking about my past to that stranger that I know I can't trust; what's even worse is the fact that my uneasy feelings have returned, along with those damn nightmares again. On top of that, I swear that I hear that man's demonic voice again; however, that can't be! I killed him with my friends' help that fateful day. Or did we?

The next day had come faster than the last. Knock, knock, knock. The knocking finally woke Bobby up. "Is it that time again already?" he asked himself.

"Bobby! That man is here to talk with you again!" the nurse yelled out. "Send him in! I'm awake and dressed now!" Bobby yelled back. The stranger quickly walked into the room with purpose. "Bobby, I know you're not going to shake my hand. And saying good morning to you is a waste of time, so what do you say we get right to work. How does that sound to you?" the man said as he took his seat and pulled out his notes from his bag.

"That's fine by me. The quicker I get you out of my room, the better I will feel." Bobby replied as he started to sit down. I wonder what's eating him, He thought to himself. There were just too many things about the man that just didn't add up, and sooner or later, Bobby was going to have to start asking questions of his own. Judging by the stranger's temperament, today just wasn't the day for Bobby to start questioning him. But that didn't stop Bobby from trying to take a glance at the man's notes.

"Start from where we left off yesterday, please," the man demanded. "One more thing."

"What?" Bobby asked.

"These are my notes, stop trying to look at them. The notes do not concern you; they are for my eyes only. Understand?" Bobby had no idea what to say back to the man, even though what the man said to him made him angry.

"And here I was thinking that I was being sneaky," Bobby said to the man jokingly. Not a single word came from the stranger's mouth. All he did was give Bobby a harsh look for his joke. "Damn. Someone is in a mood today." Bobby joked again. "But all joking aside." Bobby's facial expression changed drastically when he said, "I'm eventually going to find out more about you, and I'm going to read those notes you're taking whether you like it or not. I'm not joking about that, mark my words. But don't you worry, I'll tell you more this time."

The man glared at Bobby with a fire in his eyes that Bobby had yet to see from him, and then he motioned for him to start telling his story again. To keep the peace between them for one more day, he decided that he would talk again, just one more time. As we stood there staring into the unknown, neither of us was willing to move a muscle. You have to think we were young teens and a little nerdy at that. So yeah, we were definitely scared, especially me. It looked like the same woods from my nightmares, and I sure as hell wasn't going to lead the way into that nightmarish place.

To my surprise, Chubs was the one that took the first step forward. "Come on, guys. We don't have much longer until it's completely dark." The way I felt was if Chubs was brave enough to lead the way, then I had to be brave enough to follow him. "Chubs is right, you guys. We better get a move on; it won't help if we get lost out here at night." I said to them.

Bobby paused for a moment and then looked up at the stranger. "This part you need to understand, because if you don't, I will not even try to explain it to you. So pay close attention," said Bobby.

Now, you have to understand why the four of us were so scared. Straight in front of us was the creepiest woods you could ever imagine, and the four of us were about to venture out alone. I think what added to our fear was the fact that the area chosen for the campsite was a little clearing. I mean there were no trees in this little area, except for a few stumps and dead bushes. That was about it. That would freak anyone out, I'm sure of that. To make us feel better, we told ourselves that the counselors must have cleared the area beforehand as a halfway point, or something like that. Chubs kept walking slowly closer, and I was right behind him.

"Hell with this!" Tommy shouted. It wasn't even a moment later that Tommy pushed us into the woods. "What can I say? Those two just weren't quick enough." he joked.

"If that's the way you want to play it, then fine by me, Tommy." I screamed at him. Then I grabbed his arm and yanked him into the woods right along with us. Nick didn't view any of our actions as being funny; instead, he followed behind scolding us.

"Stop acting like little kids. I want to get this done and over with, the sun will set, and it will be night time before long, guys. So stop with the goofing off."

But that didn't stop Tommy. Ignoring what Nick said to us, he kept on pushing Chubs deeper into the woods, with Chubs cursing at him every step of the way. I was walking right behind Tommy, laughing at him and Chubs, also trying to trip them both while I was at it. It was the only way I could cope with the bad feelings I was having at the time. "If you don't mind, I have a question for you, Bobby." the man interrupted. "I do mind, but it's not like I can stop you. So make it quick." Bobby scowled.

"I know I have yet to ask this. But do you remember what year this took place?" the man asked.

"What kind of question is that?" Bobby snapped.

"Just answer my question, Bobby. It's for my notes. And I'm curious about something." Bobby glared at the man, but he knew he didn't have a choice in the matter.

"Fine, it was the year 1983. Happy now?" said, Bobby.

"No, I'm not. Do you remember the month? And what state?" the man asked of him.

"What in the hell does that have to do with anything?" Bobby asked.

"Like I said before, answer my questions," the man said to him.

"It was in the later part of July. Do I remember the exact date? Hell no, that was nearly sixteen years ago. Do I remember the state? Yeah, it happened in Kentucky. Now, are you happy?"

"Just one more question." the man said.

"What now?" Bobby asked.

"Tell me, what was the name of the camp?" he asked.

"I was getting to that part in due time. It's an important part of what I have to tell you. Can you at least wait?" Bobby said to him.

"Hmm. It's important to me as well, Bobby. For now, I shall wait." he said.

"Can I continue on?" asked Bobby.

The man looked at him and replied, "You can, but I will stop you again if need be." Bobby nodded in agreement with the man and continued on from where he was stopped. And, oh man, you could tell that Nick was getting ready to blow a gasket. I think the woods was getting to him just as much as it was getting to me, I just had a different way of showing it, or I guess you could say I was hiding my feelings. And upon noticing how pissed he was getting, I decided I had better do something to calm him down.

"I agree with, Nick. We need to start gathering the firewood instead of goofing off. We will be screwed if we don't hurry." I said. As bad as I wanted to turn around and run back to the campsite, they were my friends, and we didn't leave each other behind. We would always have each others back no matter what; at least that was the promise we had made.

"There's no need to worry. Again, like always, I have everything under control." Tommy said to us.

"And again, what do you mean by that, Tommy?" Chubs asked.

"Yeah, Tommy. Fill us in on this little secret of yours." I said to him. Nick didn't say a word; he was waiting for Tommy to say something before he would talk.

Tommy stood there with a smirk on his face, keeping us waiting in suspense as he normally does. "Spill it, Tommy," I said to him.

"I don't have time for this. I'm getting this shit started." Nick said hurriedly and with a hint of anger in his voice.

"Chill, man, chill. I have these." Tommy reached into his backpack and pulled out four flashlights.

"Where in the world did you get these, Tommy?" I questioned.

"So that's what you were doing over by the counselors before you came over and talked to all the others," Nick said.

"Shut up, man," Tommy said quickly.

"Damn it, Tommy! Did you steal the flashlights?" I shouted.

"I didn't steal them. I borrowed them. Now shut up and take one." "Tommy's right. We needed the flashlights. We can sneak them back later, Bobby." Chubs said to me after he took one from Tommy.

Nick took one as well without saying much, and I took the last one. The sun was about to set, and we did need the flashlights, so I couldn't complain much. So I pretty much ate my words and moved on to collecting firewood. After exploring the area farther, I was frightened to discover this was the same place as my nightmares! I didn't want to alarm the others, but I did want to get back to camp quickly. "Okay, guys. I think we have plenty of firewood. Let's get back." I said to them.

"What's wrong, Bobby? You look worried," said Tommy.

"I'm not worried, Tommy.  I just don't like this place." I answered.

"Aw, the poor baby is scared." he laughed and then added, "Let's explore some more; it will be payback for Mark making us come out here. And it will be fun making them wait."

"I'm not scared, Tommy. I'm worried that something bad is about to happen soon." then I looked over at Nick and Chubs. "Help me out here, guys. Don't you want to get out of here?" I asked.

"Maybe we should listen to Bobby, this place gives me the creeps, and soon it will be completely dark," Nick said.

Tommy rolled his eyes and said, "Fine, fine. Let's head back; you're all a bunch of babies."

Before Tommy could get another word out, we all heard a loud noise come from behind us. "What in the hell was that?" Chubs asked with a startled look on his face.

"I don't know what it was, Chubs," Tommy answered back with the same expression on his face as well.

"It sounds like someone is following us if you ask me," Nick said. He was right, someone was following us, or maybe it was something. I could feel every move we made being watched; it was nerve-racking for me because this was just like my dream.

"Perhaps my dreams were warnings of what was to come," I said to myself. My uneasiness was starting to grow stronger inside of me, and with good reason to. Every time one of us took a step, whatever or whoever was following us would also take a step. I knew that I didn't want to go any farther into the woods and that we should turn around and make a run for it.

However, Tommy had other ideas. "Mark! I know that's you, man! So come on out!" he shouted.

"Man, this sucks." said, Chubs.

"We're out in the middle of the woods with God knows what following us, and it's almost pitch-black. We're screwed."

That's when Nick stepped in. "Calm down, Chubs. I'm with Tommy on this one. It has to be Mark and Steve." And in an instant Nick went from being a coward to being the bravest one here, all to impress us and mainly Tommy.

"They're trying to scare us as payback for me taking their flashlights and for us befriending Nick," Tommy explained.

"That's right, guys, I believe Tommy. And now that we have the firewood, they're messing with us and trying to scare us enough that we come running out of the woods without it and scared shitless." Nick was figuring out a way to hide his true feelings, the same way I was.

I wasn't going to be persuaded to go chasing after what I knew in a way was following us. No way in hell. And just as I was about to tell Tommy how it was going to be, things went from bad to worse in just a few minutes. The footsteps drew closer and closer until they were upon us, right on top of us to be exact. There wasn't just one set of footsteps that we could hear now; as far as I could tell, there were at least six sets of footsteps that we could hear running close around us. I had no idea how we were going to get back now, it was dark as hell, and on top of that, we were being stalked, and then I remembered the flashlight I had in my hand.

"Guys, let's use the flashlights and get the hell out of here!" I shouted.

"I'm the leader of this outfit, and I say we beat Mark at his own game," Tommy yelled.

"Let's get that asshole," Nick yelled out as well. I could tell that both Nick, and Tommy were both scared stupid, but they were good at hiding it from Chubs and me. I was ready to go, and I turned around about to head back when both Tommy and Nick grabbed me by the arms and made me drop my firewood.

"Damn it, guys! You made me drop my firewood!" I yelled at them.

"Don't worry about that. We have to prove that Mark and Steve are the ones doing this," Tommy said.

They dragged me along with them farther into the woods, with Chubs leading the tail end trying to carry all the wood himself. Then I figured out something that chilled me to the bone: when we would slow down, the sound of the footsteps would draw near, and when we would walk faster, they would get farther ahead. However, Tommy and Nick were persistent in their pursuit of proving themselves right. "Let me go!" I demanded of them. "I said, let me go!" I shouted again, this time struggling with them to get myself free.

"All right, just chill out, man," Tommy said as he let my arm go.

"Sorry, Bobby. I guess we took it a little too far," Nick said as he let me go.

"Hey, guys? A little help here." Chubs said to us. He had

the firewood stacked in his arms almost up to his head; for a moment, Tommy, and Nick forgot what they were doing to quickly help him out. I didn't care about Chubs, Tommy, or anyone else at that moment. The main concern was getting out of there, and all my warnings had gone unnoticed. All my friends did was laugh at me, telling me that I was letting the creeps win. I was starting to get upset with them for blowing off my warnings, then something inside of me just snapped, and the rage that I had been suppressing took over. I ran up to them like a man possessed and started to rant and rave.

"Guys, would you just shut up and listen!" I screamed. I was starting to lose control over myself. "We've collected plenty of firewood. Let's get back to camp now. I have a bad feeling things are about to get worse. This isn't a damn game. Let's go! Now!" I pleaded with them.

"Okay, okay. Just calm down, Bobby." Tommy then looked at the others. "Let's head back, we've got what we came for. Catching Mark will just have to wait." Tommy explained.

"This place gives me the creeps anyway," said Nick.

"Too bad we can't catch Mark trying to scare us." Chubs jokingly said. He tried his best to act like a badass; you could see the relief on his face though. I was now starting to gain control back over myself and was feeling somewhat relieved at the same time, for, in fact, the noises had stopped, and I talked my friends into heading back to camp. However, that feeling of relief gave way to a horrible feeling of despair as all hell broke loose.

We were joking around, and I was starting to join in on the fun, somewhat. And as soon as we gathered everything up and turned to start making our way out of the woods, the noises started up again, even louder than before. At first, we ignored it the best we could, but we started to freak out when we could see shadows that went along with the sounds of footsteps now. Then the four of us really started to get scared when the shadows would dart in front of us; the light from the flashlights were of little use to us at that point.

Sometimes I would catch a glimpse of someone's shoes or a quick glimpse of their face. I wasn't sure if the rest of my friends were seeing the same thing. We were all scared so badly that neither one of us wanted to move for fear of what would happen next. I noticed that Tommy's flashlight was moving in all directions; he would even point it in our faces to make sure that the group was still together. "Everyone still here?" he would ask. Each time the rest of us would call out to let him know we were still there. Then again right out of the blue, Tommy yelled out. "Mark—"

That's when I cut him off before he could finish yelling, "Damn it, Tommy! You know it's not Mark!" I shouted at him.

Still, we stood there frozen with fear until we heard what seemed to be little kids laughing at us. Next thing we noticed was Nick making a run for it. "Nick, stop!" we yelled out to him, which didn't do a bit of good because he was already too far ahead of us. Tommy was the first to give chase after him, dropping his firewood in the process. I threw the stack that I was carrying onto the ground, making sure I still had my flashlight tight in hand. I then turned and yelled for Chubs to follow, for I was going to give chase as well.

"What about the firewood?" he yelled out.

"Screw the firewood, Chubs! Let's go!" Chubs then turned back around and threw his firewood to the ground as well, and he paused; he didn't move at all, which frightened me. I kept my flashlight on him as I slowly moved in closer; then I could hear a frightful, blood-chilling laugh that sounded very familiar.

At that point, I didn't know what to think. As I reached my hand out toward him slowly, Chubs turned around quickly to face me, and his face was deathly pale, and he started screaming hysterically; before I knew it, he ran past me with a wild look in his eyes.

I looked ahead to see what might have scared Chubs so badly; however, there was nothing. So I quickly turned myself around and gave chase, hopefully, he was running in the same direction as Nick and Tommy if I was lucky. I ran after him for what seemed like a good seven or eight minutes. That is until I happened upon the flashlight that Chubs was carrying lying there on the ground. I knelt down to pick it up, and that's when I felt something brush against me as it ran by. "Chubs! Chubs, is that you?" I called out as I stood back up.

I could still hear the sounds of footsteps and laughter in every direction, but in that instant alone all I could think about was finding, Chubs. I called out for him again and again and still had no answer; then something startled me as it made its way behind one of the trees straight ahead of me. My flashlight could show me but a brief outline of a figure in the darkness that had surrounded us, so I called out to him again. "Chubs, if that's you, will you at least answer me!" Right then I heard a faint cry come from behind the tree that was to the left of me, and I knew without a doubt that it was Chubs.

Just to make sure I didn't frighten my friend further, I slowly walked toward the tree. "Chubs! It's just me, come on out, please. We need to find Nick and Tommy so we can get the hell out of here." I quietly said to him. I pointed my flashlight at the tree as I drew near. I could see Chubs cowered down up against the back of it. I walked closer and closer to him. I could see that he was shaking badly and crying into his arms almost as if he were a little kid again. "Chubs, Hey, buddy, it's okay, man." I said as I reached out to touch him on the shoulder.

"Don't touch me!" he screamed out at me. Then he slapped my hand away from him in a fit of rage, almost making me drop my flashlight.

"It's me, Chubs. It's Bobby." I explained.

I think hearing my voice snapped him back to reality because he then looked up at me and asked, "Is that really you, Bobby?"

That's when I offered him my hand to help him up and told him. "It's me, Chubs, don't worry." Chubs didn't just grab my hand, but he also hugged me, which was a surprise. I could barely see his face, but the light from my flashlight allowed me to see enough. He had tears running down his face, and believe me, they weren't tears of joy either.

At least the wild, crazy look that he had in his eyes from before was starting to fade as he gained back control over his senses. However, I didn't have the leisure of time to make sure he was okay; now that Chubs and myself were reunited, it was time to find the others and get the hell out of there. But first, I needed to return something to him that he had dropped when all the chaos started. "You're going to need this back, Chubs," I said as I handed him his flashlight back.

"Thanks, Bobby. I'm glad you didn't leave me behind."

After nodding to him, I turned back around in the direction I was sure Nick and Tommy ran off in. "Are you ready, Chubs?" I asked, not even once did I look back.

"I'm ready when you are, Bobby," he answered.

We poised ourselves for what may come at us next, and then we both took off running as fast as we could without saying a word. I could hear the sounds of the footsteps giving chase. The sound of little kids laughing had also started again, and you could see the shadows running alongside us with what light we had. It was madness, I wanted to give up, and I thought over and over again that I would wake from this nightmare that was plaguing me. The nightmare never ended, and I never did wake from it.

Then I heard Chubs cry out to me, "Bobby, we're surrounded! What are we going to do!" never did I stop running to answer his question.

I just yelled out as loud as I could to him. "Ignore whatever is chasing us, Chubs! Don't stop running no matter what!" I was beginning to lose all hope of finding Nick and Tommy and getting out of there alive. But luck would be on our side this night, however, as just up ahead we noticed two silhouettes running toward us carrying flashlights.

"Bobby! Chubs! Is that you!" It was Tommy yelling.

I would know that voice from anywhere. "Tommy!" I shouted. "Over here, Chubs. Look it's Nick and Tommy." I shouted back at him.

"Finally. We can all get the hell out of here." Chub's replied. The second we all met up we were out of breath and could barely stand, but we knew that we couldn't stop running until we got out of the woods and back at camp. "Tommy, Nick, it's great to see you guys," Chubs said.

I was happy to see them as well. "Are you guys all right?" I asked.

"We're fine, now let's get the hell out of here!" Tommy answered. The laughing was getting even louder than before, and the sounds of footsteps were many. And just as we were about to make a run for it yet again, everything went silent, the noises of footsteps had ceased, and the laughter slowly faded out. This was definitely confusing and yet scary. I had no idea what was going to happen to us next.

"Is it over?" Nick asked. I surveyed the area with my flashlight a little more, waiting for something else to go wrong. I was so caught up in what I was doing that I didn't hear Nick's question.

Tommy must have noticed that fact, so he answered instead. "There's no way we will know the answer to that man," said Tommy. Tommy was right about that there was no way of knowing if it was truly over or not.

"Well, I say we need to get moving. Let's not take any chances," said Chubs.

With my friends standing around deciding what to do next, I walked off on my own making sure the coast was clear. And that's when I noticed the light of the campfire straight ahead of me. I was certain that was our camp. That means safety was right there. Hell, at that moment even if it wasn't our camp, I still didn't give a damn; we would still have the safety in numbers. I looked back at the guys and motioned for them. "Hey! Get over here!" I shouted.

The three of them ran over to where I was standing. "What is it, Bobby?" they asked all at once.

"Look over there." I pointed straight ahead. "It's a campfire. I'm almost certain that's our camp." I shouted with joy. If you could have seen our faces, you would have known what pure joy on a person's face looked like.

"What in the hell are we waiting for?" Tommy asked. "We need to make a run—" Before Tommy could finish his sentence, a dark and sinister voice came from the darkness.

"You're not going anywhere. The four of you are going to stay and play." this voice was unlike anything I've ever heard in my life; still to this day I've never heard anything like it and hope to God I never will again. Shortly after the sounds of footsteps could be heard yet again, but unlike all the other times, we could tell it was only one set that was walking closer and closer to us. This person, or thing, whatever it was, was taking its time and slowly stalking its prey, and that prey was the four of us.

None of us said a word to one another, this time we didn't scream or panic, we knew exactly what we had to do to escape. For what had us in its sights was nothing more than pure evil. And the four of us took off running as fast as we could; whatever was stalking us was running close behind. We ran and ran and ran. I didn't think we had a chance in getting out of the woods alive, for it seemed like the woods was coming to life, fighting to stop us from making it out. To my horror as I was running, the batteries to my flashlight started dying on me, and I watched as the tree branches started reaching out for us. What was I going to do now?

I was leading the charge to get us out of there; my friends were depending on me. And I was about to just give in until that damn voice started speaking to us again. "Just give up and stay. None of you will make it out of here." I could hear my friends start to freak out again behind me; if I didn't do something, we were finished.

Knowing that I had to do something to save us triggered my rage. And it boiled over inside of me, which caused my instinct to survive to kick in, and I yelled out like a madman. "You're not taking me or my friends." I then turned to my friends and started screaming at them as well. "Don't stop running! That thing shall not have us on this night!" I didn't care that my flashlight was now dead, for I could see the campfire closer than ever now. Seeing my new courage and resolve gave my friends the courage they needed to push on as well.

Tommy came running up beside me and shouted, "Stick close

to me, Bobby! I will lead us the rest of the way!" I nodded and stuck close to him and didn't leave his side; then Chubs and Nick came up on the other side of me. I could feel that thing of evil closing in on us, its breath was felt upon my neck, and I knew it was reaching out to grab at us. And just as all hope was about lost, we found ourselves tumbling out of the woods and onto the ground with everyone staring at us, like we had given them all a fright. We really didn't notice the fact that everyone in camp was staring us down, and we didn't care.

We jumped up and started hugging one another, for we had made it out of hell alive for now. Then Nick and Tommy turned their attention toward the woods behind us and started shouting at the top of their lungs. "Screw you!" they shouted at the same time.

"We beat you at your own damn game," Tommy shouted. And Nick was cheering him on; it was no surprise to me that both of them couldn't admit that something beyond their imagination happened to all of us. Chubs was more like me, he was just grateful to be alive, and nothing else at the moment mattered to him. As for myself, I was trying to wrap my mind around what happened to us out there, but for now, I was happy to be back at the camp.

Our moment of happiness was short-lived, however, because Mark had walked up behind us and started his shit. "It's about damn time you ladies got back," he said to us. Then he looked around and glared at us before asking, "Where's the firewood, ladies?"

I knew that we were going to take shit for dropping the firewood, if only he would have been the one out there, right? Anyways, I couldn't help but notice something fishy. If they didn't have any firewood, how did they start up a fire? So I decided to find out. "Hey, Mark. If you needed us to gather the firewood for you so you can start a fire, how can you already have one going?" I asked.

He looked at me and started laughing. "I knew that I couldn't count on the four of you, so I sent Steve and some of the other kids to gather the firewood for me shortly after you ladies headed out."

When Tommy heard that remark, it strengthened his resolve about the whole thing being just one big prank, and that seriously pissed him off. "You sent out Steve and a few others, huh?" Tommy asked. He then put his arm around the back of my neck and said, "Did you hear that, Bobby? Steve and a few others were out in the woods at the same time as us. Isn't that funny, man?" With plenty of light from the fire, I could see the anger illuminate in Tommy's face. He was definitely about to explode, and explode he did, and he aimed it all at Mark. "You set us up, didn't you, Mark?" Tommy angrily asked.

"I have no idea what you're talking about, Tommy," Mark replied with a smirk on his face.

"I think you know exactly what I'm talking about, Mark. You sent Steve and a few of the other kids in there to scare the shit out of us." Tommy shouted back.

Nick jumped into the argument as well, just to prove he had Tommy's back. "That's bullshit the way you had Steve to try and scare us. Do you know what we went through in there?" Nick shouted at Mark.

And I believe that Steve could hear the commotion that was going on, so he made his way over to see for himself exactly what was happening. "What's going on over here?" he asked as he walked up. When he caught a glimpse of us, he changed his tone. "Oh, the ladies finally made it back, I see. That would explain all the bitching I was hearing from over here. All I can say is that it's about damn time you ladies made it back. Candice was about ready to send out a search party!" he said to us.

"Hey, Steve. I'm glad I sent you out to gather firewood. Something scared the ladies here, and they dropped all of theirs. And now they're blaming us, or rather you." Mark said to him.

It looked like Chubs was about to say something to them; however, he did not. "I'm not in the mood for this crap right now," he said as he walked off toward the campfire where everyone else was sitting.

I tried to stop him. "Where are you going, Chubs? You're supposed to have our backs."

Even Mark mouthed off at him. "I'm not done talking yet! Get your ass back here, fat boy!" he shouted. When Chubs gets called "fat boy," he usually flies off the handle; however, this time he didn't react to what any of us had said to him. He walked straight on past me and then Mark without saying a word, and he went right over to sit down by the fire. But it didn't take long for Mark to forget about Chubs and turn his attention back on the rest of us.

"I want the rest of you to go back in there and get the firewood I asked for," he demanded.

That's when I got mad because I knew for a fact that Mark nor Steve had anything to do with happened in those woods. Deep down, I knew Tommy and Nick felt the same way. "Mark, there's no way in hell that we're going back in there! No way in hell!" I screamed.

"You heard him, Mark. No way in hell." Tommy said to Mark slowly. Nick stood back laughing at Mark and Steve, and that didn't help the situation.

That made Steve very upset, and he started yelling at us along with Mark, "Get your asses back in those woods and do what you're told!"

I could tell things were getting out of control, and if it wasn't for Candice walking up, I'm almost certain all hell would have broken loose. "Mark, Steve, what is going on over here? And what's all the yelling about?" she asked.

"These punk-ass kids won't do what they're told," Steve replied.

"What were they told to do? And I want Mark to answer this time," she said. Tommy tried to talk instead, but Candice stopped him quickly. "I didn't ask you, did I, Tommy?" She had her ways of getting men to shut up and listen, and it worked on Tommy as well even if he didn't want to admit it.

"No, ma'am. You didn't ask me," he answered.

She glared at him and said, "Then be quiet and don't interrupt me again." I think that took us by surprise. Candice has never acted like this before. I would say by the look on Mark's and Steve's faces that it had taken them by surprise too. "I'm waiting, Mark," Candice said impatiently while standing there with her arms crossed.

"I wanted them to go back into the woods and get the firewood they dropped," Mark replied.

"That's it?" she asked.

"That's it, Candice," he answered.

She then turned her attention toward us. "Now I want to hear from you, Tommy. What's going on?" she asked.

"We did go into the woods, and we did gather his stupid firewood. But as we were heading out, someone decided to scare us. Bobby and I had to drop our firewood because we had to run after Chubs and Nick because they ran off ahead of us and in different directions. Come to find out, Mark here sent Steve and a few others into the woods to gather 'firewood' shortly after we left. And now he wants us to go back in? Hell no! There's plenty of firewood. Why should we have to go back in there?" Tommy answered.

"That is odd. And I'm sorry to say, even though I don't agree with what Mark has done, or how he's acting now. There's no way possible that Steve could have even tried to scare anyone. I was with him and the others, helping them carry the firewood. I'm sorry, guys, but it's the truth. And it wasn't Mark either, because he stood there and watched us work the whole time, not once lifting a finger to help."

Now Nick and Tommy were stuck in between a rock and a hard place; they really had no choice but to back down. I could tell that it was hard for them to let the subject go, but for now, they had to accept Candice's word. "It looks like it was all just one big misunderstanding. Tommy, I don't know what happened to you or your friends out there, but I assure you that none of us had anything to do with it. I wish I knew what to tell you." said Candice.

That wasn't good enough though, for Nick and Tommy, I stepped in to make sure nothing else was said for now. "It's all right, Candice. We believe you more than we believe Mark or Steve. And besides, we should go check on Chubs. That's more important than fighting with those losers." I said to her.

"What did you call us, you little turd?" Steve asked as he started walking toward me.

Candice stopped him and said, "Knock it off, Steve! And besides, we don't have time for this."

There was no reason for me to stick around and keep arguing, so I turned and headed toward the campfire. And as I started walking back, I heard that vile voice again. "I will see you soon," it said to me. I had a bad feeling that "soon" I would be fighting for my very soul. It caught me by surprise so much so that I didn't even realize that my friends left me standing there.

After I finally had caught back up to Nick and Tommy, they had words for me. "So you finally decided to play catch up, 'bout damn time," Tommy said as he looked at me with a smile on his face.

Nick slapped me on the back. "Don't worry, we will get those assholes back soon enough." I pretty much smiled at Nick and ignored every word that he had said to me.

I was done talking about it for that night. "I'm a little on the slow side," I said jokingly back at Tommy. Then I asked, "Do you see Chubs sitting anywhere?"

Tommy pointed, "There he is." he shouted.

The three of us ran up to him. "Chubs, my man. You're one tough person to find," Tommy joked.

"Why did you leave us high and dry? Were you scared of them?" Nick asked.

I didn't like Nick's attitude toward Chubs. Nick was new to the group and had no business opening his mouth about anything, and I let him know that as quickly as possible. "Back off, Nick. You leave Chubs alone if you want to stay a part of this group." I warned him.

"Guys, would you sit down and shut up?" Chubs said to us. "Whoa, someone is cranky," Tommy said.

"Just sit down, guys, I don't feel like dealing with Mark or Steve again," said Chubs.

"Come on. Let's sit down if it makes him feel better." Nick said. He then looked at me and said, "Sorry, Bobby."

I nodded in acceptance and motioned for him to take a seat as well. "Ah, shit! Here comes Mark, and Steve is right behind him," I said.

"Well, it looks like the gang is all here." He looked at us and said, "That's good because it's scary-story time. So anyone that's faint of heart, please go back to your tents at once," he said to everyone.

Now to be honest with you, I wasn't one for scary stories. Especially when the stories are told by Mark; not once has he ever told a story that was scary. Also, I didn't want Mark to think he had me scared of him either, so I stayed put, and so did Tommy, Nick, and Chubs. "This is your last chance, ladies. You can leave now, and we can let you know when it's suppertime. Think about it, ladies," Mark said to us.

"We're not going anywhere, Mark. After what we've been through, I doubt whatever you have to say will scare us." Chubs looked at him and said. The rest of us agreed with him and refused to let Mark scare us any further.

This time around though something weird happened. Candice who usually stays to chuckle at Mark's scary stories got up and walked off toward her tent, after informing him to tell her when the food was done. "Is everyone ready?" he shouted. Everyone except for the four us excitedly yelled out, "hell yeah!" Give it some time, and that excitement will fade, I thought to myself. "Let's get started then.

No whining when done. Steve, keep an eye on the food. It's time to scare the shit out them." Mark said. He then laughed one of the creepiest laughs he could come up with, it was just lame. Then he started with his scary campfire story. "We have a good one in store for you tonight, kiddos. Tonight you will learn the secret of these woods that we are in. I see the look of confusion on some of our previous guests' faces. You must think I'm full of shit. Well, look around you. Does any of this look familiar to you in any way? Are you not wondering why we are now hiking to our destination?

After this story, everything will become clear to each and every one of you. I see that I've caught your attention. Good, good. You will need to pay close attention. Trust me." He paused for a brief moment to stare us all down and get a drink of water. Now I'm not one for scary stories but the start of this particular story caught my interest, so I sat there hanging on every word Mark was saying. After he had his brief pause, he continued on, "Supposedly ten years ago there was a camp here in these woods.

To this day what happened in these woods was a mystery. Until now, that is, I know the deep, dark secret of these woods. There was a young boy that went to this so-called camp. His name was Albert, he was more of an outcast, and he wasn't well liked by any of the other kids at the camp either. He was picked on day after day, especially by one group of the meanest teenagers you could ever meet. They made his life a living hell. They practically tortured the young boy every chance they got.

One day the boys pretended to befriend him, and they talked him into going on a one-mile hike into the woods. Afterward, the group of teens blindfolded him and left him out in the woods by himself. Albert spent three days in the woods lost and scared. He desperately tried finding his way back to camp hoping that the counselors were looking for him as well. However, not a single person cared that he was even gone, and not a single soul went out to search for him at all. Luck would, however, be on his side, for he eventually found his way back to camp, just to realize no one even noticed he was gone.

Soon though he would learn that he would have been better off if he had just stayed lost, for once the bullies learned of his return, they took their bullying one step further. And soon that would wear on the young boy, to the point he was starting to have horrible nightmares and fits of rage. One day, Albert caught the one that was always leading the charge when it came to the bullies by himself. Albert pulled his pocketknife on him and threatened to kill the teen if he or any of his friends ever touched him again.

The teen didn't take Albert seriously and laughed in his face; who could have taken Albert serious? He was a pale and frail-looking young boy who was scared of his own shadow, which in turn made him an easy target, even if he hadn't done anything to deserve it. The teen walked close to him and grabbed at Albert's shirt; that proved to be a huge mistake.

As Albert swung the blade of his pocketknife at the teen cutting his arm, the teen screamed in fear. "You'll pay for this!" But that didn't faze Albert at all; his face seemed to distort in the pleasure of causing someone else pain, rather than himself. That look on Albert's face scared the teen more than the wound on his arm, and the sadistic laugh that came from him made the teen run away in fear. At that moment, Albert felt the sensation of nothing more than pure evil run through his veins, and he loved every minute of it.

For him, that meant victory over anyone that was going to treat him badly. He learned what he believed were lessons: "Hurt or be hurt," "Do to them before they get a chance to do upon him," and the one he loved the most was "Kill or be killed. He felt powerful; however, the next day, that would be a short-lived feeling. For what had happened yesterday made the leader of the bullies pissed, and he wanted revenge, and he was going to get Albert no matter what. So the teenagers decided they would meet back up at the certain time and at a certain place, in which they knew Albert visited often.

And so later on the teenagers met up with each other to carry out their plan. They waited in complete silence for about thirty minutes, but to them, it felt like hours. And just as they were about to give up, the teenagers heard the sound of footsteps coming their way. The group of boys knew right off that it was Albert. As soon as he was close enough to them, the teenagers jumped out from behind some trees and grabbed him.

This is when things get really bad, and I do mean really bad. The teenagers, bullies, whatever you want to call the group of kids. I just like to switch it up and keep everyone on their toes. Anyways, the bullies had Albert pinned up against one of the trees now, and they started to beat the hell out of the poor kid. He was punched in the face several times, which caused his nose to be broken, and his lip was split open into several places, and one punch landed perfectly on his eye in which caused him to have a gash right above.

He was then thrown to the ground and was kicked on over and over again; he was so badly beaten that he could barely even move. He cried out as loud as he could, screaming and yelling for help, but he was too far away for anyone else to hear his pleas. The bullies, however, knew that eventually someone would either see or hear what was going on. So they made the decision to lock him in a shed that they spotted just up ahead; the lesson was now taught in their eyes, so they figured he could stay the night in there, at least until the morning or later.

The teens dragged Albert toward the shed as he was kicking and screaming and pleading for them to stop and let him go. However, the teens refused to listen to Albert, as they finally had him at the door of the shed; then they laughed and cursed at him as they threw him inside and locked the door behind him. With what strength Albert had, he made it to his feet and pounded on the door with his fist and begged for them to release him.

However, the blood loss that he had suffered from his wounds was weakening him, so much so that now he could barely even stand. He slowly slid down to his knees and lay down on the floor; his strength now was completely gone. He cried and cried; with tears and blood running down his face it didn't take him long, and out he went.

Albert started having nightmares right after he passed out. Albert didn't even know if he was dead or still alive, nor did he care. However, this time the nightmare would prove too much for him to handle. His rage was building inside of him until the point Albert was no longer the same. Everything that the bullies put him through brought out his hate for every living thing that was around him; when he awoke all he could feel was the rage. And he was like a caged animal, he clawed at the door until his fingernails fell off, and bloody fingerprints were all over the door.

He then started clawing at the floor as well; he had blood everywhere. Feeling that his pocketknife was still in his pocket, Albert gave a sadistic smile as he reached inside and grabbed his knife. After opening up the knife, he started cutting and cutting on his body all while laughing hysterically as he did so. The poor boy had gone mad and killed himself, or did he?

The very next day the bullies went back to the shed to let Albert out and tease him, for they figured he had been crying like a baby the whole night. But what they witnessed when they unlocked the door and opened it sent chills down their spins; there hunched against the wall was Albert, in a pool of his own blood. With his pocketknife still in hand, it looked as though Albert cut on his hands and face, to the point you couldn't even tell that he was even once human. He had cut the flesh from his hands, and he even cut his eyelids off so he could never shut them.

By the looks of things, he even cut a permanent smile into his face; it was pure madness. But what I believe scared them the most was the message Albert left for them in blood on the wall. And it read, "You will all die. I will kill each and every one of you. I am death, and I am coming for you."

# 5

# A Frightening Surprise

Completely freaked out by what they had seen, the teens knew there was only one choice they had to keep themselves out of trouble. So they dragged Albert's body deep into the woods and left him there until they could return with some kerosene that they had stolen from the camp counselors' cabin. Ready for the task at hand, they took the kerosene and poured it over his body. Not realizing that Albert was still alive, they struck the match and threw it on top of him and watched as his body caught fire.

The teens didn't stick around either, for they quickly made their way back to camp and got themselves ready for sleep. That night, however, there would be no sleep for them, as screams could be heard coming from the exact place they set Albert's body on fire; even though it scared them, they did their best to ignore it. The very next day the teens didn't go back into the woods; instead, they ran back to the shed with buckets of soap and water. And they cleaned the blood-soaked room from top to bottom, making sure not to miss a single drop.

One thing stood out to them, though; no matter how many times they cleaned the message off the wall, it would keep coming back. Seeing how there was nothing more they could do, the teens went back to camp to finish off the day. But before they went off their separate ways, they swore an oath to one another that none of them would ever talk about what took place. The day went on as normal as if nothing had happened over the past couple of days.

Even weeks went by and all was forgotten; the teens went back to having fun and being bullies again. The saddest part was no one noticed that Albert was nowhere to be seen; the camp counselors didn't even notice he was gone. And I don't think anyone really cared, but things were about to change.

Albert wasn't dead; the kerosene that the bullies used to set him on fire changed the looks of his skin. His skin was severely burned, but he felt no pain. The color of his skin had also changed to a white leathery-looking complexion. What was left of his lips were now black as night, and his eyes were also sunken deep into the sockets; he no longer looked human. Albert was now an insane killer, or I guess maybe you could call him a demon.

He now waited in the woods and watched everyone as he plotted his revenge; for weeks he had been waiting for just the right moment, and that moment was now. Nightfall came, and Albert was ready to make his first kill, and he already had his first victim in mind. He was going to kill one of the bullies responsible for what had happened to him and leave a warning for the rest.

As the night went on, the teenagers were back in their cabin and goofing off. That is until the sounds of footsteps could be heard outside their cabin, and everything went quiet; not even the sounds of crickets could be heard. The boys sat there in silence watching and waiting in fear, but nothing happened, and they went right back to goofing off thinking it was just the wind. But then all of a sudden the lights in the cabin went out, and the cabin door flung open violently, and all you could hear were the cries of the teens in the cabin.

Right before the lights came back on, they could hear a hideous laughter coming from the darkness over their own screams. After what felt like an eternity, the lights had come back on, and what they witnessed next would forever change everything. One of their friends was gone, and all that was left of him was a puddle of blood on the floor and a very familiar message on the wall written in blood: "You will all die. I will kill each and every one of you. I am death, and I have come for you."

The teens were now scared to death, and they wanted to get help, but they knew what it would mean for the rest of them if they did. So they hid their fears and cleaned up the blood on the floor and wiped off the blood on the wall as well. And afterward, the teens still swore not to tell another living soul of this night or any other. And they did their best to sleep; however, they could not, for they knew that because of them a monster was created with one thing in mind—to kill.

The next day the teenagers were out and about doing their usual thing but could not help to think about what horrible fate had befallen their friend. That was all the young teens could take, they knew they had to help their friend, and they needed a plan of action. Unfortunately, it was already too late; before the teens could even come up with anything, they were startled by screams of horror coming from just up ahead. In all the chaos, they could have sworn they heard something about a body; the bullies knew they had no choice but to see what was going on, so they ran ahead to take a look, and there lying on the ground was the mangled body of their friend.

Now pay close attention, kiddies, this is where the weird shit starts to happen. After close examination of the body, the counselors knew that he had been murdered and that there was a killer on the loose. The counselors had one choice, and one choice only. It was time to gather every kid and young teen in camp and get them the hell out of there before the killer has a chance to strike again. And let me tell you that's exactly what they attempted to do. Did it work? I know that's what you're all asking yourselves. I can see it on all your faces. The answer to that is, no, it didn't work.

The counselors led the group of campers out the same way they had all came in, except this time the way out only led them back in. Which meant some strong force had turned the woods into a wicked maze and wasn't about to let them out. The camp counselors would give up on this night and try again in the morning, but this time they would be another kid short because Albert would strike again. This left all in a panic, and they wanted to get everyone out as quickly as possible. Each time they attempted and failed to leave, and each time they would find yet another kid brutally murdered.

That, in turn, fueled them to get out of there as fast as they could; however, that would not happen. They tried over and over again until there was just a few of them left. Then one last time they would try, and as they got ready to lead the way, the whole campsite mysteriously burst into flames. Then a silhouette could be seen standing in the fire as if it controlled the flames themselves. Then one by one the rest of the teens and kids were found dead, blood had covered the camp in a crimson red, and the flames were burning it all down to the ground; however, one teen—just one— had survived.

He was found wandering around in the woods covered in

blood, lost and muttering about a killer boy that he and his friends accidentally created. It was a horrible sight to see—all the bodies burned to a crisp and all the blood that was also left. The parents and also the police wanted answers, and they could only get those answers from the teen they had taken to the hospital.

After a few days, the boy seemed to be back to normal, and it was time for them to ask questions. And he told them everything; it was hard to believe at first. But for the police, it was time to go search for a murderer; as hard as the police tried, they never found the person responsible for the camp massacre. So they turned their attention back on the young teen that made it out alive; unknown to them, however, that young teen would be dead.

Because on that very night, the parents would hear a blood-chilling scream come from the boy's room, and as soon as they got to his room, his mother let out a cry of sadness. For there in his bed was the teen, dead and covered in his own blood; his face and hands had been cut to the point you couldn't even recognize him. There on the wall was that same bloody message: "You will all pay. I will kill each and every one of you." Albert had gotten his revenge on everyone. The end.

"I do apologize if I lost you at anytime there. Mark wasn't exactly the brightest tool in the shed. And the stories that he told needed work," Bobby said, barely able to contain himself from laughing.

The man sat there and stared at Bobby. "I didn't ask for idle jokes, now did I?" the man said.

Bobby could tell that the man was irritated badly and that in itself was starting to wear on Bobby's nerves. "Look, I don't know what your deal is today, but I've had just about enough of you, mystery man." Bobby stood up out of his chair looking down at the man. "I'm only going to ask you this one more time. Who in the hell are you?" He really didn't want to ask the man on this day, but enough was enough.

All Bobby got for his efforts was to be told, "All in due time, Bobby. All in due time. Besides, Bobby. Look around you, all you have is time. And there's nothing you can do about it." Hearing what the man said had upset Bobby; he paced back forth thinking of a way to make the man talk. Then he had a brilliant idea, and a smile came across his face. "Do you find something funny?" the man asked.

Bobby turned to face him again and answered, "It's funny for me and bad for you."

The man's facial expression changed drastically as he asked, "What do you mean by that? You can't keep me out of here, so what could you possibly do?"

Bobby kept the smile on his face because he knew he had the man on the ropes now. "I will tell you all you need to know when you tell me everything I want to know. You have three days to make your choice. I believe you know the way out." Bobby said to him.

The stranger didn't like the fact that Bobby figured out a way to one-up him, and he didn't appreciate his attitude toward him either. "You will know my decision in three days' time. That's all I have to say for now."

Bobby had a feeling of triumph this time because he knew by the man's reactions and words that he had finally figured out how to get the information he wanted out of him. The stranger didn't have much to say this time when he was getting ready to leave, nor did he even try and shake Bobby's hand. He quickly gathered up his notes and called for the nurse to let him out.

Usually, he would turn to Bobby and say, "See you tomorrow." That wasn't the case this time around, the door opened, and before the nurse could even get a word out, the man quickly darted out past her. Bobby, on the other hand, didn't really notice how odd the whole thing seemed to be; he was to busy laughing at the man for acting like a complete child.

To him, it was a much-needed relief because he hadn't laughed like that in a long time. Even the nurse that lets the stranger in and out of the room got a little chuckle out of it as well, before looking back at Bobby with a smile on her face as she was shutting the door. Guess I pissed him off this time, Bobby thought to himself. He then laughed again before heading over to his bed to grab his journal. Bobby's fun was now over, and it was time for him to get to work.

There was one thing that was very important to him more so than anything else, and that was writing in his journal. All he could think about day in and day out was writing every little detail of his feelings and his dealings with the strange man down in his journal. And tonight would be no different; with his journal in hand, he went back over to his little table in the corner and started writing.

July 2, 1999 Today for me was a triumph, because now I have finally found my ace in the hole to use against that strange man. At first, I didn't know if it would even faze the man's resolve; however, when I played my cards, it shook the man to his core. That much I could tell. When I told him he had three days to tell me what I wanted to know or I wouldn't talk to him about my past gave me more power than I would have expected. He went quiet on me, and his attitude had worsened. I'm sure whatever had him upset today, my words had added to it. Usually, before he leaves, he turns and tries to shake my hand or attempts some kind of small talk to gain my trust. But today he was so pissed off at me that he stormed out of my room without saying a word to me or the nurse at my door.

It was like watching a child throwing a fit when he or she doesn't get their way, the way I acted toward my parents the day they sent me back to summer camp. I miss my parents, and I loved them dearly; if I had known back then that, that would be the last year I would ever see them again, I would have spent more time with them and made them both proud of me. However, you can't change the past no matter how much you wish you could. Anyways, I got a well-needed laugh at the man's reaction, and so did my nurse. She's such a nice lady and pretty as well. Who knows, maybe I will talk to her at least once before I meet my end.

It didn't take long before Bobby passed out on the table that he had been using to write on. He had been sleeping for a good few hours before a voice in the night had awoken him. "I will see you soon," the voice said to him. It scared Bobby bad enough that he jumped up and started searching around his room frantically. But after the search had proven pointless, he calmed his nerves and chalked it up to nothing more than a bad dream.

Before Bobby could even think about what he should do next, there was a loud knocking coming from his door followed by a voice. "Bobby! He's back!" It was the nurse's voice, informing him of the stranger's return. Damn. I didn't think he would be back so soon. Bobby thought to himself. He then looked back at the table and noticed he had left his journal out.

"Give me a minute!" he shouted back at the nurse as he ran over to grab his journal. But the stranger was now more impatient than ever before, and he started to force his way past the nurse and into Bobby's room. Bobby could hear his door opening and the nurse yelling at the man for what he was trying to do, as she tried her best to stop him. He quickly ran over to his bed and lifted up the mattress and tossed his journal underneath just in the nick of time.

"You can't stop me from entering this room, ma'am! Now back away!" the stranger shouted at her before both of them ended up in the room.

"What's going on? Why are both of you in my room at once?" Bobby asked. He knew he had hidden his journal just in time. However, he was still curious, and he wanted to know what was happening. "Hey!" he shouted at them. Both jumped at the realization that now they stood arguing with each other in front of Bobby.

"I'm so sorry, Bobby. I couldn't stop him from coming in. No matter how hard I tried, he wouldn't listen to me." the nurse explained.

The stranger, however, decided to argue his side of things. "She's not allowed to stop me; by law, I'm allowed in any room I please. Not a single person here can stop me, not one patient nor doctor can refuse me access! And besides, you owe me three more days per our agreement, Bobby."

A smile appeared on Bobby's face as he said, "I see. It's all right, Nurse, let him stay. He won't cause any more trouble." He looked at the man and asked, "Will you?" The man nodded in agreement and apologized to the nurse for his bad behavior, then turned his attention back to Bobby. "Looks like you have me stuck in between a rock and a hard place. I apologize, you're smarter than I thought." the man said to him.

"Remember, you have three days, and then you tell me your decision. Got it?" Bobby said.

"You win for now. It's time we get back to work," the man

replied.

And as promised, Bobby happily went back to telling his side of the story. Like I was saying beforehand, Mark definitely needed to brush up on his storytelling skills, even though you could look around at all the scared faces and clearly see he had gotten to a few of the younger kids. "Boo!" Steve yelled as he leaped out from behind the tents, making most of the younger kids jump and scream in fear. I hate to admit it, but I even jumped because that was unexpected. I could also see Tommy and Chubs jump as well. I think what happened out in the woods got to us more than we wanted to admit to.

Mark was laughing his ass off as he got a kick out of hearing almost everyone scream. "I just wanted to let everyone know that food was done. Let's eat!" Steve said to us all, also laughing as hard as he could, all the while almost falling over.

"I really hate those guys," Nick said.

"Get used to it, Nick. Because after this year, it will all be yours, man. We won't be around to have your back then," Tommy said to Nick after slapping him on the back.

"Who cares? Let's go get some food. I'm starving!" Chubs said to us. Not even the scariest places on earth could stop him from eating, and off he went without us. After Tommy realized that Candice was outside of her tent and serving food, he ran off ahead as well with Nick following behind him like always. Good thing food was only a few feet away, I myself wasn't that hungry, but I also knew I would need my energy for being on watch duty later that night, so I went and grabbed some food as well.

For the most part of the night, we sat around the campfire, eating and joking about things; not once did we bring up what happened earlier that evening.

Nor did we talk about the scary story that Mark had told either, even though it weighed heavily on my mind. Was Mark's story true? Or was it all just one big coincidence? Those were the things I kept asking myself throughout the night. Unfortunately, I wasn't going to find out those answers just yet as it was getting late and time for everyone to turn in—well, almost everyone.

"It's time to call it a night, as we will be up bright and early!" Mark explained. And afterward, he turned his attention on us. "Remember, ladies, you're all on watch duty. I would suggest that you decide who will watch first then switch every couple of hours. Now get to it," he demanded.

"You heard the man. Get to it, ladies. Time's a wasting!" Steve butted in. "You heard the assholes. Let's get going," Tommy said to us. He turned in the direction of the tent and started marching that way.

"That's right," Nick said as he marched behind Tommy. I stood there and laughed as the two marched away.

"Come on, Chubs. We better go as well," I turned and said to him. He didn't say much to me when he stood up; well, he actually didn't say anything at all as he walked off. I wondered if what happened to him in the woods started weighing on him like it was on me.

I turned and started walking away, and that's when Mark yelled out to us. "Oh, and by the way, ladies. I want my flashlights back."

After hearing those words, Tommy and Nick stopped in their tracks, and so did I. Chubs, on the other hand, acted like he didn't even give a damn. He walked straight past Tommy and said, "Good luck." I could tell by the look on Tommy's face he didn't like the comment Chubs had made. In our group, it was one for all, and all for one. You know, like the musketeers?

Anyways, if one went down, we all went down. Chubs knew that. However, I was smart, and I had put the flashlights back in Mark's backpack. I knew we would still be in deep shit later, but not on this night.

"Don't worry about it, Mark. I put them back where I got them from." I shouted back at him. Then I couldn't help but be a smart-ass. "Oh, and thanks for letting us borrow them!" I added. It was fun for me to be able to piss Mark off as much as I could.

"Just get your asses ready for watch duty!" Mark screamed out at us before turning and walking away, shoving Steve in the process.

I walked on by Tommy and nodded at him, and he nodded back at me, which let me know he was glad that I had his back as promised. But we did walk back to our tent bitching all the way there; good thing we got that out of our system because we didn't need to be bitching at each other. Teamwork was the only thing that was going to get us through the night.

"Hey, guys. Why don't you stop goofing off, and let's decide who's on watch duty first," Chubs demanded.

"Well, we can't all stay up and watch. We do need some sleep throughout the night," said Tommy.

"Hey! Why don't we flip a coin?" Nick asked.

And that's when Chubs started running his mouth to Nick. "Flip a coin? Flip a damn coin? Really?!" he screamed.

"Calm down, Chubs," I said.

That's when he freaked out even more. "Calm down you say? First, Nick here says let's flip a coin, and now I'm being told to calm down?" he shouted again.

"What crawled up your ass?" Tommy asked.

Chubs was definitely irritated and all fired up about something, and he wasn't about to stop taking it out on us. "What crawled up my ass? Look around you. How can we flip a damn coin? We have no flashlights now. How in the hell could we find the coin once it hits the ground? Oh, maybe we can hear where it lands. Who needs to see, right? Stop making stupid suggestions for one. And stop asking me stupid-ass questions." he explained.

Nick knew that he had accidentally pissed Chubs off with his suggestion of flipping a coin; even though it was just a joke, it started more trouble more than he wanted. So he came up with an idea to calm Chubs down. "There's no need to decide who will go first because I will. I've got the first watch," Nick said. Not to be outdone, Tommy volunteered to take the second shift of night duty.

"I'll take the third shift of watch duty, and, Chubs, that leaves you with the last of the watch duty. Does that work for you?" I asked.

"Do whatever, I don't give a shit," Chubs said before he stormed off inside the tent.

Tommy sighed and shook his head. "I'll go check on Chubs. Maybe I will find out what his problem is with us. You just worry about showing Nick what to do, Bobby," Tommy said before disappearing into the tent.

"You heard what Tommy said, so follow me," I said as I motioned for him to follow me back to the campfire. The fire was still burning, but I could tell that it needed an extra log of wood or two to keep it burning strong for another hour or so. "Okay, so this is what you want to do, Nick." And I pointed over to the stack of firewood. "You want to take one of these logs and throw it into the fire when the flames are looking low, like so. And then wait for a few minutes to see how well the fire starts up again.

If the flames still look somewhat low, add another log. Now listen to me real close, Nick. Whatever you do, do not throw more than two logs at a time on the fire. And do not—I repeat, do not—let this fire go out," I explained. I could see a little bit of confusion on his face, so I asked, "If you need my help, I can stay out here with you. What do you think?" Nick smiled and thanked me for the offer, but he assured me he had everything under control and that I could head back and get some sleep before it was my turn.

I took him on his word, and I headed back to our tent for some well-needed sleep, and just as I was about to go into the tent and sleep, I swear I could feel something watching me. I shook it off and went inside. I figured that whatever was out there wouldn't make such a bold move with a camp full of people. So I felt safe enough to lay down and fall asleep, and this time around as I slept I didn't have not one single nightmare. Before I knew it, I could hear Nick make his way into the tent and wake Tommy up. "Anything to report?" I asked.

I couldn't see him all that well because of how dark it was, but I could hear his voice. "Except for few noises here and there, nothing much," Nick answered. "Hey, Tommy. Would you hurry up? I would like to get some sleep now if you don't mind."

"Hey, man. Don't rush me, I'm getting up, and I move as fast as I want." Tommy replied.

"Would you guys please shut the hell up! I'm trying to sleep here." Chubs angrily demanded. I don't remember much else as I must have fallen back to sleep without even noticing that I had done so, that is until Tommy woke me up and informed me that it was my turn for watch duty. I made sure to ask him the same question that I had asked Nick, and Tommy had the same thing to say as well.

"It was the same for me, Bobby. A few noises and that was it, pretty much quiet the whole time I was out there." Now it was my turn to head out by the campfire and be on watch duty. I didn't like the thought of it, but if the new guy can do it without a problem, and Tommy also, then I knew I could as well. So I told Tommy to have a good night's rest, and off I went without saying another word because I didn't want to wake Chubs up again by accident. Who knows what kind of trouble that would have started a second time around, and I didn't want to find out either. I was feeling pretty confident that the rest of that night would finish without a problem; however, that confidence would be short-lived.

Because as I got about halfway to the campfire, that feeling of something watching me had returned. I did my best to ignore it, and I kept walking on until I was finally there, but before I took a seat on of the logs, I decided I would double check to make sure everything was in order. It looked as though Tommy and Nick had done a good job; the fire was burning strong, and we had enough firewood to get us all through the night. Afterward, I was ready to sit by the fire and try my best not to fall asleep; it had been a long day, and just a few hours of sleep just didn't cut it for me.

However, the sounds coming out from deep in the woods and knowing something evil was watching me were all I needed to keep myself from even attempting to close my eyes. As I sat there watching the shadows of the flames, a million thoughts rushed through my head. Are Nick and Tommy right? Was it really Mark and Steve that caused all of these? And if so, did they both make the others help them out?

I'm sure it would have been easy for Mark to talk the other teens into it, or even the younger kids, because that would mean being on his good side. However, to me, none of it added up. And I thought about it long and hard and tried to put it all together, but it only proved to me that Mark and Steve had nothing to do with what happened to us in the woods.

It just wasn't possible, and Candice wouldn't lie to protect Mark or Steve; she hated them both. So I believed her when she said that Steve and the few that went with him were in and out of the woods within five to ten minutes. On top of that, it would now be near impossible to convince Tommy and Nick otherwise. I also had questions for Chubs as well.

I wanted to know what scared him so badly that he ran ahead of me and almost attacked me when I finally caught up to him. I just needed to think of a way to approach him on that subject. But before my mind could be made up about all that has transpired, something happened that caused me to lose my train of thought. I felt someone touch the back of my neck. I jumped and turned around as quickly as I could; however, there wasn't a soul around. Shortly after I could hear the sounds of footsteps running away from me, and then I could hear someone laughing as if they had just pulled a prank on me.

But still, as much as I looked around the area, I couldn't see a single person around, and I know for a fact that no one can move that fast. That only happened in the comic books that I loved to read. It wasn't long after that, things started getting crazy again, just like it was earlier that night. And again that uneasy feeling was returning, as the laughter of young children could be heard right in front of me.

All I could see though were shadows dancing in the darkness; all I could tell was that whoever or whatever was doing this was no taller than me. I had no idea what was going to happen next as I sat there doing my best not to run back to the tent.

The laughter started to get louder and closer to me. I kept on looking around hoping to actually see someone—anyone at all. It was really starting to get me, and I was reaching my breaking point.

"Steve! Mark! If that's you, guys, please stop! I give up. I've had enough! You win!" I begged and pleaded with them. I waited for a few minutes for a response, but I got nothing in return. I didn't know what to do; it was either stay or make a run for it! And just as I was about to make my choice, that creepy, evil, sadistic laughter from the woods and my dreams could be heard. It was faint at first, but I knew, I knew what it was! The laughter got louder and louder until I couldn't hear anything else but that! I couldn't control myself anymore, and my rage took over yet again. I started screaming out curse words left and right, "Shit! Damn you! Damn every one of you!" I had officially lost my mind at that one slight moment.

Hell, I even started picking up anything I could find like rocks, branches, and even the firewood and throwing them into the woods screaming uncontrollably the whole time. This time around I wasn't thinking clearly at all, and in my fit of rage, I decided it was time to prove a point to myself.

So I took off toward Mark and Steve's tent, and all the noises and evil laughter in the world weren't about to stop me either. Come hell or high water I was about to prove Tommy right or wrong in one instance.

The madder that I was getting, the faster I started walking until I was full-out sprinting toward their tent. And when I finally got to the tent and quietly looked in, it was no surprise to me seeing both of them sleeping. I honestly knew they never scared us or had anyone else to scare us either. It would have been a relief to prove myself wrong, but right in front of me was all the proof I needed. There was something out there, and it was waiting for the perfect time to strike, and now I knew that I needed to prove it to Tommy as well.

But for now I had to finish my watch duty first before anything else; as I was making my way back to the campfire I could hear someone following me. Not once did I attempt to look behind me, for I knew what I would find if I had done so. Then I could feel breathing on the back of my neck, followed by a faint whisper.

"Tell everyone to turn around and go back." At least that's what I thought was said at the time. At that moment fear overtook me, and I took off running as fast as I could back to my tent. Just as soon as I ran inside, I wanted to wake Tommy and Nick up and tell them what had happened and also to let them know Mark and Steve had nothing to do with any of what happened now, or earlier either. But I didn't do it. I was so scared that all I did was wake Chubs up and tell him it was his turn now.

Afterward, I quickly crawled into my sleeping bag and covered my whole body up, even my head. I didn't say another word to Chubs, and I sent him out without a single warning of what was out there waiting for him. I didn't even know if my time was really even finished, and I didn't care, I was safe under my sleeping bag, and that was all that mattered to me at the time.

While lying there I was still shaking badly, so I took a few deep breaths to try and calm my nerves, and I closed my eyes. And as I lay there with my eyes closed and finally asleep, I thought I heard a loud blood-chilling scream coming from the direction of the campfire, along with the sounds of someone running close by. Even though upon hearing those sounds, I still refused to move a muscle, for I felt safer inside my covers at that moment in time.

And eventually, I would find myself falling back asleep, without even thinking twice about what may be going on outside in the darkness to Chubs. Yes, we were supposed to have each others' backs, but that wouldn't be the case for the rest of that night in question.

The very next day would come quicker than I could have ever imagined, and with even more problems that would be forced upon us by Steve and Mark. Tommy, Nick, and myself were awakened from our peaceful slumber by Steve's dumb-ass screaming in our ears. "Wake up, ladies! Do you guys think the shit you pulled last night was fun!" Not one of us had any idea what he was even talking about, nor did we understand why we were getting screamed at by him. He didn't even give us a chance to defend ourselves little alone find out what was going on; he just kept on screaming at us. "What in the hell were the four of you thinking?" he asked.

And again he didn't give us a chance to answer, before asking us another question. "Did you ladies think you could get away with what you have done?"

I wasn't sure how Tommy and Nick were handling things, but I was confused as hell. I just knew for sure that we were tired and barely awake, and I'm sure my friends were like me and just wanted to know what in the hell was going on. I could tell that was a fact by the same confused looks on their faces that I had on mine, and it wasn't even a second after he asked us those weird-ass questions that Steve started screaming at us again.

"Get your asses up, get dressed, and then get your asses outside with your other friend! And make it quick!" You could tell that whatever was going on that it was bad enough to piss Mark and Steve off so much so that they were willing to drag us out of our tent if need be. The whole time the three of us were getting ready, we kept giving one another the "what the hell" look. The only thing I could think of that would piss Mark and Steve off that badly would be if Nick and Tommy did something to get even. However, if that was the case, it would have been pointless of them to do so, but it couldn't have been them though.

Because if I know Tommy, and believe me I do, he would have woken me up bragging about what they had done. But, on the other hand, as I looked around, Chubs wasn't anywhere to be found, and Steve did mention joining our friend outside, which could only mean one thing. It had to have been him that did something to get us all in trouble, and we were about to find out exactly what. And he must have already gotten his ass chewed, and now it was our turn. The whole time we were getting dressed, I could hear the commotion on the other side of the tent; the other teens and the younger kids were freaking out, and I could even hear Candice yelling about how the campsite was destroyed.

"Destroyed? What exactly happened out there?" I asked myself. Tommy and Nick headed out of the tent first, and I was the last one out. What I had seen when I first walked out of the tent scared the shit out of me. The campsite was completely demolished, there were a couple of tents torn to shreds, and backpacks were thrown all over the place, all the firewood was gone, and the tents that were left standing, including ours, was covered in red-stained handprints in all different sizes.

And on top of that, Chubs was nowhere to be found; as far as I had known, Chubs could have done this all by himself. But in the back of my mind, I knew exactly what had happened, and I also knew that there was no way to explain it to anyone either. I didn't know what to say or think. I was honestly in a state of shock.

However, Tommy would nudge me and snap me back to reality with his questions. "Hey, Bobby," he whispered. "Do you think Chubs had anything to do with this?"

"You and I both know that Chubs could never pull this off without help, Tommy," I whispered back to him.

"I know, man. But this is bad, really bad. I don't see Chubs around either, and that makes it look like we were all—"

Right before Tommy could say another word, Mark rushed up to us, screaming, "What the hell! What the actual hell!" We stood there still somewhat confused as Mark was letting us have it. I then glanced over at Nick, and he was just as confused as Tommy and myself, but then he made a huge mistake, and he smiled. As soon as Mark noticed that Nick was smiling, he jumped right over and got in his face. "Do you think this is funny?" he yelled. Nick stood there frozen; you could tell by the look on his face he had no idea what to say. "Well, answer me!" he shouted.

All Nick could do was mumble out a few words. "Um. Uh. I don't know."

That just pissed Mark off even more. "What? You don't know? You don't know?" Mark screamed as he had his finger in Nick's face.

I don't think I've ever seen Mark so pissed off before, and that's when I knew I had to do something to help Nick out because I was afraid of what might happen next if I didn't. "Just what are you trying to say, Mark?" I asked.

That was enough to get his attention away from Nick, and back on all three of us. "What I'm saying is that I know that it was you guys that did this!"

And that was all it took to get Tommy fired up. "That's bullshit, Mark! We didn't have anything to do with this! Look around you. Do you see something wrong with this picture, Mark?" he asked.

"What? Besides the fact you guys took a prank way too far," Mark replied.

Tommy shook his head and lightly chuckled before saying, "Look at our tent, Mark. Why would we prank ourselves?"

Mark just stood there and glared at us with pure hatred in his eyes, and I had to get one more punch in the gut before I was done talking as well. "Hey, Mark. You might want to worry about the kids that went missing from those tents that are torn apart. And our friend is missing as well," I said to him.

Mark didn't even know what to say to us anymore, and I waited to see if Tommy, or maybe even Nick, would take another stab at him since he was at a loss for words at the moment. But to my surprise, there wasn't another word said, except for what Mark whispered in Steve's ear, which I couldn't make out, but I'm for certain it had to do with what I had said to Mark. Mark then turned to walk away, and he glared back at us as he walked toward where Candice was standing. Afterward, Steve told us that we needed to clean up the mess we had made and that they had bigger problems to deal with now.

After Steve walked off, the three of us started cleaning, but I knew that this was far from over, and Mark was going to get us eventually when the time was right. But like them, at that point in time, I had bigger things to worry about.

"Tommy, do you still think Chubs had something to do with this mess?" Nick asked.

"Well, look who got his voice back," Tommy jokingly said to Nick. "And no, I don't think Chubs would have done this by himself."

We talked about our thoughts more on the situation as we

cleaned for what seemed to be hours on end. And just as we were about finished cleaning everything up, we happened upon one of the tents that had been torn down. "What the!" Nick shouted as he jumped back.

"What's wrong with you, Nick?" I asked as I laughed at him.

"He's just being a chickenshit," Tommy said with a smile on his face.

We were still shaken up over everything that had happened, and we needed to have a little bit of fun even if it was at Nick's expense. However, just as I was getting a good laugh, I jumped in fear all of a sudden at seeing the tent move across the ground a little ways. "Did you see that?" I yelled.

"See what?" Tommy asked. "The tent moved."

"And you guys thought I was just being a baby," Nick said with a smirk on his face.

And then it happened again, except this time we heard a slight moan coming from underneath the tent as it moved, which made even Tommy jump and curse out loud. "There has to be something under there," I said.

"Don't look at me, man. I'm not going to look," Tommy said.

"Me either," said Nick. Then they both looked at me, and I knew they had both decided it was up to me to find out what was underneath.

"Damn you two," I said to them both. So I slowly started to reach down for the tent that was moving on the ground, and I pulled it away to see what was underneath, and we jumped but not in fear. Because there, lying on the ground was Chubs, and he was sound asleep. The relief that I felt at that moment was that of the world being lifted off my shoulders, and looking up and seeing the expressions on Nick's and Tommy's faces told me that they felt the same way. But now the question was, what in the hell happened last night? And I was determined to find out. "Hey, Chubs! Wake up!" I shouted at him as I nudged him with my foot.

He just lay there and moaned, and he refused to wake up, so Tommy leaned over and slapped his face and yelled at him, "Wake your ass up!" And as soon as Chubs woke up, he started screaming to the top of his lungs about evil children, and he was trying to fight us off.

And it took him a little while to finally realize that it was us that were standing in front of him and not some demon children that he had to fight. "Chubs, it's me. It's Bobby!" I shouted at him.

"Bobby," he answered back. "Bobby, it is you! Tommy, Nick! You guys are here too! Man, am I happy to see the three of you!" he said to us happily; then he jumped up and gave us all hugs.

"What in the hell happened out here, Chubs?" I asked.

"Man, Bobby, things got really bad out here. Not long after I started my turn on night watch duty, everything went to hell. Last night as I sat by the fire, I started hearing the sounds of someone running around me. At first, I thought it was Mark or Steve messing with me. Or maybe some of the other kids were playing a prank on me, but I learned real quick that wasn't the case. A few times the fire almost went out, and a couple of logs went flying off the stack.

It scared the hell out of me, and I tried my best to ignore it. And I did pretty well at first, that was until the children came running into the camp. Let me tell you now, these were not normal children either. They were pale and almost evil looking. There were a few times that I could have sworn some of them were burned or missing body parts. All I can remember is that they came running through like the wind.

I watched in horror as they forced some of the teens out of their tents and ripped out their insides before dragging their bodies off into the woods. Then the children that were left used the blood to make the handprints you see all over the tents that were left standing." Hearing Chub's recollection of the events that took place that night was absolutely horrifying; in a way the only person to blame for what happened was me. I could have warned Chubs what was happening, I could have even woken the others for help, but I didn't do any of those things. I left Chubs to defend himself.

"If all of this went down the way you say it did, how did you make it out alive?" Tommy asked.

"I hid under this tent here, and I didn't move a muscle. Sorry to say, but last night being coward saved my life." Chubs answered.

"That's the biggest bunch of shit I've ever heard, Chubs," Nick said as he jumped in the conversation. Chubs looked over at Tommy waiting for him to make a comment, completely blowing off what Nick had said. What Tommy had said next was a complete surprise to Chubs, but not to me.

"It's a lot to swallow, man. I hate to say it, but I agree with Nick on this one," said Tommy.

I could tell that Tommy's remark had hurt Chubs, but that wasn't going to stop him from defending himself. "So that's how it's going to be? You're choosing the new guy over me, huh, Tommy? What happened to watching each others' backs no matter what?" he asked.

Nick tried to say what was on his mind yet again, but Tommy stopped him from doing so. "Stay out of this, Nick," Tommy said as he held out his finger, motioning for him to be quiet before he turned his attention back to Chubs. "How do you think it looks to us, man? The campsite is a complete wreck. We get yelled and screamed at. Then we had to clean up this f— — mess. Then we find you hiding under a tent, with some lame-ass story to tell us once we found you, dog."

And of course, trying to hold this group together for what was to come, jumped in and tried to defend Chubs. "Back off of, Chubs, will you? There's no need to jump down his throat, we are friends, and friends stick together right?" I said as I looked at Tommy and Nick.

"Yeah, Bobby, we are all friends in this group. But because of him, we all got our asses handed to us by Mark and Steve." Tommy answered back.

"Who cares! At least he's all right and not missing like the others!" I said to him. "And besides, remember what happened to the four of us out in the woods last night also? You can't tell me this had nothing to do with what happened."

"Bobby, man, you know that was Steve scaring us for Mark. We know that already. I'm just pissed that Chubs did this without us, more than anything else." Tommy explained.

"Hey, ladies! If you're done cleaning, then let's go! We have to make up for lost time, thanks to you four!" Mark shouted from across the camp at us.

I shook my head and looked at my friends and said, "Let's get a move on. We better get our backpacks quickly and head over there, or this time I'm sure we will be left behind. And right now, I don't know about the rest of you, but I don't want to be left out here right now, all alone." This wasn't a good time to screw around. We needed the safety in numbers at that moment.

"Leave it to me, guys. I'll run over to our tent and grab our backpacks." Nick said. "Be back in a flash." and off he went.

"Oh, and one more thing. The others aren't missing. They were killed— killed! You got that, Bobby? How about you,

Tommy? Is what I said sinking in yet? You have no idea what's out there." Chubs said to us again. "You know what? Just forget about it." Chubs said before walking off to join up with the rest of the campers.

Just shortly after, Nick came running back with our backpacks and handed them over to us; then he looked around and asked, "Where did Chubs go?"

I reached over and took Chub's backpack away from Nick. "Don't worry about him. Let me handle Chubs. Is that clear?" I answered.

Nick didn't have much to say to my demands about Chubs, but he did agree with me, and that worked for me. "Come on you three! Hurry up, we have something important to tell everyone before we head out!" It was Candice that shouted for us that time. And a gentleman never keeps a lady waiting, so we hurried on over to where the rest of the group was waiting.

"Now that everyone is here, well, almost everyone, I have something very exciting to tell you guys. We are only three hours away from our destination! All I can say is that it's a brand-new campground, and we will be the first ones there! But wait, there's more; however, seeing how I love surprises, I will not say anything else about this place further until we arrive there. If everyone is ready, then let's move out!" Mark happily explained.

I wasn't going to say a word about the ones that were missing, because I believed every word that Chubs had said about last night. But, on the other hand, Nick wasn't about to go without finding out the truth. "What? You can't do that! Four others are still out there! We have to find them!" Nick shouted.

"Hey! Shut your damn mouth! You know the rules: if you're not back when we leave, you get left behind! I don't want to hear it from anyone. Not from the four of you." he said, and then he pointed over to Candice and Steve.

"And I don't want to hear anything from you two either. Got it?" he shouted at them too. "And for the idiots hiding out in the woods! I will deal with you later, so you don't have to hide right now! Last chance!" He waited for a few seconds and shouted again. "Fine! You're getting left behind! Try to follow if you can! Everyone, move out." Then he turned around and started walking ahead as fast as he could. He was so angry that he forgot to make us carry their bags, and I knew that meant more trouble for us later on. Steve made sure that he was right by Mark's side, and Candice stayed behind to motion everyone else ahead; if it wasn't for her, the whole group of campers would have been left behind if Mark or Steve had their way. As far as I was concerned, there was no way that any of our group would be left to defend themselves alone.

"It wouldn't do any good to go out and look for the others, trust me." Chubs said as he walked on ahead of us. Mark must have heard the remark he made because he glanced back briefly at him; however, it was just for a moment. For me, it was a no-brainer, and I followed on behind Chubs; even though I'm sure it was a hard decision for Tommy and Nick, they followed on as well. I watched as even Candice paused for a few minutes waiting for the missing teens to come running back; however, they did not, and she was forced to run back up to the front with Mark and Steve.

As we walked on ahead for what seemed at least an hour, Tommy caught up to me and asked, "Bobby. Do you believe the story Chubs told us?"

I fired him a look and answered, "He didn't tell us some story, Tommy. I'm telling you now, what he said was the truth." We walked on a bit farther, and I could tell by the look on his face that he was very confused by my answer.

"How do you know that for sure, Bobby?" he asked.

"I just do, Tommy. I just do." I replied. He walked in front of me then stopped. "What are you doing, Tommy?" I asked.

"I need a better answer than that," he said to me.

"Move, Tommy. Or we will be left behind. This isn't funny," I said back to him, a little upset.

"Bobby, I'm not moving until you answer me. I don't care if we get left behind," he said to me with a serious look on his face. "Now give me a straight up answer, Bobby. We're friends, now tell me. Please!"

I paced back and forth for a few minutes watching the rest of the group getting farther ahead of us. I stopped and stared right into his eyes and didn't even flinch as I told him the truth. "I know because of my nightmares, I know because of what happened in the woods to the four of us, I know because of Mark's story no matter how stupid it sounds. I know because it was happening to me last night, and I chickened out and made Chubs go out on watch duty alone! Is that good enough for you!"

That's when he turned his back on me and said, "I see, but I still find it hard to believe. Come on, man, let's catch back up to the group." And he started to walk away. I could hear the disappointment in his voice when he spoke back to me. Hell, I was disappointed in myself even more than he was. I didn't say anything else to him; all I did was follow behind him until we caught back up to everyone else.

"Where did the two of you run off to?" Nick asked.

I walked on past Nick and said, "Don't worry about it." I was sure Tommy was going to tell him what went down anyways, so I kept my mouth shut and caught back up to Chubs.

Bobby paused with his story and stared at the strange man for a minute before asking, "What would you have done if you were me?"

The man looked up from his notes and answered, "I have no idea what I would have done, Bobby. I guess for one I wouldn't have left my friend to fend for himself, and if something that bad was happening, I would have gone to get someone else to help out. Is that what you want to hear?"

Bobby thought for a minute before saying, "Fair enough. I should continue on now." He was also getting tired of talking, but he decided to go on for a while longer.

"What, you are going to ask me if I'm telling the truth too?" Chubs asked as he turned to look my way.

I looked at him and answered, "I'm not here to ask you anything, Chubs. I believe you, and I think I know what's going on." Chubs were relieved to hear me say that, but at the same time, I knew that he would want some answers. Here soon Chubs was going to get his chance to ask me some questions because already the younger kids in the group were complaining about needing a water break. Of course, Mark being Mark, he did his very best to ignore the cries of the group, but that would only get him so far as Candice walked up to him and demanded he let them have a break. So he turned and yelled for everyone to stop.

"Okay, since I hear a lot of whining about a water break, and my assistant here says that I have to let everyone get a break in, I will be nice enough to allow the group to take a ten-minute break. Enjoy." Mark said.

"Well, since we are taking a break now. Do you think we can sneak away from Nick and Tommy for a minute?" Chubs asked

124

me.

I knew exactly why he asked me that, so there wasn't much of a point in asking him why. Or trying to convince him to wait until later, so there was just one logical answer that I could give. "All right, Chubs." I then glanced around for a place that was just a little ways from everyone else. "Over there looks like a good place to sit and talk in private," I said as I pointed over to a log that was big enough for us both to sit on.

After we sat down, it took Chubs no time at all to start wanting answers. "Why do you believe me?" he asked.

"Think about it. What happened that night out in the woods? And, Chubs you know as well as I do that it wasn't Mark or Steve that was doing that to us." I said to him.

"You're right about that, Bobby. It sure as hell wasn't Mark or Steve, or anyone else from the group. It was something far worse than you could ever imagine." Chub's replied with a serious look in his eyes. He was right though: whatever was out there watching us was nothing more than pure evil.

"It's true, Chubs, something evil is out there. I'm not sure what happened to Nick and Tommy after they both ran off that night, but they're hell-bent on blaming Mark and Steve instead of accepting the truth. And since I'm on that subject again, what about you, Chubs? What did you see that made you run off and then try to fight me once I found you hiding behind a tree on that night?" I had to know. There was no way of avoiding the question. This was important, and I wanted to know the truth.

"It's hard to explain, Bobby."

There was no way that I was going to take that as an answer, not this time. "Try to explain the best you can. We don't have much time until we have to head out again. I want the truth."

"I want the truth too, Bobby! You haven't answered me either.

I know that you're hiding something from me!" he snapped back at me.

I couldn't hide the truth from him any longer. I had to tell him the truth even if that meant I would lose him as a friend. "Fine, you want the truth? Then I hope you're ready for what I have to say," I replied.

He paused for a brief moment and said, "Tell me."

I looked him straight in the eyes, and I told him everything that there was to tell. After hearing everything that I had to say, Chubs paced around muttering to himself and treated me like I wasn't even there; he did this for a good five minutes or so.

"Are you going to say something, Chubs?" I asked. He looked at me for a second and then went right back to pacing around without saying a single word to me. I couldn't take the silence anymore, so I snapped at him. "Will, you just talk to me already, Chubs?" I asked him loudly.

That's when he stopped pacing around and broke the silence by saying, "What am I supposed to say, Bobby? That you could have had my back last night, but didn't. That you left me out there damn well knowing what was happening? Or maybe it was the fact that you could have gotten me killed! And you lied about the whole thing to my face until now? Is that better?"

It's not like I didn't deserve what he said to me, but I wasn't going to back down either. "And what about you, Chubs?" I said.

Not taking his gaze off of me, he asked, "What about me, Bobby?"

I took a step closer to him and was just inches from his face, "You saw something in the woods last night, and you didn't say a word. You went ahead and let Tommy and Nick believe that it was all Mark's doing, as you walked away. But I knew better. Remember, Chubs, I was the one that chased you down. Me!

Not anyone else. So I ask you, when are you going to come clean and tell me what took place? What did you see?"

And right then I heard Mark yell out, "All right, everyone! Grab your shit! It's time to head out! And remember you will be left behind if you don't hurry up!"

Then I heard another voice, "I found them, Tommy!" It was Nick of course, with Tommy running up behind him.

"So this is where you two have been hiding? I would ask what you've been up to, but right now it doesn't matter, man. Mark's moving the group out right this minute, so let's get a move on!" Tommy explained.

Chubs looked at me and said, "Guess you will have to wait a little longer for your answer, Bobby." And then he walked away from me without saying anything else. I shook my head and followed behind him, and I didn't say anything to Tommy or Nick as I walked away, leaving them both behind with confused looks on their faces. I'm sure they had questions as well, but as Chubs said, it will have to wait until later.

It didn't take us long until we had rejoined the group just as they were heading out. And the whole time that we hiked we didn't speak a word to one another. I know that I was too pissed off to talk, and I'm sure the others felt the same as I did. However, I couldn't shake the feeling that we were still being followed as we hiked on, and I kept a close watch of my surroundings.

I wasn't about to give that evil force another chance to strike at us. The bad part was I could see the shadows of children now, the same as I had that night, but it was only shadows, and that wasn't enough to warn every one of the impending doom that lay in wait. And if I had tried, who would have believed me?

Anyways, after a couple more hours of hiking and watching the shadows follow us, Candice yelled out for everyone to stop and listen up. Then Mark took over. "All right, everyone, our destination is right down this hill! If you would, please step forward and take a look if you like. It's a wondrous sight! Trust me, you don't want to miss out on this from up high!" he said. I could hear the younger kids and some of the teens go "oh" and "ah," and they kept on about how amazing the campgrounds below looked.

I didn't bother to take a look, and neither did Chubs, but that didn't stop Tommy or Nick from taking a quick glance. You could hear the excitement in their voices when they both started shouting, "That's amazing! Man, this year is going to be a blast here at this place!" It was almost as if they had forgotten that it was still summer camp, no matter where we stayed out here. "And my brother has to be down there too, dogs." Tommy excitedly said. "And you know what that means, right?" he asked.

Nick didn't even give anyone else a chance to speak before saying, "Those two might get it, but I don't know what you're talking about, Tommy."

Tommy laughed at Nick and then replied, "It's cool, Nick. Stick with us, and your first year here will go smoothly. My brother is the head counselor this year, and he will have our backs. That means you won't have to deal with the bullies like the rest of us did for the past few years."

I looked away and waited for Mark to say "move out" again, but he was too busy admiring the camp down below, so that gave Tommy the opportunity to ask, "You should be happy with what I said, Bobby. What's eating at you, man?" Man, did I get pissed and rip his ass apart.

"What's eating me, you ask? Let me fill you in on something, in case you've forgotten. We have something evil out there! And it's stalking each and every one of us, and it's going to take us

out one at a time—if we don't do something about it right now!"
I shouted.

"Bobby, do you really believe that crap?" he asked. At the time
I didn't know what to think.

I wondered if he really was that damn stupid. "Yes, Tommy! I
do believe, and so should you after everything that happened
last night."

"How many times do I need to say this? There's is no evil
monsters out here watching us. The only ones that are evil are
the ones standing over there." he said, before pointing at Mark
and, of course, Steve as well. "And of course they talked some
of the other kids into helping them out—not the teens, just the
younger kids—and the only reason they are missing is that they
pulled the same shit again with Chubs while he was alone last
night.

Mark must have had them get a head start on the whole group
this morning, and they're following us right this minute just
waiting for his signal to scare everyone this time, not just us.
Mark and Steve had the whole thing planned out to make their
scary story more believable. That way he could chew our asses,
while the others made their escape this morning. Why else
would he leave those kids behind? Tell me that?"

I looked over at Chubs to give him the "what the hell?" look;
however, he would have none of it. "Mark! Can we get a move
on, please?" Chubs asked.

Mark said nothing in return; all he did was ignore what Chubs
had asked.

That was until Candice spoke up. "Come on, Mark. Let's go,
I'm getting tired of being out here. I know that you and Steve
feel the same way. So why waste more time?"

He shot her a look of anger as he said, "You heard the lady!

Everyone, move out! Head down that path over there, and we will be just minutes away!"

Bobby paused for a few minutes to take a drink of water, and right as he was about to start talking again, the stranger took that pause in the story as his opportunity to interrupt Bobby once again. "Are you finally going to tell me the name of this new camp?" he asked.

"I told you before that I was getting to it, didn't I?" Bobby answered. "If you would give me just a few damn minutes. I would have told you. Now shut the hell up and let me finish." Bobby demanded of the man.

"Okay, okay. I'll shut up and let you finish." the man replied.

"Good, because I'm ready to call it a day after I tell you this part," Bobby said to him. Like I was saying, we all had to walk down a slight hill to get to this so-called new campgrounds. Let me tell you, it wasn't easy either. There were thorns everywhere; if you were wearing shorts, you were screwed. If you happened to fall like a few of the other kids did, again you were screwed. And the four of us had shorts on, and by the time we got down the hill, our legs were all cut up by those damn thorns. I'm almost for certain everybody was hurting that day, but to be honest with you, I think everyone was too excited to even care. Well, everyone except Chubs and myself was excited, that is, but can you blame us for everything we had gone through? And as for myself, I wanted to make Chubs tell me what he had seen that night. I wasn't about to let that go not in a million years.

So the quicker we got to camp, the happier I would be, and right then Mark yelled out to the crowd of campers. "Everybody, stop! We're here! Let me be the first to welcome everyone to the newly rebuilt Camp Greystoke!" And then he motioned for all of us to be quiet. "Oh, and that secret I was talking about earlier, well, I might as well tell all while I'm at it. The reason I said rebuilt this time is that this was the exact place that story of mine happened. Have fun!" he said before turning and walking on ahead of the rest of us.

I was about to ask the guys if they thought Mark was telling the truth, but before I could get a chance to, Tommy looked over at me and said, "Don't even think about it, Bobby." Then he added, "Nobody wants to hear it right now."

By the look on his face, I knew that he was serious and would hear none of it. I didn't want to push the issue and cause a fight between us; the mood the four of us were in wouldn't end well at that point. I ended up doing the smart thing, and I let him know this wasn't over, not by a long shot. "For now I will drop it, Tommy. But later on, when I feel the time is right, I will bring up this subject again." After that, it didn't take me long to focus my attention back on Chubs. "You and me, Chubs. We need to talk, and I really don't care if you're pissed off at me or not," I said to him.

Bobby then paused again to look at the man sitting across from him. "I think we're done here for today. I believe you know the way out." The man stood up from his chair knowing that another day of conversation with Bobby had come to an end.

"I will see you bright and early in the morning then, Bobby. Have a good evening." There was no point in saying anything, so he made his way to the door once more. "I'm ready to leave, Nurse!" he shouted.

And just as he was ready to walk out the door, Bobby again reminded him of their deal. "Remember, after tomorrow you have a choice to make." The stranger briefly paused for a moment, and just like the day before, he walked out of the room without saying a word. However, this time there was something left behind on the floor that caught Bobby's attention; it was the man's black bag.

This was Bobby's chance to maybe learn something about this man or at least read what he has been writing about him. He knew he wouldn't get a chance like this again, and he wasn't about to pass it up either. He looked ahead to make sure the strange man was actually gone. And with no one in sight, not even a nurse, he jumped over to the other chair and quickly reached down for the bag. He glanced around one more time to make sure that the coast was still clear before he opened the bag.

Bobby looked and looked inside the bag for the notes or anything else he could possibly find; however, the bag was completely empty. That is until he spotted a piece of paper hidden at the very bottom; his curiosity now piqued, even more, he couldn't help but read what was written down. The note read, "Soon you will know who I am, Bobby. For now just be patient, remember a deals a deal." He wasn't happy at all about the man setting him up like that, just to make him look foolish.

Bobby ripped up the letter and threw the bag across the room and yelled, "Son of a bitch!" He was irate, now and his rage was visible by his facial expressions; he stomped across his room muttering curse words under his breath. He figured that was his chance to learn something sooner about what was going on, or who this stranger could be. But the man had one-upped him and made him look like a fool. Bobby was tired of being left in the dark, and he was also tired of the mind games that the man was playing with him as well.

However, Bobby realized that he still had the upper hand and that he needed to calm down his temper before he ruined any chances he had at getting the information he sought. Once he realized that, he was a lot calmer, and he was even smiling, just a little. And now he was ready to make another journal entry. July 3, 1999, Once again the strange man seems to be impatient, even more so than usual. He wanted to know the exact month that everything happened, and I finally got around to telling him. And then for some reason, he insisted on knowing the name of the campgrounds.

I'm beginning to think he believes that I'm lying about something. I know what happened out there, and it's all true. Why would I lie? I have no reason to. On another note, I have to say this about the man: he's very persistent. And on top of that, he also seems to have a sick sense of humor, leaving his bag behind like that with a note in it for me just to get under my skin was also smart as well. But I calmed myself after realizing I still have the upper hand on him for now.

Anyways, it won't be long until I found out all I need to know. Until then I can't let my guard down around him, and I must always stay one step ahead of him and his mind games. And like every night, it wouldn't be long before Bobby would fall asleep. But unfortunately, this night would be far different for him, as nightmares from his past would return. Bobby had a very strange, almost-realistic nightmare. The door to his room was wide open, which never happens.

There was blood on his floor leading out of his room, almost as if something had been dragged out of his room. He wasn't sure if he was dreaming or not at the time, and he was also unsure if he should go out of his room and investigate or not. But he felt this strange force pushing him forward as if there was something on the other side of the door that he had no choice but to see; once out of his room, he made his way down the hallway. The closer he got to the waiting room where the only exit out of the asylum came the most god-awful screams that you could ever imagine, and the closer he got, the louder the screams had gotten.

As he got to the end of the hallway, he slowly peeked around the corner. And what he had seen next chilled him to the bone. It was the stranger that had been visiting him for the past few days, and he was brutally killing everyone in the building, and he didn't leave anyone out. There were bodies everywhere, all the doctors and nurses were dead, and now he had started killing the patients. There were blood and body parts all over the place.

Unfortunately for Bobby, he didn't move his head back in time, and the man spotted him. "There you are! I've finally found you!" he shouted and then took off running toward Bobby. Just as the man was about to strike Bobby down with everyone else, he had awakened in his bed uncontrollably shouting at the top of his lungs. He gathered himself up enough that he wasn't screaming anymore, he still wasn't sure what had happened, and he was sweating badly. After he had figured out that it had all been a bad nightmare, he got out of his bed and walked around his room for a while waiting for the nurses to come rushing in to suppress him.

Luckily for him, not a single nurse or doctor came rushing into his room. The rest of that night he lay in bed and thought about the nightmare that he had experienced; it's been a very long time since he's had a nightmare like that one. To him the nightmare was very strange; the killer wasn't of the demon in the woods like it was so long ago, nor was it of ghosts either. But why would he dream about the strange man killing everyone?

None of it made sense to him. However, there would be no time for Bobby to dwell on it any longer, for there would be a knock at his door like the days before. "Who in the hell is there!" he shouts. Then he paused and thought about it for a moment and changes the tone of his voice. "Never mind, don't answer that. Just send him in," he says.

The door slowly opens, and the stranger walks into the room. He seems to be in better spirits than the last two days that he had talked to Bobby. "Well, Mr. Sikes. Hmm. I believe that's the first time I've said your last name since the first we meet. Anyways, let's get the ball rolling." He smiled at Bobby, knowing that that would upset him. It did exactly as the man had planned, as Bobby shot him the biggest "go to hell" look that he could give someone. "What?" the man asked, still smiling at him.

"Kiss my ass," Bobby replied.

"Come on, Bobby. There's no need for any of that," he said. "By the way, where's my bag?"

Bobby pointed over by the wall. "There's your damn bag. Now if you're done screwing around, I would like to get started." The man was acting very strange.

Bobby's words to him didn't faze him a bit. He just looked at him and said, "That's works for me. Start whenever you're ready."

Now Bobby was really getting pissed off, but somehow he managed to gain back his composure. "I know what you're trying to do. And it's not going to work. I'm smarter than you give me credit for, mister. Let's get this over and done with." Still acting like he didn't have a care in the world, the man took his seat and motioned for Bobby to do the same. Bobby smiled and took his seat across from him and went on with his story.

# 6

# Return of the Bullies

Where was I? Oh yes, now I remember. We had finally made it to our destination, and we all knew the secret of these campgrounds. The truth is, while everyone else blew it off as being a load of bullshit just to scare the whole group, I, on the other hand, knew that Mark was telling the truth even if he was using the story to scare us all. However, bringing it up now wouldn't be a good idea, but there is always a right time and a right place, and that would be sooner than later.

I even decided I would give Chubs a break and get my answers from him at a later time. Hell, I even kept my mouth shut during the tour of the place that Candice took us all on when Mark took off on her. It was a nice camp, and it pretty much had everything you could dream of at summer camp; there was a tennis court, a basketball court, and even a place to play Putt-Putt golf.

It was an amazing sight to behold, and the lake that was just a little ways ahead was a beautiful sight as well. I knew this would be the first place that my friends and I would go to first out of all others. I believe that most people would prefer swimming in a big lake over almost anything else. I know I do.

The tour ended with everyone being shown to their cabins; this was the part I hated because I was afraid that I would be stuck in a cabin with bullies. To my surprise, Candice had mercy on the four of us and allowed us to stay in the same cabin, to this day I'm not sure why she felt sorry for the four us, but she did. Anyways, this would make things a whole lot easier for me and my friends, and of course, it would be easier for me to get the answers I wanted from Chubs as well. When I was finally able to take off my backpack and relax a little, I looked for my bagful of clothes and comic books and other things. I found what I was looking for in our closet, shoved in with Chubs's, Tommy's and Nick's bags as well.

"Bag check!" Tommy shouted.

I grabbed my bag first and moved out of the way so my friends could get their things as well. Upon inspection of my bag, I noticed that everything I had brought was still in the bag; that was the first time in years that I actually had everything and nothing was missing, not a single comic book was gone. "Anything missing, guys?" I asked.

Tommy and Chubs answered no while Nick, on the other hand, was very upset that the board games that he had brought were gone. "I'm not going to let them get away with this," said Nick.

"What do plan on doing, Nick?" I asked.

"I'm going to go and give them a piece of my mind and also demand my stuff be returned to me at once!" he answered. "Nick, you might as well give up. You have no proof, and that's what they will tell you. Just chill out, it's not going to do any good, trust me. We've all been through the same damn thing." I tried my best to stop him, but he was to upset and would have none of it, as he stormed past me, and out the cabin door he went.

A few minutes later, Tommy stood up and said, "I'm going to look for my brother now. Either of you wants to come along? Bobby? Chubs?" he said.

"Not me, Tommy. I'm going to relax and read a comic book." I was too exhausted to do anything else.

"I'll go with you, Tommy. I don't have anything else better to do." Chubs answered.

Tommy asked me one more time, "Are you sure you don't want to tag along, Bobby?" I already had my comic book out and had decided which of the beds would be mine. I had no plans on going anywhere until it was time to eat. "Yep, I'm sure," I answered.

"Suit yourself, man," he said to me. "Come on, Chubs, daylight's a-wasting, and I need to find my bro." And off the two of them went out the cabin door as well. So now it was just me and my comic books all alone in the cabin; it took me a while at first to get comfortable. I had an uneasy feeling at first as if someone had been watching me from afar, but soon that feeling would fade away as I lost myself in my comic book.

At that point nothing of the outside world mattered to me; not even one thought of this place being a cursed camp even crossed my mind. I was lost in my own little world like always when I read. I was even so relaxed that I put my comic book to the side, and forgetting where I was at for a brief moment, I lay my head back on the bed, and I fell asleep. That was a big mistake on my part, for what happened next was only a warning of things to come. I had fallen asleep on the bed like I was saying before, and I heard a scratching noise coming from underneath my bed that woke me up, or so I had thought.

To me, it sounded like something was clawing at the floor, so I shrugged it off as some kind of rodent making its home under the cabin as most do. And it didn't take me long to fall back asleep. Soon after, I have awoken yet again—this time to the sound of whispering. But I couldn't make out what was being said. The whispering would go on for a good few minutes, and at first, I wasn't even scared. I just figured some other kids were standing outside the cabin talking to one another.

That was until I could make out exactly where the whispering was coming from. It wasn't coming from outside the cabin; it was coming from underneath my bed! Now I was scared! That bad, uneasy feeling that I had last night was coming back. I knew that it was the same evil force from last night. I didn't move a muscle. I was too damn scared to even think straight.

That's when I heard the words more clearly. "I'm going to get you." the voice said, followed by a faint laughter. I wanted to scream and run out of the cabin, but I didn't. I was afraid that if I did so, whatever was under my bed would get me. Then silence, it was so quiet you could hear a pin drop in the room. I thought for sure it was over, so I decided I would be brave enough to make my way off the bed. Just as my feet were about to touch the floor, the bed started to violently shake, causing me to put my feet back up from the floor as quickly as possible.

It seemed like there was something trying to keep me from getting off the bed for some reason. But I wanted to find out what was underneath, or maybe who. It was possible that someone was playing a prank on me; at least that's what I told myself anyway. So I gathered up all the courage that was left inside of me, and I slowly leaned off the side of the bed to take a look underneath.

I pulled up the covers as slow as I could and lowered my head to take a look. All there was, was darkness. I couldn't see anything at all. I took a deep sigh of relief knowing that it must have been my imagination. And just as I was about to raise myself back up on the bed, a hand with bony fingers and black sharp nails grabbed me and pulled me under the bed and into the darkness. That's when I must have actually awakened from my sleep because I jumped up looking around and patting myself and the bed down. Afterward, I must have been in a state of shock, because I didn't scream. I didn't try to run or anything like that. I just sat there on the bed emotionless, trying to figure out what had just happened.

I sat there for a good thirty minutes, before deciding to move. "I think it's time to get out of this cabin for a bit," I said to myself. As I was getting my shoes on, I happened to notice scratch marks on the floor. It looked as though something or someone had been pulled underneath the bed. I certainly didn't notice the scratch marks there before when I chose this to be my sleeping area.

The only explanation on how the marks could have gotten there was it happened while I was sleeping, or the nightmare I was having wasn't a nightmare at all, which would mean that it really happened. But if that was the case, why did I wake up still on my bed? And why am I not dead? I'm sure that whatever evil force that was behind this was out for blood. It really didn't make any sense why in the world would it let me live? Was it toying with me first, before it dealt the fateful blow? Or maybe it had a more sinister plan for me that I would discover later on.

Whatever it was, I knew it wasn't going to be good, but right now I wasn't going to set there and find out. So I made my way out the cabin door for some fresh air and to also find Chubs, Tommy, and Nick. I figured I would be safer with my friends around me. I happened to find Nick first; he was sitting not too far from our cabin at one of the benches. When I walked up closer to him, I could tell that he wasn't into good of a mood. I had a feeling I knew why, but it was best to hear it from his own mouth. "Hey, what's up Nick?" I asked.

"Hey, Bobby," he replied. "How did it go, Nick? Did you get your stuff back?" I asked.

"No. They said exactly what you told me they would. I didn't have enough proof to do anything about it, while the whole time Steve was standing in the corner laughing about it! I'm sorry, Bobby. I should have listened to you," he answered.

I tried to tell him, but there wasn't any point in rubbing it in his face now. "It's all good. Nick, have you seen Chubs or Tommy around?"

"Sorry, Bobby. I haven't seen them. Why? Are they out walking around?" "They could be by now. Tommy wanted to see if he could find his brother, and Chubs tagged along with him."

"Oh. We can go look for them if you want," he said.

We didn't know it at the time but Tommy and Chubs had already sneaked up behind us. "Find who?" Tommy asked quietly.

We both jumped. "Damn it, Tommy! Don't sneak up on us like that! Especially me!" I demanded of him.

Tommy and Chubs got a real kick out of making Nick and myself jump; neither one of them could contain their laughter for very long. "Damn, I'm good," Tommy said as he completely laughed his ass off.

"Figure of speech, just in case you didn't get that part," Bobby said to the man sarcastically.

"I got it, Bobby." the man answered. "But what I would love to find out is more of what happened out there. If you don't mind." It was as if Bobby and the stranger did their best to one-up each other.

"Whatever. Anyways, as I was saying…" Tommy had made his little smart-ass remark, and I knew that Chubs had to make his as well so he wouldn't be left out.

"You should have seen the look on your faces. Priceless," Chubs said.

"We have to give it to you guys. That was a good one," Nick said. Nick was never going to learn that he didn't have to suck up to everyone.

"Nick, you don't have to kiss their asses. It was a jerk move," I said.

"I'm not kissing their asses, Bobby. They got us good. It's just as simple as that," he replied.

"Chill, man. We're just having fun, you're being a killjoy," Tommy said to me.

"Fine, you got us good. Is that what you want to hear?" I asked.

The joke had now gotten old, and Tommy had given up on making me laugh. "Forget it, Bobby. Man, you're just no fun today," he said. "So, Nick. How did things go with your complaint?" He changed the subject quickly.

"They screwed me over, Tommy," he replied.

"I knew that was going to happen," Tommy said.

"Oh well." Nick shrugged.

"Any luck on finding your brother?"

Chubs butted in and said, "Oh, Tommy found out all right."

You could tell that Tommy didn't like what Chubs had to say, "Shut your mouth, Chubs." Chubs looked at us and smiled.

"It's a touchy subject for him to find out his brother—"

Chubs didn't even get a chance to say the rest when Tommy jumped in, "Would you shut your pie hole, Chubs! Does it look like I need you to talk for me?" Tommy was a little on the irate side after Chubs started to run his mouth.

"It must be a really touchy subject. So spill it, Tommy. What exactly did you find out? You seem really pissed off more so than usual." I said.

"Yeah. Come on, Tommy, we're your friends," Nick added.

Little did Nick know that would never work on Tommy; he just didn't know him well enough to understand. "Man, Nick. You're starting to get on my nerves. You think that sappy shit goin' to work on me, dog?" said Tommy.

I could tell that Nick had no idea what to say next, he searched for words, but he couldn't get himself to answer. And again I had to step in and stop things from getting worse. "Tommy, stop delaying. Tell us what you found out and no more bullshit, please," I demanded.

Tommy shook his head and replied, "Mark was right."

I looked at him with a confused look on my face. "What do you mean by that, Tommy?"

"Man, Bobby. My brother Jerry wasn't here because he took a certain group out white water rafting. That's why Johnny and his gang wasn't on the bus we got on. It was all planned out, and my brother never said a word to me." he explained.

"Did I call it or what, guys?" Chubs sarcastically said.

"Chubs, will you just shut the messed up!" Tommy shouted.

"Guys, calm down! And I thought I was in the bad mood." I said to them.

I just knew things were about to get completely out of control. "Well, I did say you were full of shit, didn't I?" said Chubs.

"Chubs! Knock it off! Tommy can't help what his brother did. I'm sure he had his reasons. And I'm sure Tommy will find out what those reasons are when his brother gets here. But for now, lay off him." I said as I did my best to diffuse the situation. "And,

Tommy. You didn't have to ask Chubs or me to go, right?"

He looked at me and smiled slightly. "You're right, man, I should have gone alone. In a way, I guess I had this coming, the way I bragged about my brother the whole time here."

"In a way, yes, you had it coming. But, Chubs, you tried to take it too far, and right now, guys, we need to stick together—trust me." I replied back.

"What do you mean by that, Bobby?" Nick asked.

"I'll tell you guys later. Better yet, I will show you. But for now, we better make our way to the cafeteria if we want to eat because it's starting to get late."

"You're right about that, Bobby. If we're too late, Mark might try and stop us from eating. With the mood he's in, I wouldn't put it past him either." Tommy added.

We hurried our way to the cafeteria in hopes that we wouldn't be too late to grab a bite. When we walked in, we were amazed to see just how huge and nice the place was; there were rooms off to their own, more than likely for the counselors. Then there was this one huge area full of tables and chairs, and off to the far right was where they served the food; we guessed that this must be the actual cafeteria. We looked around for some of the other kids and teens, but to our surprise, we were the first ones to arrive. Don't get me wrong or anything, we weren't complaining at all; it was great to finally be the first at something at camp for once.

And just to make sure we went up and asked if the food was done, there could have been a chance that we had gotten there way too early. But we were in luck, even the food was done, so we got a plate of food and walked around until we found the perfect place to sit down. There was a table with a huge window with a nice view of the lake, and we sat there. We might as well enjoy it while we can.

I knew that the next time we would be fighting Johnny and his gang for this spot. And for once since this whole camp trip started, we actually enjoyed ourselves, and I forgot about everything that was on my mind that day. We talked, we laughed, and we ate some decent food, which any food not cooked by Mark and Steve had to be halfway decent.

Before we knew it, the place filled up with all the others, including the counselors, and that meant Mark and Steve would be in there shortly, if not already. But the four of us decided it was time to go before they spotted us and cause us even more grief. All and all, we did have a good night, and everything was going great for us; we even played some basketball too. Even though I sucked at playing, and Tommy loved to rub it in my face as well, I still actually had fun. I could tell that Chubs and Nick were having fun playing basketball too, even though they sucked as bad as I did.

Tommy was the only one out of us that knew how to play, and he was damn good. But like I said before, he was the athletic one. I would almost bet he could have played any sport he wanted and would have done well. The night was going to end well for us, or so I had thought. That was until we got back to our cabin, and I remembered the nightmare that I had earlier that evening. "Guys, I have something I want to show you," I said. "Follow me," I added as I led them inside our cabin and over to my bed.

"What is it, Bobby?" Nick asked.

I pointed at the floor and said, "Just take a look and tell me what you see."

"Great, here we go again," Tommy replied.

"Just look, will you," I demanded.

"Fine," Tommy said before looking down at the hardwood

floor. "All I see are scratch marks."

"Yeah, that's all I see too," said Nick.

Chubs looked at the floor then back at me, then shook his head, and walked over to his own bed without saying a word. "What, Chubs, nothing to say?" I asked.

He looked up at me then turned his attention to his bag. "I'm getting ready for bed." And that's all he would say.

"Come on, Bobby. You're ruining a perfectly good night," said Tommy.

"Then tell me, Tommy, which way are the marks going?" I asked.

He looked again. "Under the bed. So what?" he answered.

"Something was being dragged under the bed, and my guess by force," I said.

"It does look that way, Tommy," said Nick.

Tommy looked over at him and said, "Don't get him started, Nick. He won't stop if you do." Then Tommy looked back at me and asked, "Why do you keep on? What happened out in the woods last night was a prank, and what happened to Chubs later that night was also a prank as well. It's just a matter of time before I prove it to you, so why do you keep on with this childish shit?"

I started to get mad, and it didn't take me long to blow my top. "What more do I have to do to prove to you it wasn't a childish prank? And furthermore, I think deep down you know what the truth is. You're just too scared to admit it! And that goes for you too, Nick!" I said to them.

"That's not fair, Bobby!" Nick shouted.

"He's right, that was a low blow on both of us," said Tommy.

I decided it was time that I come clean with them and let them know what had happened to me. "I apologize to you both. But, guys, let me tell you, I had a really bad dream, or at least I think it was a dream."

"So let me get this straight: you're all bent out of shape over a dream?"

"It wasn't just a dream, Tommy," I replied with a frantic voice.

"Then tell us, what was it then?"

"I don't know what it was, Tommy. One minute I'm reading my comic book; the next I'm hearing all kinds of weird scratching noises coming from under my bed! Then I could hear a voice whispering, and it sounded like it was coming from under the bed also, and when I tried to get up out of the bed, it violently started to shake. I was scared out of mind, and I wanted to scream, but I didn't in fear that whatever was under my bed would do me harm. Just as I had built up the courage to make the leap off the bed, it stopped, and all I could hear was the scratching noises, and so I looked under my bed, and a hand grabbed me and pulled me under." I explained.

"So you think you left those scratch marks on the floor? Is that what you're saying?" Nick asked.

"If that's what he's trying to tell us, it's too far-fetched, man," said Tommy.

I got down on my knees and slammed my hand down on the floor. "Can't you guys see that the marks go clearly under the bed? And can't you see that it's fingernail markings?" I asked.

"Man, you're losing it, Bobby," Tommy said. "And think, if it really happened, wouldn't the tip of your fingers be bleeding and nails are missing if that much force was used on you?"

I thought about it for a moment and answered, "Yeah, that's true."

Then he pointed out the fact that my fingernails were just fine, and he was right: my fingernails didn't have anything wrong with them. I would at least have had some wood under my nails, but I didn't. Now things at that point weren't making sense at all. "Now get up and sit down on the bed, Bobby," Tommy demanded. I did as he had told me to do, and I sat on the edge of the bed in a state of confusion.

"Bobby, did you fall asleep by accident?" Nick asked.

"I might have fallen asleep. I don't remember." I answered.

"That explains it—you must have fallen asleep and had a nightmare," said Nick.

"Then explain how those fingernail marks got on the floor," I replied.

"It must have happened before we got here," Tommy explained.

I looked up at him and said, "How? We're the first to visit this newly built camp, remember?" He didn't have an answer for my last question so he told me to leave it be, that I shouldn't ruin a perfectly good night with my nonsense. I really didn't know what else to say to him or Nick that would convince them into believing my side of things over theirs. Sometimes it's best to give up and try again another day, and on that night I didn't have much of a choice until I had more proof than just marks on the floor, and I had a feeling Chubs had that proof, but that would have to wait for now.

"I'm going to bed. I need sleep if I'm going to wake up early and greet my brother when he gets here," said Tommy. "And, Bobby. You need some rest. You look like shit. Whatever you do, don't bring this shit up around my brother, Jerry." And he walked off to get ready for bed.

After Tommy walked off, I wanted to ask Nick something, but he was already passed out on his bed. I looked over at Chubs and noticed that he was still awake, so I decided I would pass on a little message to him. "Chubs. I told you everything that you wanted to know, so tomorrow you're going to do the same for me. No more beating around the bush, got it?" And when I didn't get an answer from him, I glanced back over at him, and he was pretending to be asleep. I didn't say anything else. I was sure he got the message loud and clear.

I checked the area thoroughly, and as I was doing so, Tommy walked past me and said, "Man, would you just get to bed already, you big baby?" I just flipped him off and motioned for him to go on to bed. I made sure to look under the bed and inspect.

Afterward, I got myself ready for bed as well. About ten minutes after, I was finally calm enough to jump into bed. I couldn't just fall asleep like my friends did, because of what happened to me earlier that day; it took me several hours before I was able to sleep. However, nothing happened that night; all was calm even. I slept like a baby without one single nightmare yet again. However, the next day, all hell would break loose.

That morning I awoke to Tommy's voice calling out for us to wake up. "Wake up! Guys, wake the hell up!" he shouted.

I was barely awake and still groggy. "Can't it wait until later, Tommy?" I asked.

He started kicking on the edge of my bed, saying, "No! It can't wait! My brother is finally here. Let's go say hello."

I slowly crawled out of my bed. "Fine, fine. I'm getting up." I said sluggishly.

After he woke me up, he made his way over to Nick's bed and started kicking on his bed as well. "Get up, man," he shouted.

"What do you want?" Nick said as he pulled his covers over his face.

"Come on, Nick! My brother is going to be here any minute now." Tommy said. After hearing that, Nick jumped up out of bed and was ready to go in a matter of minutes; he would do anything to keep on Tommy's good side, though I never understood why; it wasn't like any of us was going to be back the following year. But, oh well, Tommy then rushed over to Chubs's bed and was just getting ready to kick it when he noticed that Chubs was already gone from his bed. "Anybody know where Chubs ran off to?" he asked. I didn't have any idea where he had run off to, and neither did Nick. "Forget about Chubs right now. Let's just hurry up and go," Tommy said. Tommy was in such a hurry that he pretty much pushed us out the cabin door.

I noticed that Chubs wasn't waiting outside for us either. "Looks like Chubs isn't anywhere to be found," I said to Tommy.

"Who cares? Hurry up and walk or better yet, run," he replied.

I knew that he was excited to see his brother, but he didn't have to be an ass about it. "If you want to run, then run. I'm not going to do that." I explained.

"Come on Tommy, let's run," Nick said excitedly. Tommy looked at me.

"Go ahead and run if you're in that big of a hurry, I'll catch up to you guys later," I said to them.

Tommy smiled and said, "All right, man, but don't keep us waiting too long. I want you to meet my brother too." And off Tommy and Nick went, running as fast as they could. I wasn't stupid. I wasn't about to run with Tommy. I knew that there was no way in hell that I could keep up with him. And if Nick wanted to try, by all means, he could go right ahead.

But I started thinking that I should at least try and make my way there a little quicker, so I walked as fast as I could—hell, I even picked it up to a light jog, but I had no chance in hell of catching up to them. By the time I got there (which was, if I had to take a guess, ten minutes later than them), Tommy and Nick were standing around waiting, and so were the counselors and the rest of the campers.

As I walked up to them, I asked, "What's going on, guys?"

Tommy turned to me and replied, "The last two buses are running late, vehicle issues or some shit like that."

I looked around at everyone else that was there as well. "A grand welcoming for them, I see." I joked.

That's when Nick turned around and noticed that it was me. "These last two buses must be important because of Tommy's brother being on one of them."

"Told you he was the main man here, didn't I?" Tommy bolstered.

"Whatever, Tommy," I said back to him.

That's when we heard Mark yell out. "They're coming! The buses are coming! Everyone, make sure to cheer for them when they get off the bus!"

I just wondered at the time why in the world did we have to cheer for them. I mean in my mind, this group of campers was just as important as them, and so were we. But for some odd reason, Mark didn't see it that way, he wanted to make them seem like they were the actual campers, and everyone else was just in the way. And there was no way in hell that I was going to cheer for a busload of assholes like Johnny. I looked over at Nick and Tommy, and both of them were cheering as well. "Come on, Bobby. Cheer for my brother's arrival." Tommy shouted at me before he started cheering again.

"I can't wait to meet your brother Jerry, Tommy. But I refuse to cheer for a bus full of assholes. Just remember who else is on those buses, Tommy," I explained.

Tommy paused for a moment. I think it took him a while to realize that he was cheering for not only his brother but for the bullies that had tormented us for years at summer camp also. He turned quickly toward Nick. "Stop cheering, Nick," he hissed.

Nick seemed to be really confused. "Why, Tommy? Is something wrong?" Nick asked. Of course, Nick didn't know, this was his first year, and he had yet to run into Johnny and his gang of thugs, so he had no idea who was waiting for us on one of those buses that were pulling in.

"Just stop cheering, Nick. You'll find out soon enough why," he explained to him. With a confused look on his face, Nick lowered his hands and stopped cheering as well. Mark looked over and noticed that the three of us weren't cheering like the rest of them.

"I said cheer—damn it!" he yelled. We ignored him and stood there watching as the buses got closer and closer to us. Mark started to make his way toward us, but it was too late; he had to stop and start cheering again. Only because the buses were pulling up and parking right in front of us, and I could see the look of excitement on Tommy's face as he waited for his brother to get off the bus.

But that excitement faded, and a look of anger went over Tommy's face as his brother got off the bus and walked straight past him, without saying a word. We didn't see Johnny get off or any of the others, but we didn't really have time to look at Tommy ran off after his brother, and Nick and I gave chase.

I didn't notice if his brother went to the campsite or not, but by Tommy's reaction, it would seem as though he had. The farther we had gotten away from the buses, the more it seemed like we were going in the wrong direction, or so I had thought. It wasn't long before Nick and I came to a screeching stop because right in front of us was Tommy talking to four other teens.

As we walked closer, I recognized three out of the four teens that he was talking to. It was Johnny and his gang, and it looked like he had a new friend as well. "Who are they?" Nick asked me.

"You don't want to know," I answered.

Johnny noticed us walking their way. "Look's like almost everyone is here, and you've made a new friend as well." he smiled arrogantly. He then gave an odd expression and then asked, "Where's fat boy?"

I was about to tell him to shut the hell up, but I didn't get a chance to. "Let me through, Johnny!" Tommy demanded.

But I was certain that Johnny wasn't done with us; he still wanted revenge for what happened when we first ran into him and his thugs. "You're not going anywhere, Tommy," he growled. Then he looked over at us. "And that goes for you two as well."

Tommy, however, wouldn't take no for an answer, and he tried to push through them, but Spike and Big Tony grabbed him by his arms. "Let go of me, assholes!" he shouted.

"I'll deal with you two here in a few minutes," Johnny said before turning and walking up to Tommy. "Why do you always have to make things hard for yourself, Tommy?"

"Why are you always such an asshole?" Tommy spate.

Johnny started laughing. "Do you know why your brother blew you off, Tommy?" he asked.

"He didn't see me! That's why! And if you would just let me pass, I can go talk to him." Tommy snarled.

"Let him go." Johnny nodded. Without a word, Spike and Big Tony let go of Tommy's arms. "Let me fill you in on something, Tommy. Your brother is one of us, he doesn't hang with losers, and as long as you chose them over us, you will be considered a loser," he said with a smile on his face. "But hey, if you don't believe, then go ask him." Johnny moved to the side. "Go ahead.

We won't even lay a finger on you," he added.

Tommy didn't even give it another thought. He took off running and left me and Nick behind. "Tommy, you can't just leave us," Nick shouted, but it was too late. Tommy was already gone. I could see the fear on Nick's face starting to build.

"You look scared, new guy. That's good, you should be scared, and you're in the wrong place at the wrong time with the wrong group of nerds," Johnny explained. "Now my boys here are about to rough you guys up. Nothing personal," he added. It was do or die time for Nick, I could see it in his eyes, and I knew that he was about to take off running, and that's exactly what he did, leaving me all alone to fight by myself.

"Spike! Tony! Go after him! Eddy, you stay here with me." Johnny ordered. And off they went after Nick; hopefully, he was fast enough to outrun them back to camp where he would be safe. "Looks like it's just the three of us now. This should be fun. You can try to run if you like." Johnny said to me. I looked around trying to figure out which way would be the best to run toward. However, the rage was coming back, and I was tired of running. Now all I wanted to do was beat the hell out of Johnny; however, this wouldn't be my brightest moment. "Aren't you going to run?" he asked.

I looked up from the ground right at him. "I'm not going to run from you anymore, Johnny."

"Oh really? What makes you think you have a chance against the two of—" Before he could finish his sentence, I ran up to this Eddy kid and punched him right in the face, knocking him to the ground. Johnny looked surprised at what I had done.

"That was pretty good. You know some moves. Guess you're not a complete wuss, more than I can say for your friends." he said to me. I was about to do the same thing to Johnny, but I could hear Big Tony and Spike making their way back, yelling at each other for losing sight of Nick. "Too bad looks like your time is up. You can't fight all four of us by yourself." Johnny was right. There was no way I had a chance against all of them, but I had to at least get one good shot in on him.

So I caught Johnny off guard by charging at him, and I punched him right on the nose; it staggered him enough that I was able to run right past him. I got a good head start, and I wasn't looking back; however, it wasn't long before I knew they had already started giving chase. I could hear Johnny screaming out that he was going to find me and kill me, and he was screaming for Eddy, Spike, and Big Tony to chase me down and find me no matter what.

"Don't let him get away! But don't any of you touch him. He's all mine!" I could hear him order. I looked around for a good hiding place because if they found me, I knew I would be a dead man. I was in luck. Just ahead of me was an old cabin or storage shed; it was hard to tell which it was. I would say it was an old run-down cabin. I mean there was no reason for a storage shed to be out in the middle of the woods. I ran quickly up to the door trying to get in; however, the door was locked, and I couldn't get the windows to open either.

I ran back to the door and pounded on it with my fist as hard as I could. "Is anyone in there!" I shouted. "Please let me in! If anyone is in there, please let me in!" I begged. It seemed as though I wasn't as lucky as I had thought at first, and I could hear Johnny and his gang getting closer to my location. I knew if I didn't find my way into the cabin, my ass was done for, and that's all there is to it. Just as I was about to give up hope, I could hear the front door slowly open.

"Hey there, Bobby. This is a cool cabin, huh? But I found it first." It was Chubs, and I didn't give him time to say anything else. I forced him back inside the door and slammed it behind us and quickly locked it.

"What in the hell is going on, Bobby?" Chubs asked.

"Find a hiding spot and do it now, Chubs!" I shouted back at him. I looked around and noticed a small hiding spot, almost like a hole in the wall. "Over there! That's where we can hide!" I grabbed Chubs by the arm and ran over to the small area pulling Chubs along with me. I could tell by the look on his face that he was confused and wanted to ask me what was going on again, but all became clear when he heard Johnny yelling.

"You can run, but you can't hide!" I quickly pushed him inside, and I followed behind him so that if Johnny or anyone else in his gang looked in the windows, they wouldn't be able to see us. My heart was pounding out of my chest as I motioned for Chubs to stay quiet. We could hear them by the windows. "Do you see anyone in there?" Johnny asked.

"There's no one in there, Johnny. And who would be stupid enough to hide in there?" Big Tony replied.

"Well, go inside and look, just to make sure," Johnny demanded.

Then we could hear Big Tony getting upset with Johnny. "I'm not going in there. If you want to go in and look, go right ahead." That's when we started hearing banging noises at the door.

"It wouldn't matter, guys. The door is nailed shut. No one is getting in there, so stop arguing." Spike barked.

# 7

# The Truth Is Finally Told

There was a knock at the door, Bobby paused and looked up at the stranger. "Looks like our time is up for today," he said.

The man shrugged and asked, "How do you know that?"

That's when the nurse opened the door and said, "Sorry to interrupt, but it's time for your weekly medicine and then sleeps for you after that, Bobby. I'll be back in a bit, so wrap it up you two."

Bobby smiled. "Told you, it was time." The stranger reluctantly agreed to leave until the next day, but Bobby wasn't going to make things that easy on him. "Remember our deal: if you want to know the whole story, then you have to tell me everything as well." Bobby reminded him.

Before leaving, the man looked back at him and said, "If I don't come back tomorrow, then I guess the deal is off." And out the door, he went.

"What was that all about?" the nurse asked as she brought Bobby his medicine.

"Oh, that? We had a deal with each other, but I don't think he will be coming back," he said to her.

She smiled at him and handed him his cup of pills and some water. "Well, that's too bad, I was starting to get used to him now. Get yourself some sleep, and if he comes back, I'll let you know like always," she added before collecting the empty cups and walking out the door. It now was getting late, and the medicine started to make Bobby drowsy, but before he slept, he was still determined to write in his journal as always.

July 4, 1999, This might be the last time I write about that strange man; it seems as though he might not be coming back. I doubt that he will uphold our deal and tell me who he is and what he really wants. Anyways, today I told him more about that cursed camp. I still hate talking about it even today. I still remembered that summer and every little detail of what happened. I'm close to the end of everything. If the stranger makes himself known, then I will tell him all.

I think tonight I will watch the fireworks before I fall asleep; that will be a nice change of pace. After watching the fireworks for a while, Bobby would soon fall asleep. And again like the night before, he would be plagued by another nightmare. On that night he would awake to scream to the top of his lungs uncontrollably. "Stay away from me! stop laughing! Stay back!" he yelled. All of the commotions brought the nurses running into his room; they've seen this from him only once, and that was years ago.

The only way to calm him down was to hold him down and do their best to wake him up. There was no way they could sedate him because in his state it could do him more harm than good. After what seemed like hours of fighting with him, the nurses were finally able to wake Bobby up. He was confused and had no idea what was going on. Bobby didn't even realize he was having a nightmare until the nurses explained to him what had happened. After completely gaining his composure, he apologized to each of the nurses and thanked them for what they had done for him. Shortly after they left his room, he noticed that his clothing was soaked and wet from his own sweat, so he called out to the nurse that waited outside his door.

"Nurse, can I get a change of clothes?"

"Of course you can, Bobby. I'll be back in a minute with some fresh clothing for you," she said. A few minutes later, his door opened, and there she was with clothing for him. "You know that you can call me by my name, Bobby," she was said as she laid out his clothes.

"I don't know your name."

"It's Julie," she said back to him.

He gave her a smile. "Julie. That's a pretty name. I'll remember that."

Julie looked back at him with a smile on her face and said, "Try and get some more sleep, Bobby. I'll be outside your door if you need anything." He smiled back at her and thanked her for being so very kind to him.

And after she walked out, he changed into his clean clothes and climbed back into his bed. He tried his very best to stay awake; he even thought about writing in his journal again for the second time that night, but in just a few short minutes, he fell right back to sleep.

The next day came, and again he had been awakened like all the other times before, but this time thinking that it might be Julie or time for his breakfast. He got out of bed and went over to the door himself; it didn't even cross his mind that it might be that strange man again, that is until he opened the door. To Bobby's surprise, the stranger was the one on the other side of his door, and he didn't look happy, but Bobby wasn't scared.

After what he had been through as a kid, he feared no man.

"Well, look who it is," said Bobby. "I didn't think you were coming back."

The man stood there for a minute staring Bobby down before saying, "A deal, is a deal, right?" Was the man there to talk? Or could he be there for another reason? Soon those questions would be answered. "Aren't you going to invite me in? Or am I no longer welcome?" he asked.

"Come on in, I won't stop you." The man walked into the room and grabbed his usual chair to sit down in; then he pulled out Bobby's chair and got it set up for him to sit down as well. "Please, take a seat." the man motioned.

"Why? Are you going to tell me what I want to know? Is that why you're here?" Bobby asked.

The man pointed at the chair in front of him. "Sit the down first." the man demanded of him. Bobby was none too happy and wasn't going to sit down until he got the response he wanted from the man.

"I'm not going to sit down unless you're going to tell me what I want to know. Understand?" Bobby snapped. The mood of the man changed even more so than usual.

"If you don't take your seat, I will walk out that door, and you will never know who I am or what I really want. Do you understand?" the man said angrily.

"So if I take my seat, you're going to talk, right?" Bobby asked.

The man pointed at the chair in front of him yet again. "If you take your seat, I will tell you everything. If you don't, I leave never to bother you again. Your choice," he explained.

Bobby thought about it for a few minutes, sat down, and he finds out everything, but then he has to finish his dark tale. Refuse to sit down and the stranger leaves never to return and bother him ever again. He glanced at the man, then back at the empty chair one more time before sitting down, he has come this far, and Bobby didn't see a reason to back out now when he was so close to the answers he sought. "Okay, I'm seated. Now tell me who you are and what you really want."

"All right, Bobby. If that's what you really want, but know you won't like what you'll hear. Are you ready for that?" the man said.

Bobby was now all business, and all hints of him joking around were now over with. "Tell me—now," Bobby demanded.

"Okay, here we go. I'm not really a doctor, wanting to make sure if you're crazy or not. I don't give a damn if you are or not, and don't get me wrong, I'm not a reporter either. I'm a detective, and I've been investigating the Camp Hell case now for a very long time. I thought for the longest that I would never solve the mystery that I had sought after, that is until I found your file. And I knew that I had to come here and find out from your mouth what had happened. I knew that if anyone from the police force found out about this, I would be fired, and then all my efforts would be for naught. So I kept everything hush-hush if you know what I mean."

Bobby interrupted the man to ask him some questions. "What's your name? I'm tired of calling you stranger all the time."

"My name is, Joe."

"Okay, Joe. Why are you so interested in what happened at that cursed place, to the point you're willing to risk everything? Why is it that important to you? It happened over fifteen years ago. Why drag it all back?"

"That's some good questions, and I hope you believe what I have to say," Joe said. He then sighed and looked Bobby straight in the eyes. "I'm John Boy's younger brother, and I'm trying to figure out what drove him crazy and why he disappeared the way he did. In your file, you talked about being his friend, and hearing your story I believe that you and he were good friends. Do you know anything at all?"

Bobby was speechless; he had no idea what to say or even what he should believe. "What are you talking about? John Boy died in the hospital. I've told you this. Why are you saying shit like that to me?"

"I'm sorry, Bobby. I wanted to tell you, but your friends didn't know the truth. He didn't die. He escaped and was never found. I was sure he would try and make his way to his friends, the only ones that would believe him, and he knew he could trust you and the others. That's what I've always thought. Believe it or not, Bobby. It's all true. I can show you the files if you want," Joe explained to him.

Bobby was lost. It was like everything was starting to happen all over again like it did when he was a kid. "I don't believe you! You're lying to me to cover your tracks!" Bobby yelled.

Joe stood up out of his chair and grabbed his black bag and handed it over to Bobby. "Here, you want to know the truth? It's all right here. Read it over if you can handle knowing the whole truth. I'm going to go and do a few things. When I get back, then we can talk further. I warned you that you wouldn't like what I had to say, remember that." Joe called for the nurse and asked to be let out of the room. Bobby didn't even notice that he had walked out the door, for he was too fixated on the black bag that he had in his hands now.

Bobby had another choice to make: look in the bag and find out if this Joe guy was telling him the truth or toss the bag aside. And again, Bobby had come this far, and all he wanted was the truth, and it was right there in front of him. Bobby closed his eyes for a brief moment then looked inside the bag; there were notes and three different files, and he read them all for hours. Now he knew the truth about what really happened to his friend John Boy, and Joe was indeed John boy's brother.

He was ready to talk and help Joe in any way that he could; he didn't understand how his dark tale would help find where John Boy ran off to so many years ago. But he would finish his story nonetheless. Joe lived up to his end of the deal, and now it was his turn to do the same, regardless of the outcome.

When Joe returned, Bobby was now ready to talk and also hear the rest of what he had to say. "Now do you understand?" Joe asked.

"I do," answered, Bobby.

"I need you to tell me everything, Bobby. Not just for, John Boy, but also for the sake of other lives that can be saved as well."

"What do you mean?" Bobby asked.

"Again, I didn't want to have to tell you these things. But the camp was rebuilt again years ago, and counselors and young kids are still dying out there, Bobby," Joe explained.

Bobby glanced away for a brief moment. "So what the files you brought in said was true. I honestly thought that we killed him, but it's true: you can't kill pure evil. I guess all we did was slow him down for a few years. Damn."

"Bobby, I need to know everything. Don't leave out a single detail, all right?" he said.

Bobby shook his head in agreement. "I'll tell you everything that happened. I won't leave anything out, but let me say this before I start again. What you hunt is no normal man; he's a killing machine that loves every minute of what he does to others. He's a monster, a pure-evil monster." Bobby said with a serious look on his face, and he meant every word of it.

"I'll keep that in mind."

"If you don't want to end up dead, then you best do," Bobby said. "Let's get serious now, shall we?"

"Let's, it's time we finish this up, and I go put an end to whatever is out there. But first, the complete and honest truth. So please, go on with your tale," said, Joe.

"Like I was saying last time, Johnny pretty much had Chubs and myself trapped inside an old log cabin; he just didn't know that because we were already hidden from him. After Johnny was told the door was nailed shut (which I thought was a little strange, because the door was locked from the inside by me), I thought that maybe he would give up.

But he wasn't about to give up that easily. I could hear him calling the others a bunch of chickenshits for not trying to kick the door in. Were they scared? I don't really know, I wasn't out there to find out. I could hear Johnny kick and kick and kick on the door until it finally gave way, and the lock on the door had broken, and in he rushed like some kind of madman.

Except for this time, Johnny was all alone, and you could tell by the sound of his voice he hated it too. "Get in here and help me look for him!" he shouted at the others.

"You know I would have your back on anything else, Johnny. But I'm not going in there, and you shouldn't be in there either." Big Tony replied. Even Spike and Eddy refused to go inside and help him look for us, we couldn't see what was going on out there, but we could hear every word that was said.

"I don't need you cowards to help me. I can find him by myself." Johnny shouted. He tried his best to find us too, he kicked things over, he threw things around, he yelled and screamed that I couldn't hide from him forever and that I was on borrowed time. I mean he did everything he could to flush me out, but I was smart, and I kept quiet, and I made sure that Chubs stayed quiet as well.

If he made even the slightest noise, the two of us would be in big trouble, and I couldn't let that happen. Without the help of his goons, it was only a matter of time before he would give up. And after about five or six minutes of searching for us, he did exactly what I thought he would do: he gave up. He walked out of the cabin called his goons a bunch of chickenshits again, and then he told them the cabin was empty and that it was time to head to the campsite, that they could find me there at some point.

Chubs and I stayed in that tiny room for a few more minutes until we could no longer hear Johnny and his gang talking; that's when I knew that we were in the clear and could come out of hiding. We crawled out of that tiny space and made our way for the door. "What was that all about?" Chubs asked.

I wasn't about to answer his question at that point, for I knew that wasn't the time or the place to talk about what just happened; we needed to get back to camp so there would be safety in numbers. "I'll tell you as soon as we get back to camp, Chubs. But for now, we get the hell out of here."

"Just tell me, Bobby," he said as we walked closer to the door.

"Not right now, Chubs." Just as we were about to walk out the door, it quickly slammed shut and locked us inside.

"Must have been the wind, right?" Chubs said.

I ran up to the door and pulled on it, but it wouldn't budge. "Damn it, Chubs! Does the wind force a door close and keep it closed!" I shouted. "Because clearly, the door isn't moving," I added. I couldn't understand how it was locked. Johnny clearly broke the lock when he kicked the door in. I could clearly see that fact right in front of me. So I looked around and couldn't figure out what was keeping the door shut on us.

"Stop screwing around, Bobby! Open the damn door!" Chubs demanded. I was scared and was starting to get upset.

"Then you open the door. I'll gladly let you if you think you can." I shouted back at him. I moved out of the way, and he came running up to the door pulling on the handle as hard as he could.

"Open, you piece of shit!" he yelled as he started kicking at the bottom of the door, all while pulling on the handle.

"Chubs, you have to calm down," I demanded.

He looked at me, and I could see the same fear in his eyes, maybe even more so than I. "Calm down." he screamed. "How can I calm down when we're trapped in here!" Then it happened right before I had a chance to try and calm him down further; we started hearing strange noises coming from inside with us. "What was that?" Chubs jumped.

I looked behind us, but I couldn't see anyone. "I'm not sure, Chubs. But I don't think we're alone." I whispered. Shortly after we started hearing someone walking around us slowly as well, almost as is if something was stalking us, as it did in the woods that night. "If someone is in here with us, you're not funny," I yelled out.

It could have been Johnny and his gang, but the more I thought about it, the more I knew that wasn't how Johnny did things. He would have already been kicking my ass, and of course the others would have been putting a beat down on Chubs as well so they wouldn't be left out. I knew for a fact that it wasn't them after thinking on it; what happened next proved that I was right all along about everything.

"Did you hear someone talking?" Chubs asked.

"Yeah, I heard it too," Neither one of us could make out what was being said. It was just a bunch of incoherent rambling. "We don't know what you're trying to tell us!" I shouted. It only got louder after I shouted, but we still couldn't understand what was being said. All of a sudden this loud bloodcurdling scream could be heard throughout the whole cabin, which pierced our ears and made us drop to our knees.

It was screams of someone that was in extreme pain, that much I could tell. The thought of Mark's story crossed my mind, and I wondered if his scary story was true and he didn't know it to be so. And what if this was the place that those teens locked Albert up in? It's very possible that it was a cabin instead of a shed. I would imagine this cabin couldn't have been that far away from the campsite back then, which would mean we were not that far away from our campsite as well if that's the case.

But it would be hard to prove it to anyone else without more proof; it wouldn't be long before I got all the proof I would need along with Chubs as my witness this time to boot. We both started kicking and beating on the door, hoping that with enough force from the both of us it would come open, and we could make an exit. But that wouldn't be the case; the door wouldn't budge no matter how hard we tried.

"We're not getting out of here." Chubs said.

I was about to tell him not to give up, but then I remembered the windows. "Chubs, the windows!" I shouted at him.

"What about the windows?"

"Use your head, Chubs. We can break one of the windows and get them out of here." I explained. I picked up a board that was on the floor and made my way over to the window, I swung my arms back with board in hand, and I got myself ready to swing away hoping that it would break the glass in the window.

I looked behind me to see if Chubs was there.

I was going to warn him that he might want to move, but he was nowhere around. I even called out to him. "Chubs! Hey, Chubs! Where in the hell are you?" I yelled. I was starting to get worried when he didn't respond back to me. But I figured that it would probably be best that I break the glass in the window first then go and find him; however just as I was about to swing the board, I heard Chubs scream out for help.

The cry came from the far room of the cabin, I dropped the board, and I made a run for the room. "Chubs! What's going on? Are you okay?" I shouted. He never responded to any of my cries to him, I thought for sure something awful had happened, and I needed to keep my guard up. I walked slowly around the room and whispered, "Chubs are you in here?" I asked. Just then I felt something grab the back of my arm and pull me backward, I tried to scream out, but my mouth was covered by someone's hand. My eyes were wide from fear, I thought for sure that I was about to die, so I decided that I would do my best to fight back.

"Stop it, Bobby. Calm down, it's me its Chubs," he whispered in my ear. "Now I'm going to let go of your mouth, just be as quiet as possible."

I shook my head in agreement, and he lowered his hand from my mouth. It took me a few minutes, but I did manage to regain my composure. "What in the hell is going on?" I asked quietly.

"Bobby, we're not alone in here." Then he pointed across the room. "Look over in that corner. Do you see him?" I could see a figure sitting in the corner of the room rocking back and forth, muttering to himself. We sat there hidden from him hoping that he wouldn't see us watching him; to us, it was a scary sight. There was blood all over the wall near him, and his hands were covered in blood as well, where it looked like he tried to claw his way out of the room. We also noticed that he was holding a pocket knife. I wondered if he found us would he use the knife to kill us both. Believe me, we didn't want to find out either.

"We need to get out of here, and now," I whispered to Chubs.

"What do you suggest we do?" he asked.

"We need to sneak past him before he notices we're even here," I said.

"How in the hell do we do that?" He looked at me and had a scared look on his face.

"Just follow me and keep quiet." We placed our backs against the wall and tried to quietly slide out of the room, and just as our escape was near, he turned his head quickly toward and screamed, "Please let me out! Please!" I paused and watched him for a few moments. I was surprised and yet at the same time a little bit confused: number one, he didn't attack us, and second, what I thought was going to be an evil man turned out to be just a teen like us. And on top of that, he was crying out for help. "It's all right, we can help you," I said to him. We stood up straight now with our backs off the wall. "I'm going to help him, Chubs," I explained.

"Bobby, don't do it! I'm telling you, you're making a huge mistake!" he said a little on the loud side. I completely ignored what Chubs had said to me, it was a warning that I should have listened to, but I didn't, and I slowly walked away from Chubs and toward the scared boy that was coward down in front of me crying.

If I would have put two and two together, I would have realized that this was the same boy from Mark's story. I put my hand out to him. "It's okay, we're not going to hurt you. We want to help you," I said. I felt sorry for him; who knows how long he had been stuck in that house and who or what put him in there. I thought for sure he was going to reach out and take my hand, but he didn't; instead, he took the knife and plunged the blade into his face.

His tears faded as he laughed hysterically, and then he started cutting parts of his cheeks off. I was caught by surprise and was horrified by what I was witnessing. Chubs noticed that I was in shock and not moving away like I should have been. So he grabbed me once again and yanked me back before harm could come to me; we both watched in horror as the boy cut his face to pieces.

Blood had now covered the floor and his face and clothing. He acted as though he was enjoying what he was doing to himself, which had me in even more of a panic. "We need to get out of here, Bobby!" Chubs shouted.

"Then what are we waiting for," I shouted back. And we both ran to the next room where I had the board; luckily it was still where I had left it. I picked it back up and swung it at the window, but the glass didn't break.

"Hit it again, Bobby!" he shouted at me.

I hit the window again and again and again to no effect, "Why isn't it breaking!"

That's when I noticed that Chubs was frozen with fear and looking in the opposite direction. I didn't even ask him what was wrong as I quickly turned to face in the direction he was staring in. And there he was walking slowly our way carrying that damn knife and covered in his own blood. The teen didn't even look human now—hell, he was no longer human at that point, I believe.

He was muttering something about killing us, but I really couldn't make out the words he was saying that well though.

Man, did I start to freak out, I hit the window as many times as I could with that board, and as hard as I possibly could, and yet it still didn't break the glass. At that point I knew that there was no escaping, and I was completely exhausted, so I gave up; if I was going to die then fine, I didn't care anymore. Chubs snatched the board out of my hands. "I will do it myself!" He swung at the window many times over, but not even he could break the glass. I knew that we were dead, and there was no use trying to fight our fate.

"Come on!" I shouted. "Come and get me!" I shouted again. All I could hear was a sick and maniacal laugh coming from him as he drew near us. Right then and there he stopped and let out this horrid scream before he burst into flames right before our very eyes! He then dropped to his knees and fell to the floor as his body was consumed by the flames; then all of a sudden we both heard a clicking noise come from the front door of the house, which caught our attention, and when we turned back to look at the burnt body of the young teen, it was gone. For some reason, the body vanished into thin air, and the front door was now open.

Chubs ran past me and out the door, screaming, "Let's go! Let's go!" I was more curious now than I was scared, and on top of that, I wanted to know where the body went, and if it wasn't for Chubs constantly screaming at me to get out of the cabin while I can, I more than likely would have stayed a while longer to see if I could find the body. But that would change once I got outside, however. I had this strange feeling that someone or something was still watching us. "Come on, Bobby! Let's get back to camp before something else happens to us!"

As bad as I wanted to stay and figure out what just happened, I knew that Chubs was right, and it would be for the best if we got out of there for now. "You're right, Chubs. Let's get the hell out of here." We walked down off the porch and turned to leave, and that was when something caught my attention out of the corner of my eye. I turned my head quickly to the left, and that's when I saw him for the very first time.

Bobby paused for a moment and got up out of his chair to pace around on the floor. "Who did you see, Bobby?" Joe asked.

"Give me a second, please," said Bobby.

"Okay, take your time," Joe replied. "Whatever you had seen, it must have scared you half to death being a kid and all."

"You don't even know the half of it, Joe," Bobby replied back.

"Then it's up to you to explain it to me, Bobby," he said. It took Bobby some time, but he managed to gather up his nerve and continue on. "I'm ready to go on now."

There he was, standing not too far from us, the so-called demon of the woods, and if you could have seen what he looked like, you would have agreed that he was nothing more than a demon from hell. I mean how can a human man look the way he did? It's not possible and still be alive! His face was a pasty pale color, and his eyes were deep, very deep inside their sockets, and the color of his eyes was black as the night sky; the same went for his razor-sharp fingernails.

The scariest part was seeing just how badly mutilated his face really was, his cheeks had been cut out on both sides of his face, which caused him to constantly smile, and his eyelids were also cut off so you could see the whites of his eyes in his sockets. One side of his face was badly burned, and he was missing one of his ears on the left side of his head, his hair was long and black, and his teeth looked like fangs, almost as if he had filed them down that way himself. This was absolutely one of the most horrific sights you could ever imagine.

172

"Who or what in the hell is that?" I shouted. I looked over at Chubs. "Do you see that!" I asked. "Or is it just me?" This time Chubs was too scared to even get a word out, his face was now completely pale, and he looked as though he was going to get sick, but I didn't care. I had a feeling that what we were seeing was the boy from the cabin we were stuck in, just minutes ago, only older. And I also believed that he was once known as Albert, the young teen from Mark's story.

"Run! Run, Bobby!" Chubs turned and shouted at me. Once I put everything together in my head, Chubs didn't have to tell me to run. I already knew that we had to get out of there and fast. We both turned and took off running as fast as we could in that moment Chubs could run, and for a few minutes, he was even running faster than me. I would turn to look back every so often, and sure as shit, he was giving chase. I don't believe that he was running as fast as he could though.

I was for certain that if he really wanted to, he could catch us without even trying, but that's when I noticed that he had something in both hands, and that might have been keeping him from catching up to us. On one hand, it was easy to tell what he was carrying; it was an ax. It wasn't one of those firewood-splitting axes either; it was more of the handheld ones. And in the other hand, it looked as though he was holding a severed head by the hair, which seemed more important to him than catching the two of us.

"There's the camp, just up ahead! We're almost there!" I yelled.

And before we knew it, we had made it out of the woods and standing in the entrance of the campsite itself. "Is he still after us?" Chubs asked. I stopped running to look behind us as Chubs was a few feet ahead of me, and there he was just standing there. He didn't chase us any farther; he actually stood there and watched us. I think all he wanted to do at that point was making himself known to us. I asked myself why, and all I could come up with was he wanted to send a message, and he wanted the two of us to deliver it to him. That he was watching and soon he would strike, at least that's what I had thought at the time. "Where did he go?"

I looked back in his direction again, and he was gone. It didn't matter at that point. "I don't know, and I don't care. We need to find Tommy and Nick and tell them what happened to us," I explained.

Chubs didn't say anything else as we ran on ahead; the two of us managed to get back to our cabin, and it was no surprise to me that no one else was around. "You're bleeding, Bobby!" Chubs said as we walked on inside.

I looked down at the blood on my shirt. "That's not my blood, Chubs. It's Johnny's blood." I told him.

"How did you get his blood on your shirt?"

"I punched him on the nose. It was either fight back or get my ass handed to me."

"So that's why they were chasing only you. I never would have thought you would be the one to hit him." And for a brief few minutes or so, we forgot all about what had happened earlier to us as we talked about Johnny and what happened before our terrifying event.

"Yep, I hit hard enough to stagger him so I could get away. I even decked the newest member of his gang and knocked his ass completely down to the ground." I bragged.

"And I missed it—that sucks," he said. "I bet Tommy and Nick got a kick out of seeing that. Did you guys split up in the process?"

"No, Johnny let Tommy pass by without a fight so he could

talk to his brother about something. And Tommy left Nick and me behind without even thinking twice."

"Sounds about right. I knew Tommy's brother being around would cause nothing but trouble for us. What about Nick, did he stay and fight?" Chubs said.

"Nope, the first chance he got he ran off and left me alone with Johnny," I told him. I could tell by his reaction he was shocked to find out that I was left to fight them alone, and just as he was about to say something else, he paused and started staring at the floor near my bed.

"Where did those marks on the floor come from?" he pointed and asked.

I was very confused by his question because he was there the night I tried to tell Tommy what had happened to me.

"Chubs, don't you remember?" I asked.

He looked at me confused himself. "Remember what?"

"You were there the night that I told everyone what happened to me. You know, how something grabbed me and pulled me under the bed, but Tommy and Nick said I just had a nightmare and those marks were from something else. Remember?" I explained to him.

"No, Bobby. I don't remember! And I'm pretty damn sure I would remember something like that!" he said loudly.

I wasn't sure what to think now, he was there in the room with us, how could he not remember? It didn't make a damn bit of sense. What in the hell was going on? "But you were there with the rest of us Chubs. You walked past me when I was telling that very story and went straight to your bed!" I said back to him.

"Bobby, that night I was so upset I stayed out by the lake. By the time I got back, everyone was asleep—even you."

"No, no, no. That's not how it happened Chubs; you were

there with us. You can even ask Tommy!" I shouted. "Next you're going to tell me that nothing happened to us in that damn cabin earlier! Or that there was no scary-looking man chasing us!" I shouted again. I had no idea what was happening, but I was damn sure getting tired of it.

"Calm down, Bobby. I remember what just happened to us. I wish I could forget about that, but how can I? It was the scariest moment of my life. And seeing that scary man for the second time proved to me that we're being chased by some killer, that I'm not even sure is human."

"A second time?" I thought to myself. And that's when I realized he had just answered a question that I had been wanting to ask him. "You saw him out in the woods that night when we were all being chased, didn't you?" I asked.

He nodded. "Yes, Bobby. I did see him for the first time that night."

Now I was scared and pissed and confused all at the same time. "Then why in the hell didn't you tell the truth, instead of letting Tommy and Nick blame Mark and Steve? You even made me look like a dumb ass by not sticking up for me that night." I said to him.

"I was scared, Bobby! And Tommy and Nick didn't want to hear it! They knew that it wasn't Mark or Steve. They just couldn't accept the fact that something beyond what they could handle was happening to them. And don't you dare act all innocent either, Bobby. You knew what was going on! And you also knew that something bad was about to happen, and you sent me out on watch duty without saying a word to anyone. You could have said something! Anything! But you chose not to. You could have prevented what happened that night to me, and the others, they died because of you. I could have died as well." he explained to me angrily.

After that outburst, I really had no idea what to say to him. He was right though. I could have prevented what happened to him on that night. But just like him, I was too scared, and all I wanted to do was hide from the world, and that cost Chubs a night full of nightmares, and it cost others their lives. And I do believe what he said happened that night, and I do believe that if he wouldn't have hidden when he did, he would have lost his as well. We were both guilty on that night of hiding the truth, and we paid dearly for it; that I much I do know is true.

"I'm sorry about leaving you out there to defend for yourself. I am, Chubs, and I wish I could take it back, but I can't. But you know what, you're just as guilty as me. If you would have just told us what you had seen as I asked you, we would have all stayed up together on that night." I shouted at him. I didn't mean to yell, and I was sure that he wasn't meaning to either. We were both just venting out of frustration, but this wasn't going to get us anywhere, and it was time that we both explained things to Tommy and Nick. "We've both made some bad mistakes, but if we don't stick together, then you know as well as I do we're all dead."

"We're all dead anyway, Bobby," Chubs replied. Now that was something I didn't like hearing, I knew things were bad, and after him saying that I knew now that it was up to me to keep it all together. My friends and I are going to have a long battle ahead of us, fighting against that demonic man and also dealing with the bullies. God save us all.

# 8

# Some Never Learn

"Bobby, your time is up for the day," Julie yelled after knocking on the door. Bobby, as well as Joe, jumped at the disturbance she had caused, both were concentrating very hard, Bobby on telling his story, and Joe was hanging on to every word that was said making sure not to interrupt him. Both looked at each other with a look of disappointment on their faces, but there wasn't anything either one of them could do about it. Joe could try, but it being this late in the evening, the doctors and nurses could actually try and have him thrown out of the building.

"It's all right, Joe, just come back early in the morning. As you can see, I'm not going anywhere." Bobby jokingly told him.

"I'm sorry, Bobby. I'm just doing my job. I'm not trying to sound rude." Julie said. "I apologize to you as well, mister."

Joe got up out of his chair, and for the first time, he smiled at her. "It's okay, ma'am. I'll just come back in the morning and talk more with him then." he politely said to her. He then turned to look back at Bobby. "I'll see you later then," he said.

"Talk to you in the morning, Joe," Bobby replied back to him.

Joe offered his hand for Bobby to shake again, and this time around Bobby trusted him enough that he didn't have any problems shaking Joe's hand. For he now looked at him as a friend, and that's something Bobby hasn't had in a long time— someone he could trust. Then he showed himself out of the room. "Looks like you made yourself a new friend," Julie said.

Bobby smiled at her for just a moment. "Seems that way."

"That's good. He seemed like a jerk at first. But today he showed that he had a nice side to him. Again, I'm sorry that I had to send him on his way. But you need to eat and rest, Bobby." she explained.

"Don't worry about it. I need my energy for tomorrow because I've got a long day ahead of me." Bobby said.

The smile on her face told that what Bobby said made her happy, she was afraid that she had upset him, and that wasn't what she wanted. "Oh, that's good, I'll go get you some food now. Be right back, Bobby," she said, before leaving the room. In a matter of minutes before Bobby could even move out of his chair, she was back with him a tray with a plate of food on it, a drink, and his meds as well.

"Hey, I'm getting to eat slop again tonight," Bobby smirked.

"I'm not the cook. I just bring the food to you," Julie said with a slight grin on her face.

"I think the cook needs to try harder. I'm not big on slop out of a can." After he made that comment he couldn't help but burst out laughing.

"Very funny, Bobby," Julie said to him. She did her best to keep a serious look on her face; however, it didn't last long as she started laughing along with him. They both were laughing so hard you could hear them from down the hall; it was a much-needed laugh for them both, especially for Bobby. After the laughter had stopped, Bobby and Julie talked for a while, and then she wished him a good night and went on her way. He waited for a while to make sure there wasn't anyone else around before taking his journal out and getting ready to write.

This time he had a lot to write about, and it would take him hours to finish updating his journal. July 5, 1999 Today I found out more than I ever thought I would: the mystery man that had been visiting me actually kept his end of the deal, to my surprise. He wasn't a psychologist like he claimed to be at first, but he was definitely good at making himself convincing enough to pass as one. But come to find out his name was actually Joe, and he was a detective for the police force and also my childhood friend John Boy's little brother.

Honestly, I didn't see that coming. I didn't even know my friend had a brother; he never talked about his family much. Come to think of it, none of us ever talked about our families much; it just wasn't the cool thing to do at summer camp with friends. He even told me that John Boy didn't die so many years ago, he had escaped from the hospital, and since his family was rich, they had it all covered up with the story that he had died instead.

They couldn't bear the shame that he would bring to the family name. That's why they felt like they had to do so. He felt so bad for his brother that he swore that someday he would find out where he went and what drove him mad. I couldn't believe it! I didn't want to believe it! I thought for sure it was all lies! That was until he handed over his bag to me, and inside was all the proof I needed contained in three different files. One was about John Boy and everything that had happened over the weeks with him was inside that file. I read it over and couldn't believe what I was seeing, John Boy did go mad, and he did attack a kid and his own parents; however, unlike what I was told, John Boy didn't die. He escaped just like Joe had said.

My heart was racing, I was afraid to learn what truths may be hidden in the other files, but I pressed on. I knew that I had to. The second file that I looked through contained information about what happened sixteen years ago at that accursed camp, along with the notes that Joe had been taking. There were also pictures of all the dead kids and counselors, their burnt bodies were placed in order on the ground for the pictures that were taken, and there were also pictures of a couple of my friends that had survived, and pictures of me as well. It was hard for me to look through that file, but I couldn't help myself.

I needed to know what was said and if they swept it under the rug. Then I happened to come across the police reports from that day they had come to rescue us, or so I had thought. Of course, the stupid idiots ended up arresting me, instead of rescuing me. When I read over the police reports I was stunned to find out what all was said.

My friends had no recollection of the events that had transpired over the last weeks of camp; they basically claimed not to be able to remember a damn thing. It was insane, and when I got to the report on me, it read that I was found soak and wet with blood from my head to my feet carrying an ax and muttering, "I killed them all. I killed them all." before passing out.

No other statement needed. No other statement needed? What the hell? I knew they made me the fall guy! Bastards! But I can't be that angry the more I think about it. I knew deep down they had done that years ago to me, and I did nothing to stop it. I didn't even try to put up a fight.

I figured that I would be better off in here, behind the safety of these walls, and I found every excuse I could to keep myself in here. But upon viewing the last file, I would find out just how wrong I was. They had rebuilt the camp, and the same thing happened that year happened to others again and again and again. Maybe it was time. Before Bobby could write another sentence, he started falling asleep and decided to end his new entry there instead of trying to go on.

That night there would be no nightmares for him, only memories of the dreadful past flooding back to him in waves until morning came, and he was awakened by the sound of knocking at his door. For the past eight days he had been dreading the visits from that man, but today he jumped up and was ready to talk and help out any way he could.

"Come on in, Joe, and let's get this show started!" Bobby shouted.

The door opened, and in walked Joe; it seemed as though he was in just as big of a hurry as Bobby was. "All right, Bobby. Let's skip the conversations for now and jump right on in from where we left off yesterday. We're running out of time, I will explain everything to you at a later time, just please trust me on this one," Joe explained.

Bobby could see the seriousness in his eyes, and right away he knew he had to do what was best and go with what Joe had said. "All right, Joe. I won't waste any time. If I remember correctly..." Chubs and I were having a heated argument over all that was happening to us. We said some things that neither of us meant, and that sort of helped gain some control back, but now it was time that we made Tommy and Nick listen to what we had to say; it didn't matter if they liked it or not. "Chubs, you know that we have to tell Tommy and Nick about this, right?" I asked.

"Yeah right, Bobby. You know how those two are. They let their egos get in the way and refuse to listen to the truth."

"I know. It's not going to be easy, but we have no choice this time," I explained. That's when Tommy and Nick barged into the room.

"Tell us what, Bobby?" Tommy asked. "Oh, man. Don't tell me you two are about to start that stupid ghost shit again? I don't want to hear any more of that shit right now."

"Yeah, that's right. Tommy's had a bad enough day and doesn't want to hear any more bullshit." Nick added.

I tried my best not to get angry, but after everything that had happened that evening pushed me over the edge, my rage finally took over completely. "Tommy's had a bad day? Really?" I shouted. "Oh, hell no. Let me tell you what a bad day is really like. It's when you think your friends have your back, then leave you high and dry when you need them most." I said.

"What's that supposed to mean, Bobby?" Tommy asked. "You really want to ask me that right now?" I said angrily.

"Yeah, I think I do, man," Tommy answered.

If that's how Tommy wanted to play, I was all for it and didn't have any problems telling him how I felt. "Fine, Tommy, I'll tell you what I mean. You walked off and left Nick and me all alone with Johnny and his gang! They offered you a free pass, because of your brother, and you took it. Leaving your true friends behind without thinking twice." I explained. Then I turned to face Nick. "And you're no better than he is, Nick. The first chance you got to run, you took it and left me all alone."

"What, Chubs magically appeared to save your ass? Is that what's going on here?" Tommy asked sarcastically.

"No, smart-ass, I ran into him later." I snarled.

That's when Nick butted in again. "How did you get away? I mean, you don't even have a mark on you. That's odd, don't you think?" Nick asked me.

"The new guy Johnny had with him wanted to be the one to

beat me up. So when he got close enough, I hit him and knocked him to the ground, and that was enough of a distraction for me to run up to Johnny and punch him too. It staggered him enough that I was able to run past him, now you know." I answered.

"You hit Johnny? That was you that he was talking about killing for hitting him when he got to camp?" Tommy asked.

"Yeah, Tommy. That was me," I answered him.

"Man, that's awesome! I can't believe he was talking about you!" he said excitedly.

"That still doesn't change the fact you both bailed on me," I shouted. I couldn't help but be mad at them, and I wanted to know why they both left me there alone with the bullies.

"What do you want me to say, Bobby?" asked Tommy.

"I just want to know why you walked away. I needed you guys to have my back," I said.

"I'm sorry, man. I really am! I needed answers from Jerry. I needed to know where he stood. I wasn't thinking. I'm sorry!" said, Tommy.

"And what's your excuse, Nick?" I asked.

"I don't have one, Bobby. I ran because I was afraid. I didn't want to get hurt. I'm sorry, I didn't mean to leave you alone against those guys," he explained. I wasn't going to calm down anytime soon. I wanted to chew Tommy and Nick up and spit them out. But all I can say was that I'm glad Chubs was there at that moment; he reminded me that we had a bigger task at hand.

"I know that you're mad at them, Bobby. But right now we have bigger things to worry about. Remember we need to tell them what happened to us when we met up," Chubs explained.

I turned to look back at Tommy and Nick. "You two are damn lucky that Chubs is here right now to calm me down," I told them. "Guys, I'm going to forgive you, for now, I don't have a choice. Now listen up, I'm not in a good mood, so please both of you sit down and shut the hell up! We've got some things to tell you, and you will both listen to what we have to say."

"I owe you that much, so I'll do as you say. But don't get used to it," Tommy said as he pulled up a chair to sit down in.

"And I will do the same," said Nick.

Chubs sat down on the corner of his bed, and I didn't sit down at all. I was way too antsy. And since Chubs was never any good at explaining things, I was the one that was going to have to explain to Tommy and Nick what had all happened and what we found out. Once I started talking, I didn't stop. I talked for hours upon end, and I explained to them everything that happened. I wasn't sure if they believed what I was telling them or not.

"Now I've heard it all," Tommy said, as he started laughing at me. Nick, on the other hand, didn't say a word. His face was a pale as could be, and for a second I thought he was going to break down and cry. "Come on, Nick. Don't tell me you believe this shit that is being told?" Tommy asked.

"It's not bullshit, Tommy!" Chubs shouted at him. "Can't you stop being an egomaniac for just a few damn minutes?" You could tell that Chubs was at his breaking point as well; he was ready to jump down everyone's throats if he had to.

"Tommy, I think we should listen to them. You know deep down that something isn't right around here, and I myself am tired of pretending that everything is all right when it's not," Nick said.

Tommy started laughing at Nick as well, "You expect me to believe that some ghost tried to get them in some cabin in the woods, and now some ax-wielding maniac has now shown up to kill us all."

"He's real, Tommy. I've seen him twice now! Once in the woods that night when you claimed it was Mark and Steve scaring us and again watching Bobby and myself as well when we came running out of the cabin! It's all true, Tommy. You have to believe us," Chubs explained to him.

"You guys are nuts; if you want me to believe you, then prove it to me. That's all you've got to do, but for now, I think you're all crazy. Oh, and my brother, Jerry, he's just as bad as the rest of them. We're alone like all the other times, dogs. So watch yourselves, it's been a long day, my ass is going to bed," Tommy said to us.

"But Tommy—"

"Save it, Bobby. I know what I did earlier today was wrong, and I'm sorry, but that's all," Tommy said as he walked past me and over to his bed.

Nick stood up and did the same, but before crawling into his bed, he turned and said, "I believe you, Bobby, and you too, Chubs. I saw him too that night, I wish that I would have said something sooner, but I was trying to impress Tommy. Again I'm sorry, guys."

It was a plus to finally hear the truth come out of Nick's mouth, but on the other hand, it was going to take a hell of a lot more than just words to convince Tommy otherwise. I think that Nick was right; deep down Tommy knew that things didn't seem right at all here in these woods, but he was just too scared to admit it, and his ego had a lot to do with it as well.

That night some strange things started to happen, and it wasn't in my dreams either like the times before. I awakened to the sounds of someone walking around outside our cabin. So I quickly made sure to wake the others up as well. Chubs and

Nick both woke up to the sound of my voice, but Tommy refused to wake up. He told me to "Fuck off." and I left him be. Then we started hearing some scratching noises, almost as if someone was running a razor blade up and down the outside of the cabin wall.

At first, I wondered if this time it was Johnny and his gang doing this to us, to pay us back for before; after pondering on it for a few minutes, I hatched a plan to catch them in the act. "All right, listen up. We're going to go out there and find out who's doing this. I really think it could be Johnny this time. So let's show them that we're not scared, and we're not going to take their shit any longer," I said quietly.

"And what if it isn't them? What happens if we come face to face with that demonic man when we go outside?" Chubs asked. I can't say that I gave it much thought. I wanted to see for myself who was outside.

"Don't you want to know? Aren't you getting tired of all of this shit?"

"Yeah, I am. Let's do it," Chubs replied.

"Are you in or out, Nick? Remember, you can stay inside if you don't want to do this," I said to him.

He thought about it for just a moment, "I'm in. It doesn't mean that I won't make a run for it though."

"Understood. Okay, guys, follow me and be quiet. We want to catch them off guard," I told them. So we made our way quietly out of the cabin, and we slowly sneaked around the corner to see who was there. I will say this, it wasn't Johnny or any of his gang of idiots. It was the demonic man Albert walking back and forth dragging his fingernails along the side of our cabin.

The three of us were damn lucky that he didn't see us, or we would have all been killed right then and there, and we took off back inside as quickly as we could, locking and also blocking the door behind us. We were screaming at the top of our lungs, and we were also scared shitless at who we had seen walking around outside our cabin. Our screams had now awoken Tommy, and he started screaming as well but for a different reason.

"What in the hell is going on!" Tommy screamed. "Some of us need sleep, dammit. And why in the hell is the door blocked?"

"He's out there! He's right outside the door!" the three of us shouted.

"Would you guys please calm down, and tell me what's going on," Tommy scowled.

I took a few deep breaths and talked as calmly as I could, "I heard noises outside our cabin, so I woke everyone up."

"That's when I told you to get fucked, I remember that part, keep going."

"Well, we decided it could have been Johnny and the goons, so we went out to take a look, and it wasn't Johnny at all," I said as I could feel myself getting carried away again.

"Chill out, Bobby, and tell me who it was," Tommy demanded.

I was scared out of my mind, but I was still able to answer his question. "It was him. It was the demonic man, Albert!" I screamed out.

Tommy busted out laughing, and then he started making fun of us, "Big bad demon man is going to get us. Big bad demon man is outside our door and wants in to kill us. Big bad demon man with an ax is going to kick our door in," Tommy mockingly said to us.

Right at that moment, Nick shouted, "Here he comes."

The four of us paused and were completely silent and waited to see what would happen next, that was until Tommy decided to be a damn prick. "Let's see who's at the door. I want to meet this big bad man myself." Tommy said as he walked toward the door. We ran after him and grabbed him by the arms, there was no way we could allow his dumb ass to do something stupid that would get us all killed. "Let go of me." he snarled.

"We're not letting you go, Tommy. We can't take any chances of you opening that door," I told him.

"I'm going to kick your asses if you don't let me go!" "Shut up, Tommy," Chubs said.

There was a slight knocking noise at the door, "Did you guys hear that?" I asked quietly.

It got silent again throughout the whole cabin, and Tommy stopped trying to fight with us. "I heard it loud and clear, Bobby," said Tommy with a surprised look on his face. "Turn the lights on, that will scare whoever is out there off." And without thinking, Nick let go of Tommy's arm and hit the light switch, and yes, before you say anything, there was electricity at the campsite.

"Shit!" Chubs shouted.

"That was a bad idea," I said.

Before anything else could be said, the sound of knocking started coming from the door again. It was light at first, and then it would steadily get louder and more violent as time went on. The demonic man known as Albert was doing all he could to get into our cabin, or was he? He had an ax but wasn't using it, and I knew for a fact that he could have gotten in if he really wanted to. I think he was toying with his prey before he killed us, and yes, we were his prey, "What are you waiting for, tough guy? Break down the door and come and get us, if you think you can!" Tommy yelled out.

That's when we heard him talk for the very first time, "All in due time, boys. All in due time. I'm going to kill you all, one at a time. All in due time." He talked slowly and his voice was rough and rugged; he didn't sound like a human whatsoever. Right after his words, there was a loud thud at the door that shook the whole cabin, or so it seemed that way to us. And then there was silence yet again that seemed to last for hours upon end; it was Tommy first that found the courage to move toward the door.

"Whoever was out there is gone now, guys," Tommy said. "I'm going to open the door and take a look just to make sure."

"Hang on, Tommy. I'll go with you," I said.

We both walked slowly to the door. "Ready?" he asked. "I'm ready when you are," I answered.

Tommy opened the door to our cabin and quickly ran outside screaming like a damn fool. If he wanted to act like an idiot, it was fine by me, but I was going to keep my guard up because this wasn't the time to have my head up my ass. We looked around the whole cabin but didn't see a damn thing. Chubs and Nick stuck their heads out the door and quietly asked, "Is the coast clear?"

"I think so," I answered.

Tommy came walking back around from the other side, "Where is the so-called demon, man?" Tommy sarcastically asked.

"Knock it off, Tommy. He was out here, that much I know for sure."

"Then point him out to me, Bobby," Tommy replied. "I knew that you guys were full of shit. If this was your way of convincing me, man, then you're going to have to do a whole hell of a lot better than this." I knew that unless Tommy had seen him himself, he wasn't going to believe in the fact that he was outside our cabin stalking us. That was until he went to shut the door.

"Come on, Bobby, let's get back inside. Some of us like to

sleep, you know," Tommy said to me as he was walking back toward the cabin door. But I wasn't ready to just give up yet, I knew there had to be something out here proving that Albert was here outside our cabin, and I was going to find it. I searched the area for another good five minutes and still hadn't found anything. That was when Tommy started to get pissed off and yelled at me, "Come on, Bobby! I haven't got all night. I will lock you out!"

At that point, I knew it would be best to go ahead and call it a night. Then I thought about it for a few minutes. I didn't need any more proof than what I already had. We all heard Albert's voice; even Tommy couldn't deny that. There wasn't any point in looking around any further or keeping my friends awake either. "You win, Tommy. I will come inside, there's no point in me staying outside any longer than I have to." I said as I made my way toward the door too. I walked inside and turned to talk with Tommy as he was shutting the door behind us. And that's when I noticed something was sticking through the door. "What in the hell is that?"

Tommy turned around to look as well and reached out to touch it. "Ouch," he shouted as he pulled his hand back quickly. "The damn thing cut my finger," he said loudly. "Just what in the hell is this thing in our door?" he asked.

"You know if you opened the door and looked on the other side, you would probably find out, Tommy," Chubs explained.

"Shut up, Chubs! I was just about to do exactly that," Tommy replied. He turned back around facing the door and reached out to move it back so he could walk out and take a look, "Hey! You've got to see this!"

"Just tell us what it is, Tommy," I demanded.

"Get your asses over here now!" he barked back.

It was clear that none of us was going to argue with him. I was the first to walk out the door and see what Tommy was talking about so excitedly. What I had seen was horrific; there stuck in the door was the ax that Albert was carrying that day when he was chasing Chubs and myself. When Chubs walked outside with us and saw the ax, I thought for sure he would flip out, but he didn't. He smiled and said, "There, now you know who it was outside our door."

"No, that doesn't prove anything. It still could have been Johnny and his gang, or even Mark and Steve. Hell, it could have even been my brother," Tommy told us.

"Wake up, Tommy! Stop acting like a badass and accept the truth!"

Nick walked out and was looking down toward the porch; his face went ghostly pale. "Is that someone's head?" he asked as he pointed.

We didn't even get a chance to answer his question or look at what he was talking about before he passed out and hit the ground with a hard thud. "Nick." I quickly made my way over to him and knelt down to make sure he was all right.

"Is he good, Bobby?" Tommy asked.

"Yeah, he's going to be fine. He just passed out is all," I answered.

"Do you see what he was talking about?" Chubs asked.

"No, I don't see anything—" I quickly stopped talking as I felt my hand in some kind of warm liquid.

"What's wrong?" asked Chubs.

I had no idea what my hand was in and why it was so warm at that time. Not knowing any better, I thought maybe Nick had pissed himself, and that was what I had my hand in. "I think Nick pissed himself, guys," I said.

"That's gross! You better wake his ass up, because I'm not carrying him," said Tommy.

I moved my hand over to get it out of the liquid, and that was when I had felt something else, "Wait for a second, guys. There's something else. I can feel it with my hand."

"Well, what is it?" Chubs asked.

Right then I jumped backward and fell on my ass screaming, "Holy shit!" I pushed myself quickly away and up against the wall. I was shaking like a leaf and muttering hysterics. I could feel my eyes bulging out of my head.

Tommy ran up to me quickly. "Are you all right, man?" I remember that I didn't answer him. I just kept muttering and pointing straight ahead. "Bobby! That's not piss on your hand. It's blood!" I don't even know if I actually heard his words; all I do know is that there was a severed head over by Nick's unconscious body. "How did you get blood all over you, man?" Tommy asked. "You sure Nick's all right?" I still couldn't find the words I wanted to say. I was in complete shock at what I had seen.

"It's someone's head! Oh my god!" Chubs started shouting. Chubs was so scared that he accidentally kicked the severed head in between my legs.

"Fuck! Fuck! Fuck!" I screamed as I jumped up and away from the head.

"Is that what I think it is?" Tommy's eyes grew wide. "It can't be real! There's no way it can be real!" It didn't matter what any of us thought at that time; the severed head was real.

I regained my composure and realized that we needed to get Nick and get our asses back inside the cabin before something else bad could happen, "Chubs, grab Nick. Tommy, help him if he needs it, forget about the head for now! We need to get back inside the cabin and lock the door," I explained.

Chubs couldn't pick Nick up by himself, so Tommy ran over to help him, and they worked together to drag Nick inside where he would be safe. I slammed the door behind them and locked it as fast as I could. It didn't take long before Tommy started to put everything together, and once he did, he started to freak out badly. "That was a real head! So, where in the hell is the body it belongs to? Who would do something like that in the first place? It's true, isn't it? Everything that you've been telling me is true! I didn't want to believe it, but now I know it's all true. Damn it! What have we gotten ourselves into? I need to warn Jerry about all of this." Tommy's little world and the bubble he had put around himself that world was starting to crumble and badly. He was losing it. I knew that was going to happen once he started to listen to what we were telling him.

"Calm down, Tommy," I said as calmly as I could. "Chubs you need to wake Nick up. I don't care how just do it," I told him. "We also need to do something with that severed head outside our door, I know that we're all scared, but if someone finds that here, they will accuse us of being the ones that killed that person." I knew these were things that had to be done if we were going to keep ourselves out of trouble. Nick was finally moving around as well, Chubs took a while, but it seemed as though he had finally woken Nick up, which was a good thing. Nick was in hysterics at first yelling and screaming about the severed head that he had seen first.

"Did you guys see the head? Where's the body! Am I going crazy? It was real, right?" Nick asked one question after another. It was hard to even keep up with him; he was talking so fast.

"Nick, it was all real. The head and all, it was all real," I answered him. Tommy was still muttering shit to himself, Chubs was trying to hold it together, but who knew how long that would last, and Nick was still trying to gather his senses.

If I was going to get rid of the severed head, I was going to have to do it myself. "All right, listen up. I'm going outside to get rid of the head that's on our porch, just watch my back, that's all I ask," I said to them. I could tell that Nick was nervous, and so was Chubs, but they both agreed to have my back when I needed it. Tommy, on the other hand, was still lost in his own little world and didn't even make a response back to me. I walked slowly to the door and stayed as quiet as I possibly could, listening to see if I could hear the slightest movement on the other side. I didn't hear anything at all, so as far as I was concerned the coast was clear, so I slowly made my way outside. I looked around all over the place, but there was no severed head to be found whatsoever.

"What's taking so long out there?" Chubs asked.

"I can't find it," I answered.

"What do you mean you can't find it?"

"The damn thing is gone."

"How in the hell does a severed head just vanish?" Chubs shouted hysterically.

"I don't know, Chubs. It's just gone." I shouted back. "How any of this possible?" Then I got to thinking the only way it could be gone is if he's still out here, and he took it; that thought chilled me to the bone. I had a bad feeling that Albert was still there and watching us, and I needed to get my ass back inside. There was nothing we could do at that moment, and there wasn't anybody we could run to and tell what we had seen; who would believe us anyways? And we weren't for sure what would happen if we tried. So we had no choice but to barricade the door and call it a night. None of us really slept that night.

I lay in bed staring up at the ceiling waiting for something else to happen. I could hear Chubs get up every hour on the hour and look out the window. Nick tossed and turned in his bed all night, and Tommy, he sat on the edge of his bed muttering to himself never once trying to lie down. So yeah, I would say not one of us slept a wink.

The next day when morning came and the sun was shining through our window, it took all we had to get ourselves moving. "What do you think is waiting for us on the other side of this door?" Nick asked.

"I'm not sure, Nick. But there's only one way for us to find out," I answered. Four teens come running out of a cabin screaming bloody murder, which was us, and of course, me being covered in blood from the night before didn't help either. It scared the shit out a bunch of little kids and made them cry, which I can understand how it would scare them. I think that would even scare the piss out of most adults. Like I was saying, we made them cry, and they took off running away screaming and crying. I felt bad for them, but I had bigger things to deal with than a bunch of whiny kids. "There's blood on the porch, but no head."

"Yeah, that's odd. He must have come back for it," Chubs explained.

"Hey! We need to talk to my brother; he might help us," Tommy said.

"But I thought you said we were on our own," I replied.

"Well, what do you suggest we do, Bobby?" Tommy asked.

"I don't know, Tommy. But if you think we should talk to your brother, then I'm with you," I answered.

"So you believe us now, huh, Tommy?" Chubs asked.

"Hey, man, I don't know what to believe. But after last night, something freaky is going on around here, that's for sure."

Tommy answered. "And I think my brother, Jerry, may be willing to help us if he hears it from me." The bad part was if Tommy's brother was like the rest of them, then he would never help us.

"Okay, okay. We will go and talk with your brother," said Chubs.

"That works for me too," Nick said.

"Good, then we're all in agreement. But first, you need to get cleaned up, Bobby. You can't go to my brother's place with blood all over you, man." Tommy was right about that. There was no way I could go anywhere covered in blood. I would look like the guilty one.

"What about the blood on the porch here?" I asked.

"You go and get yourself cleaned up, and we will take care of what's out here," Tommy told me. I nodded in agreement with what he said to me. I went back inside the cabin to get myself cleaned up, and I left them to handle the rest. By the time I was done and back outside, they had just finished cleaning up the blood.

"Hey, Bobby. How does it look?" Tommy asked me.

"It looks good; that should actually work."

"That's what I wanted to hear. Now let's go talk to my brother about what's going on around here."

"This isn't going to work, but hey, I agreed with it," Chubs jumped in and said.

"Tommy, are you sure about this?" Nick asked with a serious look on his face.

"You two just shut up, we're going to talk with Jerry, and yes, I'm sure about that," Tommy snarled.

"We said we would go, guys. Don't start giving Tommy shit about it now." I told them. What I said didn't really have any effect on Nick because he still considered Tommy his best friend;

however, I was curious about why he would ask Tommy that though. Now Chubs, on the other hand, didn't much care for my words, he loved giving Tommy shit about everything he possibly could, it didn't matter what it was about, and not being able to do so this time seemed to piss him off, because he was quite the whole way there. And as for myself, on the way there, I was asking myself, Is this a good idea? After Tommy's words last night about being "on our own" had me worried.

"Okay, guys we're here. Now before we go in, please do me a favor," Tommy said.

"What kind of favor do you want from us, Tommy?" I asked.

"Just don't take this the wrong way, but could you guys not go overboard with this whole Albert thing? I know some crazy shit has been going down, but if we tell him everything, he will just ignore us. So please just do this one thing for me, okay?" he explained.

"I can't promise you anything, Tommy, but I'll do my best not to lose it in there," I replied. Chubs refused to say anything, and Nick made a promise that he wouldn't say a word unless asked to. That was good enough for Tommy, and we walked inside what the counselors liked to call the "headquarters" cabin.

We walked around for while seeing a few new faces that would be taking over for the other counselors next year like Tommy's brother had taken over for Mark as the head counselor; even though Mark was still around, this was his last year as a counselor. The good part was Mark had no control, and there were quite a few more lady counselors around that year as well.

# 9

# Death Of A Bully

I t didn't take long for us to run into Tommy's brother as he passed us in the hall; he tried his best to ignore us at first. However, Tommy wasn't about to let him get away. "Hey, bro! We need to talk to you; it's important! And we're not leaving until you hear us out!" Tommy shouted.

He stopped and turned around and started walking back our way. "Follow me," he said. I could tell that Tommy's brother was completely pissed off, and I knew there was no way in hell that he was going to help us. I kept quiet, and to my surprise so did Chubs, and we followed his brother until we came to his office. "Take a seat," he said to us as we walked inside.

"It's cool, guys. Go ahead and take a seat as he said," said Tommy. And so we did.

"Now what do you want, Tommy?" Jerry asked.

Tommy sighed and then he told his brother everything there was to tell; he didn't leave out one single detail either. At first, his brother looked as though he was taking what Tommy was telling him seriously, but we would learn real quick that that wasn't the case. When Tommy had finished talking, his brother didn't say a word; he looked at us like we were all stupid right before he started laughing at us. That didn't sit well with Tommy. "What's so funny?" he asked angrily.

"He told that damn story over the campfire, didn't he?" Tommy's brother said as he kept on laughing.

"Who told what to whom?"

"Mark, he told that stupid story about Albert the killer, didn't he?"

"Yeah, so what's that got to do with anything?" It was like the only ones that were in the room was Tommy and his brother as they kept going back and forth with each other.

"It has to do with everything, Tommy." "But how? And why?"

"Because it was just an urban legend, some old story that we were told when we rebuilt this place. Mark overheard and must have decided to use that as his scary story, and now everyone is freaking out about it, but I didn't expect it to get to you."

So that's where he got that story from, I thought to myself. I knew that he could never come up with something like that on his own. Most of his stories sucked badly; however, the one he told about Albert the killer was unusually scary. "So you're telling me that what Mark told us as just a scary story is true?"

"No, it was just some stupid story to scare us away. None of it was real, that's what I'm telling you."

"It seems real to me, or did you not hear what I was saying?"

"Calm down, little brother, like you said before it was probably Mark and Steve screwing with you guys all along. So why worry? Enjoy your last year at summer camp."

Tommy stood up out of his chair, "Just forget I said anything at all. I knew you wouldn't help." He then motioned to us. "Come on, guys, let's go."

"Go ahead and leave, Tommy, walk on out with the nerds. You've hung out with them for so long that you've become one yourself. And you wonder why I have nothing to do with you here," his brother said.

Tommy was hurt by what his brother had said and run out of the room, Nick and Chubs went off after him, and as for myself, I couldn't leave without saying what was on my mind. "Tommy's my friend, and even though you're his brother, you had no right treating him that way. All he's been doing is bragging about how you would have our backs this year. We wouldn't have to worry about anything at all, but you know what? You're no better than the rest of 'em, if not worse. Think about one thing though, what he said was all true, and Albert is out there waiting to strike again. When he does—and trust me he will—the blood will be on your hands."

He looked at me and laughed, "Are you done? If so, get the hell out of my office."

"All right, all right. Just remember, you've been warned." Once outside I noticed that Chubs and Nick were over by the basketball court with Tommy, and I made my way over as well.

"Bobby, will you and Chubs do me a favor?" Tommy asked.

"Sure, what is it that you want?"

"I want the two of you to take me to that cabin," he said.

I agreed to take him there, and so did Chubs, but before we could leave, Johnny walked up with his goons right behind him. "Where do you think you're going, losers?" Johnny said.

"Somewhere you're not," Nick responded first.

"Now that's not nice, we're just here to talk."

"Save it, Johnny! We don't have time for your shit right now!" Tommy barked.

"There's no need to be that way. If I wanted to, I could tell my boys here to take you guys out. But I'm going to give you guys a fighting chance. Interested?"

"If I say no?" Tommy asked.

"Then I'm going to have to do what I have to do. And you know what that will mean." Hell, we didn't have time for this shit, we had other things to worry about, and I knew that at that time Tommy wasn't in the right mind frame to make deals with Johnny.

"What do you have in mind?" I asked.

Johnny laughed when I butted in; then he started to make fun of Tommy afterward, "What? Does the nerd talk for you now too, Tommy? You've become nothing more than a loser every since you chose to start being their friend. And we all had high hopes for you. Too bad."

Tommy didn't need anyone to talk for him, but still, yet he was in a bad place, and he needed to know that his true friends had his back. And I was so tired of Johnny's shit that I wasn't just having Tommy's back. I was also taking up for myself for once. "Just shut the hell up and tell us what you have in mind," I demanded.

He laughed at me for a second time; apparently, I wasn't intimidating enough to him, "I will humor you for now. We can either go ahead and kick your asses, or—"

"Or what, Johnny?"

"Or we play a game of basketball. If you guys win, you get to walk away."

"And if we lose?"

"Then you and your fat-ass friend stay here and get the ass beating you deserve, and Tommy and the other nerd does nothing about it. Deal?"

I only thought about it for a moment. "It's a deal," I answered.

"All right! Let's play some ball!" he shouted.

Tommy pulled me to the side and asked, "Are you f—— crazy?"

"Maybe I am crazy, Tommy. But I'm tired of getting pushed around by those guys, and we need to deal with them if we're going to deal with Albert."

Tommy knew that I was right, that we really didn't have a choice at that time and point. "Do you think we even have a chance?"

"I think we do, I mean yeah, three of us isn't very good, but you're damn good. And I imagine the same goes for them as well, so it will mainly be you against Johnny. Just because you're good at football doesn't mean you're good at basketball too," I explained.

It didn't take long before Chubs and Nick came over, and they were not very happy with me at all. "Really! You want us to play basketball?" Chubs shouted.

"What in the hell were you thinking, Bobby?" Nick asked.

"Guys, just chill out. Tell me which would you prefer? A chance to play basketball? Or get our asses beat right off the bat? Ask yourselves which one sounds better," I told them.

"I hate it when you're right, but I guess we don't have a choice, do we?"

"No, Chubs, we don't, not this time," He sighed and walked back on the court along with, Nick.

Tommy grabbed a basketball and threw it at Johnny, "Let's play, asshole."

"Oh, this is going to be fun! A whole hell of a lot of fun!" Johnny shouted.

We played basketball for what seemed to be hours on end. Johnny wasn't ready to name an ending score, because it was a back-and-forth battle. It was a brutal game as well, Chubs's bottom lip was already split open, and Nick had the makings of a black eye. They tried to give back as good as they got, but

I don't think either one of them had it in them to take on Big Tony or Spike. However, just causing them to be distracted was good enough.

As for me, Eddy was the one that wanted to guard me on the court. I figured he wanted payback for me knocking his lights out. Neither one of us would back down either; we were both bloody, battered, and bruised. It wasn't just a game, but it was also a full, outright fight. Tommy and Johnny played roughly as well but not near as rough as the rest of us did; they were the only two out of everyone else that could actually play, and at times it was fun to just pause for a moment and watch them go at it. I wasn't big on sports, but actually being apart of the game was actually kind of fun.

"The last bucket wins!" Johnny shouted. It was about damn time; how much longer did he expect the game to continue on anyways?

"That's exactly what I wanted to hear," Tommy said loudly as he stole the ball away from Johnny. He then motioned for me to run ahead, and he passed the ball to me. I waited for Tommy to have an opening. When he was clear enough from Johnny, I elbowed Eddy in the gut and passed the ball over to Tommy, and he shot the ball, making the winning bucket.

We cheered loudly, giving one another high fives, finally, we had beaten those damn bullies, those damn jocks at their own game. Even though we had won, would they actually go quietly without a fight? That was the question I asked myself. "A deal's a deal, Johnny. We get to leave, without any problems," said Tommy.

"Since when do we keep our deals with, nerds?" Spike replied.

"That's right, I'm not done with the fat boy just yet. I still have some fight left in me." Big Tony said to Chubs. Eddy didn't make a comment, he was just as exhausted as I was, and I was certain he wasn't up for fighting at the moment.

"Let them go," Johnny insisted.

"Did you say what I think you said?" Spike asked.

"I did, now let them go," Johnny answered.

Spike grabbed Nick by the shirt and said, "I don't think I want to let them go. What if I want to hurt them some more?"

"I'm not going to tell you again—let them go." It was weird to see Johnny upholding his side of the deal. I thought for sure he would be the one to back out and have our asses kicked. "Unlike most, we have honor, remember? Next time we beat the shit out of them, they won't have any way out. I promise you that," he told them.

Spike let Nick go and told him how lucky he was, but next time it wouldn't be the same, that he would be looking over Nick's dead body. Big Tony just walked away laughing, he could have done more, but he chose not to. "You're right, Tommy. A deal is a deal, and I honor my end of the deals. Just know that next time, all bets are off, and we will put a hurting on you and your friends." Johnny said before walking off.

Eddy looked at me, "You're tougher than you look. I think you're hiding just how tough you are. I look forward to when we actually fight for real."

I didn't know what to make of his words; it was like I earned his respect. But I think on that day we all earned some respect from the people who have been bullying us since the first day of summer camp. Too bad John Boy wasn't there to see it. "I'm sorry, Joe. I should have thought that one through," Bobby said.

"It's okay, Bobby, don't worry about it. Just continue on with your story, please," Joe said.

Anyways, Johnny walked away with his goons following right

behind him, without anything else happening or being said. "Now that they're gone, you two can take me to that cabin." Tommy looked at me and Chubs when he said it.

"Damn, and here I was thinking that you had forgotten about that," Chubs joked.

"This could be a bad idea. Are you ready for that, if something goes wrong?" I asked.

"I am ready for whatever happens. You know if you or Chubs don't want to go, you can just point me in the right direction, and I will find it myself."

"I won't do that. I'm going with you. You know that I will have your back," I said.

"The two of you ain't going without me," said Chubs.

"What about you, Nick?" I asked.

"I'm tired, I'm beaten, and I'm bruised, so yeah, count me in," he answered. It was as if the four of us were ready to take on anything or anyone after the battle we had with Johnny and his gang of thugs. "All right, Tommy, follow me," I said. And I led the way, with Chubs and Tommy beside me, and Nick was walking slowly behind us. It was a long walk, and it took us about an hour to finally make our way to the cabin. I pointed straight ahead. "There it is, the cabin of nightmares." We walked closer, and I started to get a cold chill run up my spine.

"Something wrong?" Chubs asked me.

"Nope," I replied. I was almost certain that Chubs could tell that I was lying, but I was decent at hiding my true feelings from others. Tommy, on the other hand, was very impatient as he walked ahead in a hurry and made his way over to the cabin window. "Tommy! Wait for us!" I yelled. "Come on, Chubs, we have to catch up to him!" I didn't even think about Nick being that far behind us as Chubs and myself took off running ahead without him. Which ended up being good in the end, for later on Chubs, Tommy, and myself were going to need his help. "What do you think you're doing, Tommy?" I asked. "You were supposed to wait for us."

He acted like he didn't hear a word I was saying; he walked right past me, "How do we get inside?"

"The front door, there is one of those on here, you know."

"Oh yeah, I almost forgot." He then walked past me and made his way to the front door. I could hear him start to pound on the door and cursing because he couldn't get in. "Bobby! Chubs! I thought you guys said the door was busted in." I walked around the corner of the house and found Tommy kicking at the door trying to get in. "Does this look broken to you?"

I turned and pushed on the door as hard as I could. I even rammed my shoulder into the door a couple of times. "This can't be right. This door was busted in by, Johnny! What in the hell is going on?"

Right when I thought about getting a running start and ram my whole body into the door, Chubs walked up. "What is all the shouting about? Is he here?" It was clear that we had accidentally scared Chubs with all of our screamings and shouting over the front door being locked.

"No, genius! The door is locked! Do you see any crazy killers around here?" Tommy shouted at him.

"There's no way in hell that's possible," Chubs said loudly. He pretty much shoved me out of the way and started ramming his shoulder into the door, just like I was doing when he walked up.

"What is this, some kind of joke?" Tommy asked.

"Don't even start that shit, Tommy!" I turned and shouted at him. "Well, what in the hell am I suppose to think, Bobby?" It didn't take long before Tommy and I was having a shouting match back and forth at each other.

"This door wasn't like this before now!"

"Then how did it get this way now, Bobby?"

"How in the hell am I suppose to know, Tommy?"

"You better figure it out! Because right now, I think Chubs and you are playing some kind of sick prank!"

The words that Tommy had just said completely pissed Chubs off, and he joined right into the shouting match as well. "The hell with you, Tommy! We're not playing some sick prank. Someone had to have fixed the damn door."

"Who, Chubs? Who fixed the door?" Tommy shouted back.

"There's only one person who could have wanted to fix this door, you guys," I screamed.

"Who?" Tommy asked.

"You know who," I answered.

"Don't tell me Albert the killer fixed the door, right?"

"Yeah, Tommy. I believe he did!"

"Show me the proof then!"

The three of us just kept on shouting and screaming at each other, until Chubs shouted at us, "The door just came open."

Tommy and I didn't hear him at first, and we turned and yelled at him, "What do you want, Chubs?"

He made a motion with the door and said, "Look, the door just came unlocked and opened on its own."

"What the hell?" said Tommy.

"I think someone's inside, and they want us to come in," I said to them both.

"Well, let's not keep whoever it is waiting," Tommy said sarcastically. He took a step inside and yelled, "Hello! Is someone in here? If so, you better stop messing around with us!"

"Tommy, stop. You shouldn't go in there," I said to him.

"Don't try and stop me. Now do you guys have my back or not?"

"Well, since you said it like that, then why wait?" Chubs said as he pushed right past Tommy and through the door.

Tommy chuckled a little because he knew how to push the right buttons to make Chubs do whatever he wanted. "Are you coming or not, Bobby?" he asked as he was already standing inside the doorway waiting for me.

"I'm telling you this is a bad idea, Tommy. But what would I know? Let's just get this over with," I said as I stormed past him and inside the cabin.

The three of us walked a little way inside the cabin; we stuck by each other at first until Tommy wanted to know which room everything took place in. Once we told him, he broke away from Chubs and myself and went off into the room alone. As for Chubs and myself, we were still too afraid to go back into that accursed room, that was until Tommy didn't give us much of a choice.

"Hey, Chubs, Bobby, get your asses in here quickly. Hurry!" Tommy shouted. I could tell that it was important, I could hear the urgency in his voice, and so could Chubs, and we quickly made our way to the room Tommy was in. "What is it, Tommy?" We both shouted as we entered the room. Tommy was just standing there not saying anything as he was looking up slightly. "Stay here, Chubs," I demanded.

Then I slowly started to walk toward, Tommy. And as I got closer, I reached out and put my hand on his shoulder and asked, "Tommy, are you all right?" He didn't answer me at first; it was like he was frozen in place and couldn't move. "Tommy!" I shouted, trying to get his attention. He then turned to look at me, and his face was covered with blood, and he had the look of fear in his eyes that I've never seen before in all my times of knowing him. I thought for sure that he was injured, so I started freaking out. "Tommy, you're bleeding! We have to get you out of here right now.

"I'm not bleeding, Bobby. I'm fine. The blood is coming from those," he said then pointed up. "Take a look for yourself."

I didn't get a chance to even look up because Chubs had come running over to us, wanting to know what was going on. When he first had seen Tommy's face, he freaked out just like I did, but I was able to calm him down, and I told him the blood was leaking down from above. He looked up first, and his face went deathly pale; it wasn't long before he ran over to the corner of the room and started vomiting. "Chubs are you all right?" I asked.

The only words I could make out was, "We need to get out of here, and now." Tommy had blood on his face and was scared to death, and Chubs was now sick. I couldn't figure out what was going on, but I knew my questions would be answered once I looked up. I have to admit that at first, I was too scared to look up.

However, I knew that I needed to know what was up there, and I used every ounce of courage I had left in me, and I looked up at the ceiling. It was horrible; what I have seen was absolutely horrible! There hanging from the ceiling were human body parts, and blood was dripping everywhere like rain. I couldn't believe my eyes, I've never seen anything like it and hoped I never would again. We knew whose body parts these were. "Do you think this is what happened to those missing teens from our camp?" Tommy asked with a look of fear still on his face.

"Look around you, Tommy. What do you think?" I replied.

"I told you guys so, I warned you that I watched them being killed that night. I told you that they had been cut up," Chubs said before he went back to vomiting.

"We have to get out of here before it's too late," I warned them.

Just then we heard the front door slam shut. "It's already too late, he's back," said Tommy. Chubs cowered down in the corner where he was vomiting, trying his best to hide. Tommy and I were about to do the same when we heard someone shouting out to us.

"I know that you nerds came in here! Show yourselves, and I will go easy on you! I promise!" It was Spike, and it seemed as though he followed us here by himself. I'm sure that if Johnny found out that he went against his word, he would get kicked out of the group, so he was going to enjoy himself at our expense.

"Let's take this asshole down. It's our only chance of getting out of here alive," I said.

"Yeah, it's only Spike. I'm sure that the four of us can take him, and right now we don't have a choice but to try," said Tommy.

"Get over here, Chubs. We need your help. Unless you want to wait for Albert to get back and end up like them." I said to him. He nervously walked over and rejoined Tommy and me, and the three of us went back into the other room, and our only means of escape, to confront Spike.

"That was easy enough," Spike said, smiling.

"You think it will be that easy to take on the three of us?" Tommy asked.

"I don't plan on fighting you. I'm going to kill you," he threatened, then pulled out the knife that he had hidden in his pocket. "The question is, which one of you will I kill first?"

"You damn coward!" I shouted at him.

"Don't worry, Bobby. He doesn't have the guts to use that

knife; he's just trying to scare us," said Tommy.

"Shut up, Tommy! Don't provoke him!" Chubs said angrily.

"I said don't worry about him, I know his kind, all talk, and no show. Right now, he's so scared he doesn't know if he wants to run or stay here and keep trying to scare us."

"You don't think I will use this knife? Then I guess I will just have to show you." Spike slowly started to walk our way. "Don't even think about running." With a sadistic smile on his face and knife tightly held in hand, he kept slowly walking toward us. Before I knew it, fear had overwhelmed my whole being, because Albert just appeared out of thin air and was standing right behind Spike.

"Spike, turn around slowly," I said to him.

"Now why would I want to do that? As soon as I do, I know that you will make a run for it."

"Listen to him, Spike. Turn around!" Tommy pleaded.

"I know that the three of you are scared. I can tell by the look on fat boy's face," he said as he laughed. We tried and tried to convince him to turn around, but he refused to listen to us. But there was nothing we could do to prevent what happened next. Albert grabbed Spike by his head from behind and jammed his long razor-sharp-like fingernails straight into Spike's eyes.

Blood squirted out of his sockets as his eyes were being crushed into the back of his head by Albert's fingers; it was too late for Spike, but it wasn't too late for us. We had no choice but to leave him behind and make a run for the door, but somehow it was locked from the outside now. The three of us beat on that door as our lives depended on it because it did. But it was no use; there was nothing we could do now to save ourselves from Albert's wrath.

All we could do was wait for the screams coming from Spike

to cease. I turned slightly to see if Albert was making his way toward us now. He wasn't, though; he was too busy gruesomely hacking away at Spike with an ax until you could no longer hear him screaming. The only thing we could hear now was Albert, laughing at his handiwork. He rose back up; with his ax in one hand and Spike's head in the other, I knew that now it was our turns to die. However, luck would be on our side as the door opened, and on the other side, standing there was Nick. He had no idea what was going on as we ran out the door and shut it behind us screaming to the top of our lungs about Albert the killer.

"What's going on guys? And how could you just leave me behind like that?" he asked.

I turned to him and without wasting any time, I said, "There's no time to explain. Just run, and run as fast as you can, and don't look back! Trust me!"

Tommy wasn't about to stand around and talk, for he was the first one to make a run for it, followed by Chubs. Nick was still confused and wasn't quite sure of what to make of the situation that he happened to walk in on, but after hearing a cold-blooded scream come from inside the cabin, he finally realized that this wasn't a laughing matter, and he took off running as well. I was the last to make a run for it.

You can call me stupid, but I wanted to know why Albert hadn't given chase yet, so I decided to look through the window—and watched in disgust and absolute horror as Albert took Spike's head and hung it up on a meat hook, as he did with the rest. After he did that, he went back and started hacking away at what was left of Spike's body with his ax, blood gushing everywhere as he did so. I couldn't stand watching any longer, so I turned away from the cabin window and to make a run for it.

I wasn't running fast at all, however, because I knew that I wasn't going to be able to catch up to my friends, and I also knew that Albert wasn't interested in chasing us at the moment. It wasn't long before the campgrounds were in sight, but I didn't feel any safer being back there; who would if they knew the truth? Albert could come into camp and start killing people anytime that he chooses, we're all his prey, and he's having fun hunting each and every one of us down! Besides, who's going to stop him? No one will listen to me or my friends, no one will believe us and take action before it's too late, it's just a matter of time before we're all dead by his hand!

Those were the thoughts that were going through my head at that time, and I did everything I could not lose control and run for the hills. But I couldn't do that. I wouldn't do that to my friends.

I stood outside the entryway into camp for minutes on end, hesitating whether I should make my way through or not. I was too scared of what I might find. But I had to, so I forced myself to go back to the campgrounds. I was relieved to see that nothing had happened, that everything was still normal here. Once I walked farther in, I found my friends sitting at a picnic table, staying as far away from the others they possibly could.

Hell, I couldn't blame them. I didn't want to be around anyone else either. But whether they liked it or not, we had some things to talk about, and we also had to make some plans on how we were going to survive against Albert and what he might do next. So I knew that it was up to me to get things set in motion. So I sat down beside Chubs at the table.

"It's about damn time you showed up! We thought you were dead too!" Tommy shouted at me.

"What in the hell took you so long, Bobby!" Chubs asked loudly.

That's when the three of them started jumping my ass for not being right there with them when they were running away.

"Guys! Guys! Would you please just shut up for one second!" I demanded. That got their attention. "I was making sure Albert wasn't chasing us, so yeah, I stayed behind! Someone had to." I shouted. "Also, think about this, we need to come up with a plan, or we're all dead! Understand that?"

"What are you talking about?" Chubs asked.

"What in the hell do you think I'm talking about? Do you think Albert is done? No, he's not going to stop until he has killed everyone, including us. We have to do something, right?" I explained.

"I know we can go and tell Tommy's brother what happened. If we take him to the cabin, he would have to believe us," said Nick.

"He's not going to believe us, and he's not going to help. We're on our own. And that is that," Tommy said.

"Then what are we going to do?" Nick asked.

"We have to take matters into our own hands," I said. It was time that we did something about it on our own, instead of trying to get help from the counselors. Or so I had thought, that was until one of the new lady counselors came up and started talking to us.

"What's wrong, guys? Do you not want to have fun getting to know the others that are here?" the lady asked.

We sat there and ignored her the best we could; don't get me wrong, it wasn't easy. She was even better looking than Candice and had even fewer clothes on as well. She had a smokin'-hot body and wasn't afraid to show it off either. I would imagine that she was used to getting anything she wanted. "Look, lady. We care nothing about joining in with the other campers. We have bigger things to worry about," I said to her.

She wasn't about to give up. I could tell she was going to annoy us until we did what she wanted, "Oh really? Then tell me, boys, what's so big that you can't have fun with everyone else?" she asked.

I was starting to get upset at that point, and I'm guessing that Tommy could sense that emotion in me starting to boil over, so he jumped into the conversation. "Since you asked, there's a killer running around, and he's already killed a few times. We've seen him kill at least one person. Also, he's using a cabin not far from here to hang up the body parts of his victims."

What she said next was the most ignorant thing I've ever heard come out of a female counselor's mouth. "You boys are just too cute; you're playing imaginary games with one another." Now either she was that damn stupid, or she was just trying to blow us off as everyone else had done, I wasn't sure which, but I didn't mind asking either.

"Did you really just say that to us? Are you that damn stupid? You were just told there's a killer out there, and you treat us like we're a bunch of three-year-olds."

"There you guys go again about this so-called killer. I swear you boys are just too cute. Next time though watch your language, it's not nice to say things like that. I'll leave you boys alone now so you can get back to playing your games." she said before walking off.

"That stupid bitch will be the first one to get themselves killed," Chubs said jokingly.

"Hell, I think I would be pulling for Albert on that one," Tommy said with a smile on his face.

Nick didn't find the jokes funny, I know that Tommy and Chubs were just trying to lighten the mood and all, but Nick was having none of it, "Forget about the lady and stop with the jokes."

"What crawled up your ass?" asked Tommy.

"Well for one, I got left behind in the woods," Nick said.

"We didn't mean for that to happen," Chubs said to Nick.

"We are sorry, I thought for sure you were right behind us when we went after, Tommy," I said.

"You and Chubs don't have to apologize; it was my fault. I shouldn't have taken off on my own the way I did, and I'm sorry especially to you, Nick," Tommy said.

"Nick, don't take this the wrong way, but I'm glad we left you behind," I told him.

"What in the hell is that suppose to mean, Bobby?" Nick asked.

"Let me finish what I was saying before you get all pissed off, Nick. The reason why I'm glad you got left behind is that if you hadn't been, we would all be dead right now. If you hadn't been left behind, you wouldn't have been there to open the door, you would have been stuck inside with us, and surely we would have all been killed." I explained. I believe what I said to him made sense, and he accepted my half-ass apology; it seemed as though he had calmed down somewhat. But now he was ready to ask questions that I don't think any of us was ready to answer.

"So tell me, what happened inside the cabin? Why did you guys run out screaming when I opened the door?" I looked over at Tommy, and he let me know that he wasn't in the mood to talk about what happened. And Chubs turned around and wouldn't even face Nick, which let me know he wasn't going to be the one to explain things. "What happened in that cabin? What is going on! I deserve to know, damn it!" Nick said again. He wasn't going to stop until he knew the truth, and he was right: he did deserve to know.

"All right, Nick. If you really want to know that badly, I'll tell you everything but know that it's not pretty at all. Be sure you can handle it and promise not to freak out," I explained.

"I promise, Bobby. I can handle it, just tell me what happened" I agreed to tell him everything, and that's exactly what I did. During the time I was explaining what happened inside the cabin, I could see his face turn ten shades of gray. I even had to stop a few times so he could vomit. I expected this to happen. I mean honestly, who can handle hearing something like that especially a young teenager. Once I was done, he still had some questions for me. "So the one you guys call Spike, is dead? Killed by Albert?" he asked.

"Yeah," I answered. "There were human body parts hanging from the ceiling inside the cabin as well."

"What? And you guys think it was the body parts of the teens that went missing that night when someone tried to scare us?" Nick asked.

"Yes, Nick." At that point, I was tired of explaining things to him, and I was getting tired of repeating myself over and over again. "Look, Nick. I told you everything that happened to us inside the cabin, now please stop asking me questions. I don't know what else to tell you." It was time to stop with the questions, it was time to stop ignoring what had happened, and it was time for us to do something about it, to fight back, and to protect ourselves against that killing machine that was hiding out in the woods, watching, and waiting for his chance to kill again. "Chubs, Tommy, Nick! Listen up, we have to do something, anything that we can to stop Albert! If we don't do something now, he will kill us! We can't rely on anyone else. We can only rely on one another. So the three of you need to decide right now. Are you in or out?" I said to them.

"You know me, I'm in. I don't run from anything," Tommy said.

"Count me in as well," said Chubs.

Nick stayed quiet and didn't give us an answer, but I had to know for sure if he was in or out, "Nick, what about you, in or out? I need to know."

"Come on, Bobby. Cut him some slack," Tommy told me.

This time I couldn't cut anyone any slack. I needed to know if we all had each other's back, because soon shit was going to hit the fan, and we had to get ready for the hell that was to come. "I can't, not this time, Tommy. You know as well as I do what we're up against. We have to be ready, and I need to know if he has our backs too. So again, I ask you. Are you in or out, Nick?" I wanted to know right then and there what his answer was going to be.

"I don't like this at all. I think we need help." Nick said. But then he looked me straight in the eyes and added, "I know though that I don't have a choice, so yeah, I'm in."

"Good so we're all set then, we can talk about what our next step will be later. For now, we need to try and have some fun," I said.

"How in the hell are we going to have fun, when there's a killer out there?" Tommy asked.

"We have to try, Tommy. Look at us, right now we're all so stressed and scared that we could pop at any moment." I said to him.

"He's right, Tommy. We have to do something that will help us relax, I don't know about the rest of you, but I'm up for a swim in the lake." Chubs said.

Nick finally smiled for the first time that day as he also thought swimming would be a fun way to relax and unwind. It took us a few minutes, but we finally convinced Tommy that it would be for the best if we forgot about it all for now. So we decided that we would head back to our cabin and get ourselves ready to go swimming; we did keep a close eye out for anything out of the ordinary.

Yeah, we did want to go and have some fun, but we never did let our guard down, not even for a moment. Once ready we made our way to the lake, and we got lucky that nothing else had happened yet. For two hours we had fun swimming and throwing one another around in the lake, you know, kid stuff. We forgot about everything and at that moment we could be young kids again, and all was right with the world.

# 10

# Albert Strikes Again

A knock on the door came later than usual this time. "Time's up," Julie shouted. She then opened up the door and whispered to Bobby and Joe, "I bought you guys all the time I could, but it's really late now. So if you don't mind, I need you to leave quickly, mister. I don't need to lose my job over this."

Joe smiled and replied, "Thank you, ma'am. I will leave as quickly as possible without a fight." Joe then turned to Bobby.

"Time's up, my friend, but I will see you bright and early tomorrow morning," he said before shaking Bobby's hand. Bobby shook Joe's hand for the second time.

"Don't forget, because you're very close to the end of the story and learning the truth about Camp Hell," Bobby told him.

"I won't forget, I promise you that. And I may have some more news for you as well come morning," Joe replied. He bid both Bobby and Julie a good night before walking out the door.

"I'm sorry but I also have to go," said Julie. "Don't forget to take your pills before you sleep. I'm leaving them right here beside your bed. Good night, Bobby. See you in the morning." Bobby didn't even get a chance to make a response back to her before she quickly ran out of the room. But he didn't mind as he was already preparing to write more in his journal. Like the past nights before, he again pulled out his journal from under his mattress and went over to the desk in the corner of his room and started writing yet again.

July 6, 1999. Here I writing in this journal again before I sleep; if it wasn't important to share all that I know, I wouldn't be writing at all. But let me get to the point, I'm right at the end of my story, and who knows I could also be at the end of my journey as well. Not much happened this morning, I didn't have any bad dreams, and Joe came in today in a decent mood. I know that he wants to find out the truth and that I hold the key to that truth, but he does need to learn a little patience though.

There's really not that much for me to write, I told him more of what happened at that blasted camp, and Julie bought us some extra talking time, which was very nice of her. I don't know if Joe picked up on it or not, but when I was telling him about the cabin and the body parts and what happened to Spike, I could see the way his face would change, and he looked more serious than ever, which let me know I hit a nerve with what I had said. I will have to ask him about it at a later time. I still think about the day I watched Spike die, and to this day I believe that if Albert wouldn't have killed him, then Spike would have killed me and my friends.

Some things are best left alone, I say. Bobby closed his journal and put it back under his mattress, and he was now ready for bed. He took his meds, and he got himself ready for sleep. Once in bed, it didn't take him long to fall asleep. He wouldn't have any bad dreams; however, one odd thing would happen to him the following morning. Once awakened by the usual knocking at his door, Bobby arose out of his bed to find the ghostly boy from his childhood standing at the foot of his bed. It seemed as though the boy was trying to tell him something, but before Bobby could make out what he was saying, the door to his room opened, and the boy vanished. "Great, he's back," Bobby said to himself.

"What was that, Bobby? I didn't hear what you said." Julie said to him.

"Oh, nothing, just talking to myself. If that's Joe out there, you can send him in. I'm ready."

"All right Bobby, I'll send him on in," said Julie.

Bobby could hear her inform Joe that he could go ahead and enter the room if he liked. And not even a minute later, Joe walked into the room and shut the door behind him. "We need to talk, Bobby," Joe said as he pulled up a chair.

"All right, what's on your mind?" Bobby asked.

"I believe that my brother is somewhere in town."

"Are you sure about that?"

"I'm almost certain about that, and I also think that he may be after you."

"Why in the hell would he be after me?"

"I don't know for sure. That's what I'm trying to find out. That's all the info I have for you right now. Also, I don't have time to answer any questions. So if you don't mind, I would like for us to get started."

The look on Bobby's face was that of concern, and he was feeling upset with Joe as well. But he understood where Joe was coming from, he is a detective after all, and more than likely has other cases he has to work as well. However, the concern he has about John Boy, that won't go away anytime soon, for he has to keep his guard up yet again and protect himself from what may be coming his way. But that wasn't going to stop him from helping Joe, and Bobby was hell-bent on finishing telling his side of what happened at that accursed place. "I understand, Joe. Let us get started, and who knows maybe this time I will finish my tale of horror," Bobby said to him.

As I was saying last time, the four of was swimming in the lake and having a good time of it. That was until Johnny and his gang minus Spike made their way into the lake as well. I had hoped that since it was a big-enough lake, maybe he wouldn't notice us, but I was wrong as usual. "Hey, boys! Check it out, the lake is full of nerds," Johnny said after he spotted us.

"Can we not catch a break?" Tommy shouted.

"Doesn't look like it, Tommy," I said.

"We could easily take you nerds out right now if we wanted to," Johnny explained.

"Is that right?" I asked.

"Yeah, it is, nerd."

"My name isn't nerd! It's Bobby! Get it right! And if you want a piece of us, then jump." I've had enough of their shit, and I couldn't and wouldn't take it any longer; if they wanted a fight, then I was happy to give them what they wanted. I wasn't for sure if my friends felt the same way, but I didn't care. I would take them on alone if I had to.

"Wait right there, tough guy! We would love to come in that water and drown you rats, but we're looking for someone right now!" Johnny shouted back.

"What, Johnny. Are you looking for another nerd to bully?" I asked.

"No, idiot! The only nerd I want to bully is you. Don't think for a second I've forgotten about that sucker punch! Unfortunately, right now our friend Spike has gone missing. You nerds haven't seen him, have you?" said Johnny.

Tommy was quick to answer before anyone else could say a word. "Nope, haven't seen him. Knowing that moron, he more than likely got lost in the woods." After that he shot the rest of us a look, letting us know not to say a word—otherwise… It was hard for me not to let Johnny know that his friend was dead, but if Tommy didn't want me to say anything, it was for the best.

"You're probably right, Tommy. We will go and look there, but if I find out that you're lying to me, there will be hell to pay," Johnny explained.

"You have no idea what hell is," said Chubs.

"What did you say, fat boy?"

"Nothing at all."

"That's what I thought. We'll see you later, losers. Let's go, guys." And off went Johnny and his gang of thugs.

"Hey, Tommy! Why didn't you let us say anything?" Chubs asked.

"Use your brain, Chubs. What do you think would have happened if we told him Spike was dead?"

"He would have started a fight with us."

"And?"

"And he would have forced us to go back to that cabin."

"Do you think we're ready for that?"

"No, probably not."

Tommy had a point; if we went back there, we would have gotten someone else killed. Likely one of us would be killed as well. "Chubs, Tommy! If you two are done, we should get out of here before Johnny gets back," I suggested.

"Good point, we don't need any more trouble right now." Tommy agreed.

"Besides, don't we need to prepare for what's next?" Nick asked.

That was the first words out of Nick's mouth since we started swimming. "Well, look who decided to start talking," said Chubs.

"I've been talking to you guys, Chubs. But it doesn't mean I'm not upset with the three of you."

"Oh, really?"

"Yes, really, Chubs."

"Well, get over it, Nick. We didn't mean for any of it to happen. And it wasn't our fault that there's a killer out in the woods!" Chubs and Nick argued with each other over and over and over again, and it didn't seem like they were going to stop any time soon. That's when I decided I had had enough and was just about to break them up when I saw the boy from my nightmares standing off in the distance. He was standing behind a tree, kind of leaning out watching us.

Nobody was paying any attention to the fact that we were being watched except me. I thought that maybe Tommy would notice, but he was already in the middle of Chubs and Nick's argument. So like always it was up to me to find out what the boy wanted, I knew that he was a ghost, but I wasn't scared; he seems to only want to warn me of the dangers out here. Little too late to listen to him, we were all too familiar with the danger now, and that danger came in the form of a killer named Albert.

I swam out of the lake and walked my way toward him slowly. I thought for sure I would get the jump on him this time. But it seemed as though something startled him, and he vanished into thin air; before walking back to the lake, I noticed that something was written on one of the trees, in what seemed to be red ink or blood. And it read, "He comes out to play tonight. Someone will die on this night." To me, it was another warning, and I just felt like I should run back and tell the others, and that's exactly what I did. "Hey, guys!" I shouted. "You really need to come and see this!"

"What is it, Bobby?" Tommy asked.

"Guys, just get out of the water and follow me, trust me you need to see this," I said again.

"Way to ruin the fun," said Nick.

"What fun? The three of you was still arguing in the water when I sneaked away, and when I got back just now, that didn't sound like fun to me, Nick," I said. "Now get out of the water and follow me." It took some effort, but I got them to follow me to the spot where the boy was standing.

"What did you want us to see?" Tommy asked as he walked around and if front of me.

"Turn around, and you will see it," I told him.

And he did exactly what I said. "What the?" Tommy gasped.

"It's warning," I said.

"I know that, Bobby. But from who?

"It was a warning from the boy I have been telling you guys about."

"Now wait for a second, Bobby. I don't have a choice but to believe you about the killer in the woods. I've seen him with my own eyes. But I draw the line when you tell me to believe in ghosts too," Tommy said to me.

"Well, Tommy, do you see anyone else around that could have done this?" "He's got you there, Tommy," Chubs said.

"What does it say?" asked Nick. And Tommy read off what it said to them.

"What do you think it means?" Chubs asked.

"What do you think it means, Chubs?" Tommy asked back.

"It could mean anything," Nick jumped in and said.

I laughed at his remark and explained to him what it really meant, "As I said, it's a warning. It means that tonight, Albert will kill again. And we need to be ready for him." It was crazy for me to say that, I mean four teenagers taking on one demonic killer; would we even stand a chance against such a person? And who knows, he might not even be after us, but I couldn't sit back and let him kill others without some kind of warning or fight.

"I say we go eat and get ready for tonight." For once I had my friends all on the same page, and we made our way back to our cabin to dry ourselves off and dress up so we could go eat. It seems weird that we would have to dress up nicely just to eat at a campground, but the counselors' pet peeve is that we all look nice for dinner each and every time, or we don't eat at all.

"Damn, we look good! Too bad there are no ladies around our own age," Tommy bragged.

"You never know, those smokin'-hot lady counselors might like younger guys," Nick joked.

"You're sick!" Tommy said back to him.

"Knock it off, you two, this isn't about having fun right now. We need to eat to keep up our energy, and then set a plan in motion for tonight," I told them.

"We don't have time for jokes." I know that I was being a buzzkill, and I also knew that we had to act somewhat normal, or someone might think we're up to no good. However, if Albert was going to be out tonight looking for another victim, then maybe we could find a way to stop him, or so I thought we could, but I would end up being dead wrong.

"All right, Bobby. Let's go and eat and plan out our attack," said Tommy.

"And here I was hoping to get lucky with a lady counselor tonight, damn it all," Nick said as a joke.

"Enough of the jokes, Nick. Let's just get this over with." I could tell by the tone in Chubs's voice that he was not happy with me and also by the way he stormed past me, and out the door, he went without saying another word to me at all.

"We better catch up to him. Who knows what he might try and do." Tommy said. Nick didn't say anything; he turned and chased after Chubs. My guess would be he heard what Tommy said and went after him. "Let's get this show on the road, shall we?" Tommy turned and said to me.

"Let's. Oh, and, Tommy."

"What?"

"You know that when the time comes, Nick and Chubs won't be of use. I need to know that I can count on you."

Tommy thought about it for a few minutes and replied, "Yeah, man. I know that Chubs and Nick will more than likely run, but know that I have your back no matter what happens. But, Bobby, when that time comes, you better have my back too."

"I will, Tommy." Then we bumped knuckles and walked out the door and caught up to Nick and Chubs. That night we would eat as much as we could handle, and everything that looked good we grabbed. Yeah, it got us some unwanted attention, but on that night we didn't care. It could very well be one or all of our last meals, so we made sure to enjoy it, and we made a pact that no matter what happens, that whoever survives eats like this every night until it's the last so that we could remember the fallen. After the four of us were done, we decided it was time to come up with a plan of action for tonight. "It's time, guys."

"Time for what, Bobby?" Chubs asked.

Now I know that Chubs was just being himself and making light of the situation to make himself feel better and all, but that was starting to get old for me. "I know what you're trying to do, Chubs. But in all seriousness, this is a bad time to be joking around, don't you think?" I said to him.

"Come on, Bobby. Sometimes you still need to laugh about things."

"As I said before, the time for joking can wait," I told him.

"Lighten up a little, man," said Tommy.

"Yeah, dude. What's eating you?" asked Nick.

"Seriously? What's eating me?" I responded.

"That's what I asked."

"Well for one, we have a maniac that wants to kill every single person here. Or did you forget about that?"

"No, Bobby. I haven't forgotten about that, but it doesn't mean we can't joke about it."

"Nick, if you want to get yourself killed, do it on your time, not mine."

That's when Tommy decided he would stop us before things got out of hand, and it was a good thing he did because I was getting ready to kick Nick's ass. "All right, stop it, you two. Fighting isn't going to solve the problem, is it?" he said."If we're going to come up with a plan, we had better do it now. Or do you not realize how late it's getting?"

I wasn't paying attention like I should have been. I was too busy arguing with Nick, and Chubs. "Damn it. Enough of the bullshit! We're almost out of time. Does anyone have any ideas?" I said almost in a panic.

"No, I'm sorry, Bobby. I have no idea what we should do, to be honest with you," Tommy said.

I then turned and looked at Nick, "What about you?" I asked.

"I got nothing, Bobby," he replied. This was going to be tough, not one of my friends had any good ideas so far.

"Bobby, if this is what you want to do so badly, then you come up with some kind of plan. You're the one dragging the rest of us into this. As far as we know he might not even want to go after us until last. So why should we worry about it right now?" Chubs said to me.

I was getting more and more upset by the minute that I was the only one that cared about Albert stalking everyone and waiting for his time to kill again, which was obvious by the warning that kid left us it was going to happen again on that night. "I'm not dragging anyone into this; remember you made a promise that you was in on this. I gave all of you an option. If you want out now, then say so and go run and hide until he decides he wants to kill you next.

Be my guest! Who knows who he will kill tonight! But it's your choice, not mine." Nick and Chubs apologized to me for the way they were acting; they explained to me how scared they were and didn't believe that we stood a chance in hell at stopping Albert from killing anyone. And was also afraid that if we tried, he would more than likely kill one of us in the process. Then at that moment, a plan came to mind. "I have an idea guys, I don't know if it will work, but just hear me out," I said.

"We're listening, Bobby," said Tommy. "Right, guys?" Both Chubs and Nick agreed to listen to what I had to say.

"All right, now I say we keep an eye out for anything odd, and I mean all four of us to stick together no matter what. And if we see anything out of the ordinary, you know the siren the counselors use to keep up with the time?" I said.

"Yeah, what about it?" Tommy asked.

"We use it to our advantage," I told them.

Tommy slapped me on the back and said, "That's a great idea. I don't know why I didn't think of that." He seemed to be the only one that was getting what I was trying to say.

"Just what are you telling us, Bobby?" Nick asked.

Tommy turned to me and said, "I got this, Bobby." He then

turned back to look at Nick and said, "If we see anything weird, and damn sure if we see that demonic man, we break into that small building, and we set off the siren that alerts the counselors of the different times to do things."

"But won't that get us in even more trouble?" Chubs asked.

"Yeah, Chubs, we're going to be in a shitload of trouble for doing this. But ask yourself, would you rather be in a shitload of trouble? Or would you rather be dead?" I said to him.

"Good point, Bobby. So when are we putting this plan into motion?" he asked. I looked out the window, and then I looked back at him and said, "We better do this right now before it's too late." We didn't have much time left before it was too late for us to sneak out of our cabin in the middle of the night, counselors were supposed to be on watch duty at night, but yeah right, that hardly ever happened, but we couldn't take that chance.

So we made sure to wear as much black as we had, which wasn't that much, and we made our way out of the cabin and sneaked into the woods to keep an eye out for Albert. I remember that night well because it was a little colder than usual, and on most nights you would be able to hear crickets and wolves or at least an owl or two.

But on that night all was silent, except for the few counselors who were out and about doing their thing, and believe me, it wasn't watch duty. None of us even spoke a word. The four of us just sat there waiting for something to happen, waiting for Albert to show himself. Hours had passed and nothing; the only thing interesting that happened was seeing Candice run by without her top on, and that got Tommy going. "Did you guys see that," he asked loudly.

"I'm going to remember this night forever," Chubs said jokingly.

"Wow. I could die happy right now," said Nick. But we would be disgusted by what we saw next. It was Mark chasing her, and he was completely naked. I mean he had no clothing on at all.

"Guys, you don't want to see who's chasing her, trust me," I said as I turned away. I could hear the other guys yelling about how they didn't want to see that, and it ruined seeing Candice running around topless. And that it was gross thinking about Candice and Mark hooking up with each other. I have to admit it turned a bad night for me into a worse one. But our moment was short-lived as we watched in horror as Albert was now sneaking up on Mark!

We may not have liked Mark, and yes, he was a total ass, but we didn't want to see him dead. We yelled and screamed out to him, "Mark! Mark! Look out! He's behind you!" But we were too far away for him to hear us, and he wasn't able to see us either, for we were in the woods and not close enough to the lights.

"The siren! We need to get there and set it off!" I shouted. "Come on! Hurry up!" I didn't even think twice as I took off running as fast as I could, we had only one chance to save his life, and we needed to hurry. I didn't even bother to look behind me to see if the others were keeping up with me. Luckily I wouldn't have to as Tommy ran past me and took the lead; he would end up being the first one to the small building. He didn't even stop; he kicked the door in and went right on inside. The rest of us stopped outside the door in awe at what Tommy had done.

"What the hell," Tommy gasped. I could tell right then that something wasn't right, Tommy may have been a jock, but he could work electronics very well.

I ran inside. "What' wrong, Tommy?" I asked.

"Look around and see for yourself!"

"Who could have done this?" Someone had broken inside and destroyed everything. There was no way of warning anybody now. "Shit! We still have to warn, Mark! Forget about this right now, Tommy! Let's go!" I shouted before running out the door with Tommy hot on my heels.

"What's going on?" Nick shouted.

"There's no time to explain, just run!" Tommy shouted back. But by the time we got to Mark, it was already too late. Albert had him by the hair of his head, and Mark was fighting back the best he could, screaming madly at him. We stopped in our tracks and watched in fear as Albert lifted up his ax and swung it down between Mark's legs.

The blade of the ax went straight through Mark's crotch and right into his pelvis; blood was gushing everywhere even out of his mouth. You could see the look of fear and disbelief in Mark's eyes as he fell to his knees, then face-first into the dirt. He was dead on the spot. That's when Candice came running back outside and saw what had happened to Mark; she let out this bloodcurdling scream and fainted right after, and on the ground, she lay as well. You could hear this sinister laugh coming from Albert at what he had done; it was a laugh that I was all too familiar with now, from in my dreams and in person.

It looked as though he was going to go after Candice next, but Tommy wasn't going to have any of that. "You stay away from her, you freak!" Tommy yelled as he charged at Albert. I didn't even have a chance to react, or I would have stopped him, but he was just too damn fast for me. Tommy was charging at him at full speed and lowered his shoulder like he was going to try and tackle him to the ground.

However, that didn't do Tommy a damn bit of good, because once he was close enough, Albert swung his arm almost effortlessly and knocked Tommy a pretty good ways away from him, and into a tree knocking him unconscious. It was insane to witness such strength come from just one man, which proved Albert was not a normal man whatsoever. If Albert had gone after Tommy or Candice, we would have run over too and tried our best to stop him.

But he wasn't interested in either one of them; instead, he reached down and grabbed Mark's body by the hair of the head, raised back up smiling at us, and off he went dragging the body behind him, disappearing into the woods. After he was completely out of sight, I quickly ran over to where Tommy was lying to make sure he was all right. Then I yelled for Nick to run and get some help. Once he was gone, I instructed Chubs to check on Candice.

Luckily Tommy just bruised the back of his head, and Candice was breathing just fine; the shock of seeing Mark being murdered was just too much for her to handle. The shock on the four of us was great as well; that was the second time we had to stand there and watch someone being killed right in front of our eyes. "How's Tommy doing!" Chubs shouted.

"He's all right. He just hit his head." I replied. "How's Candice?"

"She's all right! She just fainted is all!" he shouted back at me.

About the time Tommy started coming to, Nick was coming back with some help. There were at least four other counselors with him, but Tommy's brother was nowhere to be found, or so they said.

The counselors didn't seem to give a damn about Tommy, and they sure as hell didn't want to hear about what had taken place; all they wanted to do was get Candice back to her room. "Doesn't anyone want to know what happened?" I shouted. None of them even responded to what I said. "Hey! Do any of you care that

Mark is dead!" I shouted again. It was like I wasn't even there. "Hey!" I screamed.

That's when Nick walked up to me and said, "Leave it be, Bobby." I was starting to get upset, and on top of that, I was so confused I didn't know what to think.

"Why should I let it go?" I asked.

"Because Tommy's brother told them to ignore us. He would deal with the matter later tomorrow." That didn't make any sense to me. Why on earth would he say that? I wasn't going to just let things go that easily without knowing why?

"That's not good enough for me! Another person has been killed. He has no choice but to do something about it now!" I shouted.

Tommy was awake now but still somewhat out of it. But he could still understand what was going on. "Jerry wants to cover it up, at least that's what I think anyway," he said.

"Why would he want to do that for?" I asked.

"Think about it, he's the head counselor. Rebuilding these campgrounds was more than likely his idea, and if he was given warnings about what could happen out here from others, and he ignored them, that means his ass would be on the line. Would you want anyone to find that out if you were him?" he explained.

It all made sense to me now, that's why his brother refused to listen to us in the first place, and if he's willing to go this far, who knows what he might do to keep what happened quietly from all the others that are here as well. "Hey, look, there's Steve. I'm sure he'll listen to us." I said.

"I doubt it," said Tommy.

"It never hurts to try." I motioned for Steve to come to me, he tried to ignore me at first, but when I started yelling at him, he finally gave in. I could tell how angry he was as he walked over toward me.

"What in the hell do you guys want?" Steve asked. "We know what happened here, Steve," I said to him.

"More lies coming from the four of you? I don't want to hear it." He responded back.

He turned to walk away, and that's when Tommy shouted at him. "So you don't give a damn that your friend Mark is dead?"

Steve turned back around to face Tommy. "What did you say?" "You heard me, Steve!"

"You're lying to me."

"No, I'm not lying to you, Steve. Mark is dead."

"And let me guess, the four of you witnessed the whole thing?"

"Yeah, Steve! We did see the whole thing go down."

"Then which one of you wants to tell me what happened?"

"Don't look at me, I'll let Bobby tell you. He's better at explaining things than me." Tommy said. Great, I thought to myself.

Steve turned and looked at me. "Let's hear it," he demanded.

"Don't get pushy with me, if the two of you are done arguing, then I'll tell you exactly what happened," I told him.

"Fine, just tell me what you know," Steve said to me.

This time around I had Steve where I wanted him instead of the other way around. I turned to only see Tommy by my side, Chubs and Nick were nowhere to be found, also Candice and the other counselors were gone as well, so I thought maybe Chubs and Nick went along with Candice to make sure she was all right.

"What are you waiting for? I don't have all night." There for a moment, I forgot about Steve standing there waiting.

"Oh, sorry about that," I said. Before I started, I explained to Steve that it wasn't something he was going to like, but he demanded that I tell him anyways. And I did exactly what he demanded of me. I could see the look of disbelief on his face, even a hint of anger, and maybe even fear. But still, he acted like he was big and bad.

"I still don't believe you. But if it's true, then I say Mark got exactly what he deserved. Now you two should find your loser friends, then get your asses back to your cabin. And don't say a damn word to anyone about this. Now go!" he demanded of us.

It didn't take long for him to storm off shortly after. I looked at Tommy all confused. "What was that all about?" I asked.

"Let's go and find Chubs and Nick. I'll explain it to you while we walk." Tommy said to me. We walked around looking everywhere for them, but we weren't having any luck, so I decided to ask Tommy to explain some things to me.

"Why did Steve say Mark deserved to die?" I asked.

Tommy looked at me and laughed a little. "You don't get it, do you?"

"Get what?" I replied.

"That figures, you've probably never liked a girl yet, have you?" he replied.

"What in the hell does that have to do with anything?" I asked angrily. He laughed again and that seemed to really piss me off. "Stop laughing, Tommy!" I said. "And this isn't the time to be laughing, Albert has killed again, and this time it was Mark. And Steve claims Mark deserved it! So just tell me what you're talking about. Would you?"

Tommy stopped laughing, and he got all serious real quick. "It means that Steve had a thing for Candice!" Tommy said to me.

"And?" I replied. I have to be honest, I didn't really get a word he was saying to me, I didn't get the whole relationship thing until he made it all crystal clear.

"Look, Bobby. It's clear that Mark knew about Steve's feelings for Candice, so to rub it into Steve's face, he hooked up with her. Only Mark wasn't planning on getting himself killed; he was more than likely just hoping that Steve would see them running around naked with each other. And then he would figure out what was going on after that, only things backfired, and Steve didn't catch him. Albert did, and we both know what happened after that. He was trying to crush Steve, that's all there is to it." he explained. "Now do you understand?"

"Yeah, Tommy. I think I get it now. Maybe Steve is right. Mark may have deserved that one." I said. Why would someone want to hurt their friend like that? But then I remembered that Mark never really saw Steve as a friend; Steve was more of his slave, a nerd that wanted to be like Mark. And Mark treated him like shit. I think Mark only let Steve hang around so he could have someone to bully. So I hate to say this, but if one person deserved his fate, it was Mark.

"Hey, Bobby. Let's head back to the cabin. Chubs and Nick might be there by now." Tommy suggested.

"Okay, Tommy." Maybe he was right. It was possible that they had returned to the cabin and waiting for us; it only took us a matter of minutes to get there. It wasn't like we were that far away. Albert was gone, and we were safe for now, at least until the next night when he would come back out to kill again. But it didn't matter right then; we had to figure some things out, as we walked inside the cabin Chubs and Nick was there to greet us.

"Hey, Chubs! Bobby and Tommy are here. Where have you two been? We've been worried about you guys," Nick said.

Chubs stuck his head around the corner. "It's about time! What have you two been up to?"

"We talked with Steve. Where in the hell did the two of you go?" Tommy asked.

"We wanted to make sure Candice was all right," Chubs said.

"That's right, we couldn't just ignore the fact that she also watched Mark being killed," Nick jumped in and said.

"How is she doing?" I asked.

"Not that good, she was screaming a lot and talking about some kind of monster killing Mark," Chubs replied.

"Well, what do you expect?" Tommy said.

"We're scared out of our minds. I could only imagine what it's like for her." Tommy was right.

The four of us was barely hanging on by a thread; what she's going through must be hell for her right now. "But she's tough; she will pull through. You said something about talking to Steve?" Chubs said.

"Yep, we talked to Steve. Well, Bobby did anyways," said Tommy.

"How did that go?" Nick asked.

"It didn't go the way it should have. I don't know if he believed what happened or not. All I know is that he said if Mark was really dead, he deserved it. And that means until Candice pulls through, or Steve gets his head out of his ass, the four of us are still on our own." I explained to them.

Just then we heard a knock on the door, which made us jump. I went to answer it, but Tommy stopped me. "What in the hell do you think you're doing?" he asked.

"I'm going to answer the door. What else would I be doing?" I replied.

"You don't know who's out there, man. It could be him."

"Tommy, he's gone for now. And I doubt he would be knocking at our door."

Then we heard the knocking again followed by a voice, "Is anyone in there? If so, you better open this door right now!"

I looked at Tommy. "Is that good enough for you?" I asked. He let go of my arm, and I opened the door; it was one of the counselors standing on the other side.

"Is there someone by the name of Tommy around?" the person asked.

"That would be me," Tommy answered.

"Would you step outside for a moment? I have a message from your brother." the person said.

"Sure, why not, you guys stay here, I got this," Tommy said to us as he walked past me. I shut the door and walked back on inside the cabin.

"I wonder what's going on," said Nick.

"I don't know, Nick. But we will have to let Tommy handle this one by himself." I said.

"Or we can listen from the window." Chubs said jokingly.

"No, we're not going to do that. If Tommy wants to tell us what's going on, he will." I said to them both.

Then the door opened, and Tommy reappeared back inside the cabin. "What was that all about, Tommy?" Nick asked.

He didn't answer Nick's question. Tommy just walked right past all of us and started getting ready for bed. "Hey, Tommy. Are you all right? What did he say to you?" Chubs was now asking his own questions as well.

"Back off of him, Chubs," I said. I walked over to, Tommy. "It must have been pretty bad, huh? But don't worry, Tommy. We will leave you be until the morning." I said to him before I walked over to my bed. That night I had trouble sleeping again, and so did Tommy; he tossed and turned the whole night. I wasn't sure about Nick or Chubs. I didn't hear any movement at all coming from them whatsoever. Lucky for us nothing else happened the rest of that night.

However, the following morning, Tommy was up and running. "Get up, guys! Now!" he shouted at us.

"Chill out, Tommy. I'm already up." I said.

"What has you so motivated?"

"I don't have time to explain, Bobby! Just trust me on this," he answered. I promised to have his back no matter what like he did the same for me, so I helped him wake Chubs and Nick up as quickly as I could. Neither one of them could figure out what all the rush was about, and I didn't have any answers for them either. Tommy rushed us out the door once we were all dressed and ready.

"What is your problem, Tommy?" Chubs asked.

"We have to be somewhere right this minute. We don't have any time to spare." Tommy said with a hint of urgency.

"Tommy, I know that I said I would have your back, but I want to know what's going on," I said to him.

"Just come on and don't fall behind."

Chubs stopped walking and said, "I'm not taking another step until you tell us all what's going on." And he wasn't joking, Chubs didn't take another step forward, he stood his ground on this one.

Nick even went against what Tommy was wanting of us. "Sorry, Tommy. I'm with Chubs on this one; we have a right to know what's going on."

"What about you, Bobby?" Tommy asked me.

"I want to know what's going on too, Tommy. But I will still have your back even if you don't tell us." I answered.

He paced back and forth for a second. "Okay, fine, I'll tell you what's going on." We waited in silence for what Tommy was about to say. "Last night I was told my brother wanted to speak with us at this time today. I don't know what for though so don't ask," he explained. "Is that good enough?"

It was good enough for us, we had no choice but for it to be, Tommy was a friend, and that's what friends are for. "That works for me, Tommy. Let's get a move on. We don't want to get into a fight with your brother for us being late." I turned to look at Chubs and Nick. "Right?"

"Yeah, yeah. Let's be on our way." Chubs replied. Nick agreed with Chubs again, which is weird because usually, he's always against everything Chubs says and always sticking by Tommy's side. But things seemed to have changed, and quickly, Nick was realizing that he finally had to stand on his own two feet. It's about damn time he figured it out because like I said before, once that year was over, he was on his own. Anyways, we turned and followed Tommy on into his brother's office; maybe after last night, he was finally going to listen to us. However, once we got into his office, we realized that wasn't the case at all.

"What do you want from us now?" Tommy asked. Not once did we ever hear him call his brother by his name since he got to camp. There must be a lot of hate between them at the moment.

"I want to know exactly what happened last night, little brother," he said.

But still, Tommy wasn't about to back down from his brother. "Why don't you ask, Candice," Tommy said back to him.

"I tried; she just keeps on about some kind of monster killing Mark. So tell me, did you and your nerd friends play a prank on her?" he said with a hint of anger in his voice. Now there was no way in hell that Tommy was going to take that from anyone, not even his own brother.

"What in the hell do you mean by that?" asked Tommy.

"You know what I mean, did you have anything to do with what happened last night?"

"No, you idiot, we tried to stop what happened last night. But we failed, and Mark was killed in the end."

"Then why don't you tell me everything that happened. How's that for starters?" Tommy got pissed at his brother, but he still told him everything about that night.

"You expect me to believe that?" Tommy's brother asked.

"You're my brother; of course, I expect you to believe me. You need to do something about this, or we will all be killed by the maniac. And you know as well as I do who that maniac is, don't you?" Tommy said to him. I wanted to say something to show I had Tommy's back, but Tommy refused to let any of us talk for him this time.

"Get out of my office, now! All of you get out here!" Jared yelled. "And don't any of you say a word to anyone about this! Or you will pay, got it?"

"You can't just sweep this under the rug. I won't let you. I don't give a damn about your reputation. Damn it, man, you're going to get us all killed." Tommy told him. "Come on, guys, let's go. We have things to take care of." Tommy said to us before storming out the door. I wanted to give Tommy's brother a piece of my mind, but I knew that it wouldn't do any good. He knew the truth, but he didn't want to risk his good name by helping us, because that would give away the fact that he knew what was going on the whole time.

# 11

# All Hell Breaks Loose

"All right, Joe, I think we've talked enough for today. I'm sorry, but I don't want to get Julie in trouble. She's helped us a lot already." said Bobby.

Joe stood up. "Its all good, Bobby. I understand where you're coming from, and besides, I have a few things I need to do before nightfall." Joe responded.

"Well, you take care of yourself, Joe," Bobby said. Then he offered Joe his hand first to shake this time around.

"There's a first time for everything," Joe said with a smile on his face, before shaking Bobby's hand. Joe called for the nurses to let him out, then opened the door, and Joe hesitated for a moment and just walked right on out the door. That confused Bobby for a brief moment, but he eventually shrugged it off as just Joe having some odd behavior; he was a detective after all. Later that evening, Bobby had discovered that he cut Joe's talking time with him short for no reason. Julie didn't show up for work apparently. Now, why would Julie not show up for work? That job meant the world to her; all the years that Bobby could remember she never missed a day.

To him it was odd; he even made up his mind that if she didn't show up tomorrow, he would ask Joe to look into it for him. It was nice to have a friend in high places. But Bobby was too curious and didn't want to leave it be without asking around about Julie first. So the first chance he got at dinnertime to ask some questions, he took it.

Normally Bobby didn't like to talk to the other nurses, because of how rude they always were to him. But he was worried about someone he cared for deeply, and that was enough to make him look past all of that crap. As one of the other nurses brought him his food and meds in the room, he figured now was the time to ask. "So what happened to Julie?" Bobby asked.

"What do you mean?" The nurse responded.

"I mean, why did she not show up for work? Was she sick, or did something else happen that made her miss?"

"Bobby, I don't know what happened. All I know is that she didn't show up for work. There's not much more I can tell you." He found out as much as he was going to at that point, and for now, he decided he would leave it be. He finished his food, took his meds, said thank you to the nurse, and went about his nightly routine. He wasn't quite sure what to make of what all happened today, he found out that one of his childhood friends are trying to find him, and of course Julie not showing up for work was very odd to him as well. So instead of thinking about things and keeping himself up all night, he decided he would write down his feelings in his journal.

July 7, 1999, So today like all other days, I talked with Joe again. He told me that John Boy was basically on the hunt for me. At least that's what he thinks his brother may be up to now; it was insane. I didn't know what to think, but still even in my state of shock, I told Joe more of what happened at that horrid place. This time things were getting more gruesome. I didn't know how much more of the truth he could handle hearing, as his facial expressions told me all I needed to know. I knew that no matter how bad things were about to get, he was going to see it through till the end.

Also, another thing that is bothering me as I write is that Julie didn't show up for work. She didn't even bother to call in, which isn't like her at all. I know for a fact that working at this place that I'm locked up in is very important to her, and she would never miss like this. I asked a few of the other nurses, but I got nowhere with them. I am still not sure what to make of it all, but I do know if she doesn't show up tomorrow, I'll ask Joe to look into it for me.

It didn't take long for Bobby to fall asleep right after he put his journal away; that night he would have another encounter with the ghostly boy from his memories. Like the last time, he would be given another warning, and he would hear word for word what the boy had to say this time. "She's dead. He's killed her, and you will be next," the boy said to him, before vanishing into thin air yet again. Bobby jumped up quickly, but he's never fast enough to catch the boy, to try and talk with him.

Before he could think about what to do next, there was a knock on his door. It was Joe that much he was sure of. "Send him in, please."

The nurse that opened the door wasn't Julie like he was hoping it to be, "Where's Julie? Has she not come back to work yet?" Bobby asked.

"Don't worry about it, Bobby I'm sure she will show up." the nurse smiled as she let Joe into the room. Joe looked a little perplexed by the situation he walked into; it was different than the normal routine he was used to.

"Is something wrong, Bobby?" Joe asked.

"I think there is something wrong, badly wrong," Bobby responded.

"Is there anything I can do to help?" Joe asked.

Bobby looked at him with a smile. "Actually there is something you can do for me, Joe."

"Name it, and I will do what I can," said Joe.

Bobby motioned for him to take a seat. "You know that nurse that usually lets you in my room?"

"Yeah, what about her?"

"She hasn't been showing up to work."

"Why is that so weird?"

"She never misses work, ever. No one has heard from her or even knows where she's at. I find it odd that someone like her would never call in and inform her bosses that she would not be in for work."

"So you want me to check in on her?"

"If you don't mind, Joe." You could tell by the look on Joe's face that he found it an odd request, but he still agreed to check in on her for him as a favor for a friend. Bobby thanked him kindly.

"Are you up for continuing on from where you left off yesterday?" Joe asked.

"Of course I am," Bobby answered.

"Are you sure?" Joe replied.

"Yeah, I'm sure." And just like the day before, Bobby went on with his horrifying tale. Like I was saying before Tommy's brother had refused to help us for the second time, and he even threatened that we would be in deep shit if we told anyone.

"What do you think your brother would do if we did try to warn the others?" I asked.

"If I know my brother, he would probably try to have us locked up in one of the cabins," Tommy replied.

Chubs started laughing thinking everything was a joke like always. "You're funny, Tommy. That's a good one." Chubs said.

Tommy didn't think what Chubs said was funny in the least. "I'm not joking, Chubs. Try, and see what happens."

"That's bullshit!" Nick snarled.

"I know that, Nick. But there's nothing we can do about it right now." Tommy responded back to him.

"We can't count on Tommy's brother, we know that. But maybe we can still count on Candice or Steve for help later on." I insisted.

"We need help now, Bobby." Nick gasped. "Calm down, Nick," I said to him.

"Calm down? Calm down? You want me to calm down? I don't know if you remember but we have a killer that seems to always be one step ahead of us."

"You're right, Nick. I'm sorry." I replied.

"I'm sorry too, Bobby. I'm just so damn scared, one of us could be next, and there's nothing we can do to stop it either." Nick said.

I could see the fear in his eyes as he spoke. "I'm not buying that! We can stop him—damn it. All we need is a better plan of action." I said to him.

Tommy decided that he would cut me off right there. "Bobby, how can we stop him? Somehow, he knew what we were going to do with the siren, and he destroyed it." I didn't get a chance to respond to what Tommy had said, because unbeknown to us, Johnny and his gang were standing right behind us.

"What's up, losers?" Johnny said to us. It startled us only for a moment.

"What do you want, Johnny?" I asked.

"Well, how nice of you to ask me."

"What, do you want to play another game of basketball?" Tommy asked him.

"Nope, that's not what I want this time," he replied as he laughed at us. I looked around and happened to notice that Eddy wasn't with them this time, but I didn't have time to ask any questions.

"Well, what do you want?" Nick asked.

"I'll tell you what I want, nerds. I want him." he pointed straight at me as he spoke.

"What do you want me for?" I asked.

"I want you to fight me one on one, just you and me. Nobody else will get involved, I promise."

"And why should I fight you?" I asked him.

"Because you owe me for that sucker punch from a few days ago. Now I'm giving you an option: fight me fair and square or we force you into a fight. Your choice, nerd."

I thought about it only for a brief second. "You're on," I smirked.

Tommy, like always, pulled me to the side and asked me if I was crazy, and I explained to him that I knew what I was doing and that I had everything under control. And then I told him to look around, that Johnny only had Big Tony to watch his back if he jumped in, the three of them could take him on easily. Tommy reluctantly agreed that I was right, but he said if Johnny pulled anything funny that, he would jump in and stop the fight, right then and there. I also reluctantly agreed with him as he did with me. Tommy then turned his attention back on Johnny and said, "Okay, Johnny, you can fight my friend here, but if you'll try any funny business, I'll jump in and put a stop to it."

Johnny laughed. "I doubt that I will need to cheat to win

against your friend, Tommy, but sure whatever you say." I think Chubs and Nick were stunned to find out that I was willing to fight Johnny without help, they were both speechless. "Come on, nerd! I've been waiting to kick your ass!" Johnny shouted at me.

I didn't say anything back to him; all I did was smile. I could also feel the rage inside of me start to boil over again, and to me, that was a good sign of things to come. For once I knew I had the upper hand against Johnny, he had no idea that over the past winter, I had been taking karate and preparing endlessly for this one moment. "What are you laughing at? Oh, I see you're so scared that you have to fight me, and now you've lost your mind," he said as he laughed.

"This isn't going to be as easy as you think it is, Johnny," I replied back to him.

"Why's that? Unless you have some kind of nerd power, this is going to be simple for me."

"Well, let's find out, shall we? Come on, Johnny. You can even throw the first punch," I said, smiling at him. And he did so; he came charging right at me and swung at me. I sidestepped and tripped him, and he fell straight to the ground.

Man, was he pissed after that, he jumped back up on his feet, and he came at me again. That time I managed to grab his arm and flip him over my back and dumped him onto the ground yet again. "Are you done yet, Johnny?" I asked. He punched the ground with his fist out of rage and again came at me. This time I sidestepped him again, and instead of tripping him, I kicked him in the stomach, and he almost dropped to his knees from the pain. "I'm going to kill you nerd!" he screamed. I didn't give him a chance to come at me again. I spun around kicking him right in the face, sending him straight to the ground. I turned to look at my friends, and I could see the look of disbelief on their faces, they had no idea I could fight like that, and neither did Johnny, until now.

But I didn't knock Johnny out, I just busted his nose like I did last time, and that gave him a chance to call out to Big Tony. "Get him, Tony!" Johnny shouted.

That's when Tommy jumped in right beside me. "I don't think so, man!"

Chubs and Nick also jumped in. "We've got your back, Bobby!" They both said. It seemed as though we would all have to fight, but that wouldn't be the case. Coming from the woods just a little ways away from where we were standing were loud horrid screams of death; that is the only way to explain it. It even startled Johnny and Big Tony.

"That's Eddy! Come on, Tony, we have to help him!" and off they went into the woods.

I turned to my friends quickly. "We have to help them, come on."

But my friends were unwilling to help out Johnny and Big Tony. "Now why would we want to do that?" Nick asked.

"I know that they've treated us like shit, I realize that. But it's not right letting them face Albert alone. They will be killed." I explained. "Please." They lowered their heads and refused to help even me, because of their feelings toward the others. "Screw you, guys! I'll do it by myself!" I yelled. I didn't waste any time turning around and taking off after Johnny and Big Tony.

I didn't like any of them, but if I could help prevent another death, then that was what I was going to do. I could hear Johnny shouting for Eddy nearby. I didn't want to just run up on them out of fear of what they might do to me. So I took the smartest way possible, and I sneaked up on them as quietly as I could. I could now see Johnny and Tony off in the distance, and it looked like Eddy was with them as well, but something about Eddy just wasn't right.

As I was getting close to see what was exactly was going on, I felt someone's hand on my shoulder. I jumped and wanted to scream, but my mouth was covered as well, I was scared shitless, I thought for sure I was going to die right then and there.

"Calm down, Bobby. It's just us." Tommy said quietly. "So what's going on?"

"I don't know, I've been trying to get close enough to see, all I know is that something isn't right," I replied. "Are Chubs and Nick with you too?"

"They're right behind me, Bobby."

"Good, I'm glad you're all here. Now let's try and get closer." I led the way quietly with my friends following right behind me; it was good to know that my friends had joined in to help. I tell you now, sometimes I wished that I had listened to my friends and had just stayed put. For what we saw next was even more horrifying than all the other deaths we had witnessed. Eddy was standing right in front of Johnny and Big Tony, but they weren't alone.

Albert was standing behind Eddy, and he had him by the back of the neck, Eddy was doing his best to fight off Albert, but his grip was too strong, and Eddy couldn't break free. He yelled for his friends to help him, but Johnny and Big Tony were too struck with fear to even move. "Let him go!" I shouted as I jumped out from behind the tree. That snapped Johnny out of it, and he realized that if he didn't try and do something, his friend would die.

"Hey ner—I mean Bobby, right?" Johnny said.

"Yeah, that's my name. What do you want?" I said.

"Try and distract that man, and I will jump him from behind," he answered.

"That won't work." I said

"Why not?" he asked.

"Because we tried that last night when he killed Mark, and it didn't work. He has some kind of superhuman strength." I replied.

"Someone help me! Please!" Eddy cried out. None of us knew what to do. Albert was toying with us; he knew that he could kill Eddy anytime that he wanted. It was one big sadistic game to him, and Big Tony seemed as if he had enough of just watching.

"I'm going to save Eddy! You chickenshits can watch me do this by myself." Tony bolstered.

"No, don't do it! You don't know what you're dealing with!" I shouted at him. I tried my best to stop him, but it didn't do any good. Big Tony took off running right at Albert and punched him in the face. It didn't faze Albert none whatsoever. All he did was smile and show his razor-sharp teeth at Tony before grabbing him by the throat and lifting him up off the ground.

He let out this scream as his throat was being crushed by Albert's strong grip, and Albert started laughing his sadistic and vile laugh because now he had two teens in his grasp, and he wasn't letting them go until they were dead. Albert turned to look at us all standing there, as Tony was trying his hardest to gasp for air.

You could tell by how red Tony's face was getting that Albert was now squeezing his neck even harder than before; then blood could be seen running down his face from his eyes, even from his mouth. Albert turned his attention back to Tony and smiled at him again. "Fuck you!" was the last words that Tony would ever speak as Albert squeezed hard enough to break Tony's neck, and he threw his body to the ground like it was nothing more than trash.

"No!" Johnny screamed. "I'm going to kill you!" But Tommy and I grabbed him and held him back.

"Don't do it, Johnny," I said.

"He'll kill you too," Tommy explained.

"He still has Eddy!" Johnny screamed. "Let me go, you cowards!"

"Eddy is already dead! He will kill you too!" I shouted at him.

"Somebody help me!" Eddy begged. But it was too late for him. After Albert figured out that none of us was going to try anything else, he stuck his fingers in Eddy's mouth and proceeded to rip the top of his head off, and blood spewed everywhere, even on us. Johnny completely flipped the f—— out and managed to get away from us, but he didn't try to fight, he turned and took off running as fast as he could.

I can't say I blame him; he just watched as his last two friends were killed right in front of his eyes. Now as for us, we had no idea what we should have done. We stood there covered in blood and watched as Albert grabbed both bodies, threw them over his shoulder, and disappeared into the woods. We noticed after each kill that he usually doesn't kill again unless he has to or wants to; he will usually grab the bodies of his victims and walk off doing nothing more than that.

But on that day it seems like he decided to start killing even more, and now that posed as a bigger problem that we had to deal with because nightfall had even yet to come. That night we were afraid that he would come back, and he would kill again, and we needed to be ready now more than ever. And if we could find Johnny, maybe he would help us with the fight now. "There's nothing more we can do here, guys. Let's go." I said to my friends.

"Yeah, you're right, Bobby, let's get out of here." Tommy agreed. Chubs and Nick still didn't say much. I think it was the combination of watching two more people getting killed and the fact of me running off to help Johnny, and I'm sure while I was gone Tommy made them follow behind me. Things at that point were just becoming too much for any of us to bear, but we were just kids with so much on our shoulders with no one to help us and just trying to stay alive. We were back at the campgrounds before we knew it, and the first thing we did was look for Johnny.

I know that we fought over the years with him, but right now we needed all the help we could get. We had forgotten that we were all covered in blood at that point and walking around out in plain sight; we were stared at multiple times. Some of the other kids even ran away from us. But we hadn't really paid any attention to that fact; we just had one thing on our minds, and that was finding Johnny. We tried our best, but he was nowhere to be found.

I was worried that he might have tried to leave the woods on his own. And if that was the case, Johnny was already dead, and we had to accept the fact that we were on our own yet again. That's when I heard a few screams coming from the younger kids, and I thought for sure Albert was back already before nightfall, but they weren't screaming because of him; they were screaming because they were scared of us.

That's when it finally sunk in that we needed to make a run for our cabin and get ourselves cleaned up. If we get caught looking like we did, we would be the ones in trouble, and we didn't need that to happen. "We need to get back to the cabin," I shouted.

I think it started to sink in with Tommy as well when he noticed all the young kids were staring at us like we were monsters. "Shit! I didn't even pay attention to the fact that I was covered in blood." Tommy said in a panic.

"You're not the only one, look at my shirt," said Chubs.

"We're all covered in blood," Nick said, looking around at everyone watching. "Let's calm down, and get back to the cabin," I said. I motioned for them to follow me, and we took off running back to our cabin to get cleaned up. We got ourselves cleaned up and decided to grab a quick bite to eat and quickly made our way back to our cabin to plot our next move. It took us a couple of hours for any of us to finally speak, we paced back and forth inside, we had no idea what we should do at that point. "All right, listen up. There's only one thing we can do now." I said.

"And what's that, Bobby?" Chubs asked me.

"We have to arm ourselves and kill Albert before he kills everyone else, including us," I explained.

"What? Are you serious?" Nick jumped in and asked.

"Nick, that was a stupid question. Just look into his eyes, and you will know that he's not joking, and I agree with him. It's time that we stand our ground and kill that maniac." Tommy said to Nick.

"Where are we going to get weapons?" Nick asked.

That's when Chubs joined back in on the conversation. "I know where."

"Where, Chubs?" I asked happily. I was excited that we might have a plan that could actually work this time.

"There's a shed not too far from here. That's where they keep things like axes and chainsaws and those big-knife things. It's what they use to keep this area cleared off." he explained. I could see Tommy's face light up as well after hearing what Chubs had said to us.

"This is a bad idea. I think we should lock ourselves inside our cabin tonight and just try and rest." Nick suggested.

"If you don't want to come with us, then stay here, Nick. I won't force you. It's up to you." I said to him. "But we're going. Chubs, take us there. It's getting late. We need to prepare ourselves, for tonight we kill Albert for good." On that night Nick stayed behind, he no longer wanted anything to do with the goings-on at the camp. We got dressed in our black clothes again like the night before, and it was time for us to go on the hunt. I turned to look at Nick before leaving. "Lock the door and don't let anyone in except for us and take care not to go outside," I warned him. Nick wished us luck and shut the door and locked it behind us. "All right, Chubs. Lead the way."

"Follow me and don't wander off. I can feel someone watching us from afar." In my whole time knowing Chubs over the years I've never seen him so serious. That to me was a warning that I was going to take seriously, and Tommy did the same. In a matter of minutes, we happened upon an old, beat-down shed.

"And there you have it." Chubs pointed. "We're here, all we should need is right in there."

"Well, what are we waiting for?" Tommy asked.

"Just chill, Tommy. We need to take this slowly. We don't know who could be in there." I said to him.

"Okay, okay, Bobby. Have it your way," he said before turning and kicking the door in quickly. I shot him a look from hell. "What? We don't have time to be sneaky," he said with a smile on his face as he walked on inside the shed.

"Let's just get what we need and go, you jackass," I said jokingly as I followed him inside. We were looking things over, and I picked out my weapon of choice, a machete. It suited me well.

Tommy grabbed the long-handled ax, "All right, I can do some damage with this bad boy."

"Hey, Chubs. You need to get in here and pick out something for yourself."

Chubs came dashing into the shed. "Hide and hide quickly!" he shouted hysterically. Before I even got a chance to ask why Chubs was already hiding under a work table that was in the shed. He was trying to get us to hurry up and hide under the table with him. Tommy didn't waste any time in hiding under the table with him. I was too confused, and I wanted to know why I had to hide so quickly.

So I took a peek out the door, and it was Albert walking towards the shed. This must be the place he keeps his tools of the trade, and if that's the case, we were dead, or so I thought. I quickly hid under the work table as well, but I had a feeling we were dead meat regardless. I mean we did kick the door open to the shed, and we took some of his blades that he liked to kill people with, and I'm sure he would notice that if nothing else.

We couldn't see a damn thing, but we could hear him walk inside quickly. I could hear him looking for whoever trespassed into his domain; he started throwing things around, demolishing everything in his path until he found who he was looking for, and that was us. He even took one of his blades and shoved it through the top of the table; the blade ripped right through the side of my pants, barely missing my leg. I'm not sure how we did it, but not a single one of us screamed out. I was almost certain that he was about to look underneath the table; it was the one place he had yet to look for us.

But right as he was about to look, there was some sound of commotion that came from outside. It sounded like gunfire, and some men and women were screaming about something. It wasn't any of the counselors or teens from our campgrounds, that much I was sure of. It must have been a different group of people throwing a party out in the woods. I hate to say it, but it turned out to be our lucky break because instead of trying to find us, he went after them.

"He's gone, now let's get the hell out of here." Chubs demanded. And the three of us got out of there as fast as we could and made our way back to the campgrounds. Once we got to a certain spot so we could see every angle perfectly, we made that our waiting point. I have to admit that on two occasions, I wanted to give up and run back to our cabin where Nick had locked himself in safely.

I mean fear was setting in, and the fact that Albert almost caught us didn't help, and the fact that we had to sit there and listen to screams and gunfire coming from the darkness over and over again until all was silent, scared the shit out of me. I knew what was happening, and so did my friends that were sitting there with me. Albert was out there killing whoever was throwing the party in the woods.

And what did we do about it? Nothing! Not a damn thing! We ran back to the campgrounds and lay in wait for Albert to return so we could ambush him, and as bad as we hated it, there was nothing we could do for the others. It still eats me up that people died, and we did nothing to stop it, nothing to warn them of the hell that was on the way.

"I don't know what happened, or the hell you went through. But it sounds to me like you and your friends did the only thing you could do." Joe said to him.

"I don't know about that Joe. Until this day, I still don't know. What if we could have done more? But I will never know the answer to that, will I?"

"No, Bobby. I guess you will never know the answer to that. But at least you're making sure it will never happen again," Joe said in return.

"We'll see, Joe. We'll see." So again, just like the night before we sat there in silence, waiting for any sign of Albert, or anything that might seem out of the ordinary. It was possible that since he had already killed that night, he might not show up again until tomorrow. But I would be proven wrong as Albert soon made his presence felt yet again. There were two younger teens screaming to the top of their lungs as it seemed like they were running away from something or someone.

"That's our sign boys. Let's get that bastard!" Tommy shouted as he took off running that way. Chubs and I gave chase and yelling for him to wait for us to catch up to him, but he was acting like a badass with that ax in his hands and refused to wait up for us. Once we caught up to Tommy, I chewed his ass.

"What in the hell was that all about, Tommy?" I yelled. "You said you would wait for us? What is your deal?" Tommy acted like he didn't hear a word I said. "Are you listening to me?"

He walked straight past me, "Hey, Chubs."

"What, Tommy?" Chubs asked.

"That night when all hell broke loose and you were on watch duty by yourself, you said something about young kids attacking you that night, right?"

"Yeah, why do you ask me about that now?" Chubs replied.

I didn't think things could get any worse, but it did. "I see what you're saying, Tommy," I said.

"What? What am I missing here?" Chubs just couldn't figure it out on his own.

"We got set up, man. That's what." Tommy said angrily.

261

"What are you talking about?" Chubs was completely clueless. "Think about it, Chubs. We walked into a trap." I explained. Chubs didn't get a chance to make another response, because we were interrupted by the sound of laughter coming from behind us. We turned around slowly, and standing there were five young teens, probably around our age or younger. We tried to talk to them, to warn them they needed to run away, that it was too dangerous out here, but something didn't seem right. They were dressed in old, ripped clothing, and their hair was the same as Albert's. Come to think of it, they looked exactly like Albert. "Keep your guard up," I warned my friends.

Tommy chuckled at me and said, "They're just children. What are they going to do? They're just scared like us, man."

They pointed and started laughing at us, and the one in front who seemed to be the leader said, "Die." And before we could even make a move, they came running at us carrying small blades that they started stabbing us with. I didn't want to hurt them, but if I didn't want to die there, I had to fight back. So I took a swing at one of them with my machete and cut off one of their heads. It was like something out of a horror movie, stuff like that never happened in real life, but it was all real whether I wanted to admit it or not. But I noticed the blood coming from the one I killed was different; the blood wasn't a flow of crimson red like you would expect. It was clumpy, almost as if it wasn't blood at all.

Then it dawned upon me that these kids were already dead, don't ask me how they just were. "Fight back," I shouted. "They're already dead. Trust me." I started swinging at them left and right, and so did Tommy and Chubs. We took out at least three of them all together before the last two took off running away.

"Those were the ones I was telling you guys about." Chubs said hysterically.

"Who cares about them right now? Are you guys all right?" I asked.

"I'm all right, just a few cuts on me is all. And you, Chubs?"

"I'm fine, just a few small wounds for me. Are you okay, Bobby?"

I looked myself over, and I only had one decent-sized stab wound, but I would live. "All good here," I answered. I started to ask myself, What in the world was that all about? Then it hit me. Albert must have known that we were in the shed, so he must have sent them to slow us down, or maybe even kill us. Just as I was about to tell the others what was going on, screams came from the cabin that was a little ways away from us. "Come on, we have to go check it out." And off we ran toward the cabin, the door was locked, and we did our best to get inside.

I could hear someone crying out for help from within. We kept ramming the door with our shoulders, but it still wouldn't budge. Tommy would even get running starts and kick the door as hard as he could, but still nothing. Then everything just went silent, and the door came unlocked and opened on its own. We slowly made our way inside the cabin hoping that it was just some kids goofing off, but it wasn't a prank; it wasn't kids having fun or goofing off. There was blood all over the walls and on the floor; even the beds were soaked with blood. It wasn't a pleasant sight whatsoever; it looked as though Albert had come and gone leaving a path of death once again.

There was nothing we could do now except leave the cabin as it is and hopes that one of the counselors will find it like it is now and do something about it. It was a long shot, but there clearly wasn't any other way to go about it. In the end, we were unable to stop Albert yet again. Once we got back to our cabin, we knocked on the door and yelled for Nick to let us in. He was hesitant at first, but once he realized it was truly us, he was more than happy to let us back inside. I would say that the look on our faces told how things went, but Nick wasn't exactly the brightest tool in the shed if you know what I mean.

"How did it go? I see you have blood on your shirts. Did you kill him? Is it finally over?" I didn't want to answer him. I just wanted to get cleaned up and take care of my wounds and rest. Besides, I didn't have the heart to tell him that we failed again and more people have died.

So I just explained everything in one brief sentence, "We were attacked by a bunch of knife-wielding punk kids, and Albert killed again, this time just a few cabins down from us. That's all I'm saying." I grabbed some of the last clean clothes I had left and was making my way towards the door.

"Where in the hell do you think you're going?" Tommy asked.

"Look, Tommy. I'm tired of smelling like blood. It's been almost five damn days since I've had a shower because I have been too scared to do so. I'm going to get myself cleaned up for real this time, so you guys can come with or stay here. I don't care." I answered. Then I turned and walked out the door. I didn't give a damn at that point if Albert came after me or not. I was tired of living in fear of him.

"Wait up, Bobby!" I heard someone shout. I turned, and my friends were running up behind me.

"I guess you guys feel the same way as I do? Let's face it, guys, we stink." I said to them.

We made our way inside the shower building, "Remember the rules, don't try and sneak a peek at my package. It's for the ladies only," Tommy joked.

I laughed a little and told him to shut the hell up and take his damn shower, and yeah, we jumped into the shower stalls quickly and jumped back out just as fast. The four of us needed a shower pretty badly, but we weren't stupid enough to stay in there too long. Once done I decided I was tired and ready for some rest, and my friends all agreed that they felt the same way. When we finally made it back, I noticed that our cabin door was wide open. "Look, the door is wide open," I said nervously.

"Great, now someone broke into the cabin, can we ever catch a break?" said Tommy.

"You two should be quiet. It could be you know who," Chubs said to us.

"Well, if it is, I'm not going in there. You three have the weapons." Nick sighed.

"Really, Nick? Do we look stupid enough to walk around with those things in plain sight?" I asked him.

"Well, what in the hell are we going to do now?" Nick asked. That stupid idiot shouted as loud as he could without even thinking. I thought for sure Albert was going to come running out of the cabin at us, or those damn demon children of his.

That's when we heard a voice scream out to us. "Get your asses in here right now!" That surprised the hell out of us to hear Steve screaming at us from inside our cabin. We didn't say a word to one another; the only thing we did was get our asses inside as fast as we could. That was scary for me because Steve would only scream at us like that when Mark was around, but he's dead now, so I wondered what was going to happen once we were inside. "Care to explain this?" He pointed to all of the bloody clothes that we had pilled up on the floor.

"We've already told you, Steve," Tommy answered.

"Then explain to me why you have that ax covered in blood

and those two machetes there beside your clothing?"

"I will tell you why," I said to him.

"Go on, let's hear what you have to say before I report you guys to the authorities." Now those words confused me; how could he report us to the authorities way out here in the middle of nowhere?

"How can you possibly do that, Steve?" Chubs asked.

"We do have a broadcast radio out here, you fools," he answered. If we would have known that, we could have prevented all the deaths that took place already. Damn Tommy's brother to hell.

"Now explain to me what all of this is about, and do it now," Steve demanded again.

"We tried to kill Albert by ourselves, only we failed over and over again. And because of our failure to do so more people have died. That's why our clothes are covered in blood." I shouted at him.

"Nobody would listen to us or even try and help us, so we did what we thought was best," I added.

"How many have died! I want names as well—tell me damn it!"

"There was a few the first night that we hiked here, then a few more tonight, those are the ones we don't know the names of, because we never got the chance to hang out with them." I replied.

"And the ones you did know?"

"Eddy, Spike, Big Tony Parks, Mark. And if not for us, Candice would have been killed also. Oh, and few people that were partying out in the woods. If Johnny is still alive, find him. He will tell you about his friends being killed if he's not already dead by now. And Candice can tell you about Mark. She witnessed the whole thing," I explained. A scream echoed throughout the whole building that completely scared both Bobby and Joe; on instinct, they both bolted out of the room and ran down the hall to where the screaming was coming from. At the end of the hall in the janitor's storage room was the mangled body of Julie.

# 12

# The End Of Everything Is Near

That evening everyone was silent, especially Bobby. A good nurse and even a better human being was found murdered; it was heartbreaking. Bobby was more hurt more than anyone else, this was someone he could trust, and he cared for her with all of his heart; he was just always too scared to tell her how he felt. Now she will never know. He felt lost now, and he was unsure of how he would go on, his past was catching up to him, and the people he cared for were being murdered around him yet again. Because of Julie's death, Joe was able to stay just a while longer. "Bobby, are you all right?" he asked.

"I don't know, Joe. I just don't know anymore. Talking about all of this, trying to help you out, finding out about John Boy—I think all of this brought back some old demons, and that got Julie killed, and so did me having feelings for her." Bobby answered.

"It's not your fault, I promise you that I will find out who did this, and I will make them pay for you, Bobby."

"I know who did this, and here soon, so will you."

"Then why don't you just tell me?"

"That's all I can say, for now, Joe. Be here tomorrow bright and early we have work to do. I won't let him get away with this any longer."

"I will, Bobby. I promise, take care of yourself. I have to go now and report this to the higher-ups." Joe did his best to sneak out the door and out of the asylum before any of the other cops recognized him. Bobby didn't talk to anyone, nor did he eat or take his meds, he was still hurting now more than ever, and he was pissed off at himself and at the demon he knew had killed Julie. This night wasn't like all the others. It took Bobby hours before he would even be able to sit down and write in his journal.

July 8, 1999; I can't believe what has happened. Julie wasn't late, she's dead! She was found dead in the janitor's storage room. I could hear the other nurses and doctors asking, "Why would someone do this to her?" I knew the answer to that question. It was Albert! It had to be him; who else could kill someone that I cared about? Who else would be so cold and soulless? I was sure that he would never find me here, but somehow he has.

Or maybe he has been watching me the whole time waiting for his moment to kill me off, and this was his warning for me. I don't know what to think anymore. Right now I want to give up and find another place to hide, but if I do, he will just kill again and again and again until he gets to me. I can't let that happen, I just hope finishing my tale will help Joe find that answer, and we can finally kill that bastard! That reminds me that I need to warn him that he needs to watch his back or he could end up being next.

And if John Boy is really out there, I hope that he's safe and watching his own back, for I don't know when Albert may strike again. But I do know someone who might, if I can stay awake tonight, maybe I can catch him at the right time and have a word with the ghostly figure that has haunted me for almost my whole childhood. Just maybe, he will have the answers I seek. That night Bobby had a plan of action, he was unsure if this would work though, he could end up falling asleep, or the nurses could catch him not sleeping, which would be bad for him, and that's something he didn't want to happen.

And on top of that, who knew if the young boy would even show himself? And if he did, would he even talk to, Bobby? These were all things that he was unsure of, but still, yet he had to try. So, he got into bed and pulled the covers over him and pretended to sleep; he kept a close eye out for any kind of movement in his room. And yet there was nothing, he waited for hours, but there was no sign of the young boy. He almost fell asleep several times, but somehow he fought his need for sleep back.

When all seemed pointless to him, and the rays of light were shining through in his room letting him know morning was close, the boy finally appeared at the foot of his bed. Bobby jumped up quickly but made sure he didn't get out of his bed. He waited for the boy to speak before he would say a word. And speak the boy did of another ominous warning. "He's coming for you and more people will die. Be ready or you will die too." the boy said with an eerie voice.

"Who, who is after me?" Bobby asked. "And who killed Julie?"

"It's not who you think." was the last words the boy would speak before vanishing yet again. Bobby jumped out of bed and threw his blankets across the room in a fit of rage; he yelled and screamed and cursed out loud. He was letting out all the frustrations that were boiling over inside of him; the nurses at this point would usually come running in and sedate him.

However, this time they understood the pain that he felt; most of them who knew he was feeling the same as he was. Once Bobby had gained back his senses, he realized that Joe had yet to come walking through his door. He paced back and forth in his room, but still, there was no sign of, Joe. He yelled for one of the nurses. "Has that man that was here to see me yesterday came by at all this morning?" Bobby asked.

"No, you have yet to have any visitors as far as I know." That wasn't the response he was hoping for. Bobby was now worried for the safety of his friend, but there wasn't anything he could do being behind locked doors. He wanted to tell the nurses to call the police; however, if he did that, he would blow Joe's cover, and that could get him in deep trouble, and Bobby didn't want that to happen either. He was now stuck with a difficult choice, wait a while longer for him to show, or call the police and blow Joe's cover in the process.

Bobby didn't know what to do, and just as he was about to call out to a nurse, the door unlocked, and Joe came walking into the room. "It's about damn time you showed up!"

Joe was surprised at Bobby's words, but in a way he understood. "Calm yourself, Bobby. Remember, I was looking into what happened to Nurse Julie." Joe explained to him.

"Sorry, Joe. I'm just worried is all."

"I know, Bobby. But I can take care of myself."

"Yeah, I guess so. So did you find anything out?"

"No, but I will Bobby, but for now we need to get started as quickly as possible."

"I understand, Joe. No rest for the weary. I will start where I left off."

If I remember correctly, Steve was in our cabin accusing us of doing those horrible things; it didn't help that our clothes were on the floor covered in blood, beside our weapons that we were going to try and kill Albert with. I thought for sure that once I explained to him what had really happened, he would back off and would be willing to help us. Instead, he demanded that we stay inside our cabin because he was going to go and call the authorities. "We will stay right here, Steve. Go ahead and try, but you will be right back here having no choice but to help us," I said.

"And why is that?" Steve asked.

"Because Jerry wants to keep everything covered up. He's not going to let you call anybody, Steve. How many times do we have to tell you this?" I answered.

"We'll see about that. The four of you stay put! You got that?"

"We're not going anywhere, Steve. This is the only way to make you believe us; then so be it," I said.

Steve turned and left out the door as quickly as possible. "Do you think this is a good idea?" Tommy asked.

"Do we have a choice, Tommy?" I replied.

"Damn! Right now we don't have any choices," said Tommy.

"What do you think will happen?" Chubs interrupted.

"How in the hell would we know the answer to that?" Tommy replied.

"If I had to take a guess, Steve will be back soon," Nick butted in and added. That's when I figured we had to take a different approach as bad as I hated to.

"We need to have Steve talk with Candice when he gets back, I know that she's in bad shape and all, but we don't have a choice," I explained to them.

"Then what do we do?" Nick asked.

"We sit and wait, that's all we can do," I answered. We didn't talk much, we felt as though we were under house arrest.

It was now getting later into the evening, and Steve had yet to return, "Do you think Steve was able to make the call?" Nick asked out loud to anyone that would listen to him.

"It's possible but highly unlikely. Knowing my brother he's probably threatened him to keep his mouth shut or else," Tommy replied.

"No use thinking about it; we knew it would happen," I said. Steve all of a sudden came walking through the door, and believe me, he was pissed, he didn't look at us, he just paced back and forth muttering to himself.

"What's wrong, Steve?" I asked.

"Tell us, Steve. What's going on? Did my brother let you make that call?" Tommy jumped in and asked.

"Both of you shut up!" he demanded. "I'm trying to think damn it." Not even he knew what to do. I could tell by the look on his face just how bad the situation was for him.

"He didn't let you, did he?" Tommy asked.

"I said to shut the hell up!" he fired back.

"Steve, you might as well tell us what is going on," I said to him.

He paced back and forth for a few more minutes without saying a word; then all of sudden he stopped and turned to face us. "Your brother didn't let me make the call; he claimed it was all one big prank," Steve explained to us.

"What do you think, though, man?" Tommy asked.

"Yeah, Steve. Will you finally listen to us for once?" Chubs said to.

"Look, I don't know what to think. I don't even know what to do if what the four of you are telling me is true, then we need to get everyone out of here. But how can I be sure?" Steve was confused and conflicted.

"We should talk to Candice. She can tell you what she

witnessed that night," I said to him. "What do you say?"

Steve gave me a look like he was thinking hard whether or not he would go through with what I suggested or not. "I will go speak with Candice. You four stay here. It's for the best until I get things sorted out. Also, pack your bags. If she agrees with your story, then I'm getting everyone out of here," he explained to us. Moments later he was gone again.

"You heard the man—pack your bags!" Nick shouted happily. I wasn't sure if this was such a great idea. I was sure that Tommy's brother wasn't going to let any of us leave without a fight, and there was also Albert to deal with as well. If he finds us trying to leave, he may decide to go ahead and kill us all.

"Hey, Bobby?" Chubs shouted. I was in a daze and didn't realize he was talking to me. "Hey, Bobby?!" he shouted again.

I shook my head to focus again, "What?"

"Pack your bags," he said. Nick and Chubs were in a major hurry to get their bags packed.

Tommy and I didn't even bother to try and pack ours. "This is a bad idea, and everyone in this room knows it," said, Tommy.

"Tommy's right, even if we are able to leave the campgrounds, Albert will make sure we never leave the woods alive. If we want out of here, someone has to deal with him first," I tried to explain.

But apparently, Chubs and Nick had selective hearing and completely ignored everything that I had just said, "We're all packed and ready to go." Nick and Chubs shouted.

"Why haven't you two packed your bags yet?" Chubs looked at Tommy and me and asked.

"Have you not heard a damn word Bobby just said?" Tommy said to them.

"We're not packing our bags. It's pointless, we will never be able to leave," I also told them.

"Wait for a second, do you hear that?" Nick asked.

"I didn't hear anything," said Chubs.

"Just shut up and listen, Chubs," Tommy hissed. There was some kind of commotion going on outside. It sounded like someone was fighting. If I had to take a guess, it was Steve and Tommy's brother going at it. I even heard a female voice screaming, and that had to of been Candice. I mean who else could it have been, right? "Let's go see what's going on."

Hell, at that point it didn't really matter if we went outside and watched or not. Who was going to stop us with all that was going on? "Sure, after you," I said to him. I didn't move until my friends were out the door. They would have run me over if I would have gotten in the way. Even if there is a killer on the loose, it wouldn't stop them from letting the excitement of things get to them. When I made my way out, I could see Tommy's brother, Jerry, yelling at Steve, and Candice was right in the middle of them, trying to calm them down with all the other counselors and kids watching.

Steve was demanding that he be able to use the broadcast radio, while Tommy's brother refused to hear any of it. He told Steve that he bought into our bullshit, and he was about to make a fool of himself in front of everyone. And Steve told him if that was the case, then why was it such a big deal for him to make one emergency call?

Even Candice stepped in to explain everything that she witnessed that night, and that still didn't change his mind. Steve then demanded that if he wasn't going to let him use the radio, then he and Candice would lead everyone out of the woods and back to where it would be safe. Jerry didn't like that idea, and he refused, telling Steve there was no way in hell he would let that happen. That was until Tommy stepped in and tried to change his brother's mind.

"Listen to them! They're only trying to help, or do you want to see us all killed? Man, I'm your brother. Do you want to see me killed? Because that's at will happen if something isn't done!" Tommy shouted at him.

"Shut up, Tommy!" Jerry shouted back at him.

"Then do something about this. You know you can do so easily," Tommy retorted.

"Fine, you want me to do something about it, little brother? Then how's this, whoever wants to leave, then follow Steve and Candice out of here! That goes for any of you kids and counselors alike! It's your choice: stay and enjoy this beautiful campsite or make a fool of yourselves and follow those two out of here!"

"That's the smartest thing you've done since you got here," Steve said to him.

That wasn't going to work, even if we tried to leave, it wouldn't do us any good, "Leaving won't do us any good! Albert will find a way to stop us. We would be better off using the radio."

Jerry walked up to me and said, "You've caused enough trouble, so shut your damn mouth! You have a chance to leave, take it or leave it. I've had it up to here with this whole Albert-the-killer bullshit." He pushed me to the side, almost knocking me to the ground, and he walked off back into the counselors' cabin.

"Everyone, listen up! You can choose to follow us, or you can stay here! We won't force anyone to follow us against their will. If you want to leave, you have five minutes to get packed and get back here to this very spot! Starting now!" Steve shouted.

"You heard the man, get a move on!" Candice shouted out to us all.

Chubs and Nick took off running back to our cabin to get their bags, while Tommy and myself just stayed put. "What are you going to do, Bobby?" Tommy asked.

I looked at him and answered the best I could, "I'm going to go with them."

"Why? It doesn't make any sense to go. You said it yourself."

"Someone has to go along and try to talk them out of it, and besides, they don't know what to expect out there—we do. So I feel like I need to go," I answered. "And besides, what are you going to do, Tommy?"

"I'm going to stay with my brother. Maybe I can get him to listen to me with no one else around. He may be an ass right now, but he's still my brother, and I know that he's a good guy."

"Good luck, Tommy."

"Same to you, Bobby." We shook hands and Tommy turned to follow his brother on the inside, as Nick and Chubs ran up with their bags.

"Where's he going?" Nick asked.

"He's decided to stay with his brother and try to talk some sense into him."

"We don't have time to worry about that. Steve and Candice are getting ready to leave," Chubs explained as he walked up. There were only about three more counselors and half the other kids that showed up to leave. I expected as much to be honest. It was a matter of time before shit would hit the fan, and all of this would take place.

"Is everyone ready to get out of here?" Steve asked. "All right, let's go! And try not fall behind. Trust me, it won't end well for you if you do." And Steve led the front, while Candice brought up the rear. It was clear that neither one of them was going to leave any of us behind, as Mark would have. It was already getting late, but we still had a few hours of daylight left still yet. And Steve moved the group as fast and as hard as he could; however, I noticed that we weren't taking the same way out as we did getting here.

"Steve, why are we taking a different way out?" I asked loudly so he could hear me.

"We're taking a shortcut that will save us at least five hours on our time."

"Why didn't we take that way here on the first day?" I asked.

"Because, Mark, wanted to take the long way so he could tell his stupid, scary story!" he replied.

"Did you know that the story was real?" I said to him.

"I heard the warnings like he did, as we all did. I just thought it was crazy talk," he answered. "Now I know the truth, I wish I would have done something sooner. I'm sorry, everyone."

"If you blame him, you will have to blame me as well! I thought it to be a wildly made-up story, an urban legend. I'm sorry too," Candice interrupted.

"You do know he will never let us leave, right?" I said to them.

"I don't think that psycho will stop us," Steve said.

"And why's that?" I asked.

"Because we have this." he said and then he pulled out a gun and showed it to me, "Now focus more on walking instead of talking."

I couldn't believe that he had a gun, but would that even work on Albert? I asked myself. Hell, would anything work on him? Could he even be killed? Could you even kill the devil himself? Because I really did view Albert as the devil. "You worry too much, Bobby. We're getting out of here—be happy." Nick said to me.

"Don't get your hopes up, Nick. We're not out of the woods

yet," I told him.

"Don't worry, if something happens, I have a backup plan," Chubs reassured us. "And what's that Chubs?" I asked.

That's when Candice yelled at us, "Stop talking and focus on walking like he said, We're not stopping anytime soon, so save your energy!" After what Candice had been through, she was all business, and she meant what she said, and it was best not to upset her any further than she already was at that point. "That goes for anyone else as well. Shut up and walk!"

I decided that I would keep quiet and watch my surroundings for anything out of the ordinary. Which meant if something odd was going on, then Albert was close by, and that would be danger for the whole group. Nothing seemed out of the ordinary just yet, but there was a faint smell of smoke in the air. There could have been a fire farther away, so I just shrugged it off and kept following the group not saying a word. That is until the smell got stronger, and you could start to see the smoke too. "Don't stop for anything. We have to keep going no matter what!" It was obvious that nothing was going to keep Steve from getting us out of those woods.

"Steve! We need to turn back. This isn't good!" I yelled.

"No, we have to press on!" Steve demanded. Steve and Candice did exactly that: they pushed the group farther ahead. The smoke started to get thicker and thicker almost to the point I could barely see anything in front of me of me at all.

"Steve, we need to turn back right now!" I shouted again.

"We can make it through. We just have to keep going!" he shouted back.

"Look, Steve, we can barely see anything! Can you even see the group behind you?" I replied. There wasn't much time for him to answer before screams started coming from within the group.

I could also see a shadowy figure stalking us from within the smoke, and that was what was causing the screams. "It's Albert! He's here." I yelled so Steve could hear me. I could hear the cries for help as Albert would run through the group. I couldn't see exactly what he was doing, but I knew he was picking us off one at a time.

"Fall back, now! Candice, get everyone out of the smoke!" Steve ordered.

"Everyone, hurry up and go back the way you came! Follow the sound of my voice and I will lead you out!" Candice screamed. I thought for sure we were all dead, but I could hear Candice screaming, and I followed those screams, and so did Nick and Chubs and only about half the group did as well.

"Where is the rest?!" Steve shouted. You could still hear screams of terror coming from the rest out of the smoke. "I'm going back in there. Someone has to save them!"

I grabbed him by the arm. "You can't save them! They're already dead!" I said, "Help me out here you guys."

Chubs and Nick ran up and grabbed a hold of Steve to help me try and stop him. I could hear Candice demanding that everyone get as far away from the smoke as possible but not to run off away from what was left of the group. Once she noticed us struggling with Steve, she ran over to help. "Steve! Listen to them, they're just trying to help! We can't save them! If we try, then we will die too!" she said to him. She then told us to let go of him. "Steve, I can't stop you from going back in there, but I won't go with you. I'm sorry, but they're dead, Steve. I need you to help me get the ones that lived back to camp, please."

Just as it seemed Steve was finally going to listen to reason and help Candice lead us back out, the unthinkable happened. Albert swung his ax out of the smoke, and straight into the top of Candice's head, blood and pieces of her brain splattered on us, including Steve. "No! Candice!" he screamed. He reached out and tried his best to grab her arm, but Albert was quicker and pulled her body into the thick smoke, with the ax that was lodged in her head. "Bastard!" he screamed and then dropped to his knee. It was something horrible to see indeed; however, we didn't have time to feel fear. We didn't have time to cry over what happened to Candice either.

I know it sounded heartless, but if Steve didn't pull it together now and lead us all back, the rest of us would die as well. "Steve, pull it together! Do you think Candice would want us to die with her?" I asked. He didn't say anything at all. He just stayed on his knees crying into his hands. Steve was of no use to anybody now, and it was up to me to lead us back to camp. I was glad that my good memory would finally be of some use. But still yet Chubs and Nick were worried, and so were the others.

"Is Steve going to get up and lead the way back?" Nick asked.

"Can't you see that Steve is no longer of use." Chubs jumped in and said.

"Then what are we going to do?" Nick asked scared out of his mind.

"I don't know, why don't you ask him?" Chubs replied. Nick wasn't happy with Chubs's response, and he pushed him and told him to shut the hell up. Chubs pushed Nick back and told him to stop acting like a damn baby. I jumped in between them and demanded that they both knock their shit off if they wanted to live through this. "Well, what in the hell do you suggest, Bobby?"

"I will lead us back to the campgrounds. You know how my memory is, Chubs. So, everyone, listen up! I know the way back to the campgrounds, follow me, and make it fast! If you don't, you will be killed," I said. "Chubs, Nick. You will both just have to trust me," I said to them. I then put my hand on Steve's shoulder and told him that I was sorry about Candice and to be safe. "Let's go! Let's go! Let's go!" I yelled, then ran ahead, and motioned for them to all follow me as fast as they could. I ran as fast as I could back toward the campgrounds, or in the way, I thought the campground was, but I wasn't going to tell anyone else that.

Hell, I was so scared that Albert would catch up to us that I never looked back to check on anyone, not even my friends. I know it wasn't right, but if they couldn't keep up, then they would be left behind, that was all there was to it. After running for hours without stopping, the campgrounds was straight in front of me. I stopped and motioned for the group to run on ahead. "Go! Go! Go! Safety is just up ahead!" Yeah, I lied to them and told them the campgrounds are safe, and yet they're not.

Albert will come back to the campgrounds to kill again tonight. What was left of the group of kids came running out of the woods and into the campgrounds screaming to the top of their lungs, and some were crying their eyes out. The counselors that stayed behind came running out to tend to us and find out what had happened. Most of the kids were in too much shock to talk a single word, and the kids that did talk told them about an ax-wielding monster that came running through smoke and was killing everyone. They came around to ask me and my friends what happened as well.

"I'll tell you what happened, Albert damn near killed the entire group." Chubs shouted at them. Nick fell to his knees and started crying, so he couldn't give them a straight answer either.

"Albert set a trap for us. He set part of the woods on fire. The smoke got so thick that you couldn't see who was even in front of you, and that's when he ambushed us! What you see is what's left of us. Candice is dead too." I explained. They didn't believe me at first, which wasn't much of a surprise. They accused my friends and me of playing another prank. They were either afraid of Tommy's brother or too damn stupid for their own good. To this day I still don't know which it was. I did everything I could to convince them of the truth, but they didn't want to hear it, that is until Steve walked out of the woods covered in blood like us.

"It's the truth, over half the group is dead, and so is Candice," Steve told them. He looked like a zombie, his will to live was gone, and before he walked off, he said something that stuck with me for a long time. "Stay, go, it doesn't matter. We're all going to die here because you can't kill the devil."

As he walked off, Tommy came running up, "What happened?"

I told him every little detail of what happened as we tried to make our escape out of the woods. He couldn't believe that over half the group, including Candice, were dead. I could tell that he wanted to break down and cry, but he did like me and held it all inside and channeled it into anger. He turned to walk away. "Where are you going, Tommy?" I asked.

"Just follow me!" Tommy hissed.

Chubs was already walking behind Tommy. And Nick, well, he was in no shape to go anywhere. The shock of watching more people die and the realization that there was no way out of the woods without Albert killing us was just too much for him to take, and he finally broke down. I had no choice but to leave him there on the ground and walk away; it was time we took the fight straight to Tommy's brother. I had a feeling we were about to use the broadcast radio whether Tommy's brother liked it or not. We walked inside the building with Tommy still leading the way.

"What are you going to do?" I asked him.

"Just shut up and trust me on this," he demanded. I didn't ask another question I followed him straight to his brother's office door. He knocked on the door at first demanding that his brother let him inside. When he didn't get an answer, Tommy got upset and started kicking on the door violently until the door gave way, and in the room, he went.

"Are you crazy?" Jerry shouted.

"No, brother. This is crazy!" Tommy shouted, and then he punched his brother right in the face sending him down to the floor. His brother was knocked out cold, "We need to tie him up."

"Are crazy, Tommy? You've already knocked his ass out. Why should we tie him up?" I asked.

"Yeah, Tommy. Let's just make the call and get out of here." Chubs added.

"Just help me tie him up," said Tommy.

"Why?" I asked.

"Think about it, you two. When he wakes up, he will make sure we're locked in our cabin. Then what will we do when Albert comes back?"

"You've got a point, Tommy. Let's help him tie up his brother, Chubs." Yes, I know, it was crazy what we were about to do, but it wasn't like we had a choice, and who was going to really stop us? So we lifted his brother back into his chair, and we found some rope, and we tied him to his chair, and then we gagged him so he couldn't yell for help.

"Look for the radio!" Tommy ordered. I searched the room in every little area there was to search, and I found nothing.

"Tommy, I can't find the radio anywhere. How about you,

Chubs?"

"Nothing on my end, Bobby. Hey, Tommy, have you found anything?" Tommy searched and searched and searched.

"I can't find anything either," he replied.

"He must have hidden it, Tommy. Can you think of where he would hide things in here if he could?" I asked. I could see the wheels turning by the look on his face, and right then I knew that he had figured it out.

Tommy walked around the room running his hands over the walls; then he stopped and shouted, "I think I've found something!" Chubs and I went quickly over to him.

"I don't see anything," I said.

Chubs looked at the wall, "Found what?"

Tommy pointed to a switch that was oddly placed on the wall. "Watch and be amazed," he said. He flipped the switch, and part of the wall slid open, revealing a small hidden room where we found the broadcast radio. Unfortunately, someone else had beaten us to it, the radio was all busted up, and virtually unusable. "What the——!" Tommy gasped.

"Who could have done this?" Chubs asked out loud.

"There's only one person that could have done this." Tommy stomped. "And I'm going to make him tell us, why." Tommy was pissed, and I believed he was about to take it out on the wrong person, and he went and found some water and poured it over his brother's head. "Wake up asshole!" Tommy shouted at him.

He then raised his hand up in the air and swung it down, slapping his brother across the face. "I said wake your sorry punk ass up!" he shouted again. Tommy's brother finally came around and realized we had him tied down to his chair. He was gagged and couldn't talk, but that didn't stop him from trying to get out of his chair. I could see the anger in his eyes as he fought to get free, but we had him tied down pretty good. Tommy slapped him again, and I was for certain that was just because he felt like it. Then he removed the gag from his mouth.

"If you slap me again, little brother, I will beat your ass! Now untie me right now!" he barked.

Tommy laughed and slapped him yet again. "What are you going to do about it?"

"Untie me! Now!" he screamed. I waited for one of the counselors to come running in, but lucky for us they were still outside tending to the wounded.

"I'll untie you once you tell me why you busted up the radio!" Tommy told him.

"What are you talking about? The radio is fine, and who said you could use it?" Jerry yelled.

"We didn't use it. It's completely busted up!" Tommy shouted back at him. He ignored Tommy and turned his attention toward Chubs and me. "What are the two of you doing back here? I thought you left with the group?"

That's when I flipped out on him, "We did go with the group, but we're back. Albert caught us off guard and killed almost everyone, half of us managed to get away, Candice was killed as well! You heartless prick!" I went to punch him, but Chubs grabbed me and pulled me back, telling me that I needed to stay calm just in case something else happened.

"You're lying! All three of you are making this shit up! My own brother is even involved in this! What a bunch of losers!" Jerry said to us.

"Losers, huh?" I broke free from Chubs and grabbed the chair and started pushing him out the door and toward the entrance to the building.

"What do you think you're doing, nerd?"

I laughed at him and said, "We're going for a ride."

Chubs wanted to stop me, but Tommy wouldn't let him. "Don't, Chubs! I know what Bobby is up to, and I hope it works." Tommy told him.

I pushed Tommy's brother outside and told him to look at what was left of the group, look at the wounded, look at the younger kids covered in blood crying out for their parents, who can't come to the rescue this time. "Take a good hard look, because this is all your fault!" I shouted in his ear. "Tommy, untie your brother and let's get out of here," I told him. Tommy did as I had told him, but he was none too happy; he wanted his brother to pay a little more for the pain that he had caused. Tommy's brother stood up out of the chair and watched in horror at all the chaos that was in front of him. "Come on, guys, let's go see if we can help with anything," I told them.

Before we could walk off, Tommy's brother asked us to wait for him; he wanted to join us and see the damage up close and personal. As we walked over to the where everyone was at, Jerry started asking us a few questions. "So Albert killed Candice? And he set a trap for you guys?"

Tommy wouldn't answer him; you could just see the disappointment in his eyes when he would even look at him. Chubs didn't want anything to do with answering his questions; he blamed him for Candice's death. Like always, it was left to me to answer his questions, even though I couldn't even stand to look at the guy, to be honest. "Yeah, he set a trap for us. I warned everyone that he wasn't going to let anyone leave these woods alive. So he set the woods on fire to smoke us out. When that didn't work, he started to pick us off one at a time into the cloud of smoke. And yes, Candice is dead, so are half the group and all the counselors except for Steve." I explained.

"Why didn't you turn back when you started to smell smoke?"

"Steve wanted to press on. He refused to stop for anything. No matter how hard I tried to stop him."

"Where is Steve now? I want to talk with him," he said.

"I don't know where he's at. When we got back to camp, he said a few things and walked off." We walked around and asked if there was anything we could do, but we were informed that everything was under control. "Looks like we're not needed here," I said.

"So now what?" Chubs asked.

"I want you three to help me find Steve—is that clear?" Tommy's brother demanded.

"If that will get you off our backs, then let's get it over with," Tommy said to him.

"There's only one place that I think he will go," I said. "So we might as well start there first."

"Where do you think he will be?" Jerry questioned.

"He loved Candice, so we will more than likely find him in her cabin."

Tommy's brother didn't say anything else; he immediately headed for Candice's cabin and kept motioning for us to follow him. I think he was scared of what Steve would do to him, so he wanted us for backup just in case something happened. "Don't expect us to help you if Steve tries to kick your ass. You will be on your own," Tommy said.

"I never asked for your help, little brother, so just keep walking," Jerry responded.

"Why don't the two of you just shut up. We're trying to find Steve, not fight all the way to the cabin. And also show some respect for the dead. Do you think, Candice, would want everyone fighting?" I explained.

Those two really seemed to hate each other, must be how brothers are supposed to treat each other. But I wouldn't know. I was the only child in my family. Anyways, before we knew it, we were standing outside the cabin door. "Do you think Steve is really in there?" Jerry asked me.

"I believe so," I answered.

"What are we waiting for? Let's just go in and take a look for ourselves" Tommy said. And then he rushed right past us and inside the cabin. We didn't know what to expect once inside, so we stood outside looking in at first, scared that Steve would come rushing out at us. Then we could hear Tommy screaming from inside, and I didn't care what could happen at that point. My friend needed me, and I promised to always be there when needed.

I rushed inside without thinking twice and found Tommy staring at a body hanging from the ceiling; it was Steve. He had hung himself inside Candice's cabin, but then something else caught my attention. Before Steve hung himself he wrote a message on the wall using lipstick. It read, "You can't kill the devil. He kills you." It was an ominous warning for each and every one of us that are still alive.

I looked back at Tommy's brother and asked, "Do you believe us now? Or do you need another reason?" He turned and took off running back to where his office was at. And of course the three of us gave chase; we didn't have a chance in hell of catching him, though, for fear makes you run faster than you normally would. I thought for sure he was going to run back into his office and lock himself in leaving everyone to fend for themselves.

I wasn't about to let that happen; he was going to make up for his mistakes—like it or not. We chased him inside his office and into his secret room where he had the radio hidden from us;

once we caught him, he was cursing at the top of his lungs over the radio being broken into pieces.

Jerry turned and started screaming at us, "How could you? How could you break the radio? It's our only way to communicate with the outside world!"

"Fuck you!" Tommy snarled. "It was you that broke the radio, that way Steve couldn't make a call for help, so you don't look bad. Don't you dare blame us."

"Where do you get off talking to me like that?"

"Then stop acting like a damn fool and I won't talk to you like one!"

Those two looked like they were ready to rip each other heads off, so I stepped in before the situation got too far out of control. "Stop it! Both of you, knock your shit off! We have bigger things to worry about, and first of all, we can't leave Steve like that. Two, we can't get help out here, so we have to be prepared for tonight."

"What happens tonight?" Tommy's brother asked.

"Albert always comes out to kill at night." Chubs said quietly. He really hated Tommy's brother.

"Is he telling the truth?"

Tommy exploded at him again, "What in the hell do you think? We've been through hell for weeks, and not one person has been willing to help! So yeah, he's telling the truth. Albert will kill again tonight. He doesn't stop."

"And the radio?"

"Albert must have broken it, I don't see how he's always one step ahead of us no matter what we do," I replied.

"Well, the only thing he will be getting tonight is a shotgun up his ass." Jerry bragged.

"What do you mean by that?" Tommy asked.

"Just move out of my way, little brother, and let big brother take over from here," he said. Then he showed us another hiding place where he kept a twelve-gauge shotgun and plenty of ammunition to take on an army.

"Why didn't you tell me about this? We could have used this to take him out a few nights ago!" Tommy shouted.

"Well, don't worry, this so-called killer is a dead man tonight," he said as he loaded the gun and placed more shells in his pockets. "Take me to the best place to watch for him—now!"

"What about, Steve?" I asked.

"We will take care of Steve once we kill Albert," Jerry said. "Don't make me say it again—take me to the best spot!" Jerry was the man with the shotgun, so of course, we were going to do what he said without back talk.

"Follow us," I said with a smile on my face. Tommy also shut up real quick and was doing exactly what he was told. Chubs, on the other hand, didn't give a damn. As we led the way, Chubs stayed in the back and was constantly pushing his buttons.

"Why are you helping us now?" Chubs asked.

"It's the right thing to do," Jerry answered.

Chubs started laughing, "Now it's the right thing to do? Really? You expect me to believe that?"

"I don't care what you believe."

"You don't care about anyone but yourself. If you did, you would have done something sooner."

"I know, I'm sorry about not believing you guys. And yeah, I wanted to protect myself as well. You guys can hate me, but I will do my best to help out all I can now."

"Prove it. You owe Candice and Steve that much and everyone else that has died here."

I started getting tired of hearing Chubs go on and on. "Shut up, Chubs! This isn't the time or the place, and you know it." I said to him. He glared at me, but now it didn't matter. We were at the place we had waited for Albert last time and was attacked by some demon kids. It wasn't dark yet, so we had to wait for hours upon end; it was so quiet you could hear a pin drop. Not a single word was spoken between us at all as we waited for any sign of Albert, now it was dark, and I had a bad feeling Albert was about to strike again. I had hoped that we would be able to put an end to Albert once and for all. However, I would be sadly mistaken. Things were about to take an awful turn that none of us seen coming.

"Bobby times up," a nurse shouted. Without thinking, he responded by calling her Julie; that was hard for everyone there to hear her name being said. Bobby felt bad and tried to apologize, but the nurse was nice and would hear none of it.

"Well, Bobby, you heard the lady. I better be on my way and don't worry about me. I can take care of myself, and by tonight, I will find out who did this to Julie, my friend. Until then take care and rest well." Joe said before leaving in hurry. That took Bobby by surprise. Joe has never taken off without shaking his hand first. Things were about to take a very bad turn for everyone. Bobby knew that deep down inside.

# 13

## One Nightmare Ends And Another Begins

That night Bobby was quick to eat and take his meds. He wanted to write in the journal as quickly as possible. He knew that he wouldn't be bothered again on that night by the nurses; he grabbed his journal and hurriedly went over to his table to write. July 9, 1999; It seems as though I'm getting closer to the end of my nightmarish tale. I hope that I have helped Joe out enough that he can finally end Albert's reign of terror.

It's hard to believe that someone like me has been through so much, but right now this isn't about just me; it's about saving others as well. On to another subject that's bothering me. That boy that appears at the foot of my bed said that the one that killed Julie would strike again, another person would die, and more than likely it would be me, but nothing happened today. And I'm still kicking, so I'm proof that the boy was wrong, I hope.

Maybe I can catch him again in the morning, who knows, it's worth a try. And another thing, I have a bad feeling about John Boy as well. I don't know what his intentions are, but I hate to even think about it. I believe that he may be up to something sinister. I also believe that he may even be the one responsible for the death of Julie, not Albert.

But Albert may have some kind of hold on him as he did with those other kids so many years ago. One last thing before I call it a night, once all of this is over, I plan on getting out of this place and starting a new life. It's time I start to live instead of hiding in fear; this could possibly be my last entry if all goes according to plan. Or if I die tonight, and Joe is reading this, I hid everything you will need to know in a small hole in the wall under the bed.

Bobby would end up being so tired and mentally drained that he accidentally fell asleep on his table while writing. He did try his very best to stay awake, but the human body can only handle so much before it shuts down altogether on someone. Once morning came, the nurses had gotten so used to Joe that they went ahead and let him into his room. Joe quickly spotted Bobby asleep at his table and blocked the nurse's view of the room. "It's okay, ma'am. I have it under control from here," he assured the nurse.

She agreed and slowly shut the door, keeping a close eye on him. Once he heard the click of the lock, he knew the coast was clear, and he went over to wake Bobby up. "Wake up, sleeping beauty, we have work to do," Joe shouted and clapped his hands loudly by his ear.

Bobby jumped up and asked, "Where's the boy?"

Joe gave him an odd look, "What boy?"

Bobby glanced around the room quickly, "Never mind."

Joe noticed that he was also writing in a journal, "Keeping a journal now, are we?"

"Someone has to write," Bobby replied.

"You're right, Bobby. Write in that as much as you can. I have a feeling someday it will come in handy." That piqued Bobby's curiosity, but he would let it go for now; he had other things on his mind.

"Any news for me?" Bobby asked.

"I do have some news for you, Bobby, but it can wait. I need you to finish your story today, I can't explain why, but know that it's very important you do so. Understand that there can be no distractions right now, okay?"

Bobby didn't give it a second thought. He trusted Joe's words, "I understand where you're coming from, Joe. I won't ask any questions until I'm done with my tale. I will begin right away." he assured him. And Bobby did exactly like he said he would and jumped straight into where he left off yesterday.

Like I was saying, Tommy's brother had the shotgun ready and waiting for Albert to show up. The coast was clear, there were no screams coming from the cabins, all the injured had been moved inside to the cafeteria, I mean there was no sign of Albert at all. All was quiet for a long while, and Tommy's brother was getting just about ready to call it a night when all of a sudden screaming could be heard.

"Somebody, help me! Help me, please! He's after me! Please help me!" I knew that voice. It was Johnny, I thought for sure he was already dead.

"Johnny! Over here!" I screamed. We now could see Johnny running our way, and sure as shit, Albert was right behind him. He was running as fast as he could, and as soon as he got close enough, Tommy's brother yelled out for him to hit the ground. And Johnny made a jump in the air and landed on the ground stomach first.

"I see you, you son of a bitch! Now it's your turn to die!" he shouted. I found it strange that even though Albert had seen the shotgun, he still charged straight at us. Seconds later, Jerry pulled the trigger, and the gun went off. The blast echoed throughout the woods like thunder. It was such a violent blast that it sent Albert flying backward and onto the ground. Jerry started laughing as he walked up to Albert's body. "How do you like that, you piece of shit." Jerry spate.

Tommy and Chubs cheered on thinking that Albert had finally been dealt with. I wasn't too sure that the devil had been killed just yet, "He's not dead. You can't kill him." Johnny shouted from the ground.

Jerry walked over to Johnny and helped him up off the ground. "Oh, he's dead all right. Nobody can survive that." But he couldn't be more wrong, as Albert was moving around on the ground. "That's not possible." he gasped in disbelief. Tommy's brother walked up to Albert and pointed the shotgun right at him and pulled the trigger again, and another blast echoed throughout the woods yet again.

He turned to us and said, "Now the bastard is dead!" And he spat on Albert's body. However, none of us was cheering him on this time, for we were all frozen with fear. Albert was back on his feet and standing behind Tommy's brother, and he didn't look happy at all.

"Look out!" Tommy shouted.

Jerry turned around quickly to find Albert on his feet. "No way! It can't be!" He pulled the trigger on the gun again, but nothing happened; the gun was empty. In a panic, he fumbled with the shotgun shells that were in his pockets and dropped them to the ground. There was no point in reaching for them. Albert was already upon him. "You son of a bitch! I'll kill you one way or another!" he screamed as he tried to hit Albert with the butt of the gun. However, that turned out to be his mistake, as Albert caught the gun and quickly grabbed him by the throat and pinned him up against a tree.

Tommy tried to run and help his brother, but we quickly tackled him to the ground. Tommy was furious with us and demanded that we let him go. "Stop, Tommy! If you run over to him, you will get yourself killed as well!" I knew that his brother was already dead, and I wasn't about to let Tommy get himself killed too. I knew that it was Albert's way of trying to sucker us into running over to him. And just like all the other times before, once he figured out that we weren't falling for his trap, he killed Tommy's brother.

Albert took the barrel of the gun and shoved it through Jerry's mouth and out the back of his head with such force that barrel of the gun even went right through and into the tree itself holding his lifeless body upright. The only thing we could do at that point was run away and drag Tommy along with us. That night we sat in our cabin with a new guest. I decided that it would be safer if Johnny stayed the night with us. It was a sad night for us all, especially for Johnny, Tommy, and Chubs. Johnny lost the very last friend he had. Tommy lost his brother.

It must have been damn hard on him to see his brother killed right in front of his very eyes, and Chubs lost whom he thought was the love of his life in Candice. And poor Nick was still in a state of shock; all he did was stare at the wall nonstop. But someone had to break the silence, so I decided that I might as well try. "I know that it has been a rough night for us all, but I think we should all try and rest. And then come up with something in the morning," I said.

Tommy agreed with me, which was a huge surprise until he added in what his plan was for tomorrow, "Bobby's right, get some rest, you're all going to need it."

"What do you mean by that, Tommy?" I asked. He looked at me with this look of vengeance in his eyes; it was like his eyes were filled with the flames of hell in which I've never seen before.

"We take the fight straight to Albert, in the morning. We're going to beat him down with those weapons over there, and then we're going to set his ass on fire and send him straight back to hell! Sleep now and decide if you want to go with me or not. You can all tell me in the morning." Tommy explained.

I had questions for Tommy, but it was clear he wasn't going to say another word until morning came. None of us said another word, we just curled up where we sat, and we passed out from complete exhaustion. Once morning came, we weren't woken up by Tommy as I expected. We heard screams coming from outside, and that was what woke us. I was the first to run outside to see what all the screaming was about; apparently, Albert wasn't done killing for the night like we thought he might be after killing Tommy's brother. There was smoke coming from the cabin right beside ours. I didn't even think about what I was doing. All I remember is that I ran inside the cabin, with Tommy right behind me. And there lying in their beds were the bodies of the youngest of the kids at the camp.

They had been burned alive while sleeping. It was a gruesome sight to behold. Tommy was angry and seeing that sent him into a complete rage, and out the door, he went. I was about to give chase until I noticed that something was written on the floor in what looked to be blood: "Tonight you will all die by my hand." is all it said. But it was enough to let me know if we didn't do something, we would all be dead by the end of that day. So now Tommy's plan didn't sound so crazy after all. I ran out the door so I could catch back up with Tommy.

"I'm in, Tommy. But we need to kill him before nightfall," I told him.

"We better make it quick then," Tommy replied as we walked back to our cabin. Chubs and Johnny were up and ready to go.

"What was all the screaming about?" Chubs asked.

"Did they find Steve's body or something?" Johnny also wanted to know.

"No, Albert killed again last night," I answered.

"Who was the victim this time?" Chubs asked.

"It was the youngest ones here, the boys that stayed in the cabin right beside us," I replied.

"Hey! We don't have time for talking! Are you with me or not?" Tommy said.

"What do you think we're up for? Let's go kill that bastard once and for all," Johnny answered.

"I just hope this works," Chubs replied.

We grabbed our weapons and were getting ready to leave when I noticed that Nick was gone. "Has anyone seen, Nick?" I asked.

"He was already gone when you two first ran out the door," Chubs answered.

"Worry about him later! Let's get this over with!" Tommy told us. "Are we ready to go?"

The three of us told him that we had all we needed and that we were ready to go and finish that bastard off and send him back to hell. As we were making our way through the woods, there was something that was bothering me, and I just had to ask, "Where are we going to get the gas to set his ass on fire, Tommy?"

"You don't pay attention to your surroundings, do you?"

"What are you talking about?" I asked.

"The cabin where Albert keeps his trophies, there were also

jugs of gas and plenty of matches. That's where we will get what we need, and then we burn it down to the ground," Tommy explained.

"And what if he's in there?"

"Then we end him right then and there, Bobby." Tommy wasn't going to back down, he had a plan, and he was going to see it through to the end. If he went down, he was going to make sure Albert went down with him; he was hell-bent on killing Albert no matter what it took. "Now be quiet. We're getting close. We don't want him to hear us if he's in there."

I was questioning Tommy's plan the whole time there. I mean not even a shotgun could kill Albert. How was a bunch of kids with an ax and machetes going to take down a demon like him? And would setting him on fire even finish him off? I wasn't sure that this was going to work, but that was going to be our last chance. If we couldn't kill him, then all of us and everyone back at camp was going to die; that much I was sure of.

It wasn't long before when the cabin was right in front of us; we decided that we would spread out and do some looking around before we would meet at the door and rush inside. I readied my weapon and went around the back of the cabin. I didn't see Albert anywhere outside lurking around. So I figured I would have a look through the window Chubs and myself busted out to escape so many days ago. But it was a no-go, Albert had already boarded up the window, and there was no way for me to see inside, so I went ahead and made my way around to the front door of the cabin.

"Did you see anything?" Tommy asked as I walked toward the door.

"No, I couldn't see a thing. And Albert already boarded up the window we busted out. Did you see anything, Tommy?" I replied.

"Not a damn thing," he answered. Right then Chubs and Johnny walked around the corner. "Anything?" Tommy asked them.

"There's nothing odd going on out here," they both answered.

"Well then, there's only one thing left to do," Tommy said. "Ready yourselves, guys! We're about to bust down this damn door!"

I shook my head and pushed on the door, and it opened right up. "Remember, Tommy. Check your surroundings." I said with a smile on my face. "After you, fearless leader," I added. As he walked in the door first, he turned to me and called me an asshole. "Just trying to lighten the mood, Tommy." I grinned.

"Just get your ass inside and be quiet," Tommy demanded. I smiled and walked on inside, I knew I had lightened things up even if it was just for a moment. We searched for Albert first as we walked through the cabin; however, he was nowhere to be found, not sure if that was a good thing or a bad thing.

"Where's the gas and matches?' I asked quietly.

"It's in his trophy room—pay attention, Bobby," Tommy said to me.

Sometimes you forget things easily when you're scared to death, "Albert's not here. We might as well get the gas and get out of here." Chubs said.

"We're going to get the gas, but this place will go up in flames before I leave here," Tommy told us. We agreed with him and went along with what he said, and we made our way into Albert's trophy room. This time around he had some new trophies hanging from the ceiling; it was Mark's, Johnny's friends', and Tommy's brother's body parts. I could see the anger starting to boil over on Tommy's face, and Johnny did his best not to break down and cry. I grabbed the jugs of gas and told Tommy to get the matches. We didn't need to stay in that room any longer than we had to, and we made our way outside without any sign of Albert.

I handed Johnny and Tommy both a jug of gas. "Burn it down like you want, Tommy. Johnny, you deserve to be a part of this as well," I said to them. And they went to work pouring gas inside and out; they both made sure to soak every inch of that cabin. Once done. Tommy took the matches from me, and he set the cabin ablaze. The old dried-out cabin didn't take long, and it was completely engulfed in flames.

"Burn! Burn to the ground!" Tommy screamed.

"We need to get out of here before he gets back!" I shouted. I knew that this would get Albert's attention, and he would be pissed and come for us first before he attacked anyone else. And that would be our own time to carry out the last part of Tommy's plan. But I couldn't have been more wrong, and I will explain why in a few minutes.

We took off running back toward the campgrounds, but Tommy stopped for a brief moment. "Did you guys see that?" he said quietly.

"Yeah, I did. Someone's following us," I answered.

"Is it Albert?" Johnny asked.

"No, Albert would come straight out in the open and kill us where we stand," I told him. And then Nick came running up to us; he was covered in blood. At first glance, I could see that it was his blood. He was holding his hand against what looked like a huge gash on his stomach. He must have lost way too much blood, for he fell to the ground. Tommy and I pulled him over to one of the trees and leaned him up against it; he was barely conscious but fought it off long enough to tell us what happened.

"Albert attacked the campgrounds, everyone is dead, I barely made it out alive," Nick said as he gasped for air. That's not possible. The message he left on the floor said he would kill everyone tonight, I thought to myself.

Then it hit me, the claw marks going under my bed, the message wrote on the floor—they were all warnings for me to find and me alone. That's why no one else could see them but me. It wasn't warnings for when Albert would show up. Those were warnings for me to get the hell out of there. The ghostly boy was trying to scare me away so Albert wouldn't kill me. But now it was just us. We were the last five people alive out in these woods; however, I couldn't accept that fact without seeing for with my own eyes. I looked back at Nick to tell him to stay here and rest, but he was already dead.

It was more than a gash on his stomach. Nick had been holding his intestines in with his hand the whole time so he could stay alive long enough to find us. I used my hand to close his eyes, and now it just looked like he was sleeping. I sat there for a moment holding back my tears, I felt myself starting to break down, but I pulled it together, and anger had now taken me over.

"Get the last jug of gas and matches, get your weapons ready. We're heading back to the campgrounds right now!" I ordered them. Tommy tried to tell me that there was no reason for going back, that we should focus on finding Albert. That wasn't going to work for me at that moment, I needed to see for myself, and besides, I also knew that Albert would find us there as well. "Don't question me! Let's go!" I wasn't about to give them another chance to question my reason for going back, so I took off running as fast as I could back toward the campgrounds, hoping that my friends were right behind me, if not, then I would handle things on my own if need be.

I had finally made my way back, and the campgrounds were right in front of me; to my dismay, everything was engulfed in flames. I could hear cries for help, screams of agony coming from within the flames. Just then Tommy, Johnny, and Chubs came running up behind me; it was a horrible sight for them as well. It was hard for them to accept the fact that there was nothing they could do to save the ones burning alive in the flames.

"Are you happy now?" Tommy asked.

"No, I'm not happy, Tommy! I had to see it for myself, that's all!" I answered.

"Why? Why come back here and see this and hear those screams, knowing that you can't help? That none of us can do a damn thing! So tell me, why?" he yelled.

"I had to know! I thought I could do something, anything at all to help!" I yelled back. Right then I caught a glimpse of Albert walking away from his handiwork. "There he is!"

"Get him!" Tommy screamed. He led the charge after him, and I was right behind keeping up the best I could, with Johnny and Chubs running right beside me. But once we got to where Albert was seen, he was already gone or hiding off in the distance watching us, waiting to take us out. The way I see it, I believe that he was going to try and have fun to kill us slowly, but what he didn't know yet is that we set his cabin on fire and that now we were hunting him like he had been hunting us.

"Where did he go!" shouted Johnny.

"He more than likely went back to his cabin to start working on his new trophies," I said.

"But we set that cabin of his on fire," Tommy said.

"He doesn't know that yet, but once he does, he will come back for us," I explained.

"Then what should we do?" Chubs asked.

"I say we stay here and wait. If we give chase now, then we become vulnerable to whatever attack he throws at us." I told them. I had Tommy and Chubs to agree with me, but Johnny called us stupid for wanting to sit there and wait to die. He took off, and we haven't seen him since. I just hoped he hadn't run into Albert because alone he wouldn't have a chance in hell at fighting him off. And Johnny's a hothead, and he's pissed that Albert has killed all of his friends and ruined summer camp for him. Yeah, even though Johnny was upset, he still found ways to make it all about him, but that doesn't mean that he should die.

"Should we go looking for, Johnny?" Chubs asked.

Tommy was upset that Johnny ran off and left us behind. "We're not moving from this spot. Johnny is on his own from here on out."

Now usually I'm all about running off and helping someone that needs it, but Johnny chose his path, and he would have to see it through on his own this time. He had been gone for so long that he was beyond help; he was more than likely dead already. "Tommy's right, we can't take any chances. It was his choice to leave the group. We need to stick together from here on out," I said. It was now getting late, and there was still no sign of Albert. I thought for sure he would be back looking for us by now.

The sound of a phone ringing could be heard, and that broke Bobby's concentration. "Sorry, Bobby. I need to take this. It's a phone call that I've been waiting for." Joe said. Joe walked out of the door and down the hall, Bobby would have given chase, but if he left his room, he would have been in some serious shit.

Bobby just stayed put and paced back and forth waiting for Joe to return; he waited for what seemed a good hour. But Joe had yet to return, and Bobby was curious as to what was going on outside his door. All he could do was wait. Once Joe returned, he started asking questions.

"What was that all about, Joe?"

"It's not something you should concern yourself with right now."

"Sorry, Joe. But that's not good enough for me. I want to know what's going on, I know when someone is hiding something from me, so you might as well come clean with me, Joe."

"Look, Bobby. It's not something you should be concerned with right now."

"Joe, just tell me what's going on."

"I can't right now, Bobby. You need to focus on finishing your story. Remember the deal we had?"

"I do, Joe. But you also said you would no longer hide things from me, didn't you?"

"Bobby, I'm not hiding things from you. Trust me, the quicker you finish your story, the quicker I can get things done, and the faster I can tell you what is really going on."

"Just tell me the truth, Joe. I deserve that much. I'm not going to wait." Bobby said to him. It wasn't like he was hiding anything from; him he was just trying to protect him from the truth, and he also wondered if Bobby could even handle the truth at this point. But Joe had no choice but to tell him what he now knew.

"Okay, Bobby. I won't hide it from you. I will tell you the truth."

"Just say it, Joe. I've been through hell my whole life. I think I can handle anything you can tell me by now. You know this about me already," Bobby told him.

"I'm just trying to protect my friend, the same you did for me," Joe explained. "And what was it you said to me? I can take care of myself just fine. Well, I've looked out for myself for years without anyone there to look out for me. Not even my friends or family gave a damn about me. I can handle myself just fine." said Bobby.

Joe was still hesitant about telling him, but he still did as Bobby asked. "I know who murdered, Julie."

Bobby's eyes lit up upon hearing what Joe had just said to him. "Who was it, Joe?" Bobby asked. Joe paused for a moment until Bobby asked him again. "Who killed Julie?"

Joe looked up at him and said, "It was John Boy, my brother, and your friend, that killed Julie." he said in a panicked voice.

"You think John Boy killed Julie?" Bobby asked.

"You don't understand, I know for a fact that it was, John Boy," Joe answered.

"How can you be sure?"

"There are cameras all over the place in here, Bobby. So I asked for the tapes and sent them to a friend of mine to be viewed, and I also gave him pictures of my brother. He said the whole murder is on the tape, and he's almost for certain it's the same person from the pictures, but something was way off about the guy. And tonight, when I'm done here, I'm supposed to go and watch the tape myself."

Bobby couldn't believe what he was hearing. Could John Boy have actually done something like this? Were his bad feelings about John Boy true? "Why would he do something like this?" Bobby asked.

"Remember, Bobby. The John Boy we knew from long ago is no longer there. Who knows what he could have become now?" Joe answered.

"Then let's end our conversation here, so you can head out and view the tape," Bobby said, with a hint of panic in his voice.

"No, I can tell that you're at the end of your story, and I'm this close to knowing the truth of what happened out there. You can't stop now. Once you're done, then I will go and view the tape; that's the only option." Joe was right, Bobby was at the very end of his story, at the end of what really happened out there, and the truth was far different than what the police reports had said sixteen years ago. But that just let him know that the police never really looked into anything that they were told. They had their target even though he was just a victim that survived pure hell.

"I will do as you ask, and I will finish my story. You're right, I'm right there at the end of my horrible tale of summer camp gone wrong. I might be worried at this point, but I'm not scared—let's continue," said Bobby. After we had waited for so long, I started to get antsy, and I couldn't handle waiting there for Albert to show up any longer. All of a sudden the rage that had left me for so long returned with a vengeance. I started screaming and going off like some kind of crazy person.

"Albert! Albert! Show your sorry ass! I know that you're out there, you chickenshit! Come and get me! I'm the one that burned down your house of horrors! You're nothing but a coward! A damn bully! Why don't you grow a pair and face me like a man!" I had lost control of all my senses, I was like a man possessed, and all I could see was red.

All that I wanted to do was find Albert and kill him, and I don't mean just kill him. I wanted to try and make him suffer the way he made everyone else suffer. Chubs and Tommy tried to calm me down, but it didn't work. I felt so much anger and rage toward him that I wanted to be the one that sent him back to hell, even if I had to drag him there with my own hands. "I said come out and face me, Albert!" I screamed again.

"What are you trying to do, Bobby? Get us killed?" Tommy yelled at me.

I ignored what Tommy said to me, and I kept on screaming for him to come out and face me. Chubs grabbed me by the arm and demanded that I stop before I get us all killed. I pushed him to the ground and yelled at him, "Get us all killed? Look around you, Chubs. We're the only three left alive!" Chubs' face was that of fear toward me now. I didn't apologize for what I had done to him either; if he didn't want to help get Albert to come after us, then he needed to get them out of my way.

The sun was starting to set, and I knew that Albert was at his strongest at night, and we didn't have any source of light to help us fight back against him this time either. We would always use the lights from the camp to aid us; however, the camp had been burned to the ground. "Don't the two of you see that if we don't get his attention now, we're dead anyway! Look around and tell me what light source we have to use this time. We don't even have flashlights! We're sitting ducks if the sun goes down!" I explained to them.

Tommy looked around, and it sunk in that I was right. If the sun went down, we were dead. He started freaking out as well and started picking up rocks and tree branches and anything else he could get his hands on to make noise. He even started screaming to the top of his lungs daring Albert to show his damn face! Chubs were scared of both of us now. I imagine that he was hoping that Albert was done killing since he whipped out everyone that was left at camp and burned it to the ground. "Why call out to him? We should try getting out of here?" Chubs said to us.

"There's no way in hell he will let us live, Chubs! And even if he did, I couldn't live with myself if I left without doing something to put an end to this!" I explained. I was about to tell Chubs that if he wanted to try and leave, he could. I wouldn't blame him a bit. But I didn't get a chance to as Albert made his presence known by throwing Johnny's severed head right in the middle of us. I freaked out for a moment and wanted to make a run for it, but I didn't. I stood my ground and waited for him to show himself to me. Chubs crawled quickly over to one of the trees and hid behind it, but Tommy stood beside me.

"I told you I would have your back, man," Tommy said to me.

"Are you ready for this, Tommy?" I asked.

He had his ax in hand, "I'm ready."

"Then let's finish this and send that bastard back to hell," I said.

And just minutes later, Albert came running out of the woods right at us, I swung my machete right for his head, and he raised his hand, and the blade sunk into his skin, and blood went everywhere. It was like it didn't even hurt him, he just looked at me with his dark soulless eyes, and he smiled.

"You bastard! You killed my brother! Now die!" Tommy screamed as he swung his ax right for his stomach, and it landed solid right into his rib-cage. It still wasn't enough to bring him down; he grabbed Tommy by the throat and lifted him up off the ground. It was clear that he was going to kill him if I didn't do something to stop him. I dropped down and pulled the ax out of Albert's stomach and swung for his right leg as hard as I could. It was a flush hit. Now he had blood gushing from his leg, and that was enough to make him drop Tommy.

"Are you all right, Tommy?" I shouted. He was gasping for air, but he gave me the thumbs-up letting me know that he was okay.

310

Albert just stood there laughing that creepy bloodcurdling laugh of his, like he was enjoying what was happening at that moment. Before he turned, he swung his ax at me catching part of my leg ripping it open, now I was bleeding and in more pain than you could imagine, but my hatred and rage pushed me on.

"Bobby!" Tommy shouted he was clearly worried. So he got back up on his feet and dared Albert to bring it, that got his attention away from me, and now he was going after Tommy. He kept laughing and laughing as he walked toward Tommy, and he took a big swing at Tommy's head with his ax. Tommy ducked under the attack just in the nick of time for me to throw his ax back to him, and he turned quickly and sung it toward Albert's back, and it landed flush, causing him to stumble for a moment. "What will it take to put him down?" Tommy shouted.

"I don't know! Just keep hacking away until he goes down!" I yelled. I didn't know what else to say. It was like trying to bring down a giant redwood tree. If a shotgun blast couldn't take him out, how could we? It felt like a never-ending nightmare; there had to be some kind of weak point on his body. We just had to find it is all. I still didn't have my machete to fight him off with, so I made a bold move to get it back. He didn't notice me as I ran up behind him and swept his legs out from under him, and he hit the ground. I quickly reached down and yanked my blade out of his arm and blood spewed on my face as I did so. I took a step back, and when I did, Albert caught me on my other leg with his ax, causing me to have another wound to my legs.

I was lucky, if I hadn't moved as fast as I did, Albert would have cut my leg off. With Albert down, I thought that would be the opening we needed to chop his sorry ass up, but he was quick to his feet. Both of us were tired and were running out of strength quick due to the blood loss from our wounds. I didn't know how much more I could take. I was almost ready to just give up.

But something willed me on to finish what I had started, we just needed to find a way to get him down to the ground one more time, and I was sure we could finish him off. But now with gashes in both my legs I wasn't able to move fast enough to sweep his legs out from under him again, nor did I have the strength.

Then Albert did something unexpected. He started jumping around chanting, "You're going to die! You're going to die! It's just a matter of time before you die!" His voice was dark and sinister, but sometimes squeaky like a clown's; it's the only way to describe it. Then he just stopped all at once and looked at us smiling. "You will be the start of my new collection! I can see it now!" he shouted as he laughed at us.

I hated that voice; it was the same one from my nightmares that almost drove me completely mad. "You're not taking me as a trophy, you sick bastard!" Tommy yelled. Albert stopped talking and laughing altogether and raised his ax and went straight for Tommy. I thought for sure Tommy was going to die.

But Chubs came running from behind the tree and hurled his body into Albert's, sending him crashing to the ground with enough force that he dropped his ax too. That was the chance that Tommy and I needed. "Now!" I screamed as loud as I could. It was like everything was in slow motion as we ran to Albert and started attacking him with everything we had left inside of us. Albert's blood was spewing all over my face and clothes, as I kept hitting him over and over and over again with my machete. I looked over at Tommy just for a second, and he was doing the same thing as me, and screaming for him to "die" as he did so.

There for a moment, I blacked out. I was like a savage beast killing his prey. I just couldn't make myself stop hitting him. Pure hatred for this demon had consumed my whole being. it was like I was losing what sanity I had left. I was completely covered from head to toe with his blood from how many times I hit him with the blade. Tommy dropped his ax and ran over to pull me away from him, and he would pull me away for a second or two before I would run back up to him and start the attack all over again.

"Die! Die!" are the only words that were coming from my mouth as I constantly attacked him with the machete. Tommy would keep trying to get me to stop, but I wouldn't stop until I took out all of my rage on that piece of shit I wanted him to suffer, I wanted him to feel the same pain he caused everyone else. I wasn't going to stop until Albert took his last breath; it took both Chubs and Tommy to stop me, and finally, I gave in. I was so tired I couldn't lift the machete, not once more.

"It's over! It's over, Bobby!" Tommy told me. "He's dead. It's finally over."

I looked at Albert's motionless body lying there on the ground. Is it really over? I thought to myself. I watched for any signs of life, but there was none. I started telling myself that it was over, that we had finally sent him back to hell from where he came. However, the demon was not quite dead. He grabbed Chubs by the leg quickly trying to pull him to the ground.

But Tommy was quick to grab Chubs by the arms, and he started kicking Albert in the face. It wasn't enough to make him let go of Chubs leg. I watched in horror as Albert grabbed the ax that was lying beside him. He was about to try and cut his leg off. I wasn't about to let that happen though. I quickly grabbed the machete from the ground, and I stabbed Albert in the face with such force that the blade went straight through his face and out the back of his head. He fell back to the ground and released the hold he had on Chubs, then he started squirming back and forth trying to get the blade from his face. I knew that there was only one way left to finish what we started.

"Get the gas and matches! Let's roast his ass!" I shouted. Tommy came back with the jug of gas and soaked Albert from head to feet with it, and Chubs came back with the matches, and I demanded that he hand them over to me. I struck one of the matches, and I looked at him, and I said, "Go back to hell, bitch!" And I threw the match on him, and he burst into flames instantly.

I sat there, and I didn't move an inch until I made sure he was no longer moving. I thought for sure this time it was over, but somehow he still got to his feet and was walking toward us as his body was engulfed in flames. Everything he touched caught on fire, before long the forest was ablaze, but that didn't stop him from still trying to kill us.

"What the hell!" Tommy shouted.

"Why won't you just die," I screamed.

Just then Chubs ran up with another jug of gas, "I had a feeling we might need this."

"What are you waiting for Chubs? Throw it at him!" I shouted back. Chubs took the top of the jug off and hurled it at him, and the next thing I know, you could hear this loud boom, and the flames from Albert looked like they shot straight up to the heavens. And the heat that came from that explosion was so intense I thought my skin was going to melt off of me. After that Albert took two more steps and fell to the ground, and this time for good.

He never moved again. To be honest with you, I'm not sure what happened after that, I passed out. All I remember was being woken by raindrops hitting me on the face. Chubs and Tommy were nowhere to be found, and I wasn't even near the campgrounds or where we put an end to Albert.

I was dazed and confused and couldn't figure out how I got way out into the woods like that. It didn't stop me from trying to find my friends though. I searched for them for days in the pouring rain, calling out their names, but it didn't do me a bit of good. It was like they vanished into thin air. It was just like my nightmare. I was completely alone. The next day as I went searching for them again. I was grabbed from behind, and a voice said, "I gotcha."

Whoever had me in their grasp didn't realize that I was like a wild animal. I fought, clawed, kicked, and bit. I wasn't going down without a fight. "Calm down!" the voice said. "We're here to help you. It's okay, you're safe now." It wasn't the voice of a killer, and it didn't seem as though the person meant me any harm.

And for the first time in a long while, I felt safe. I even broke down and started to cry my eyes out. The person put a blanket around me and led me to where a helicopter was waiting for me. Chubs and Tommy were also on the helicopter as well. When I tried to talk to them, they both acted like they didn't even know me. The nurse that was overlooking them told me that both were in extreme shock, and that was causing memory loss.

She was very surprised that I wasn't the same way when she started looking me over. However, she did find the gashes on my legs and cleaned and wrapped them for me. I thought she was going to start crying when she noticed just how badly hurt the three of us were. "It must have been hell for you guys out there."

"You have no idea, lady. We're just lucky to be alive." I replied.

As the helicopter flew over the campgrounds, I looked out the window and saw all of the carnage that Albert had done. There were bodies everywhere: some were burned, and some were chopped up, it was a bloody and horrific sight, there were no survivors except for us, and the campgrounds were completely burned to the ground. It was hell.

"So after all of that, what happened next?" Joe asked.

"Well, I was flown to a hospital where they cleaned me up and kept me for a few days. My family visited me only once. They acted scared of me for some reason. And I would find out why later. The cops kept asking me all kinds of questions every single day. I never lied, never once lied to the cops, I told them the truth no matter how many times they asked me.

The cops acted like they didn't believe me, and with Chubs's and Tommy's memories gone, they couldn't back me up on what I told the cops. Before I knew it, I was being handcuffed and blamed for the murders, the cops used my story against me, saying I was the instigator and that I was the violent one. I got upset and started killing everyone, and Chubs and Tommy had escaped my grasp just in time to be rescued. "There wasn't enough evidence for them to send me to prison, so the judge took it upon himself to send me here. And that's pretty much the end of my horrific tale."

"So now I know the truth, not a damn thing from the police report sixteen years ago was true at all. Damn bastards." Joe said. "No wonder those old farts at headquarters never wanted me to look into this case. They knew that I would find evidence that would get them in a ton of shit and blow the top off of things that they had covered up." Joe was clearly upset, and he felt betrayed by his fellow superiors on top of that, but Bobby knew that they had more pressing matters at hand to deal with.

"Forget about that for now, Joe. You need to go and watch that tape and find out if it really is, John Boy, or not." Bobby told him.

"You're right, Bobby. We can deal with them later. I'm sorry that no one believed you back then. But I believe you now, Bobby. And I can finally go and shut that camp down for good, and it's all because of you, thank you for helping me." Joe said to him.

"Hey, this isn't over. You have to come back and tell me what you found on that tape. Trust me, it's important that you do so," Bobby explained.

"I will, Bobby. But it will be sometime tomorrow morning. We have our work cut out for us, so get some rest tonight, Bobby." Joe told him. He stood up out of his chair and yelled for the nurse to let him out of the room, that he was done for the evening. Before leaving, he turned to Bobby and said, "I'll see you soon." Joe had no idea just how soon he would be back to the asylum on that night. Joe decided that he will head straight over to meet with his friend so he could view the tape as quickly as possible, even though his friend lived over an hour away from where he was now.

He figured that Bobby would be fine for now, for he was in a well-protected room. Once there Joe rushed up to the door and started knocking. He was starting to have a bad feeling that he couldn't explain, and that was agitating him badly. His friend finally opened the door, and Joe rushed inside. "Do you have the tape ready for me to view?" Joe asked.

"Yeah, I do. What in the hell is eating you?" the man asked.

"I don't have time to explain right now, Bill. Just show me the tape."

"Chill, dude. It's right in here, and let me warn you, it's scary."

Bill said as he led him into a smaller room. "Just walk up to the VCR and press Play."

Joe did exactly that, it only took watching part of the tape for him to realize that Bobby was in danger, and he needed to get back to the asylum as fast as he could.

After Joe had left, Bobby felt uneasy. He was unsure if he should go to bed or try and stay up late. But that decision was made for him as his meds contained a dose of sleeping aid, unknown to him.

And he would find himself fast asleep; however, a loud bang at his door that night would wake him from his deep sleep. Once up and out of his bed, he realized that his door was unlocked and wide open. That could only mean one thing: the one that killed Julie was now waiting outside that door for him. He wasn't afraid though; he had been through far worse to back down from some murderer now.

Actually, Bobby was happy that he would get to kill Julie's murderer with his own two hands, but once outside of his door, those feelings would change to pure fear. For as he walked down the hall, blood was everywhere, and the bodies of the doctors, nurses, and yes, even the inmates could be found. It reminded him of the killings from his childhood, and he feared that Albert had finally come for him, so many years later.

Only moments later, the killer made himself known. It was John Boy, not Albert, and he had a large knife in his hand. Bobby wanted to try and talk to him, to ask him why. But it was clear that he wasn't the friend that he remembered from long ago. He had a wild look in his eyes, and the only thing he knew was how to kill now. He looked at Bobby and smiled; then he rushed right at him. Bobby didn't have any way to defend himself, but still, he learned how to fight a maniac like him.

Once he was close enough, Bobby grabbed him and slung him to the ground. It wasn't enough to make John Boy drop the knife, and he started slashing it at Bobby. He did the only thing he could do, and he grabbed the blade with his hand, and it cut right into him, but he didn't have a choice if he wanted to live. Bobby held on to the blade as tight as he could, and with blood running down his hand, he started punching John Boy in the face with his free hand as hard as he could, over and over again, hoping that he would at least drop the knife. Instead, John Boy was able to pull the knife blade free from Bobby's hand and turned the tables on him.

John Boy, raised the knife above his head getting ready to make the final attack on him. Right then Bobby, thought for sure he was dead where he lay until he heard a gun go off, and John Boy fell to the ground dead.

He looked back up and saw Joe standing there with a gun in his hands. Joe walked up to the body of his older brother and said, "Now you can rest in peace, brother." He looked back up at Bobby and asked, "What made my brother do this? And don't give me that 'I don't know shit' either. I want the truth!"

Bobby picked himself up off the floor; then he looked over at Joe and said, "This isn't the time or the place for small talk, Joe. For one, I need a doctor. The knife wounds I have been bleeding out pretty badly, and two, look around you, there are bodies everywhere. Who do you think will be blamed for this?"

"True, this place looks like a war zone, and I'm sure the police will be here any minute. You can answer me once we get out of here." Joe replied. They both ran out of the asylum, and Bobby was finally free. Hours later, while Joe was driving them both down the highway, Joe said, "Now you can answer my question."

"All right, Joe. I'll do my best to answer you," said Bobby. "If

I'm right, John Boy was under Albert's control. Or at least his body was."

"What do you mean, Bobby?" Joe asked.

"It's hard to explain, Joe. I believe that Albert has a way to control others through their dreams. And I also believe he has a way to keep them alive as long as he's alive. That's all I can tell you for now." Bobby answered.

"That makes sense. That would explain why it was hard to kill those kids you were talking about. And if my brother was out of his mind trying to kill you, then that means Albert is definitely alive and still killing everyone that goes to that campsite." Joe explained.

"Seems that way. But what now?"

"You know what we have to do now, Bobby."

"I know exactly what we have to do. It's time to put an end to Albert once and for all."

"Are you ready for this, Bobby? It's going to be a long tough road ahead." "It doesn't matter if I'm ready or not. I have no choice but to stop that monster, and if I have to give my life to do so, then I will. It's time I stop running and hiding. It's time I finish what I started. I'm going to kill Albert!" And the two men drove away, heading straight for hell!